P

M000158996

Perilous Shore

The Sixth Carlisle &
Holbrooke Naval Adventure

Chris Durbin

To

Jan Guidoboni

The first reader of Carlisle & Holbrooke

Editor: Lucia Durbin.

Cover Artwork: *Returning Under Fire* by Bob Payne.

Cover Design: Book Beaver.

Visit my website at:

www.chris-durbin.com

First Edition: 2019

CONTENTS

Chris Durbin

LIST OF CHARTS

NAUTICAL TERMS

Throughout the centuries, sailors have created their own language to describe the highly technical equipment and processes that they use to live and work at sea. This holds true in the twenty-first century.

When counting the number of nautical terms that I've used in this series of novels, it became evident that a printed book wasn't the best place for them. I've therefore created a glossary of nautical terms on my website:

https://chris-durbin.com/glossary/

My glossary of nautical terms is limited to those that I've used in this series of novels, as they were used in the middle of the eighteenth century. It's intended as a work of reference to accompany the Carlisle and Holbrooke series of naval adventure novels.

Some of the usages of these terms have changed over the years, so this glossary should be used with caution when referring to periods before 1740 or after 1780.

The glossary isn't exhaustive. A more comprehensive list can be found in Falconer's Universal Dictionary of the Marine, first published in 1769. I haven't counted the number of terms that Falconer has defined, but he fills 328 pages with English language terms, followed by a further eighty-three pages of French translations. It is a monumental work.

An online version of the 1780 edition of The Universal Dictionary (which unfortunately does not include all the excellent diagrams that are in the print version) can be found on this website:

https://archive.org/details/universaldiction00falc/

***

PRINCIPAL CHARACTERS

Fictional

Commander George Holbrooke: Commanding Officer, *Kestrel*

Major Hans Albach: Commander of the Dol de Bretagne Militia Artillery

Captain Charles Overton: Company Commander, the Thirty-Fourth Regiment of Foot

Lieutenant Charles Lynton: First Lieutenant, *Kestrel*

Lieutenant Colin Treganoc: Officer Commanding Royal Marines, *Kestrel*

Josiah Fairview: Sailing Master, *Kestrel*

Ishmael Renouf: Channel Pilot

John Edney: Midshipman, *Kestrel*

Reverend John (David) Chalmers: Chaplain, *Kestrel*

Jackson: Bosun, *Kestrel*

Jacques Serviteur: Captain's Servant, *Kestrel*

Martin Featherstone: Corn Merchant in Wickham

Sophie Featherstone: Martin Featherstone's Wife

Ann Featherstone: Martin Featherstone's Daughter

***

Historical

Lord George Anson: First Lord of the Admiralty

Duke of Marlborough: Commander of the British Expeditionary Army

Duke d'Aiguillon: Governor and Commander of the Army of Brittany

Admiral George Forbes: Lord Commissioner of the Admiralty

General Bligh: Commander of the British Expeditionary Army

Vice Admiral Sir Francis Holburne: Port Admiral, Portsmouth

Commodore Richard Howe: Commander of the Inshore Squadron of the Channel Fleet

Captain Sir Richard Hughes: Resident Commissioner, Portsmouth

Captain François Thurot: Commanding Officer, *Maréchal de Belle-Isle*

Captain John Campbell: Commanding Officer, *Essex*

Mrs Winter: Owner, Deptford Wharf Boatyard

***

Chris Durbin

THE ENGLISH CHANNEL

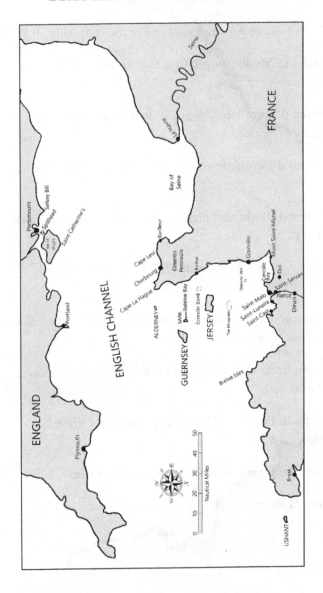

THE SAINT-MALO RAIDS

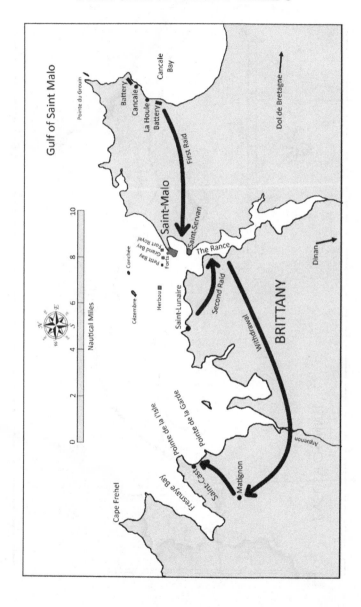

THE CHERBOURG RAID

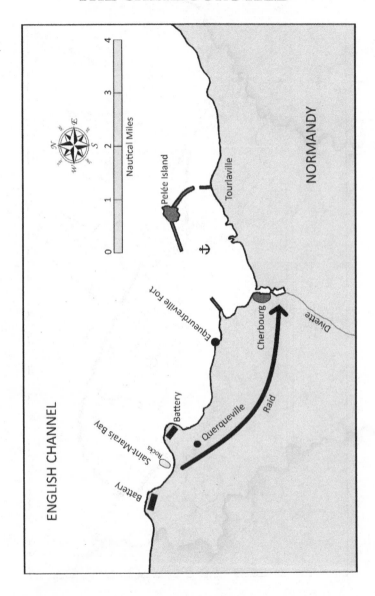

'Like breaking windows with guineas'

***

Henry Fox, 1st Baron Holland, Paymaster General of the Forces.

Describing the failed raid on Rochefort in September 1757 which had cost around a million pounds and achieved almost nothing.

***

Chris Durbin

INTRODUCTION

Pitt's Campaign of Descents

Since 1756, the British government had been under intense pressure from its continental allies to contribute to the war in Europe. There was a great reluctance to send British soldiers to campaign in Germany, instead the government tried to fulfil its alliance obligations with monetary subsidies to Prussia and the German states that were fighting the French. The Army of Observation, led by the Duke of Cumberland, the King's son, was funded by Britain, although no British units were on its fighting strength.

In 1757 the pressure intensified. In response, William Pitt devised a strategy of raids on the French coast with the principle objective of drawing French regiments away from Germany. He called the raids *descents*, and they were not intended as permanent invasions, but temporary occupations. The army was to be withdrawn after the target area was devastated and before a French field army could appear on the scene.

The first of the descents, on Rochefort in September 1757, didn't go well. The expedition was plagued by delays to the frustration of the naval commander, Admiral Edward Hawke. When it arrived off the French coast, the vital island of Île d'Aix was quickly captured, but the army commander Sir John Mordaunt refused to land on the mainland. After destroying the fortifications on the island, the force sailed for home. It was a failure and the troublesome paymaster of the forces Sir Henry Fox, eloquently described it in parliament as *breaking windows with guineas*.

Despite this initial setback, William Pitt was determined to continue the campaign of descents in 1758. In April, after the worst of the winter weather was over, he set the next phase of the strategy in motion.

Carlisle and Holbrooke

1758 was a momentous year for our two heroes. Holbrooke, newly promoted to commander in the sloop *Kestrel*, was sent to blockade Emden on the North Sea border between the Netherlands and the German states. His story in the first quarter of 1758 is told in *Holbrooke's Tide*, the fourth of the Carlisle & Holbrooke Naval Adventures.

Meanwhile, Carlisle in his frigate *Medina* was sent to take part in the siege of Louisbourg, in Nova Scotia. The story of that vital precursor to an invasion of Canada is told in *The Cursed Fortress*, the fifth in the series.

Holbrooke returned from Emden find himself ordered to join the Inshore Squadron of the Channel Fleet under Commodore Howe. Pitt's strategy of descents on the French coast was about to have a dramatic effect on Holbrooke's career and his hopes for the future.

The story continues...

***

PROLOGUE

The Privateer

Friday, Twenty-Sixth of May 1758.
Maréchal de Belle-Isle, at Sea. Off Montrose.

This time, François Thurot wasn't quick enough. That wasn't usually a criticism levelled at the celebrated Frenchman, sometime privateer and now an officer in the French navy. Speed of thought and action were the hallmarks of his successful career, along with boldness and a keen understanding of the profit-and-loss accounts of his trade. It was in recognition of those qualities that the French navy had sent him on this cruise of pure commerce destruction.

He'd been away from Saint-Malo for ten months and so far, his cruise had been successful. Over the past few weeks alone he'd taken seven laden colliers out of Newcastle to add to his long account. But now he'd let himself become trapped between two British frigates. He hadn't immediately recognised them for what they were, perhaps because they were in company with two smaller vessels, and their identity was hidden behind his legitimate prey. Now his attackers were so close either side of him – little more than pistol range – that he couldn't turn in either direction. He was forced to run to the east, away from the Firth of Forth where he'd hoped to pick up some lucrative merchantmen.

The *Maréchal de Belle-Isle* – named after his noble patron – was the strongest of the three, a forty-six gun frigate, almost a ship-of-the-line in weight of broadside. Nevertheless, she was at a decided disadvantage against the two small sixth-rates who could muster over forty guns between them and haul up on either side of him. And the long cruise had taken its toll; he had barely enough men to work both batteries simultaneously.

'You may start firing,' shouted Thurot at his first

lieutenant.

Crash! went the larboard battery and the *Belle-Isle's* deck tilted to starboard, throwing Thurot off balance.

Crash! The starboard battery fired but Thurot was ready for it this time.

Now the noise had become constant with the better-drilled gun crews reloading and firing more rapidly. There were sixty or so guns in action counting the ten or twelve each side for the British frigates. Thurot desperately wanted to get away, but he could see no chance. Five hours they fought, with dead and wounded aplenty on each side, and there seemed no end to it. Then there was an explosion alongside to starboard. A lucky shot had hit a powder ready-use store and one of the frigates started to drop astern. This was his chance and Thurot piled on sail and turned across the stricken ship's bows. One raking broadside from right ahead and he was gone, leaving the frigates to lick their wounds as he headed out into the anonymous wastes of the North Sea.

***

CHAPTER ONE

The Dockyard

Wednesday, Twenty-Ninth of March 1758.
Kestrel, at Anchor. Portsmouth Harbour.

Lieutenant Lynton's left foot was resting on the anchor cable as it inched inboard through the hawse. He felt a jolt then a sudden easing of the tension as the anchor broke free from the stinking black sludge of Portsmouth Harbour.

'Anchor's aweigh,' he called in a conversational tone, directing his voice to the quarterdeck.

There was none of the usual hustle and bustle associated with a ship leaving harbour. No tops'ls were loosed, no jibs backed, and no helm orders given, for His Britannic Majesty's sloop-of-war *Kestrel* was merely moving from her anchor berth in Portsmouth harbour into the wet basin, to await her turn in the single dry dock at its northeast corner.

Josiah Fairview, the sailing master, stood on the quarterdeck from where he could see the cut in the masonry of the dock wall that led into the basin. It was just a hundred yards on the larboard bow, and the gate had been floated into the basin to allow *Kestrel* to pass through. He could see that the last of the flood tide was carrying the usual harbour flotsam in through the entrance.

'Pull away the longboat,' he shouted through the copper speaking trumpet.

The hands at the windlass rushed the last few fathoms of cable through the hawse with practised ease, the pawls clicking in short, staccato bursts as the men leaned their weight against the handspikes.

'Larboard anchor's catted,' reported Jackson, the bosun.

'There's just a mite of flood tide still, sir,' said Fairview, 'we're just a glass before the top of the tide. I'll put her alongside larboard side to, with your permission.'

George Holbrooke, the master and commander of the sloop, studied the walls of the basin entrance. The light breeze from the southwest would naturally push them to the north side of the entrance; that and the flooding tide meant that Jackson would have to be fast with his rattan fenders to avoid damage to the sloop if they berthed as Fairview suggested. He didn't often contradict his sailing master but on this occasion, he knew that the job could be done more elegantly.

'Starboard side to on the southern side of the entrance, if you please, Mister Fairview. I fancy the longboat's crew will get the for'rard warp ashore fast enough to stop us drifting across the gate. The yawl can hold our stern until we can hand the aft warp across.'

This was to be Holbrooke's last act of ship handling for a month or two. From the moment that *Kestrel* was secured to the dockside, the sloop would be the responsibility of the master attendant. He wanted this manoeuvre to be done as best it could be, particularly with a small crowd of dockyard officers and supervisors watching. If he'd let the master do as he'd wanted, it would have been hard to prevent a heavy berthing with both the wind and the tide setting them on. The master's suggestion was the safe one but would inevitably leave a few fathoms of scraped woodwork and paint for the dockyard to deal with.

Holbrooke's way would have the sloop brought gently alongside on the southern side of the entrance, with the wind and tide keeping her off until the hands on the warps hauled her in. Of course, there was a chance that his boat's crews would let him down, that they'd drop the warp as they transferred it from the longboat to the dockside, or that they'd be slow in taking the weight. Then it would be a hard berthing indeed as they'd drift across the basin entrance to the north side. However, he'd sailed with these men for half a year now – some of them for much longer – and he trusted them.

'Aye-aye sir,' replied Fairview, 'starboard side to it is.' If he was at all disturbed at his advice being rejected, he didn't show it. 'Longboat! Take your warp to the southern side of the entrance and look lively with taking the weight,' he shouted.

The longboat was in the charge of Midshipman Edney, while Midshipman Turner had the yawl at the stern of the sloop. Edney waved in reply and under the coxswain's urging the men hauled at their oars, towing the sloop against the light breeze and fading current.

Holbrooke looked over his shoulder. There was no need to give Turner any orders, the yawl was in her ideal position, close to the sloop's starboard quarter, holding the slack of a warp that ran through the after gunport and onto the bitts.

Kestrel moved slowly forward. He could see a stirring of interest among the dockyard officers and riggers as they realised his plan. If it worked, it would make their task of moving the sloop into the wet basin that much simpler, as the wind would tend to keep her off the wall and allow her to be easily moved through the entrance.

Fairview timed the manoeuvre carefully. At the point where the entrance was alongside the sloop's waist and still a ship's length away, he signalled the longboat. Now the timing of the operation became critical. The bosun eased the tow rope to give the longboat enough slack to reach the wall. *Kestrel's* forward movement stopped and for a breathless minute, her way kept her in place. With the weight of the tow rope reduced, the longboat made a dash for the wall. The lighter warp was handed up and the bow oar dropped it over the bollard and made a crossed-arm signal to the sloop.

'Heeeaaave, the fo'c'sle,' urged Jackson, stretching out the vowels to stimulate the men's efforts.

Kestrel's bows turned quickly to larboard under the influence of the tide, the wind and the strain on the warp. Fairview waited for the right moment.

'Avast,' he shouted, 'hold her there, Bosun.'

Now it was the yawl's turn. Turner had to hold the

sloop's stern against the wind and the tide until the aft warp could be passed.

Kestrel's bows were now only two boat's-lengths off the dock wall. Jackson took up the heaving line and stood at the starboard cathead. He flung the coil and the longboat's coxswain caught it and handed it forward. The bow oar scrambled up the dockside again and hauled the line in hand-over-hand. The second warp was attached to its end and when that came snaking over the masonry, he slipped the eye onto the outer bollard.

From there it was easy. Very slowly, *Kestrel* was drawn into the basin entrance by a steady pull on the two warps. Her bows passed through the gap and now the last of the flood tide pushed them gently inwards.

The rattan fenders compressed with that gentle creaking sound – so known and loved by sailors as marking the end of a spell at sea – as *Kestrel* was hauled firmly alongside.

'Fore and aft springs if you please, Mister Jackson,' said Fairview as the sloop came to rest starboard side to with her bows just thrusting through the cut and into the wet basin.

***

'It'll be six weeks I don't doubt, Captain Holbrooke,' said the master attendant, 'maybe two months if we can't get her into the dry dock this time next month. I expect you'll be looking forward to a little shore-leave.'

The master attendant was inclined to be talkative. He was evidently well-pleased that *Kestrel* was being turned over to him so quickly. He had a constant multi-dimensional battle with the Admiralty, the navy board and the sea officers in which the sustained employment of his teams of shipwrights, caulkers, riggers and all the other trades tended to be forgotten. There was plenty of work in the commercial yards that lined the Solent and its tributaries, and his waking nightmare was to lose his best men during a quiet spell when he couldn't employ them.

'Yes, I must pay my calls in London, but otherwise I won't be going far. My home's in Wickham and I plan to visit the yard every other day. Mister Lynton will be on hand too.'

The master attendant looked doubtful at this news; he didn't relish the thought of a ship's captain looking over his shoulder. But Holbrooke was determined that *Kestrel* should be ready for sea by the end of May, and if he had to ruffle a few feathers to ensure that the work continued apace, then so be it. The master attendant shrugged his shoulders in a gesture of resignation.

'We'll warp her into the basin now and close the gate while the water's good and high. I can see the ordnance yard's wagons ready to take away your guns and powder. We'll put the victuals and stores into the number two shed,' he said. 'They'll be safe there, under lock and key.'

'What will you do first?' asked Holbrooke, intensely interested in this hitherto neglected part of his profession. He hadn't stood by a ship undergoing this kind of work before.

'It's all about the wait for the dry dock, sir. Your sloop needs to be scraped and re-caulked and given a couple of coats of the good white stuff. But as you can see,' he waved his arm towards the already occupied dry docks, 'we'll have to wait our turn. I can be sure of a dock in four weeks'– barring accidents – whereas if I try for one in the next few days, we could be disappointed at the last moment and lose all those days of waiting. Their lordships are demanding ships be made ready for the summer and that creates a very high take-up for docks. As for the work, I'll start on shifting the magazine and fitting your port-lids tomorrow, but the wheel can wait. We can even fit that while she's docked down, being as it's all inboard work.'

Holbrooke and the master attendant watched a cheerful procession of sailors making their way ashore. Each man carried his entire belongings in his sea-chest and a canvas bag, and they were lugging two of each between every pair of men. The chests were bound for the store while the bags would accompany them on leave. There was much to be cheerful about because all but two of the ship's company had been given a pass for four weeks' leave. Most would disappear into the boarding houses and sailors' lodgings of Portsmouth Point. Some had family close by and a small group was heading for the carrier's cart to take them to London. The two who had ties in Plymouth had left the day before. The purser had begged a working passage for them on a chartered coasting hoy and with this wind they could hope to be there in two days.

'Don't you fear that they'll run, sir?' asked the master attendant, looking doubtful as each man knuckled his forehead to the first lieutenant. 'I saw the clerk of the cheque going out to you yesterday, so I suppose they've been paid.'

'Yes, they've been paid, but we've been lucky with prizes and I doubt whether any of them will forego their share for a life on the run. In any case, they're good men, and I don't have any real fears. No doubt there'll be a few stragglers, and we'll have a week or two to round them up before we sail. But desertion? I think not,' replied Holbrooke as he acknowledged the more exuberant seamen who waved in his direction.

No, he wasn't worried about losing his crew; in fact, a few of them had asked whether they could bring friends or relatives back with them, landsmen hoping to try their luck at sea. Amazingly, they seemed to like service in *Kestrel*. It was undeniably more comfortable work than signing on to a short-handed merchantman and the food was generally better. And even though it was more dangerous, they had a better chance of staying out of a French prisoner-of-war camp than they would in a merchantman, with the enemy privateers being so active. Certainly, in a merchantman the pay was better with the inflated wartime rates, but the past few months had shown the potential for taking valuable prizes in a small, fast cruiser. Only two men had been denied leave, incorrigibles whom the master-at-arms had identified as likely to abscond. They'd already been sent to the receiving ship and with any luck they'd be snapped up by the port admiral and drafted to a ship-of-the-line before the sloop was ready to be handed back. Lynton had made it quite clear to the second-in-command of the old *Minotaur* hulk that *Kestrel* would make no fuss if they were never seen again.

The master attendant gave Holbrooke an old-fashioned look and shrugged again. He'd seen ships come and go and he'd seen young commanders with these egalitarian ideas before. Privately, he expected there to be a significant delay when *Kestrel* was ready to be handed back, while Holbrooke frantically tried to gather his crew together. The captain was probably right that there would be few genuine deserters, a term that they both understood to mean those men who had no intention of returning and relied on losing themselves among the shifting community of itinerate seamen. But he'd seen ships held up for weeks while three-quarters of their people took their leisure ashore, judging to a nicety the point where straggling, which was rarely punished at all, became desertion with the threat of serious reprisal.

'Do you have a few moments to see the drawings, Captain? I think you'll like the way we're going to lead the wheel tackles and you'll see that we'll be encasing the tiller on the upper deck, so it won't disturb your cabin at all.'

That avoided the usual disadvantage of fitting a wheel in a flush-decked sloop. It still required a long tiller attached to the head of the rudder to provide the leverage to move it, and usually the tiller would be moved from the upper deck to the deck-head immediately below, and that was the captain's cabin. The master attendant's proposal kept the deck-head of the cabin clear.

'You'll have your very own two-foot-high poop-deck, sir, just like a flagship, and a stylish taffrail to match. You won't be flush-decked any longer,' and he smiled happily at his own joke.

'Well, the men already talk of the fo'c'sle, the waist and the quarterdeck, just like a frigate, even though we have a clean sweep from forward to aft. I expect they'll have no trouble in adapting to a poop-deck.'

'Just so long as they don't give themselves airs and graces, sir, that never leads to any good.'

***

Holbrooke went below to see to his own things. His servant had already packed up his personal belongings and was busy transferring them to a cart that would take them to the Dolphin on the High Street. His servant was a freed slave from a French plantation on San Domingue; the only surname he'd ever known was Serviteur, a working name if ever there was one. He'd been the major-domo in the great house and his knowledge of looking after a gentleman far exceeded the needs of most sea officers. Serviteur would accompany Holbrooke and the chaplain to the Dolphin.

'Your furniture will be going to number two store, sir, but everything else will be going with you.'

'Thank you, Serviteur. I hope we won't be gone too long,' he said as he looked wistfully around the cabin.

He'd grown fond of the sloop, having taken it from Dutch pirates in the Caribbean. He felt more ownership than if it had been an anonymous ship allocated to him by a soulless Admiralty.

'Do you wish to have any leave, Serviteur? The first lieutenant tells me that you didn't request any.'

'No sir. I know nobody in this country except the Kestrels. I'd like to see London one day, but otherwise I'm content.'

'Then when I visit the Admiralty, you'll come with me.'

Holbrooke still found it a novelty to have a servant. He'd grown up in a cottage on the outskirts of a small Hampshire market town. On washing days his mother had been helped by a local girl, but she could hardly be called a servant. Serviteur could have taken advantage of him, he knew, but so far there had been no sign of that kind of behaviour.

'If that's all done, then I think we'll get underway,' he said. A servant might have been a novelty to Holbrooke, but since taking command of *Kestrel* he'd never once set foot off the sloop without the ritual of pipes, doffed hats and attendant sideboys. Now, with the ship in dockyard hands, there was nobody to see him over the side. He walked over the gangway as if he was walking off a Gosport wherry.

***

CHAPTER TWO

Blessings of the Land

Thursday, Thirtieth of March 1758.
The Dolphin, Portsmouth High Street.

Holbrooke's face was studiously expressionless. 'I wonder – just hypothetically – what would be a suitable time of day to call upon a young lady?' he asked, 'at her family home,' he added, for context.

Chalmers paused, fighting hard to keep the smile from his face and searching back through his memory to a time when he too had paid calls on young ladies.

'Well, it depends on the circumstances of the hypothetical case,' he replied with unnatural solemnity. 'If the caller hasn't chosen to obtain permission from the young lady's father, then I would say any time in the middle watch would be appropriate, and a ladder of an appropriate length may come in handy. At what height is this hypothetical lady's chamber?'

Holbrooke looked at him sharply, then his face creased into a grin.

'I'd never associated you with facetiousness, David,' he replied. 'The location of the lady's chamber is not an important factor in this question. You may assume that the hypothetical father's permission has been sought and obtained.'

Chalmers gazed discreetly out of the window; Holbrooke was blushing, the bright crimson colour creeping up from his stock to his cheeks. It was hard to imagine a person less suited for deception than George Holbrooke. Not only had he ordered breakfast at a distressingly early time, but here he was in his best frock coat and he'd shaved so close that the rush of blood to his face threatened to break through what was left of his epidermis.

14

They'd taken a pair of rooms at the Dolphin, a newly established inn on the busy main street of Portsmouth. It sat opposite the church of Saint Thomas whose gilded weathercock in the form of a ship under sail watched over the proceedings of the great port city. The Dolphin was a convenient distance from the dockyard gate, close enough to walk to the wet basin in about thirty minutes and ideally suited to accommodate a sea officer and a chaplain whose mark was accepted everywhere, in consequence of *Kestrel's* known accomplishment in taking prizes. They were sitting now in Chalmers' room which had half of a shallow bay window that looked left towards the Square Tower and the Sally Port, and beyond to the Solent. Portsmouth Point was – thankfully – out of sight to the right of the tower.

'In that case, eleven o'clock – six bells in the forenoon watch if you prefer – is generally considered a suitable time in London town, but anywhere between ten and twelve. If you call before ten you risk embarrassing the family before they've composed themselves. After twelve gives the impression that you expect to be invited for dinner. Elsewhere, outside London, I can't say, but I imagine that it won't be so different.'

Chalmers looked at his pocket watch.

'If you ask the landlord to hail a carriage now your timing will be about right.'

'You make some unwarranted assumptions about my destination, David,' Holbrooke retorted.

'Perhaps,' he replied, 'and yet only yesterday I distinctly heard your clerk announcing a letter from a Mister Featherstone in Wickham which you hastily forbade him to open. After your visit to your father in December you mentioned, in passing and yet not without a certain *je ne sais quoi* in your tone, a young lady named Miss Featherstone. And of course, you sent a letter to a gentleman of the same name on Tuesday morning. There are few secrets in a sixteen-gun sloop George, and it doesn't take the intellect of an archbishop to make the connection.'

Holbrooke laughed out loud.

'Few secrets indeed,' he said, privately pleased that there was no more need for subterfuge. 'Would you care to join me? To visit Wickham, I mean, not to call on the Featherstone family.'

Chalmers paused a moment. He'd been planning to explore Saint Thomas' church. Then, if there was time, to look into Domus Dei, the church at the seaward end of the high street where Charles II had married Catherine of Braganza. It had been used as the Portsmouth garrison church for several decades, but he hoped some trace of its glorious past may have survived. However, a trip to Wickham was attractive. He'd like to call on the senior Holbrooke whose cottage lay just to the north of the village. The trout on the river Meon were just starting to fatten up after the winter and the Holbrooke cottage had fishing rights on a stretch of the stream. After all, he *had* been invited...

It had been many years since he'd cast a fly, but William Holbrooke had repeated the offer – quite insistently – in a letter earlier in the week, and the weather was fair with a light breeze from the west. The Meon trout never rose beneath an easterly wind, he'd been assured.

'Delighted. I'll be ready by the time the carriage arrives.'

***

'Captain Holbrooke, sir,' announced the flustered maidservant, making an inexpert curtsey and offering a calling card on a tray, a combination of movements that almost toppled her. 'He's calling on Miss Featherstone,' she continued with an unconcealed look of wide-eyed wonderment. 'I've offered him a seat in the lobby, sir,' she added.

Martin Featherstone was a big man, a substantial person in this small market town on the tail of the South Downs. He stood a similar height to Holbrooke, but where the younger man was slender, Featherstone had put on weight with age and good living. He had a large, angular face –

considered handsome by many women – and powerful neck and shoulder muscles that gave him the poise of a prize bull.

On Thursdays Mister Featherstone would usually have been about his business. He was a corn merchant and even at this season of the year he was busy cutting deals with farmers and mill-owners, engaging carters on forward contracts and selling his stocks of grain to traders from London and beyond. However, the family had been set into a spin when a letter arrived from the young sea officer whom the whole town was talking about. His breakfast had been unaccountably delayed, and no iron had yet been applied to his shirt, even though he'd been informed by his wife that he couldn't possibly leave the house in an un-ironed shirt. All this inconvenience, as far as he could tell, was so that his daughter's wardrobe could be overhauled. Consequently, and most unusually, Martin Featherstone was at home on Thursday morning and not in the best of tempers.

Naturally, Featherstone knew nothing of the letter that his daughter had sent to Holbrooke in January, that was a matter between his wife Sophie and her stepdaughter, his own daughter, Ann. He'd been surprised, therefore, to receive a letter from Holbrooke on the previous Tuesday asking his permission to call on Ann. Of course, he'd heard of Holbrooke's latest exploits in his sloop *Kestrel*; it was the talk of the town. He'd been with Commodore Holmes at Emden, apparently, and had taken prizes! Featherstone was a commercial man; he knew all about the naval prize system, so he was aware that Holbrooke was unlikely to be penniless.

Perhaps a little rashly, Featherstone had replied to Holbrooke giving his permission. Meanwhile, he'd determined that he should know more about the naval rank system. At Christmas, Holbrooke had been introduced as a *captain*, and yet in the letter he'd described himself as *master and commander*. The subtlety of the distinction eluded him, but he felt it might be important. He'd agreed to meet a retired sea officer in Soberton later that week, to gain a better understanding. After all, he had only one child and he was a man of means. Martin Featherstone had ambitions for his daughter, and she was not to be given away to the first adventurer that crossed the threshold.

The pace of life of a provincial corn merchant hadn't prepared Featherstone for the rapidity of action that characterised the sea service. He'd expected a week or two to fritter away before Holbrooke appeared. Yet here he was, only a day after the earliest that he could have received Featherston's reply, seated in the very lobby of Bere Forest House in Wickham's square

Martin Featherstone stared hard at the maidservant. Sophie oversaw the domestic affairs of the household and on principle he didn't interfere, but his forbearance had been sorely tested this morning and this very maidservant was at the centre of the affair. It was *she* who should have laid out his breakfast and *she* should have ironed his shirt. But oh, no! She was too busy fussing around his daughter in the expectation of this visit.

When one has spent a full two hours in a bad temper, it's difficult to snap out of it with any grace, but Featherstone made his best attempt. After all, his beloved Ann had never had a gentleman caller, and he vaguely understood that it was probably a significant moment in her life. He wouldn't willingly spoil it for her.

'Thank you, Polly. You may inform Miss Featherstone of her caller. I'll send for her shortly,' he said with an expression that hovered somewhere between an unnatural smile and a grimace. 'And when you've done that Mister Holbrooke and I will have coffee in the drawing room. I assume it's fit for visitors.'

'Oh yes, sir,' Polly replied, 'Mrs Featherstone gave me particular instructions yesterday that the drawing room was to be ready for visitors at a moment's notice. That's why your breakfast wasn't ready, sir, nor your shirt, I was smoothing the covers.'

There was a looking glass in the library. Featherstone took a moment to adjust his expression; he didn't want to appear discontented when he met this sea officer. Where was his wife when he needed her? Why was the whole routine of the household thrown to the winds for this visit?

***

'Good morning, Mister Holbrooke. How do you do?' asked Featherstone. By a feat of superhuman self-will, he'd almost wholly restored his natural geniality in the half dozen steps from the library to the lobby. 'Will you join me in the drawing room?'

'Thank you, sir,' replied Holbrooke, nursing a hand crushed to half its usual size by the steel grip of Featherstone's handshake. 'I'm very well, thank you.'

The drawing room at Bere House was comfortable in a provincial, unshowy way. It faced southeast across the square and caught the best of the morning sun. Today it was unusually splendid; there were flowers on the sideboard and fresh linen covers had been laid across the backs of the chairs. The glass in the windows had evidently been cleaned that very morning and there was a pleasant smell of beeswax polish in the air. By chance Martin Featherstone hadn't visited the drawing room yet, having been taken up with fuming about the lack of breakfast and a clean shirt. He was startled by what he saw but managed to stifle an impolite expression of surprise.

'Please take a seat, Captain Holbrooke, the maid will be here in a moment. Will you take coffee?'

They settled into comfortable chairs with a view of the bustling town. For a small settlement of perhaps a thousand souls, it was remarkably busy. There were carts and drays, horses and oxen, women and men, all mingled and all crossing each other's path. The peculiarity of Wickham was that the shops and inns, the dwellings and businesses were scattered democratically around the square, offering no natural routes for an established pattern of movement. They looked out upon a glorious confusion of movement.

'I'm happy to see that you've returned safely. Have you seen your father yet?'

'Not yet, sir, I'll call on him later today, although my chaplain is with him now and no doubt, they're on the stream casting a fly for the trout.'

'I read with interest about the capture of Emden,' continued Featherstone who was no angler, 'I understand your ship was there with the famous Commodore Holmes.'

Holbrooke smiled ruefully. Holmes, of course, was taking all the credit, but he'd only arrived on the Ems the day before Emden's fall. All the hard work had already been done by *Kestrel*.

'Yes, my ship was part of Mister Holmes' squadron,' he replied modestly. There was no benefit, he knew, in explaining the niceties of the commodore's position in relation to a mere commander. '*Kestrel's* in the yard now, probably until the end of May, so I'm shore-bound for a few months.'

'I see,' Featherstone replied.

There was an awkward pause. I may as well take the bull by the horns, Holbrooke thought.

'I called in the hope of seeing your daughter, Ann,' he said.

'Of course, of course…'

The maid came in bearing coffee. The cook had been ordered by Mrs Featherstone to keep a pot of water near the boil until further notice, and its rapid arrival confused Featherstone.

'Polly, would you tell Miss Featherstone that Captain Holbrooke is in the drawing room?'

Polly curtsied to Mister Featherstone, then in defiance of protocol, she quickly curtsied to Holbrooke, looking him full in the face as she did so. After all, her routine had been turned upside down in anticipation of this visit, she deserved to see the man who was causing such expectation.

They sat in silence for two minutes, not knowing quite what to say. Neither of them had been in this situation before.

Shortly there was a knock on the door and Sophie and Ann came in. Mrs Featherstone brought a much brisker atmosphere to the gathering; she knew exactly what to do with gentleman callers. There were renewed introductions, then farewells from Martin Featherstone who, with a sigh of relief, felt he really should see to his business.

Sophie Featherstone was not embarrassed at all by the meeting. She liked Holbrooke and loved her stepdaughter as only a childless woman can. She'd already decided that they were a good match and had determined to make it her business to promote the friendship.

'Goodbye, dear,' she said to the retreating form of her husband. His business was only two hundred yards away and there was no ceremony about his coming and going. Even so, he felt that his wife could have walked him to the door…

'Now,' she said, turning back to the drawing room where Holbrooke and Ann were coyly considering each other across a small card table, 'we dine at two in the afternoon, Captain Holbrooke, and I've taken the liberty of assuming you will stay to join us. Mister Featherstone will be back promptly at that time as he missed his breakfast.'

She didn't look too contrite at her husband's missed meal, nor did she pause to hear whether Holbrooke would in fact like to stay for dinner.

'I have business with the cook and the maid.'

She looked out through the window at the beautiful spring morning.

'When we last met, we played whist, so I know very well that it's not your favourite pastime, Captain. I propose to leave you two alone. It's a beautiful day for a walk, and if you'll take my advice, there's a good path down to the dipping hole and along the stream from there. Ann, you should wear your walking shoes for it may be a bit damp underfoot. But of course, you were brought up in the town, weren't you, Captain? You'll know the path well.'

And with that, she was gone. They could hear her voice fading away to the back of the house as she called her servants to her.

***

Sophie Featherstone would have given David Chalmers a run for his money in the understanding of human nature. She knew very well how awkward it was to become acquainted with someone while regarding them across a card table in the confines of a drawing room, however sunny. When walking, on the other hand, the two people were not committed to staring at each other, with all the self-consciousness that it caused. They could converse much more freely looking at the buildings and trees, passing the time of day with friends and neighbours and looking out for tree roots and stones in the path.

Holbrooke and Ann walked side-by-side along the square towards the dipping-hole. They did indeed encounter friends. In Sophie's case it was a matter of a passing greeting, but in Holbrooke's it required a longer pause; apart from his short visit last Christmas, he hadn't spent any time in his hometown for years. And he was locally famous! People with the slightest acquaintance wanted to speak to him, to congratulate him on the victory at Cape François, where he'd been in temporary command of a frigate, and Emden, although they were hazier about his role in that affair.

Past the dipping-hole they continued walking upstream on a flint-laid path that followed the Meon. Holbrooke knew it well; half a mile further on they would pass on the other side the cottage where he'd grown up. In his youth, he'd known it as the *poachers' path*, because the boys of the town set their night lines here and in the height of summer tickled the tiny trout from under the alder roots. Once a year, in May, it became a dangerous place as the itinerate traders at the Wickham Horse Fair claimed their share of the catch.

Holbrooke's rather vague memory of Ann had been of

a shy girl who blushed when she met his eye, but something had changed. It would have been an exaggeration to suggest that in the past three months she'd become bold, but she'd certainly gained confidence. Whereas before she'd been a pretty young woman who had to be coaxed to talk, now she was positively chatty. Perhaps her nature thrived in small groups rather than the horde of people who had shared Christmas dinner at Rookesbury House, or perhaps it was the fresh air.

'…and did you really persuade the French to leave Emden without having to fight for it? That must have taken some diplomatic skills.'

'Not really,' replied Holbrooke, 'they knew that they couldn't hold it against a determined attack, all I had to do was persuade them to leave before they were forced to. But that's enough about the war, let's talk about something more cheerful.'

'Captain Holbrooke! How could you? Don't you know how much it's worth to me to hear these things from you who were there? My company will be sought for months to come, just so that I can re-tell the stories!'

'Oh, but I was hoping to hear something of yourself. I know that you like gardening and sewing and reading…'

They walked on up the stream, past Holbrooke's father's cottage and on through the Rookesbury estate.

'Is that your father?' asked Ann, pointing to two figures casting upstream, with their backs necessarily turned to walkers from downstream.

'Yes, that's my father and my chaplain…'

'You have a chaplain? How grand, may I meet him? I know your father fairly well; we pass the time of day when we meet in town or at church.'

'Unless we turn around, I fear that a meeting is inevitable,' Holbrooke replied. 'Shall we see how close we can get before they see us?'

They walked on quietly, avoiding the tree roots and the larger stones until they were only ten yards behind the two anglers.

'There!' whispered William Holbrooke. 'Do you see him, or rather his tail, just this side of that patch of weed? He rises! To an early March Brown I expect.'

Chalmers counted to ten to let the trout settle again after his mouthful, then he cast his own imitation. It landed six feet ahead of the trout, in between two thick patches of trailing weed that created a temporary channel in the stream. The trout's tail flicked faster in agitation; he'd seen the fly. When it came, the rise was lightning-fast, faster than Chalmers could react. He struck, but the canny trout had already discarded the tasteless confection of feather and iron, and with a disdainful flick of its tail it cruised away to the safety of the far bank.

***

For the next six weeks, Holbrooke was a regular visitor at Bere Forest House. He called once or twice a week and usually stayed for dinner. The invariable arrangement was for him and Chalmers to take a carriage in the morning and visit the cottage. Holbrooke would walk into the town leaving Chalmers to pester the Meon trout with William. They'd stay the night with Holbrooke's father and in the morning take a carriage back to the Dolphin. They were pleasant weeks of glorious spring weather, a growing fondness between Holbrooke and Ann, company for William and the occasional unwary trout for Chalmers.

However, a sea officer in 1758 could count himself blessed with every week that he had away from his duty; for the King's service was relentless. In early May a letter arrived for Holbrooke at his lodgings: orders, and an end to the halcyon days.

***

CHAPTER THREE

Commodore Howe

Wednesday, Tenth of May 1758.
The Admiralty. London.

The early morning light picked up the motes of dust in the board room of the Admiralty building in London, where Lord Anson was chairing an extraordinary meeting.

'I repeat, Gentlemen, we must comply with Mister Pitt's wishes, and I must say that there is some merit in them.'

'Merit you say, My Lord, yet we proved at Rochefort that these *descents'* – Forbes spat out the word as though it was something distasteful – 'can't work. The army's heart isn't in it and we're too vulnerable during the landing. And all for what? A possible – and I emphasise *possible* – diversion of French forces from Hanover. We have better things to do in the Americas and the Caribbean. Even West Africa for God's sake! This is a poor use of our naval superiority.' Forbes was not a man to hide his feelings.

'Nevertheless, we are bound to support the ministry. In any case, Mister Howe is gathering his ships, the Duke of Marlborough is mustering his forces, and the flatboats are a-building. I suggest we salvage what we can out of this and choose the objectives that most suit the war at sea. Now gentlemen,' he looked around him at the three civilian members, Hay, Hunter and Elliot, and Admiral Forbes; Boscawen wasn't there, he was on his way to Louisbourg. 'Perhaps we should start with that nest of vipers in Saint-Malo. We can deprive that scoundrel Thurot of his home base and clear out the rest of the privateers. That will get King Louis' attention…'

***

Holbrooke's longboat rowed him out into the choppy waters of the Solent. Not for the first time he wondered

how many sailors had been drowned in this small area
between the Hampshire coast and the Isle of Wight. With
the majority of the navy's men-of-war anchored at Spithead
or St. Helen's, it was quite usual for ships' boats and the
various craft that serviced the fleet to put out from
Portsmouth in the unruliest of weather. Today the Solent
was in turmoil, with the ebbing tide meeting a sturdy
sou'westerly breeze, raising a chop that would soon
overwhelm a poorly handled boat. He watched in awe as
Dawson steered effortlessly towards *Essex*, a third rate of
sixty-four guns, flying Commodore Howe's broad pennant.

'Good morning, Captain Holbrooke.' said John
Campbell, the captain of the flagship. His native scots
accent had persisted through twenty years of service away
from his home, and no amount of exposure to the
southerners had managed to modify it. 'Have you met the
commodore yet? No? Well, you'll find him bursting with
energy and ready to sail, if only the damned army would
move a little faster.'

Holbrooke had met Campbell at dinner a week before.
He'd been a sailing master before he'd passed the
lieutenant's examination and his rise had been rapid since
then. The navy had few enough examples of this
transformation from a warrant officer to a commission
officer, and he was noteworthy among his contemporaries.

'You've had your orders to join the squadron?' Campbell
asked.

Holbrooke patted his breast pocket.

'They arrived yesterday. I'm to join the Inshore
Squadron of the Channel Fleet under the commodore.'

'You and many others,' Campbell grinned, 'it's a
monstrous great squadron for a commodore, five of the
line, ten frigates, seven or so of your kind and over a
hundred transports, victuallers and storeships.'

Holbrooke whistled softly.

'You know that Hawke has hauled down his flag rather
than suffer the disgrace of giving way to a junior officer?'

'I'd heard so, sir,' Holbrooke replied, not wanting to commit himself to an opinion on the rights and wrongs of admirals' actions. He remembered the strained atmosphere in the navy over Byng's court martial.

'Of course, it was all a misunderstanding. The commodore merely requested some charts of the waters about Rochefort. Hawke's soundings were presumed better than anyone else possessed, seeing as he spent considerable time there last year. Hawke concluded from that that this secret expedition was bound again to Rochefort and that their lordships had decided that a captain could make a better hash of it than an admiral.'

Was that a hint, thought Holbrooke, that the expedition was not bound for Rochefort after all? The talk of London and Portsmouth was of a second expedition to that important naval port.

'What you've probably not heard is that Hawke was at the Admiralty yesterday, and they were none too sympathetic. They cleared up the misunderstanding but declined to restore his command. Anson has the Channel Fleet – again – and Hawke will have to sail as his second.'

'Then does Commodore Howe report to Lord Anson?'

'He does not. The Channel Fleet will cover the expedition, but the inshore squadron reports directly to the secretary of state, to Mister Pitt himself. You can imagine how that was perceived by Hawke!'

They had stopped outside the commodore's quarters for a moment, not wanting to enter in mid-conversation.

'You said you hadn't met the commodore.'

Campbell had a way of keeping people on the back foot by imparting critical information and following it with an innocuous statement. Holbrooke had no time to digest the vital issue before he had to respond to the lesser. Hawke resigned! That was news indeed. Britain didn't have enough admirals of his calibre that it could afford to lose one. It was fortunate indeed that he'd agreed to reinstatement.

'No, I haven't. I know him only by reputation.'

'Well, I'll say no more, but be prepared for a surprise! By the way, I hear you have Josiah Fairview as your sailing master. He was my mate in *Centurion* in '44, and a damned good one. Give him my best, will you?'

'I will, sir,' replied Holbrooke, 'but before I meet the commodore, can you tell me where we're bound?'

'Now that I can't,' he replied. 'It's a secret that only the commodore may divulge. I expect he'll tell you but be prepared to be sworn to secrecy. He's cleared the cabin of hangers-on, it'll be just you, the commodore, the secretary and me.'

***

Meeting Richard Howe was a shock. Holbrooke knew that he was young for such a significant command, but it still came as a surprise. He appeared to be around thirty, and a youthful thirty at that. Holbrooke knew the bare bones of Howe's career. He'd passed for lieutenant at nineteen and had been made commander almost immediately. He'd been posted less than a year later, still in his twentieth year. It hadn't slipped Holbrooke's notice that he could emulate Howe if he was posted in the next six months. And it seemed quite possible. Both men had profited from the promotion opportunities that the war brought, and this one had every prospect of lasting long enough to see Holbrooke a post-captain. Of course, Howe was the second son of an Irish peer, and that helped…

'Captain Holbrooke, how pleasant. I regret that I haven't had a chance to meet you socially before we dive into business, but time's a-wasting and we have great deeds to do. Nothing less than to take the war onto French soil!' Howe jumped up from his chair as though it was suddenly too hot for him and strode across the cabin to greet his guest. Holbrooke had heard of the commodore's restless energy, but he'd been unprepared for its full impact. Most senior offices affected an air of indifference, a detachment from the hurly-burly of daily affairs. But not Richard Howe.

There was a chart of the French coast laid out on the

dining table, from The Bay of Seine to Ushant, encompassing most of the north of Normandy and all of Brittany's channel coast. Coloured paper markers had been pinned to some of the principal ports: Le Havre, Cherbourg, Granville, Saint-Malo. That was all that Holbrooke could register at a quick glance before he had to give his attention to Howe.

'We're going to make a series of *descents* – Mister Pitt's term, not mine – on French ports. Put the army ashore, take a port, hold it or sack it and re-embark. What do you think?'

So that was it! He'd heard that an army was heading for camps on the Isle of Wight. In fact, he'd seen some of the marching columns embarking on transports at Portsmouth. It was a strange place to position an army either for attack or defence unless it was merely to hold them in readiness for an expedition. But what did he think? That was an awkward question from a commodore to a commander. What would his friend and mentor Captain Carlisle say? And what would Chalmers say? Given this opportunity, neither would satisfy themselves with sycophantic platitudes, and neither would start at the bottom.

'It sounds very alluring, sir, but if I may ask, what is the objective? What does Mister Pitt hope that we will gain from this?'

Howe exchanged a glance with Campbell, whose secret grin hadn't left his face.

'That's a very pertinent question, Captain Holbrooke. I can see that we'll agree very well.'

Howe paused; one foot perched on the seat of a dining chair.

'No doubt we can do this – if the army is game, that's a separate question. But *why* should we? Why indeed? Why not send more ships to the Americas to squash French resistance? Why not the sugar islands, the East Indies or the Guinea Coast? In each of those places a squadron such as the one that I've been given could turn the tide of the war, could establish local supremacy and take valuable territory.

So why Normandy and Brittany? An excellent question.'

He turned to his secretary.

'Bring that globe over here would you?'

It was a medium-sized globe on a carved mahogany stand, the sort of ornament that a well-to-do merchant would have in his drawing room; it would have looked well at Bere Forest House. Somehow it was out of place in the great cabin of a ship-of-the-line; too frivolous, too pretentious, not a serious navigational instrument.

'This has become a global war, a war for ownership of the raw materials of the world and the trade routes that bring them to our industries. It's not a series of separate campaigns as some would see it, nor can it be addressed by a succession of unconnected decisions: should we defeat the French in North America? do we defend Hanover? can we protect our Caribbean islands?'

He moved his hand restlessly across the globe, spinning it rapidly to make his points about the nature of the war.

'That's a small-minded way of looking at it. They're all linked, and a blow to the French channel ports will reverberate around the continents.'

Howe stood back. He swept his hand through his wig in a gesture of mental fatigue, his agile mind running far ahead of his tongue.

'Let's say we strike at Saint-Malo, just for example,' he said with an odd knowing look. 'First, we can clear out that privateers' nest so that the likes of Thurot have no safe base for their operations. That will allow some of our cruisers to be deployed elsewhere and the City will give thanks to the government.'

He tallied the points on his fingers.

'Second, the French army will have to deploy regular foot regiments, and horse and artillery, to protect their own coast. The coastal militia will never be up to the job. That'll take the pressure off Prince Ferdinand and ease Hanover's immediate danger, but you'll know all about that,' he added with a wink.

Holbrooke nodded. It was good to hear that his exploits in Emden were appreciated. After all, he'd secured the surrender of the first European city to fall to Britain's forces in this war, even if Commodore Holmes was taking all the credit.

'The King, of course, will be delighted that his beloved Hanover is being cherished, and the King's delight is a public service in itself.'

Howe paused again, perhaps marshalling his thoughts.

'Third, this blow can be struck without weakening the Channel Squadron, and that is the pivot on which all our sea-power balances. If we should lose superiority in the Channel, the French army will be on the Sussex coast before you can say *call out the militia*. Much good it would do anyway.'

Howe evidently shared the prevailing view of the effectiveness of militia regiments, whether French or British.

'And finally, all of this prevents the French from putting their resources into building ships to reinforce North America or protect their trade in the Caribbean. The beauty of this strategy is that it hardly dissipates our naval strength at all, we just use it more effectively. And the soldiers … well with Mister Pitt's reluctance to send them to the continent, they're all under-employed anyway.'

'The strategy is sound,' said Campbell interjecting. 'Nevertheless, there's unease after the disaster at Rochefort last year.'

'You know what happened, Holbrooke?' asked Howe.

'I know that the army chose not to land,' replied Holbrooke cautiously. The navy's view of the operation was that the debacle had been the fault of General Mordaunt, who had commanded the land forces. It was probably quite safe to take that line with Howe, but then again, Holbrooke had no idea of Howe's allegiance; he could be a close relative of the general.

'And the fools on his court-martial board *chose* to

exonerate him! It's put the blame back on the government and now there's only lukewarm support for another attempt. You know what that radical Fox has been saying?'

Holbrooke did know, but he kept his peace.

'*Breaking windows with guineas*, he calls it, and that kind of trite slogan plays well with the mob. It can be chalked on a cart-tail and its very brevity gives it an air of authenticity. God preserve us from democracy! And you didn't hear me say that.'

There was a pause while each man considered the cost of the Rochefort enterprise. A million sterling, it was estimated. Mordaunt was lucky that he hadn't suffered the same fate as Admiral Byng, who'd been found guilty of *not doing his utmost* and shot on the quarterdeck of a third rate no great distance from where *Essex* was anchored.

'Well, our expedition will be closer to home this time. Now, this is of the greatest secrecy; you understand Holbrooke? Not a word to anyone, not your first lieutenant, not your family. Nobody!'

Holbrooke nodded, his heart beating faster at the prospect of knowing where Pitt's next blow was to fall and knowing *Kestrel's* part in the enterprise.

Howe moved over to the chart.

'Here,' he said, pointing to the southern end of the bay that stretched south from Jersey and Guernsey, 'at Saint-Malo. If we can take the town, then with command of the sea we can hold it as long as we like, a running sore in the French flank. If we can't, then we can at least clear out the harbour and make the privateers think twice about using it as their base of operations. In either case the French army will be forced to react, to move at least a portion of their power west away from Hanover. Go on, out with it man! I can see your mind whirring!'

Holbrooke gulped. Did Howe really want his opinion, or was this a trap? Was the commodore angling for an excuse to have him relieved by a more experienced commander? Holbrooke almost responded with a banal comment on what a great stroke it would be for King and country, but he was again saved from such a timorous response by a recollection of what his mentor Captain Carlisle would say, and what his friend Chalmers would advise. Both would say that he must seize his chances, and it wasn't every day that his opinion was sought by a man who commanded such a squadron as this.

'Benbow tried it '93, sir, and the fortifications have been extended since then…'

'Ah! You're correct, of course. But I don't intend a direct assault from the sea, and nor does the duke, I hope.'

Howe saw the questioning look on Holbrooke's face.

'His Grace the Duke of Marlborough, grandson to the famous one, on his mother's side. He's leading the army that we're to throw ashore at the French,' said Howe. 'We're to work together on this. I lead the force until the army's ashore, and the duke takes over from there, although of course I must consult with the duke as we select a landing site.'

Holbrooke was wondering why he was being brought into the commodore's confidence in this way. Howe must have quite enough to occupy his mind, being sent on a combined operation where his opposite number was a lieutenant-general, in his fifties and an *English* peer, while Howe himself was merely a commodore – a substantive post-captain when all was said and done – and a mere honourable, the second son of an *Irish* peer.

'No, we won't assault Saint-Malo directly. However, there's one condition that may persuade me to do so. Bring over that chart, would you?' he called to his secretary.

'You see the approach to Saint-Malo? It's well defended with batteries all along the channel. As you pointed out, Vauban's engineering works have been completed since Benbow anchored his bombs within range of the city. This island here,' he pointed to a speck on the chart just two miles north of Saint-Malo, 'is La Conchée Fort. It's a whole island covered, every inch of it, by fortifications. It effectively prevents any seaborne approach from the north and east.'

Holbrooke could see what he meant. Back in 1693, La Conchée was still under construction and Benbow had easily captured it and bombarded Saint-Malo from the very position that the fort was now covering. Even then, Holbrooke reflected, Benbow had been unable to subdue the city.

'Now, this island a mile or two to the west, Cézambre Island, guards the outer end of the channel. If we could sail up that channel, we could batter the city into submission. There've been strange rumours that the guns on Cézambre have been removed. I doubt it, I very much doubt it, but I need confirmation. And as soon as that's confirmed, I need the more likely landing site to be investigated.' He moved his finger east. 'Here at Cancale Bay on the other side of the peninsula, just seven miles from Saint-Malo by land.'

He looked directly at Holbrooke.

'So those are your orders, Captain Holbrooke. I need certainty as to whether Cézambre is armed. As soon as your sloop is ready for sea – and the yard tells me that will be no more than two weeks from now – you're to sail for Saint-Malo and then Cancale Bay.'

***

Howe had appeared to lose interest in Holbrooke after that. He fussed around with his charts as Campbell and the secretary filled in the details. It was only as Holbrooke was leaving the cabin that Howe seemed to remember his existence.

'We'll do well together, you and I, Holbrooke. Two boys let loose with the toybox. We'll do great things.'

Campbell laughed as they reached the deck.

'There's no stopping Richard Howe,' he said. 'He sees the absurdity of his position. Barely thirty and in command of all this,' he said, sweeping the anchorage with a wave of his hand, 'yet he doesn't let it weigh upon him. If I may give you some advice: play the same game. You're very young for your position if you don't mind the observation. Don't use that as a reason to keep your head below the hammock-netting. Commodore Howe will never criticise you for pushing yourself forward.'

Holbrooke was on the verge of a short answer. He was exhausted by the interview and now he suspected he was being patronised. But he stopped himself just in time. Campbell was no competitor, but perhaps an ally in a strange sort of way.

'Let's stretch our legs for a moment then I have to give you the part of your orders that Mister Howe omitted. Don't worry,' he said as he saw the look of concern on Holbrooke's face, 'it's nothing of any great consequence.'

***

'Even their lordships learn their lessons, slowly and reluctantly, but eventually when all else has failed they try something new,' Campbell stated in a loud voice.

Holbrooke was faintly shocked; not at the sentiment, but at the public utterance. There were half a dozen officers within earshot – this being a crowded flagship – and any one of them could store up those words to fling at their captain in some future dispute.

'You heard about the command arrangements. It's now quite clear that the army has little to say until they're on dry land, but that's just the start of it. There are to be new boats to put them ashore, no more making do with the squadron's longboats and yawls!'

Now, this was interesting. Holbrooke had been aware of the weak link in a landing operation: the long, long process of putting the soldiers, their artillery, horses, ammunition and supplies ashore. Ship's boats just weren't made for that; they were designed principally for their seaworthiness. Their carrying capacity and ability to land on beaches came a long, long way down in the list of design criteria.

'Last month the Admiralty ordered two examples of launches to be constructed to a navy board design. Thirty-six feet long with a flat bow and a forefoot that cuts back by a fathom or two, so that they can easily run up a sand or shingle beach. I don't know much more. What I do know is that Mrs Winter's yard at Deptford Wharf built one of them and she's reckoned to have lost a good sum of money doing so, the clench-work being so difficult around the bow. Be that as it may, they clearly passed muster, and now all the capable yards have been given orders to build them as fast as they can.'

Holbrooke had heard rumours of something of this nature. It was supposed to be confidential, but there was little hope of the shipwrights not talking in the taverns.

'And your part in this? If all goes well, you're going to have orders to test the first of the boats when they're delivered to Portsmouth.'

***

Dawson kept the oarsmen to a steady pace as they stroked back towards the Sally Port at the southern end of High Street, only a short walk from Holbrooke's lodgings. The wind had dropped since their outward journey, and the tide had slackened. The clouds had fled away to the east, leaving the Solent sparkling in the sunshine with only the occasional small wavelet slapping against the longboat's quarter.

Holbrooke had thought he knew all about commodores in all their variety. After all, he'd served under a good selection of them. There was George Edgcumbe in Minorca, a commodore by courtesy as the peacetime commander-in-chief of the Mediterranean Squadron. Robert Jermy in *Wessex* was also a commodore by courtesy, but he died of an illness in the Windward Islands. Arthur Forrest commanded three ships-of-the-line and Holbrooke's frigate at the battle of Cape François, winning a significant victory over the French. Then there was Holmes, a real commodore appointed by the Admiralty to blockade the Weser, Elbe and Ems.

The rank of commodore was their lordships' means of side-stepping the unwieldy naval promotion system. It allowed them to place the right people in command sometimes decades earlier than if they had been forced to wait until they hoisted their flags as rear admirals. It meant that they could pluck people like Richard Howe out of the obscurity of the bottom half of the post-captain's list and place them in control of significant expeditions such as this. Many a senior post-captain and admiral was infuriated by the system that left them on the beach or in minor commands while men much younger than them had all the glory. Yet Holbrooke could see the value of it, and so long as the post-captain's list was so inflexible and promotion to admiral was on seniority rather than merit, some such system was surely necessary.

**

CHAPTER FOUR

The Flatboats

Wednesday, Twenty-Fourth of May 1758.
Kestrel's Longboat, Fareham Creek.

The muddy waters of Fareham Creek looked forbidding on this dark, overcast morning. There had been heavy rain overnight and the Wallington Brook had flooded the area above the tidal mills, bringing down the forest litter in great rafts of old leaves, branches and the remnants of last year's bracken. It was the bottom of the ebb and the mudflats seemed to stretch for eternity on both sides of the creek. Holbrooke was shivering in the unseasonably cold weather.

This was the supplementary duty that Commodore Howe had failed to mention. Campbell had been right; it was nothing much. In fact, if the weather had been warmer, it would have had the character of a yachting trip.

'Here they come, sir,' said Jackson, shielding his eyes against the diffused glare of the mid-morning sun. He pointed south to where Portsmouth Harbour was hidden behind a bend in the creek.

Now that his attention was drawn to them, Holbrooke could just see the two low, wide craft moving slowly towards the longboat. It was a curious sight, the brown of the unpainted hulls merging with the grey waters of the creek, while a solid block of red and yellow, topped by the glint of the polished metal of the musket muzzles showed where the soldiers were crammed into their places on the thwarts. The oars completed the picture as they regularly dipped and rose like the wings of some stately bird, drawing the boats ever closer.

'I wouldn't like to handle them in a seaway,' said Jackson, shaking his head. 'Look at the way they yaw to the slightest ripple.'

Holbrooke had his telescope out and was keenly studying the strange boats. He was here to witness a part of the trials for this new type of vessel. Their design was born of the experiences of the first few years of this war, when assaults had been hampered by the lack of specialist boats to land the soldiers. These were the fruits of the first contracts. There were two types of flatboat, one a little smaller than the other, but the two that were to be tested today were both of the larger variety. The expedition was due to sail in a week so unless there were some serious flaws, these were no prototypes, but the final design, and there was no time for anything other than minor modifications.

Yesterday they'd seen the boats being hoisted into and out of a ship-of-the-line and a transport and they'd seen the soldiers scramble down into them. The transport, with lighter spars and rigging than the ships-of-the-line, had been modified with a strengthened main yard and lifts. Special tackles had been rigged to take the ponderous weight of the boats. It had been fascinating to see how all the internal fittings, the thwarts for the oarsmen, the seats for the soldiers and the steps for the masts, were made to be removed so that the boats could be nested on the upper deck.

Some of the transports would be without their mainsails until the landings were over. The flatboats sat high on the booms and cradles that had been installed for them and consequently they fouled the feet of the mainsails so that they couldn't be set. But speed was never a key consideration for that type of ship.

Holbrooke and Jackson weren't alone in the longboat. Colin Treganoc, the sloop's marine lieutenant, had recently returned from Emden, and he was seated in the stern sheets with his captain. Jenkins, the master of the Portsmouth boatyard, was also there; he was responsible for the building and maintenance of the boats for the fleet. He'd personally supervised the fulfilment of the contracts by the half-dozen commercial yards scattered across the shores and inlets of the Solent.

Fareham Creek had been chosen for this trial for two reasons. First, because it had a variety of the kind of shorelines that were likely to be encountered in an assault. The coastline showed monotonous stretches of mud at this stage of the tide, but with the water near its highest –when amphibious operations typically took place – there were sand beaches, reed beds, gravel banks, even a few rocks. The second reason was to maintain some sort of secrecy about the proceedings. This upper limit of Fareham Creek was about as unfrequented as anywhere in the area. There was just the tidal mill at its head and a few isolated cottages dotted along the shore.

The two boats nudged up to where the longboat was waiting. They were rowed by sailors from the squadron, and the Thirty-Fourth Regiment of Foot, the Earl of Effingham's, was supplying the soldiers. The larger of the two boats held a captain of the Thirty-Fourth, presumably the man in charge of the detachment.

'Good morning to you, sir,' he said, removing his hat. 'Captain Overton at your service. I'm pleased to place my men under your command,' he said formally. 'And good morning Mister Treganoc,' he continued with a theatrical flourish, 'the hero of Emden, I presume.'

Treganoc's was the name of the moment among the British soldiery. He'd received a fair share of the credit for the military occupation of Emden earlier in the year and had in fact only just returned from there.

'Thank you, Mister Overton,' replied Holbrooke, relieved to see that he was dealing with a man with a sense of humour. God knew they would need it today.

'You perhaps don't remember me, sir?' Overton continued, 'we met under less pleasant circumstances.' He was looking expectantly at Holbrooke with a queer sort of shy smile.

Holbrooke racked his brain, there was something about the man... Of course! The Thirty-Fourth Foot had been at

Fort Saint Philip in Minorca two years before. Holbrooke looked intently at his face. Yes, this was the same soldier whom he'd met twice at that little jetty in Saint Stephen's Cove. Holbrooke had been sent to the fort in a captured barca-longa to carry messages between the garrison and the small naval force waiting for Byng's squadron to arrive. He shivered slightly as he recalled the hellish scene: the massive impacts of the siege artillery, the bombs bursting all around, the mighty fortress being reduced before his eyes, and the shattered garrison clinging on in the hope of a relief that never came. He looked again at Overton, remembering how his appearance had changed as the siege wore on, how his hand had shaken uncontrollably when they finally parted. He recalled his own shame at sailing back to the relative safety of the frigate *Fury*. It would be understandable if Overton nursed a hatred of the navy after that disgraceful episode.

'Yes, I remember you now Mister Overton. I'm happy to see you under more congenial circumstances. You endured some trying times.'

'That's one way of describing it!' he laughed. 'But without that siege, I'd be a subaltern still.'

Holbrooke looked quizzically at him.

'My regiment lost two captains and a lieutenant; killed or wounded beyond further service. I owe my promotion to them,' he said simply.

Holbrooke smiled grimly. It was uncomfortable to be reminded of the regiment's losses, at least partly the fault of the navy. And yet, it was a similar set of circumstances in that same campaign – the loss of *Fury's* first lieutenant in action with a French frigate – that had set him on the road to his present position. He ranked with a major now and was distinctly senior to Overton.

'Good morning Mister Fitzalan, Mister Johnstone,' he called out to the two master's mates in command of the boats, to break the awkward silence. 'Have you seen the schedule of trials?'

'We have, sir,' replied Fitzalan from the larger boat as he patted the pocket of his coat. 'You're to choose the landing sites, sir, and then we'll run in from at least a hundred yards each time.'

'My soldiers and I will be cold and wet by the end of the day,' said Overton, looking up at the dark clouds that drifted listlessly overhead.

Holbrooke nodded and studied the two officers seated in the stern sheets. They'd come from Howe's flagship, *Essex*, and he'd met them briefly the previous day. The naval crews were at a bare minimum to work the boats, such was the need to carry the greatest number of soldiers. The master's mates acted as both commanders of the boats and coxswains. They weren't much younger than Holbrooke. They'd be hoping for his good word from today's work, another testimony to help propel them to the lieutenant's examination and the unspeakable glory of a commission. They looked eager enough in any case, keen to catch Holbrooke's eye.

'Describe your boat, if you please, Mister Fitzalan,' asked Holbrooke. He hadn't had the opportunity to see the flatboats at close quarters before today. He'd heard all about them from Jenkins who was the navy board's representative at this trial, but he wanted to hear from a sea officer.

'Certainly, sir,' the young man said, stumbling over his words in his haste to impress. 'She's clinker built, fir on oak frames and she has an elm keel, although it's hardly worth the name, the bottoms being so flat. Most of the fittings are oak,' he pointed to the thwarts and benches. 'She's thirty-six feet long and ten feet, two inches in the beam. Fully loaded she draws an inch under two feet. We pull twenty oars and we can rig lugsails on a main and a foremast, but we're not carrying the sailing rig today. There's an anchor stowed in the bow and a grapnel for a kedge at the stern,' he said patting the small anchor that was seized outboard of the transom.

There really was no room for anything superfluous in the

boat. It was just possible, Holbrooke could see, for the two masts and the sails to be stowed between the feet of the inboard-facing ranks of soldiers. Possible, but uncomfortable.

'They're moderately well built, sir,' Jenkins interjected, 'if you don't mind commercial yard standards. Of course, we could have done a better job in the King's yard, but we weren't asked.'

Holbrooke knew very well why the job hadn't been given to the Portsmouth yard; the boats would never have been completed on time. It took the commercial pressure of a contract to be fulfilled, on time, to a minimum specification, with payment by results to ensure that the flatboats would be ready for the campaigning season.

Holbrooke cast his eye over the two ranks of blue-jacketed seamen seated on their truncated thwarts. There were grins and nods in reply, and a touch of the cap from a man he'd served with as a midshipman. The oars were shorter than in any other boat of this size, deliberately so because the rowing positions were so close to the gunwales that the oarsmen couldn't apply enough leverage to manage long oars.

'You can see that the soldiers all face inboard on those fore-and-aft benches, except the fourteen in the stern sheets and the four in the bows. I can carry fifty soldiers at full load,' continued Fitzalan.

'That's half a company, more-or-less,' added Overton, 'a real, solid force to put ashore in one boat. These two boats carry all the combat elements of my company between them.'

It was an impressive sight, Holbrooke had to admit. There were a hundred tough-looking fighting men here, dressed in their regimental colours of red with yellow facings. Most of the soldiers were musketeers and wore black tricorns, but the eight men nearest the bows of each boat were grenadiers and wore a tall red and yellow mitre. The officers were distinguished by a silver gorget at the neck, a silver aiguillette on the right shoulder, silver lacings to the coat and a crimson sash. The spontoons that the officers carried – not unlike an ornamental boarding-pike – gave them a slightly old-fashioned look. The Thirty-Fourth evidently valued the traditional ways.

'And we carry a half-pound swivel for'rard, sir, with five loads of ball and ten of canister.'

The quarter-gunner in the bows trained and elevated his gun theatrically, to prove the officer's words.

'Let's hope you don't have to use that, Mister Fitzalan.'

'Amen,' said Overton. 'It'll be damned unpleasant if your broadsides haven't cleared the beach before we get there, sir. However, it's a reassurance, certainly.'

Captain Overton was evidently not a man to be left out of a conversation.

'How do the soldiers get ashore, Mister Fitzalan?'

The master's mate pulled a long face.

'That's the unsatisfactory part of the design, sir,' he replied. 'They have to jump off the bows and that may mean getting wet, and possibly broken bones, with fifty of them performing that caper. But we have no gang-board.' He shrugged helplessly.

'That's the part that we must practise before any landing,' said Overton. 'You sailors may laugh at us but it's of the utmost importance that my men get ashore with dry boots and no breakages. It makes little odds immediately, but after an hour or so marching it can be the difference between men ready to fight and men nursing swollen and blistered feet. These brave men,' he pointed to the first and second oarsmen on either side, 'must leave their oars and leap into the water to make like human stanchions for my musketeers to steady themselves as they leap.'

'Well, we're in two fathoms of water here, so I don't expect them to carry out that part of the drill just yet.'

He looked at the shipwright.

'Mister Jenkins. I'd be obliged if you'd pay close attention to the disembarkation. I'll be asking your opinion on how some sort of a gang-board may be made to help the process of getting the soldiers from the boat to the shore.'

'Aye sir,' Jenkins replied, 'I can see what you mean,' he added studying the stem of Fitzalan's boat.

There was an essential principle that Holbrooke needed to confirm. Captain Overton had a lieutenant in each of the boats. All three of the commissioned soldiers were senior to Fitzalan and Johnstone, and that could lead to difficulties. Holbrooke looked directly at the younger of the two master's mates.

'Who command's this boat, Mister Johnstone?' and he made a motion with his hand to prevent Captain Overton from answering.

Johnstone looked startled and glanced nervously at Fitzalan. He hadn't spoken yet and he was clearly the junior partner in this two-boat enterprise. Johnstone was wedged uncomfortably close to the tiller, and it seemed to hinder his powers of expression. There was a pause.

Holbrooke kept his eyes fixed on Johnstone's, waiting for a response.

The lieutenant next to Johnstone nudged him with his elbow.

'I... I command this boat,' Johnstone stammered, 'and I'm responsible for placing the soldiers ashore, sir, then Mister Draper,' he motioned towards the officer sat beside him, he of the sharp elbow, 'assumes command of his men.'

'And if there's a disagreement on the way to the beach? Mister Draper, perhaps you could tell me how that is to be handled.'

The lieutenant was an intelligent, self-confident young man and he knew the answer by heart.

'Mister Johnstone is obliged to take my views into consideration, sir, but the decision as to where and when to land is his. I am little more than a passenger until he puts me ashore.'

'Very well.'

Holbrooke was pleased to hear that the new orders for

combined operations had been passed down to the men who must implement them. In a rare instance of co-operation, the Admiralty and their colleagues at Horse Guards Parade had agreed on groundbreaking new command arrangements for landing operations. There must have been huge pressure on them after the failures in 1757 where divided command led to embarrassing and costly debacles. Now, the navy commanded any landing until the army was established ashore. That arrangement held good equally at the highest level of command and this, the lowest. Holbrooke glanced at Captain Overton. He evidently understood his relationship to Fitzalan, who commanded his boat, and he bowed slightly to the younger man.

'Thank you, Mister Johnstone, Mister Draper. Then perhaps we should start with an easy one? There's a nice stretch of gravel even at this state of the tide, over by the mill,' he said pointing. 'Your men can stretch their legs and that will be one trial cleared away long before we're due to start.'

***

CHAPTER FIVE

Disturbing the Peace

Wednesday, Twenty-Fourth of May 1758.
Kestrel, at Anchor. Portsmouth Harbour.

Dawson, Holbrooke's coxswain, took the longboat to a position just under the mills where he had a clear view of the beach. Despite the loneliness of the location, an interested crowd had gathered beside the tall wooden buildings. The windows that looked out over the creek each had an occupant, some scowling at this interruption to their ordered existence, but most waving cheerfully at the sailors in the longboat. So much for the seclusion of Fareham Creek. Holbrooke watched as Fitzalan positioned his two flatboats a cable distance away from the shingle beaches. The signal that the boats were ready was a red flag raised on a short pole in the stern of each boat. Holbrooke would respond with his own red flag and when he was ready to start each trial, the longboat's flag would be dipped.

'They're ready, sir,' said Treganoc who was watching the boats.

Holbrooke took another look at the shingle. There were no locals down there. It hadn't occurred to any of them that the flat bottoms would be landing, otherwise they would have flocked to the scene and caused a dreadful confusion, prejudicing the trial and perhaps even forcing it to be abandoned.

'Dip the flag,' Holbrooke said

Dawson emphatically lowered the flag and immediately the two wide, low craft could be seen moving forward. The crowd at the mill realised where the boats were bound and the more energetic started to run around the back to the narrow path that led down to the beach. The boats were slow, even slower than Holbrooke had imagined, and the

47

mates were clearly having difficulty preventing them yawing. Of course, the rudders didn't reach far enough into the water to have the amount of bite that was needed. That was a sacrifice made for the greater good of a shallow draught. Each time they deviated from their course their speed decreased and a portion of the efforts of the oarsmen was wasted. It was becoming clear that the crowd would be at the beach before the boats and the capering idiots were quite likely to wade into the creek in a misguided attempt to help with disembarkation. Holbrooke could see his carefully laid plans coming to nothing.

'Dawson, raise the red flag again.'

It took a few moments for Fitzalan to see the flag, but when he did the rowers tossed their oars and the boats slowed, stopping half a cable from the beach.

'Pull over to meet them, Dawson.'

'Mister Treganoc, kindly request a file of men from each of the boats and a reliable sergeant and take them to secure the beach. I'll land you at the mill so that you can stay dry on this occasion.'

Holbrooke eyed the gathering of locals dubiously.

'I fear that they won't easily tire of such good sport and they're likely to follow us as we move down the creek. I can't promise that you'll stay dry next time.'

Ten minutes later Holbrooke had the satisfaction of seeing the crowd pushed back to the line of trees at the back of the beach. The sergeant that Overton had provided was a great bull of a man and, halberd in hand, he made an imposing figure whom few civilians would choose to defy.

The boats moved back to the other side of the creek, ready to make a second attempt.

'Make the signal again, Dawson.'

Holbrooke tried to give the boats his whole attention, but the crowd at the back of the beach was in a festival mood. There was an audible gasp of appreciation as they saw the boats start to move again.

'A whiff of canister from a boat gun would clear them,

sir,' muttered Dawson.

Holbrooke could smile at that. He remembered just such a blow against a mass of French infantry on the Ems river in Germany, was it only six weeks ago? They'd recovered the last of the marines, led by an insouciant Treganoc, and Dawson had expertly manoeuvred this very same boat so that the two-pounder covered the jetty they'd just left. The single shot had been but seconds ahead of what would have been a deadly volley from the Frenchmen, but after the canister had done its lethal business, not a musket was fired at them. By the time the surviving Frenchmen had recovered, the longboat had followed the rest of the flotilla and vanished downstream into the night.

'I think perhaps we should treat our own countrymen a little better than that, Dawson. However trying they may be, they are, in fact, friendly civilians.'

Dawson knuckled his forehead. 'Treat with respect. Friendly civilians. Aye-aye sir,' he replied impassively, staring ahead.

The longboat's crew were all grinning. With only one exception, they'd all been there on that night. It was a story that had been told and re-told in the inns and bawdy houses of Portsmouth Point and many a free mug of ale or tot of rum had been obtained on the strength of it. To a man, they were proud to be in Holbrooke's boat crew.

Holbrooke returned his attention to the flatboats. Fitzalan and Johnstone had evidently profited from the abortive first run. They had a better understanding now of handling the strange craft when they were at their full stretch, so different from their behaviour on the slow passage up the creek. Now they had their boats under better control. They'd learned that each wave and each breath of wind had more effect than they would on an ordinary ship's boat. These flatboats hardly drew anything at all, they had no keel to speak of and no forefoot to grip the water. Both mates, he could see, were standing up now, the better to read the water ahead of them and feel the breeze. Whether they would choose to do so under fire was another matter.

As they reached a point four boat-lengths from the shore, there was a splash from the stern of each, and the kedge anchors dropped away carrying the cables that had been flaked onto the transoms and held by a slipknot. The operation of letting go the kedges didn't interrupt by even a second the business of making the shore.

The instructions for sand, shingle or mud had been to go at the shore as fast as the oarsmen could propel the boats. And that was just what they were doing. They reached the shingle almost simultaneously, and their squared, cut-away bows tilted upwards as their momentum thrust them half a dozen yards past the point where they first took the ground. It was comical to see the seated soldiers lurch sideways in their benches with the muzzles of their muskets, still equally spaced, swaying with them. So closely were they packed that none moved as much as an inch in their seats.

The four oarsmen in the bows swivelled their oars under those astern of them and left them trailing by the grommets that held them to the ash thole pins. They dropped over the side into a few inches of water and ran forward and held the bows with a shoulder ready for the grenadiers and musketeers to grab hold of. There was a breathless pause while Fitzalan and Johnstone checked that all was secure. They nodded to Overton and Draper.

The sound of a single whistle blast pierced the silence. Two files of grenadiers leapt from each boat with a splash of boots in the shallow water and ran forward. They were the skirmishers establishing a perimeter to allow the main body to form up into tactical units. The grenadiers stopped ten yards short of the trees and dropped to their knees, fixing their bayonets and levelling their muskets at the shocked crowd. It was gratifying to see the most forward of the civilians shrinking back from this menace.

Three blasts of the whistle and the remainder of the soldiers filed between the rowers and dropped over the bows onto the hard shingle. Only one soldier lost his footing but was saved by one of the oarsmen who pushed him firmly back into place. The sergeants shoved the duller ones into place and in no more time than it would have taken on the Fort Cumberland parade ground, they were in their fighting formation, ready to deliver that devastating mass of musket fire that won battles.

The marvellous thing about these flat-bottom boats, Holbrooke was learning, was their carrying capacity. The logistic elements would have to follow separately, of course, but there before his eyes was an infantry fighting unit, delivered ashore in just two boats. The boats were stationary, the forward four oars trailing and the other sixteen tossed. The seamen were still on their rowing thwarts, although nothing could keep them as immobile as the soldiers. They saw no wrong in waving to the girls in the crowd and passing comment on the proceedings, but that was the way British seamen were, and Holbrooke wouldn't have it any other way.

At a word from Captain Overton, the company moved forward ten paces, the skirmishers rejoined the ranks and the whole formation froze. It was a tableau, a scene from a demonstration at Hyde Park for the amusement of the King. The crowd of onlookers burst spontaneously into applause while Treganoc's sergeant and his two files of soldiers kept them back.

'Put me alongside Mister Fitzalan's boat, Dawson,' said Holbrooke. He didn't want to get his own feet wet, even though all the soldiers had the prospect of a day with soaked boots.

Overton saluted with an elaborate wave of his hat as Holbrooke walked up to inspect the company.

'That went well, Mister Overton,' said Holbrooke.

'It did, sir. As a demonstration of how to land when we're not under direct fire it was very creditable. Of course, we still must re-embark, and I hope we'll do that in good order also. We have another trial at this site, and with your permission I'd like to assume that we are under musket fire from the tree-line, just where those yokels are gawping from.'

'Very well. I'll stay ashore this time. You may start when you see the red flag dip from that rise in the ground over towards the mill.'

Holbrooke turned away, then stopped abruptly.

'Captain Overton.'

'Sir?' he responded.

'There are to be no civilian casualties.'

Overton merely grinned in response and raised his hat in salute.

***

The second assault was quite different and had a much more dangerous quality about it. The boats came crashing onto the shore as before, but this time, the grenadiers were leaping into the shallow water over the shoulders of the rowers before the boats had taken the ground. There were wild yells and now one-in-four of the soldiers ran forward as skirmishers while the remainder formed a much hastier double line on the beach. As soon as the line was formed Overton gave the order to fire, and Holbrooke could hear the clicks of the flintlocks as the hammers descended upon the empty pans. The next order was to fix bayonets and then to charge. This time the civilians fled as the soldiers gave a cheer and a line of bayonets rushed towards them, stopping just a few yards short. It was an impressive display with only one man left back at the boats nursing a twisted ankle, a casualty of the rapid disembarkation.

This time when Holbrooke inspected them, they were breathing hard and a few had a wild look in their eyes. It was as well that they were under firm discipline, because some of them may otherwise have continued into the crowd of civilians, such was the realism of the exercise and the excitement of the men.

***

While the soldiers rested, Holbrooke walked over to the flatboats.

'Well, what do you think?' he asked them, 'how do they handle?'

The two master's mates glanced at each other before Fitzalan answered.

'It's fine at slow or moderate speed, sir, but it has a will of its own when the men put their backs into it. Any sort of wind just takes the bows away in a flash and any waves do the same. There's nothing in the bows to dig into the water, and naturally when the men are pulling hard, they're less in time, one side with the other. The steering's all over the place when we rush into the shore. It's much simpler when the men are pulling easy.'

That was much as Holbrooke had thought. A square bow with a forefoot that cut sharply away to a fundamentally flat bottom would always be challenging to steer. But that was an essential part of the design.

'If we had a deeper rudder it would help, sir,' said Johnstone.

'Let's see it then,' Holbrooke replied. 'Unship the rudder and bring it into the boat.'

It was a big, heavy rudder, suited to a boat of that ponderous size. Holbrooke could see that it was cut flat at the bottom at about the same depth as the lowest part of the keel. That was a typical arrangement to protect the rudder in groundings. However, in most boats the keel was deep enough to allow a bigger rudder; not so in these flatboats.

'How easy would it be to unship the rudder in the last few yards? That way it could be made deeper.'

The two men looked at each other.

'No go, sir. It takes two of us to shift it and you saw how long it took. We'd need to start a hundred yards before the beach, then without any steering we'd broach, for sure.'

Holbrooke nodded. They were right, of course. In those last crucial yards as the boat followed the surf onto the beach the rudder was essential. If the boats had to make only one run inshore, then a deeper rudder wouldn't matter as the damage could be repaired at leisure. But Holbrooke knew the scale of the forthcoming raids and calculated that each boat would need to make twenty round trips just to put the fighting units and their logistics tail ashore, and then another twenty to bring them back.

If there was time, perhaps something could be done to fit two rudders to each boat; that would give a greater surface area for more positive steering.

'What do you think, Mister Jenkins? Two rudders joined by a yoke with a single tiller, could it be done?'

Jenkins scratched his head.

'The boats are being delivered a couple every day. My boys could do the work, but we'd need drawings, and agreement from our masters at Seething Lane. Maybe a month and we could have the first one ready for trials. A month, perhaps six weeks,' he added doubtfully.

Holbrooke knew there was no time for that kind of process. The boats would start bringing the battalions from their camps on the Isle of Wight tomorrow and they'd be hoisted into the transports in less than a week. They'd go into action as they were.

'And a gang-board, Mister Jenkins. How would you go about building that?'

Jenkins was not a man to be rushed. He ambled to the bows of the nearest flatboat uncoiling a knotted cord that he drew from some inner pocket.

'Is this perhaps a typical sort of beach, sir?' he asked tentatively. 'Not wanting to pry about your destination of course.'

Holbrooke exchanged glances with Overton. 'You may take it as typical, Mister Jenkins.'

The shipwright measured the height of the bows off the sand and their width to the turn of the gunwale. He looked dubiously at the protruding stem-post with its iron bracket for the swivel-gun. He had Fitzalan hold the string at the stem head while he stretched it to a point on the shingle four paces from the bow. Pulling a thin piece of wood from another pocket he made cryptic marks with the stub of a pencil.

'That old stem-post is in the way, of course,' he said at length. 'Could it be sawn flush? You'd lose the swivel gun though.'

Holbrooke remembered the Ems river and the French infantry preparing to fire into the boat. He looked over at Treganoc who slowly and unequivocally shook his head.

'The swivel and the stem-head must stay,' he replied, 'can't the gang-board be made to fit over it?'

'It'll be a weakness, sir, and you'd still have the problem of the swivel when it was shipped.'

'Why not two gang-boards?' asked Fitzalan. 'The bows are wide enough, and they could clamp handily over the capping. There's no breast-hook to get in the way.'

It was true; the peculiar design of the flatboats did away with the need for a breast-hook. In fact, the run of the bow either side of the stem-post was almost perpendicular to the fore-and-aft line.

'Two gang-boards would mean faster disembarkation,' added Fitzalan. 'They can be stowed either side of the keelson, between the soldiers' knees.'

Holbrooke looked expectantly at Jenkins.

'Three deals and four foot of elm board, sir, an' a pound o' tenpenny nails,' he announced, referring to his scribe-board. 'That'll make you one gang-board twelve feet long and near three feet wide, with treads so the soldiers don't slip and clamps for the gunwale capping. Any longer and the boards will bounce when the soldiers march on them, any shorter and they'll be too steep. You can double those quantities for the two. Naturally they'll have to be built specifically for each boat so that they're a good fit.'

He paused as though considering.

'It's a yard job,' he declared finally, triumphantly.

Holbrooke smiled; Jenkins was still trying to drum up

work for his yard. Well, the yard would be disappointed, there was no time for that. He'd recommend to Howe that the job be given to the carpenters of the ships that were carrying the flatboats and that they draw the materials from the storeships. Howe needed no delays at this point.

'The army will thank you if you manage to get those made, sir,' said Overton, clearly impressed by the speed that Holbrooke was making decisions. 'Lord knows how we would ever gather this much expertise in one place to come up with specifications at this speed. And the wrangling…'

***

The commodore was expecting a pencilled report within the hour, even before Holbrooke returned to *Kestrel*, and he needed to make a few important points in his account of the trial. He smoothed out the sheet of paper on the thwart in front of him. For a start, despite the success of the trial landings, he needed to make clear the limitations of the design of the boats and how badly they handled at speed and in disturbed water.

Then there was the training. The master's mates and midshipmen who commanded these boats needed guidance and rehearsal before any landing, they couldn't treat the flatboats as just another type of ship's boat. They needed to be exercised not only in handling them at different speeds and in different conditions, but also in the command arrangements and the signals. It would be a tall order for such junior officers, and possibly he should recommend that every fourth boat or so was commanded by a lieutenant. Or perhaps that was going too far.

Holbrooke was sketching out in his mind the substance of his report. The gang-boards would need to be mentioned of course, and the bill of materials to fabricate them. That would mean a mention of Jenkins' name. He reflected that there really was no end to the subjects that a sea officer was required to master, writing a confident report about the design of gang-boards was just the latest.

***

The longboat led the two flatboats down the creek and back into Portsmouth Harbour. They'd carried out the last trial at the top of the tide when they ran the boats into the reed beds on the western side of the creek. Overton held his whistle to his lips and his soldiers paused on their thwarts waiting for the order to disembark. Holbrooke could see that the boats could only run so far into the reeds and that the soldiers would have to wade through two feet of water and a foot of stinking mud to reach the shore. He deliberately raised the red flag to see it answered by both flatboats. There was nothing to be gained in sending the already exhausted soldiers into that quagmire. They'd be cleaning their kit until late tonight in any case, but at least it was mostly water and not mud.

Holbrooke watched the two flatboats over his shoulder as they left the shelter of the creek. The light breeze had whipped up a series of shallow waves that hit the flatboats' starboard bows, knocking them off course each time. The coxswains were obviously struggling, even though the wind was not strong, and the waves were much smaller than they could expect in the open sea. Once again, the similarity to a great stately bird came to him as he watched the banks of oars rise and fall and the boats yaw jerkily a point or two either side of their course.

'There's an old heron, sir,' said Dawson, looking over the starboard bow, 'he's following the ebb. He'll be after a fish or a frog that didn't reckon the tides right.'

Holbrooke nodded and half smiled. He could afford to allow this kind of familiarity after a long day in a boat.

Then it came to him. A heron, of course! The flatboats were just like the grey heron in flight; slow and lumbering with the wind catching their broad wings and giving them a randomly undulating flight. He smiled covertly, pleased to have identified the simile. He just hoped the flatboats were as adept at surviving persecution as the trout-stealing herons that made their living on the little Meon stream beside his father's cottage. Neither gun nor hawk had any effect on their numbers and the dog wasn't yet bred that could take those master fishermen unawares.

***

Captain Campbell ran down into Holbrooke's longboat as it lay alongside, waiting for the commodore to dismiss it. His officers had no time to react, he was over the gunwale, scorning the entry port, before they knew what was happening.

'First things first, Holbrooke; orders,' he said handing over a package. 'The commodore wants you to look at Cancale Bay from the shore. It's up to you how you do it, but you're not to be caught!'

Holbrooke took the package gingerly. He'd heard of such things but never thought he'd be personally involved in espionage.

'You can read the orders at your leisure; they tell you what the commodore wants to know. Meanwhile, he's scanned your report,' he said moving on hastily. 'He wants me to tell you that each division of four boats will be under a post-captain.'

Holbrooke was reeling from this rapid change of subject. He looked sharply at Campbell to make sure he wasn't jesting. A post-captain in command of boats? And yet, it made a sort of sense. These boats carried a highly valuable cargo that must be delivered intact at the right place. And the weight of the rank would be useful to counter the colonels, majors and captains of the army.

'He saw your recommendation of a lieutenant for each division and it made him think. He's an all-or-nothing man, you know, in this case it's to be post-captains or nobody for him! That'll make the army sit up and take notice,' said Campbell. 'Perhaps now they'll take their own duties seriously.'

He paused a moment.

'The gang-boards won't happen though; there's not enough time and anyway that's something the army should be asking for. Let 'em learn the hard way! The commodore's determined that the duke and his staff should take some responsibility for these new ways of doing things.'

Holbrooke nodded. This new commodore was undoubtedly stirring things up. But it was a shame about the gang-boards.

***

CHAPTER SIX

Stone and Iron

Friday, Second of June 1758.
Kestrel, at Sea. Cézembre Island South one league.

It had blown hard all night, one of those summer gales that had bedevilled seamen in the Channel for millennia. Now the wind had dropped, and the hard rain had passed through, leaving behind a low, damp, overcast sky that drizzled its displeasure over the sloop. The grey sky faded into the slate sea offering no hint of a horizon, just a featureless disputed region with indefinite boundaries. Only one point of land was visible in this first light of a new day, a small, rocky island three miles to the south that seemed to rise naturally from the sea, as though it were a part of it.

'That's it all right,' said the sailing master, 'Cézembre Island. It would be hard to mistake that north face, just look at it!'

Josiah Fairview was an anomaly in an unrated sloop; a sailing master of considerable experience and a Channel Pilot to boot. By rights he should have been in a ship-of-the-line. The circumstances of him being sent to *Kestrel* were obscure, and Holbrooke had no wish to pry; he was too conscious of his own good fortune in having such a capable senior warrant officer.

'This side is all rocks and narrow indents, there's no chance of a landing; the south side is more sheltered. There's a sandy shore and a good anchorage at high water, used by fishing boats and the like. But it's shallow, you can almost walk to the island from Saint-Malo at low water springs.'

Holbrooke studied the island through his telescope, intent on determining whether its batteries were operational. Sixty years ago, Louis XIV had commissioned his military engineer Vauban to fortify the place against English raids, but it had always been a half-hearted affair. There was a general feeling at the court that the privateers of Saint-Malo should pay for their own protection, but the men of commerce – the owners of the privateers – were not inclined to spend money on military fortifications. In any case, the obvious direction to attack Saint-Malo was from the north, and that approach was covered by the fort on Conchée Island. The best contribution that the burghers of the city had offered was to establish a quarantine hospital on Cézembre Island to guard against the plague being brought from the Mediterranean by sea. How that would help when the British arrived was unclear.

Whether Cézembre was or was not fortified had, thus far, hardly been of great interest to the British navy. But now, with a force of five of the line, ten frigates, seven smaller men-of-war and over a hundred transports heading for Saint-Malo, the question had become urgent. A well-served battery on the island could close off the only passage into the port.

'What do you think of this weather?' Holbrooke asked, still studying the island through his telescope.

Fairview looked thoughtfully to the west for a moment before answering. He held up a wetted finger to the listless breeze.

'There's no sign of it breaking yet, but it will, probably in the morning watch tomorrow.' He looked right around the horizon. 'When the wind starts to veer again you can reckon on an hour or two more of this clag,' he declared. 'It's mostly a predictable pattern, the wind works itself up into a sou'westerly gale, then it veers into the west, the wind drops, and you get this God-awful miserable dampness for half a day. But then it veers again into the nor'west, and you can expect a fresh breeze and clear skies.'

Holbrooke didn't need this gratuitous lecture on the typical weather patterns around the British Isles; he was as familiar with it as any other sea officer. However, he'd come to accept that preaching on weather forecasting formed part of Fairview's makeup. It came with his excellent ship handling and his intimate knowledge of every rock and shoal in the English Channel; you couldn't have one without the other.

'The Old Bank's four miles to the west-southwest, sir. There are some nasty rocks at the southwestern end, all covered at high water but still shallow enough to rip out our bottom. We should give it a wide berth. Otherwise we're in the clear here, about thirty fathoms of water I would guess, but I'd like to heave the lead, if you please, sir.'

'Very well, Mister Fairview. Heave the lead and take us in closer to the island. Let's see if we can tempt the batteries to reveal themselves.'

'Beat to quarters, sir?' asked the first lieutenant.

'Let's not make a drama out of it, Mister Lynton. Have the bosun call the men to quarters, dowse the galley fires but don't clear for action. I have no intention of engaging any batteries that may or may not be on the island.'

'Aye-aye sir,' he replied, 'I'll just clear away the great guns. The swivels and muskets won't be of any use to us.' Holbrooke and Lynton had served together since the old days in the Mediterranean in *Fury*; they'd joined the frigate together in September '55 at Port Mahon. Holbrooke had been a master's mate then, and Lynton a midshipman. They'd both come a long way.

The bosun called to a short seaman with arms almost longer than his legs, who hurried away for the deep-sea lead. Jackson had heard Fairview's estimate of the depth, so he knew that he didn't need all the elaborate arrangements that usually went with a cast in very deep water. With an expectation of only thirty fathoms, and the sloop making less than three knots, a man with a strong arm could treat it as a cast of the normal hand lead, albeit with the longer deep-sea line. No need for the gang of seamen calling *watch* as each let go their bight of the line in sequence.

Kestrel ghosted towards Cézembre under easy sail.

'And a half, twenty-eight,' called the leadsman from the main chains. He hauled the line in so that Jackson could examine the tallow-filled indent in the bottom of the lead.

'It's gravel, with maybe a little broken coral,' said the bosun, studying the sample of the seabed that had been brought up.

Fairview nodded complacently to Holbrooke.

'Just so, sir. It'll shallow steadily from here. I wouldn't want to take her past the ten-fathom line without some good purpose, there are hidden rocks and shoals all along this coast.'

'What depth do you expect a mile to the north of the island?'

'It wants an hour of the ebb and we're four days before springs,' he looked thoughtful for a moment, 'perhaps twenty fathoms, sir.'

Holbrooke remembered catching a glimpse of the quarter moon during the middle watch, in a break in the clouds, four days before spring tides sounded about right.

'It's deep water right up to the north coast of the island, but there are a few outlying rocks.'

'Hands are at their quarters sir,' reported Lynton.

On a flush-decked sloop like *Kestrel*, the captain had an uninterrupted view of the main armament. All sixteen six-pounders were in his sight and from his vantage position on the new grating covering the tiller he had a slightly elevated view. The dockyard had done an excellent job on the wheel. It was placed just forward of the numbers fifteen and sixteen guns and abaft the mizzen. The tiller to which it was connected was hidden below the grating that Holbrooke was standing on. The wheel ropes had been carefully led below the gunwales and close into the scuppers so that the guns could be run out without fouling them. A new taffrail completed the illusion of a tiny poop deck. The sloop wasn't quite so flush-decked anymore.

Kestrel was barely heeling with the westerly wind, and the waves from last night's gale were flattening out with every mile that they penetrated deeper into the bay. The land forty miles to the west trended north until it ended at the Bréhat Isles. With the Cotentin Peninsula to the east and the Channel Islands to the north, this out-of-the-way corner of the channel where Normandy met Brittany – The Gulf of Saint-Malo – was open only to weather from the northwest. However, it had its own navigational problems and its brutal tides and treacherous shallows demanded a high degree of navigational expertise.

'You can just see the Conchée Fort now sir, on the larboard bow.'

Holbrooke trained his telescope to follow Fairview's extended arm. He knew about the Conchée Fort, another of Vauban's creations. The master engineer had taken over the whole of a small, rocky island to build this defensive work. Sixty-five years ago, while it was still being constructed, Benbow had captured it briefly. But now, with the work completed and the batteries manned, there was little chance of a fleet once again lying to the north of St Malo, as Benbow's bomb vessels had done. It would be hard to bombard Saint-Malo from the sea without forcing a passage past Cézambre or Conchée.

Commodore Howe had told Holbrooke his plan for the attack on Saint-Malo, or at least as much as he'd been able to decide upon before he'd heard the results of *Kestrel's* reconnaissance. And it was, of course, subject to discussions with the Duke of Marlborough. If Cézembre was toothless then there was a possibility of sailing brazenly into the town, although the twin forts before the city and the guns on Herbou Island across the channel would suggest that it would be a bloody business. The part of his orders that Holbrooke hadn't yet divulged, even to his first lieutenant, suggested an alternative. Having probed Cézembre, *Kestrel* was to sail around Pointe du Grouin and look at Cancale Bay. From there it was a march of only seven miles over easy country to the walls of Saint-Malo.

'What's the range to the island now, Mister Fairview?'

asked Holbrooke, more to stop the master fussing with the sails and the ship's course than anything else; he could estimate the distance as well as the master could.

'Let's say a mile and a half, it's not less than that and we're safe for another five cables.'

Holbrooke studied the high, indented north coast of the island. If there were active batteries they'd surely be at the western end where they could overlook the main passage into Saint-Malo. Conchée Fort lay to the east with a maze of rocks and shallows between the two islands. Any batteries that didn't cover the channel to the west would be a waste of effort.

Was there something far over on the western side of the island? Holbrooke lowered his telescope and rubbed his eye. There was just a hint of a straight vertical line, a suggestion of geometrical order among the riot of rocks and dull green scrub. Before he could replace the glass, he heard a hail from the maintop.

'Deck there! I can see a flagpole at the windward end of that island, sir. There's no flag flying but I can just make out some walls below it. Maybe a battery, sir.'

Now, wasn't that just typical. Holbrooke had the best telescope that the shops of Portsmouth could offer, bought against the almost unlimited credit that the proprietors were falling over themselves to extend to successful cruiser captains. It was by a new maker, John Dolland, and had the clearest, least distorted lenses he'd ever seen. Fairview coveted it most irreligiously. Yet his lookout could see the tiny flagstaff better than he could. Some allowance could be made for the height of the mainmast and the thickening of the atmosphere near the surface, but still...

'Mister Edney,' he said to the signal midshipman. 'Take a glass up to the main masthead and tell me what you see.'

Holbrooke could see the flagstaff quite clearly now, and there certainly was masonry below it, regular stonework that might be the walls of a battery. It could be an abandoned position, or one just temporarily unmanned. Or it could harbour half a dozen forty-two pounders loaded and primed, their gunners blowing on the slow match, waiting for this obviously British sloop to come within range.

'Mister Fairview, haul your wind, I believe we've come close enough.'

There was a flurry of activity as *Kestrel's* bows moved closer to the wind that had already veered a point. Sheets were hauled, bowlines shifted, and the sloop settled on a course parallel to the north coast of the island. They were still drawing closer to the battery, for Holbrooke was now sure that there was a gun emplacement there although not yet satisfied that it was manned. They were closing the battery, but they were doing so obliquely.

'Captain sir!'

That was Edney from the maintop.

'There's definite activity under the flagstaff. There's a cloud of dust... Ah! there's a flag, sir.'

The Bourbon white of France!

No sooner had the flag soared up the mast than a single puff of smoke erupted from a point below it, quickly followed by the flat boom of a heavy artillery piece. A column of water appeared two cables to starboard of *Kestrel* and a cable to seaward.

'Poor practice,' said Lynton. 'They should know their ranges with nothing better to do all day but prepare for this moment.'

Holbrooke looked thoughtfully at the point where the plume had shown itself.

'Bring us about, Master. Set a course a league clear of Conchée then to round Cancale Point.'

Kestrel came sweetly through the wind and had barely settled on her new course when there was another hail from the masthead.

'They've fired again, sir! A whole battery, maybe four pieces.'

Edney's shout was only fractionally ahead of sound of the guns, then the sea off the larboard quarter erupted as a close grouping of balls plunged into the waves just a hundred yards from the sloop.

'Thirty-six pounders,' commented Lynton casually, as though nothing untoward was happening, as though they hadn't cheated death by only a minute or two.

Fairview avoided Holbrooke's eyes. That was where *Kestrel* would have been if they hadn't tacked – if Holbrooke hadn't ordered the ship about. The battery commander must have carefully adjusted his guns after the first round, but he'd reckoned without *Kestrel's* handiness in stays. Having seen *Kestrel's* turn, he'd probably ordered his guns to fire in exasperation, knowing that they must miss but unwilling to waste time in moving their point of aim. He'd made a mistake. *Kestrel* was bowling along at six knots, so every five minutes – the probable time it would take to reload and point the guns – took the sloop five cables further to sea. *Kestrel* would have to endure another salvo, but it would be at maximum range this time.

Holbrooke felt a slight twinge, not of fear, more of nervousness as he waited for the next salvo. He looked furtively at his watch. Four minutes, five, six. He smiled, not even the slowest gun crew would take more than six minutes to load and fire again, and certainly not the superb Royal Artillery of France, the monarchs of a hundred battlefields.

Lynton looked at his captain and grinned. 'Any moment now,' he said, almost as though he was looking forward to the iron balls plunging down upon the frail timbers of his ship.

Another minute passed, and the hypothesis that Holbrooke had been working on became a certainty.

'I believe that's the last we'll hear of the battery on Cézembre Island, gentlemen,' he said complacently. 'Those guns are sited to cover the passage into Saint-Malo, so they're pointing west. We just sailed nor'east out of their firing arcs. That's why the battery commander wasted his only salvo, he knew that was all he'd get.'

His officers were looking at him strangely, and he

realised that it was admiration. None of them had thought it through, they were all too carried away by the moment.

'Mister Fairview. Plot the line from that battery where he fired the salvo. It'll be useful information for the future.' He paused for effect. 'You may label it *Fairview's Arc of Safety* on the chart, if you please.'

Everyone on the deck heard the captain's joke, and at quarters that meant most of the ship's company. There was a murmur of laughter across the gun crews. What they didn't know, but Holbrooke did, was that Fairview saw it as no joke at all. Holbrooke was morally certain that at some point he'd be asked to initial a notation on a carefully copied version of the chart, stating to the officials at the navy board that the line of safety off Cézembre Island bore the name of Sailing Master Fairview. The master had a streak of vanity and self-promotion that would surprise many of his friends.

'A ring of stone and iron, sir,' said Fairview, already planning how he would render the lines on his draft chart. 'With batteries on Cézembre and Conchée, not to mention Herbou and Fort Royal and the bay forts when you get closer, there's no approaching Saint-Malo from the sea, not without the whole Channel Fleet behind us.'

***

CHAPTER SEVEN

Cancale Bay

Friday, Second of June 1758.
Kestrel, at Sea. Off Cancale Bay.

The wind was fair to round the dangerous reefs that thrust northeastwards from Cancale Point. With the breeze on her quarter and stuns'ls set, *Kestrel* ran down the ten miles before the men had been called to their dinner. The visibility hadn't increased, and the land was only a hazy line to starboard.

'When can we veer, Mister Fairview?' asked Holbrooke. He was anxious to fulfil the second part of the orders that had come to him under Howe's signature. The orders that he'd shared with nobody.

'I don't have a good fix, sir, and the tides can be all over the place in a little corner like this. I'd prefer to be safe and stand on for another glass, if it doesn't interfere with your needs.'

Holbrooke recognised that Fairview was fishing for information, and he couldn't blame him for doing so. Lynton had done the same over a late breakfast, and Midshipman Edney was loitering within earshot now, just in case his captain should let anything slip.

'In that case, we'll shorten sail now and let the men have their dinner, the officers too. At two bells I'll want you to stand in for Cancale Bay.'

Fairview ruminated on this information for a moment. At Holbrooke's request he'd found the best charts of the Gulf of Saint-Malo that were available, but his captain had remained close-lipped on the reason, and he hadn't specifically mentioned Cancale Bay. However, the vast camp on the Isle of Wight, the flatboats and the mass of transports in the Solent told their own story. It was common knowledge that something was to be attempted against the

French coast. It had been a matter of speculation in the gunroom ever since they'd been ordered to sail ahead of Howe's squadron. With this new information, it wasn't hard to guess that Cancale was a potential landing site for the army.

There was a flurry of activity as the hands were called to shorten sail. The bosun, of course, was supervising from the deck although his mates were doing all the bawling while Jackson stood impassively beside the weather mizzen shrouds, watching the complicated manoeuvres. Jackson had only held his warrant since the previous year. When the captured Dutch pirate ship *Torenvalk* had been bought into the service in Port Royal, Holbrooke had been promoted to commander to take her to England with dispatches. He'd used every ounce of the minuscule amount of leverage that he possessed to bring Jackson from their frigate *Medina* into His Majesty's newest sloop-of-war, the newly renamed *Kestrel*, as his bosun. That leverage had been well used, for Jackson had transitioned with ease from the lower deck to the lofty heights of a warrant officer. Holbrooke could hardly imagine sailing without his old shipmate.

'Mister Jackson, do you have a moment, in my cabin?'

The quarterdeck officers stared. The captain asking to speak privately with the bosun was hardly unusual, but to do so when stuns'ls were being struck and the courses handed was unprecedented – this was the bosun's reason for existence.

'Aye-aye sir,' he replied, knuckling his forehead, a gesture that he hadn't lost from his days as an able seaman. 'My mates can handle this. Keep an eye on them, would you, Mister Fairview?'

***

'Sherry, I think, Serviteur,' he said to his servant, who had also come to *Kestrel* from *Medina*. He'd volunteered off Cape François just minutes ahead of the bottom of his fishing boat – his only source of income – parting company with the rest of the ramshackle vessel. Had he not reached the frigate, he would at best have been destitute, at worst his flesh would have been feeding the very fish that he'd planned to catch. Serviteur had at one time been the property of a wealthy French plantation owner for whom he carried out the function of major-domo. He was a very superior captain's servant for a sixteen-gun sloop, very superior indeed, and he had the distinction of being the only black man on board.

Serviteur brought the glasses of sherry on a silver platter then withdrew to the scullery.

'I must ask for your assistance, Mister Jackson, in a dangerous undertaking,' said Holbrooke, after taking a first sip of the sherry.

Jackson wondered whether Holbrooke understood what a thrill it was to hear himself being referred to as *mister* by a man holding the King's commission. He'd come from the humblest and most deprived of beginnings and the thought of one day holding a warrant rank had for most of his life seemed an unobtainable dream. And it would have remained unobtainable if Holbrooke hadn't fulfilled his promise to secure a bosun's warrant for him in his first command. Now this man was asking – *asking*, mind you – for a favour.

'Yes sir, whatever you wish, of course.'

Holbrooke held up his hand and laughed.

'You haven't heard what it is yet,' he said. 'You may not like it when you've heard my proposal.'

'Doesn't matter, sir,' he said and stared doggedly back at Holbrooke, 'if you need something done, I'll do it, whatever it is,' he ended in an embarrassed mutter.

Holbrooke gazed abstractedly out of the cabin windows. What had he done, he wondered, to deserve this kind of loyalty? Jackson had saved his life in Kingston and had seconded him in everything he'd attempted since. All Holbrooke had ever done in return was to obtain a warrant for him, and after all that was only self-interest born of his knowledge of Jackson's qualities.

'Very well, but you still have the option to change your mind.'

Holbrooke took a deep breath.

'This afternoon we'll sail boldly into Cancale Bay to determine whether it's a suitable place to land the Duke of Marlborough's army.'

Jackson had already guessed as much, there must be more.

'I'll take the sloop as close in as Mister Fairview will let me, and I hope that we'll get some sort of an idea of the suitability of the beaches. You've seen the flatboats and I'll value your opinion.'

Jackson nodded cautiously; he knew there was more to come. There was no great danger for him in bringing the sloop into what was likely to be an undefended road.

'However, my orders are broader than that. Commodore Howe doesn't believe that we can learn enough from an inspection from the sea. Therefore, as soon as we've seen all there is to see, we'll withdraw to the north out of sight of the coast.'

Jackson looked puzzled for a moment.

'So,' he went on, 'after sunset we'll return and put a boat ashore to examine the beach and the land behind it. There'll be at least four hours of darkness. Twilight will end about ten o'clock, then if the master's prediction is correct, with this thin, low cloud still covering us, it'll be black as pitch until the moon rises at four bells in the middle watch. That should give us plenty of time. I'm ordered to go myself, and I'm hoping that you'll agree to join me.'

'Yes, sir,' replied Jackson, 'of course I will, we'll need a good boat's crew and we'll need to be armed ourselves.'

'I'm not sure that weapons will help us,' Holbrooke replied, 'but I suppose it would be as well. I'll wear my uniforms and you must carry your warrant. If we're captured, we must give no excuse for being taken as spies.'

'You speak good French, I remember, sir.'

'Well, it passes for conversation, but no Frenchman

would ever be deceived, my accent would give me away in a moment. It's a weakness of the plan, but as far as I'm aware I speak the language as well as any officer in the ship.'

Both men were lost in thought for a moment. Holbrooke's mind registered the sounds of plates being moved around in the scullery, but it didn't rise to the surface of his consciousness, it was just his servant preparing to offer his captain an early dinner before the sloop moved inshore. They sensed rather than heard the tall figure of Serviteur walk across the cabin.

'Sherry, sir?' he asked, offering the decanter on its silver tray.

Holbrooke nodded distractedly and Serviteur filled their glasses. He straightened to return to the galley, hesitated a moment, then turned back to Holbrooke.

'Sir, if you will excuse me, I speak perfect French,' he said softly, and stood rigidly still, the perfectly mannered servant.

Holbrooke and Jackson stared at him.

'You heard our conversation, Serviteur?'

'It would be hard not to, sir,' and he motioned to the scullery only eight feet away. 'And furthermore, sir, my old master's family was from this area and my French has an authentic Breton accent. I can also understand some Breton, although I've never tried to speak it.'

Holbrooke opened his mouth to dismiss Serviteur with his thanks; a captain's servant had no place on clandestine missions such as this. He must remember in future that nothing that he said in his cabin was secret unless he sent his servant away. Then he looked up at the man standing so respectfully beside him. He had to acknowledge that there was a germ of sense in what he said. Holbrooke's imperfect French accent *was* the weak part of the plan. If all went well and they met nobody, it wouldn't matter, but if they had to talk their way out of a difficult situation… Well, he knew that his accent and his stilted vocabulary and grammar would give the game away instantly.

'If I may, sir? This is a nighttime expedition. I have a certain advantage at night.'

Holbrooke smiled while Jackson laughed outright. Serviteur, a freed Caribbean slave, was of course a black man, and he was well known for his nighttime invisibility. While the faces of all the other members of the crew shone like a full moon on the deck at night, Serviteur blended into the surrounding darkness.

'You know how unusual this is, Serviteur, for a man in your position to offer his services in these circumstances, and the impossibility of me to even considering your offer seriously?'

'I only want to be given a chance to prove my worth, sir.'

Holbrooke had never seen his servant discomposed before, not even when he came on board *Medina* off Cape François, as his fishing boat sank alongside. He looked positively nervous, swaying slightly from side to side, more than was necessary to keep his balance against the ship's motion

'Good God, man. Didn't you do that back in January, off Borkum? You saved my life, if you remember.'

'As did Mister Jackson, in Jamaica, if the stories are true...'

Serviteur stood his ground, every inch the deferential servant but unwilling to withdraw from this battle of wills.

Jackson looked at his captain and nodded almost imperceptibly. There was no doubting it, Holbrooke thought, Serviteur would be an asset on this mission. He was a formidable man who'd shown his ability to think quickly in a crisis. If he hadn't been lurking in the scullery back in March, as he was today, Holbrooke would probably have been killed or at least severely injured by the drink-maddened first lieutenant who attacked him. Serviteur had struck fast when he saw the danger, breaking Deschamps' wrist so that he dropped the wicked little dirk that was aimed at his captain's gut.

'One moment, if you please.'

Holbrooke could think more clearly looking out of the windows at the ever-changing vista of scurrying clouds and waves. He'd never seen a view to rival that from the great cabin of a man-o'-war. His mind registered the fact that they were moving more slowly now, under reduced sail. The sun had still not broken through and the grey ocean slipped away slowly in their wake. A seagull, the sort they called a herring gull, slid silently into view from the starboard quarter. The bird's smart grey-and-white plumage looked as though it was created specifically for this sea, this sky. The gull looked at him knowingly through the salt-stained glass, its yellow-rimmed eye mocking him for his timidity. With a derisive squawk it tilted its wings and was gone, lost from his view as it soared away to starboard and upwards to berate the topmen in its own environment.

'You understand the danger, Serviteur?' he said, still looking out of the window.

'I do, sir.'

Holbrooke turned, it was like seeing a frozen moment of a play, the actors caught on stage in the middle of a scene. Neither Jackson nor Serviteur moved a muscle, they appeared not even to be breathing.

'Then put away your tray and take a seat, we have much planning to do.'

***

The reconnaissance had gone well. *Kestrel* had sailed brazenly into the Gulf of Mont Saint-Michel in the middle of the afternoon watch, then hauled her wind to beat into the road at Cancale. Holbrooke hoped that it all looked very casual, a British sloop eager to surprise an unwary privateer anchored away from the protective guns of Saint-Malo, rather than the precursor to the landing of an army. Of course, all they found was a dozen fishing boats hauled up on the beach and a sleepy village watching over the scene. The battery at Cancale had raised a flag and fired an optimistic gun in their direction, but it fell short. It was useful though for Holbrooke to hold the picture in his mind so that he could describe it to the commodore. The wide beach sheltered by a rocky outcrop at its northern end, the land rising gently from the shore, riven by small valleys where watercourses had flowed into the bay at some time in the past. It was a near-perfect place for a landing; a safe anchorage for the squadron, a good, sheltered beach for the boats, a safe area for the battalions to form into columns and easy access to the hinterland. Holbrooke knew that the duke intended to fortify the beach as soon as he had landed; for without the beach secured, his withdrawal route was at risk. He could see how readily it could be achieved by throwing up earthworks above the beach.

Howe had planned to sail from Portsmouth on this very day, but it would take time to marshal his great squadron, and he was unlikely to clear the Solent until tomorrow or the next day. Holbrooke expected to meet him off Alderney perhaps as early as the third of June, certainly no earlier. That set the time imperative for this reconnaissance.

The master took soundings as *Kestrel* beat into the road, then reached across parallel with the beach, but that was normal for any British cruiser in inshore waters. There was no reaction to their incursion except for that single optimistic shot from the battery and frantic efforts to haul the fishing boats further up the beach. Much good that would do them if Holbrooke took a fancy to let his broadsides loose.

The master's weather prediction was proved correct; the wind held steady and the blanket of cloud persisted. That was important to Holbrooke's plan. A clear, starlit night could frustrate them entirely and then he'd have a choice: risk discovery as the boat pulled into the beach or confess to Howe that he'd failed.

'Have you selected the boat's crew, Mister Jackson?' Holbrooke asked as Point Cancale dropped below the horizon astern.

'Your own crew, sir, they all volunteered. I'm shipping a swivel and the gunner's mate will be with us, just in case.

And I've arranged the light signals with Mister Lynton.'

Fairview and Lynton were drawn into the conversation. They all knew the plan now; it could hardly be kept secret any longer. There had been polite protests from both of his senior officers. Lynton thought that he should go instead of his captain, but Lynton spoke almost no French, and besides, Commodore Howe had been specific in his instructions that Holbrooke should be the one to lead the shore party. Fairview didn't want anyone to go at all. He thought it madness of the first degree to go traipsing around on the shores of an enemy country.

Kestrel had spent the dog watches lying-to fifteen miles north-northwest of Cancale Point, just to seaward of the Chausey Islands and well clear of their hidden rocks and banks. If anyone saw them from the islands, they had no means of communicating quickly with the mainland and no real incentive to attempt to do so. As the last dogwatch ended, the sloop filled her sails and bore away with a quartering wind for Cancale Bay.

***

'You see that light on the shore, Dawson?'

The coxswain nodded in reply, his movement barely visible in the darkness. There was no need for silence this far from the shore, but the mood of the boat said otherwise. The crew was to a man as worried about this as the master and first lieutenant.

'There's your mark, the church at the village of La Houle. Aim for a spot half a mile to the left, that'll keep us well clear of the fishing boats.'

Kestrel's reconnaissance hadn't been wasted. They'd confirmed that the bay to the south of the village and the area where the fishing boats were hauled out was deserted, a perfect place for a clandestine landing.

Holbrooke remembered the concern on the faces of Lynton and Fairview as he gave his last instructions before descending into the boat. He just hoped that everyone remembered their parts and held their nerves. Edney was the key to it all. He would command the yawl and it was he who would have to make the decision to withdraw, leaving his captain on enemy soil, if the shore party didn't return by one o'clock. The timing was critical, the cloud was thinning and even though the starlight couldn't penetrate it, a quarter moon would, and then the sloop would be immediately visible. Until moonrise, under reduced canvas, she would only be visible from the shore if she was expected. It was imperative that she should be underway thirty minutes past one, captain or no captain. Holbrooke expected, no, he hoped, that they could conduct their business in the three hours of darkness, but he knew that any number of factors could hold them ashore: an encounter with the locals, a militia patrol, a missed turning. It was as well to be prepared.

***

The yawl thrust its forefoot into the sand, and the two bow oars dragged it as high as it would go. There were no lights at all, even the light in the church at La Houle had been extinguished when they were only halfway to the shore. Dawson had steered the remainder of the way by the feel of the wind on his cheek with Edney watching the faint glimmer of the wake to check that they weren't going around in circles. It was hardly surprising that there were no lights; the people of a poor, remote place like La Houle would hardly waste their tallow dips, and certainly not their expensive candles or lanterns, after their evening business was over. The end of vespers would be the signal for everyone to bar their doors and take to their beds. There was little chance of an encounter with the locals.

'All set?'

Answering nods from Jackson and Serviteur.

'Remember, Mister Edney,' Holbrooke looked at both the midshipman and his coxswain, to ensure that both knew the importance of the timings, 'you must be gone from here at one o'clock. If we're not here, then we'll see you in the same place at midnight tomorrow.'

***

CHAPTER EIGHT

An Old Friend

Friday, Second of June 1758.
Kestrel, at Anchor. Cancale Bay.

It was a strange sensation to be standing on enemy territory. After they had splashed through the little waves that caressed the shore – they were so gentle that they couldn't be said to be breaking – the sand felt hard and dry underfoot. There were four and a half hours to high water and when the boat came back for them, they'd be meeting it two hundred yards further up the beach. Edney would have to remember that. There was a huge tidal range in this Gulf of Mont Saint-Michel, and it would be easy for the longboat to be left high and dry by the retreating sea.

They were travelling light. There was no need for packs, but they each carried a sword or cutlass and a single pistol. Serviteur, ever mindful of other people's comfort, took some bread and beef in his pocket, wrapped in a napkin. Holbrooke carried a small telescope on a sling over his shoulder. It wasn't as good as his new glass, but his four feet long Dolland would have been a ridiculous impediment when scrambling among dunes.

They kept low as they hurried up the few hundred yards of the beach. They could see the small squat church tower of La Houle over to the right, and the vague shapes of the fishing boats below the houses. The sand became softer as they moved upwards, and they were soon pushing their way up low dunes with coarse grasses growing in tussocks. Their feet slipped as the sand gave way beneath them and ran in rivulets down the sides of the dunes. This was what they had come to see, the land beyond the high-tide mark.

Holbrooke held up his hand for a pause. They crouched down between two tall tussocks. There was no need to talk, nothing had yet changed to require an alteration to the plan.

After two minutes to catch their breath, Holbrooke motioned off the right and led the way along the line of dunes, keeping just below the crests. Still there were no lights, and soon the church tower rose in the dark sky in front of them. They angled slightly inland, aiming to determine how far back from the sea the houses spread. Holbrooke counted his paces. After fifty he signalled for another turn to the right, to probe the limits of the village. Still, not a light showed, the world was in darkness.

Holbrooke heard Jackson hiss. A warning. The bosun pointed ahead of them, and there was the shape of a building.

'A barn, sir,' he whispered, and Serviteur nodded his agreement.

That was as far as Holbrooke wanted to go. He knew that the village buildings on this southern side extended about fifty yards past the church and perhaps eighty yards behind. At a quick calculation that would make maybe twenty houses if they each had land for chickens and net drying. Come to think of it, he could smell the sharp odour of drying fish; perhaps each family preserved a portion of its catch for the winter when the weather would make fishing difficult.

The wind was from the nor'west now, so their own smell was unlikely to carry to the dogs of the village. However, the veering wind would bring clear weather. God send cloud for another four hours, Holbrooke prayed in silence.

With a motion of his hand the little band turned their backs on the village and started to move south, following the line of the beach but now on the inland side of the dunes. After a hundred yards, when they reached one of the narrow cuts in the range of dunes, Holbrooke called a halt and again they took advantage of the tussock grass.

'We can speak now, so long as we keep our voices low,' he said.

'The sky's clearing,' said Jackson. 'I saw a few stars a moment ago.'

It was true, there was a definite lightening of the sky, and now that he thought about it, Holbrooke could see the outline of the dunes.

'Jump up to the crest and let me know what you can see of the bay.'

Jackson only had to crawl about twenty yards, and he was lost in the darkness before he'd reached the top of the dunes. He was only gone a minute, but it was still a surprise when he came sliding back down into their refuge between the tussocks.

'It's still black over the bay, sir. No chance of seeing the sloop, let alone the longboat. Not unless this cloud completely disappears,' he said in a low voice.

'Good, then let's press on, but keep below the summit, just in case.'

They scrambled down into the cut between the dunes and then up the other side. It was more difficult than Holbrooke had imagined, with the sand giving way beneath their feet, the tough grasses obstructing them and the need to bend almost double to keep low.

They crept another hundred yards, down another cut and then up the other side.

Serviteur was the first to the top; he seemed to have inexhaustible stamina that made nothing of the difficult conditions. Holbrooke was behind him when suddenly he felt a strong arm pushing against his shoulder.

'Ssss,' hissed Serviteur. Nothing could be seen of his features, but the soft sibilant carried a clear warning. All three slid quietly back down the dune and crouched in a small dell, sheltered by the grasses and a single, bent tree. There was enough breeze to allow for speech without the fear of being heard.

'What did you see?' asked Holbrooke.

'A soldier,' he replied.

Holbrooke nodded, trying to look as though this happened to him every day. He hadn't expected to see French soldiers in this out-of-the-way place, and certainly not French soldiers roaming around at night. Militia, almost certainly. The French army would hardly deploy its regular battalions to such an obscure, unimportant place, unless they'd had warning…

'What else?'

'He's carrying a rifle slung over his shoulder,' Serviteur replied, 'and he was just standing there. I couldn't see anything else, no camp, nothing.'

'Was he looking out to sea?'

'No, sir, he was below the crest of the dune.'

'Then we must know more. Jackson, climb back up there and see what he's up to. No soldier would be out on the dunes at night without some purpose. Take your time but stay this side of him. I don't want us to be split up.'

'Aye-aye sir,' Jackson whispered.

Holbrooke and Serviteur saw his figure slip out of the dell and then he was gone.

The seconds passed like hours, but Jackson had probably been gone no more than five minutes. Serviteur saw him first, sliding back down the side of the dune; the sky had cleared that much.

'There are four or five of them, sir. They've pitched two tents about thirty yards back from the top of the dune and there's some sort of wooden ramp that they must have been working on in the day. I can see the glow of a fire from behind the tents. It looks like they're building artillery emplacements, but I can't see any sign of their guns.'

Holbrooke thought for a moment. It was hard to keep his mind on the subject when both of other men were waiting expectantly for him to declare a plan. There was nothing to be gained from loitering here now. It was too risky to skirt around the embryonic battery and in any case the next tiny village, even smaller than La Houle, was only half a mile further south. The French must have decided to place a small battery here between the two villages, to cover a gap in the defences. He wished he could see his watch, but it was still too dark. He'd expected to be able to judge the passing of time without the help of his timepiece, but he was starting to understand that his perception of the hours was contextual, and this unfamiliar situation – creeping around on a hostile shore – was giving him few clues. Nevertheless, they must have been ashore for an hour and a half at least, and it would do no harm to wait in shelter at the place where he expected his boat, rather than blunder around and risk detection. And yet…

'I want another look at this camp,' he declared in a whisper. He looked up at the sky. It was becoming perceptibly lighter, but still dark enough for three stealthy men to remain undiscovered.

'Jackson on my left, Serviteur on my right,' he whispered. 'No more than a head above the crest, keep close to a clump of grass and when I move back you follow me. Understood?'

Jackson and Serviteur nodded but kept silent.

Holbrooke crawled up the side of the dune. It was like his childhood games, but now it was deadly serious. He'd brought his commission, but he wasn't sure that it would do any good if they were caught. There was a fine line between legitimate scouting and the deadly sin of spying, and a French military court may draw the line in a different place, to his disadvantage.

Slowly now, moving stealthily as they came near to the top. He selected a clump of grass for cover and brought his head carefully over the rim to look down on the scene. He could see Jackson and Serviteur being equally cautious a few yards either side of him.

As Jackson had said, there were two conical tents thirty yards to the right. They could only be seen because they were silhouetted by a fire behind them, or rather the remains of a fire that was being allowed to burn itself out. But there was something else, perhaps the light had grown better since Jackson looked. Three platforms were being built and they were in an advanced state of completion. Already there were gabions in place to protect the guns, for this was

undoubtedly an artillery emplacement. The man that
Serviteur had seen – how close they were to stumbling upon
him in the dark! – was evidently a sentry. He looked alert
enough, but he didn't expect any intruders; the way his
musket was slung over his shoulder proved that. He could
hear voices now and saw a bulky shape detach itself from
the nearer tent. It moved towards the sentry and stopped.
Perhaps this was a sergeant or an officer checking on
security before turning in. The language was French, and the
new arrival spoke loudly, the common questions of a
superior to a man in a lonely post, just waiting for the hour
of his relief.

But there was something about the voice of that man.
French wasn't his native tongue and he spoke it with a thick,
guttural accent. The starlight was strong enough now for
Holbrooke to see some more details. He wasn't wearing the
Bourbon white, but then the French artillery and the militia
wore dark blue, mostly. Nevertheless, this uniform looked
even darker than that. Then the man gave a loud laugh at
something the sentry had said. All three watchers glanced at
each other to confirm their own suspicions. They knew that
laugh, they knew that dark uniform and that guttural accent.
Unless Major Albach, of the Austrian Imperial Artillery had
a twin brother, he was standing before them now!

Holbrooke signalled back over his shoulder and all three
men slid carefully down the dune and back to the relative
safety of their dell

'We've seen all we need to see, and some things we
didn't expect to see,' he whispered. This was no time to
discuss the sighting of their old friend Albach.

'Serviteur, you lead the way. Jackson, bring up the rear
and we'll go back to where we came ashore.'

They followed the line of the cut; confident that they
couldn't be seen in the deep gloom between the dunes and
paused before coming out onto the seaward side. Serviteur
touched Holbrooke's arm and pointed back at the place
where they had spied upon the camp. Major Albach's profile

was distinctive in the growing light. He was standing on the crest precisely at the spot where Holbrooke had lain. He appeared to be looking out to the north, but his posture was again unmistakable. He was relieving himself before bed, and had they not retreated, he would have been doing so over the hidden form of Commander George Holbrooke!

***

They made slow progress, scrambling back along the base of the dunes, trying to keep close to the tussocks that so effectively broke up their outlines. When they reached the point – as far as Holbrooke could judge – where they had first entered the dunes, he again looked to seaward, but there was no sign of the longboat. It was just past high water and if the boat had been there, they would have seen it only tens of yards from their position. Holbrooke had to accept that he'd badly misjudged the time and they were far too early at the rendezvous.

The three men huddled deep under a tussock and prepared to wait. There was no doubt now that the sky was lightening as the clouds swept away westward.

The minutes passed.

Holbrooke felt his arm clutched by Jackson.

'Someone is moving out there,' he whispered.

Holbrooke could hear nothing. Then as he filtered out the sounds of the sea, he heard it. Someone out there was trudging through the dry powdery sand, but he was making heavy work of it. It sounded as though he was dragging something substantial. Now they could hear him cursing as he slipped and pulled himself back on his feet. There was no doubt, this unknown person was dragging a hefty weight along the base of the dunes. He would certainly stumble across the trio, and there was no escape. They'd be discovered as soon as they moved, and they'd be trodden upon if they didn't.

Holbrooke tapped Serviteur on the shoulder and pointed towards the sounds.

Serviteur slid quietly away and disappeared into the

gloom. Holbrooke and Jackson waited in apprehension.

In no time, they heard voices. Serviteur was talking to someone, who was replying. The voices started quietly, then Serviteur's voice rose. He was berating the unknown man, not quite shouting but certainly making his point. They heard the man retreating towards La Houle, no longer dragging whatever his load had been.

After a minute, Serviteur slid back into their space below the tussock.

'It was a thief, sir. Stealing an anchor from a fishing boat. He came from the village over there,' he pointed south. 'I sent him on his way, telling him that the Seigneur of Cancale was engaged in private activity in the dunes, and he'd be best to make himself scarce.'

'Do you believe he's convinced?'

'Oh yes, sir. He's terrified. There's a rough sort of justice in these parts and his life's forfeit if he's found stealing. He's convinced that he's had a lucky escape. He'll say nothing to anyone, I'm sure of that.'

***

They ate the bread and meat that Serviteur had brought. Holbrooke guessed that another fifteen minutes had passed when they saw a dark shape moving stealthily across the silvery-black sea. It nudged up onto the beach just over to their left. It was only minutes past high water, and they had no more than fifty yards to cover. They did that at a jog, glad to be leaving the place. Edney met them with a smile and pointed to the sky. The cloud was rolling away to the east, exposing the stars and they could see the faintest hint of a glow in the east where the moon would soon be rising.

In ten minutes, they were back aboard *Kestrel* and before the moon had shown its face above the horizon, they were far to the north of Cancale Point and heading for the rendezvous off Alderney.

***

CHAPTER NINE

The Duke

Saturday, Third of June 1758.
Kestrel, at Sea. Off Alderney.

Serviteur had resisted all attempts by the ·gunroom steward to serve breakfast to the captain and his guests. The cabin was his domain and besides, he had no faith in the abilities of the old, worn-out seaman who looked after the officers.

'Coffee, sir?' he asked, just as though he hadn't shared the dangers of a night on enemy territory with this same captain and with this same bosun.

'Thank you, Serviteur,' Holbrooke replied. He was feeling refreshed after three hours of sleep but had not yet managed to put the events of the night into a proper order, nor to draw conclusions from them. His clerk, Pritchard, was poised, quill in hand and inkhorn wedged between a salt-pot and the table's fiddle, ready to record the key points.

'Let's get down what we do know, Mister Jackson. First, La Houle appears to have no garrison at all, otherwise we'd have seen some sign of it, some lights or a sentry.'

'That's right, sir,' replied Jackson, eating a piece of toast from the last of the fresh loaves out of the Portsmouth bakeries. 'A tiny place,' he added, 'just a little fishing village with enough people to work those half-dozen boats we saw.'

'And then the empty beach stretching to the south for a quarter mile or more.'

'There was a good old rise-and-fall there,' said Jackson. 'Maybe three-quarters of a mile of sand at low water.'

Holbrooke nodded.

'What did you make of that camp, Jackson?'

'A small battery, sir, for certain. At the second look I saw three platforms started but there may be more. There's a deal of work to be done before they mount any guns, and then there are the guns themselves. They'll have to build a road for them, there'll be no dragging them over that soft sand, not even with campaign carriages.'

Lynton was looking over the chart, stepping off distances with his fingers.

'It's a good spot for a small battery. We know there are already a few guns in Cancale, and there's maybe a mile-and-a-half between them. That's about right for twenty-four pounders.'

'Then there's the strange encounter,' said Holbrooke. 'It was Major Albach, wasn't it?'

'As sure as anything, sir,' replied Jackson. 'I shared a mess with him for long enough, I wouldn't mistake that laugh anywhere, and the accent. He could never remember that we didn't speak French in the mess and was always starting a conversation in that back-of-the-throat way of speaking, then he'd stop when he remembered that nobody understood him and bark out that laugh. It was him alright.'

'Serviteur,' Holbrooke called into the pantry, 'what do you think? Was that the major?'

'It was sir. He spoke to me many times, as we shared a language, and Mister Jackson's right, I couldn't mistake that accent.'

'His build was right, even his way of walking,' said Jackson.

'But what's he doing here?' asked Lynton, frustrated at being absent from the expedition. The tale was so fantastic that he was hardly able to believe the eye-witness accounts.

'He's an artillery officer, so that part of it makes sense, and Austria is allied to the French, even if they're officially at peace with us.'

Chalmers had remained silent so far. He had nothing to say about the ranges of guns or the height of tides, but he understood people better than most, and he'd made the naval and military mind his particular study.

'I'm merely hypothesising now, but our friend Hans was

concerned about how he would be welcomed back to the Austrian Army. He'd been away long time on a politically controversial posting. I assume he made it back to the Austrian Netherlands; if so, there's been plenty of time for him to feel the chill wind of official antipathy.' He tapped gently on the table, marshalling his thoughts.

'If, for example, he was offered another remote posting, filling perhaps a gap in the skills of the French *Milices Gardes-Côtes*, in a remote part of Brittany, would he not have taken it?'

Holbrooke looked affectionately at his friend. He'd come to value his insights.

'With all the French artillery sent away into Germany, a professional gunner from a friendly country would be welcomed with open arms. The militia may be able to train infantry and even cavalry, but field artillery takes years of dedicated study.'

Holbrooke looked again at the chart.

'It'd be a major's command to fortify this side of the bay, and that major would certainly need to inspect the new batteries as they are being thrown up. But there's little point in speculating. I must admit I was tempted to leave him a message. Perhaps *Kestrel* and *Emden* written in the sand.' He smiled at the memory. 'Thank God I restrained myself! Perhaps we should leave any mention of Major Albach out of the report, Pritchard, it'll only set hares running.'

***

It was a hard beat north to the rendezvous between Alderney and Cape La Hague, and they needed the help of the wind, which backed two-points in the afternoon watch, to make it on a single tack. The breeze dropped as it backed, and in the end, it was only the tide rushing between the mainland and Guernsey that propelled them to the agreed place to meet the squadron. Holbrooke had to admit that it was an impressive sight. A hundred and fifty ships in two divisions were crammed into the eight-mile gap between the island and the mainland. A huge squadron indeed, but it was nevertheless in good order. *Essex* was in the lead with a sloop on each flank. Holbrooke was interested to see that they were both smaller than *Kestrel*. He could see two frigates on either side of a great mass of transports and storeships, and dimly in the distance he could see the two fourth rates *Portland* and *Deptford* behind them. And that was just the first division! The second division was similarly organised with another fourth rate, *Rochester*, bringing up the rear. The Channel Fleet must have been stripped of frigates to provide Howe with this escort. The same Channel Fleet that was now on its way to Brest to blockade the French so that the Duke of Marlborough's army could be put ashore unmolested. If Holbrooke knew anything about Anson, his blockade would be loose, hoping to tempt the French out to destroy them in a single battle.

Yes, a magnificent sight. Even so, Holbrooke was acutely aware that the whole body of ships was going backwards. At this state of the tide and this age of the moon, the stream was rushing nor'east through the gap at a full six knots. Even with the wind on their beam, the laden transports could sail at no more than four knots, so the whole squadron was involuntarily retreating before an inexorable force of nature.

Fairview thought it vastly amusing.

'They're making good time back towards Portsmouth, sir,' he said.

'I expect they are, Mister Fairview,' Holbrooke replied, hoping against all his previous experience that the master would take the hint and mind his own business.

'Two knots over the ground I reckon they're doing.'

He rubbed his hands in glee.

'Mind you, it's past its worst, the stream will start to weaken now.'

He looked around for an audience but met only blank, abstracted faces.

'Mister Howe's problem,' he declaimed to the stony-faced quarterdeck, 'is that he has nowhere to anchor this many ships until he's well south of Alderney. He must make the best of it that he can and hope that the ebb will take him as far as Sark. There's a good anchorage at Baleine Bay in the southeast of the island, you could anchor the whole navy there. Ten or fifteen fathoms and a clean sandy bottom. With this wind there's no chance of dragging. I'll put a guinea on it that he's heading for Baleine Bay!'

But the master was speaking to himself and nobody was paying attention. In any case, it would be a foolish man who staked his guinea against Fairview's knowledge of the Channel.

'Mister Edney, you have the signal book ready?' asked Holbrooke sharply.

'Aye-aye sir,' Edney replied, and pulled the book out from behind the binnacle.

Howe had issued the most comprehensive set of signals that Holbrooke – or anyone else – had ever seen. Pages and pages of diagrams and text. There were flags and lights for almost any situation, but what Holbrooke was most keen to see was the signal for him to report aboard the flagship, a blue flag at the starboard foretopsail yardarm.

'Then let's see your telescope trained on the flagship, Mister Edney, and have the acknowledgement bent on. I want no delay when he hangs out the signal.'

There was a brief flurry as two master's mates and three midshipmen fought savagely but silently over the two remaining telescopes.

In truth Holbrooke couldn't fault the preparations. All his officers were on deck, his boat's crew was lurking forward of the mainmast bitts and the yawl was on a short painter ready to be brought alongside in an instant.

'Mister Fairview, how far does the squadron have to run for Baleine Bay now, and how far will it be from the bay at slack water?'

Fairview paused for a moment, his brain whirring.

'Well, it's maybe twenty or so miles from here. There's another three hours before the tide turns, but it's slacking all the time and soon they'll be making way. Let's say twenty-four miles by the turn of the tide at six o'clock. The wind's failing us, so I expect we'll be anchoring soon after sunrise to wait out the flood.'

Holbrooke nodded. The infuriating thing about Fairview was that in navigational matters he was invariably correct. Howe would like to hear that assessment because he'd be reluctant to anchor this great squadron in the dark. If he could get underway from Sark in the dog watches tomorrow then, even if the wind should fail entirely, he could be at Cancale Bay by the fifth. He made a mental note of those timings in case the subject should come up when he met the commodore.

'Signal from flag, sir,' called Edney in an important voice. 'Captain of *Kestrel* report aboard the flagship.'

'Very well, make the acknowledgement.'

It was a little thing, but senior officers tended to become irascible when their signals were ignored or acknowledged late. And Holbrooke sensed that this interview was important – vital even – to his career.

In this case, the commodore had no cause to complain as *Kestrel* answered in less than a minute after the blue flag had soared up to the flagship's yardarm.

'Mister Fairview. Lay me alongside the flag starboard side at half a cable. With all speed, if you please.'

***

The great cabin of *Essex* was full of officers, a mix of soldiers and sailors, with the Duke of Marlborough and Commodore Howe holding court at the table. It was littered with maps and lists and a heated debate seemed to be taking place.

'Mister Holbrooke, sir, from *Kestrel* with his report of the reconnaissance,' announced Captain Campbell.

All conversation ceased and twenty pairs of eyes turned on Holbrooke.

Howe looked irritated. It dawned on Holbrooke that they'd been discussing the best place to land the army, and he wasn't pleased to be doing so in front of such a large audience.

'Clear the cabin if you please, Captain Campbell,' he said. 'This is a naval matter and I'll hear Mister Holbrooke's report alone. Your Grace, would you care to stay? and you, Captain Duff?'

The cabin emptied as the staff officers left, some looking cheerful but most disgusted that they weren't being invited to hear this report. They all knew that a sloop had been sent ahead to look at Saint-Malo and at Cancale Bay, though few knew the name of the sloop and none other than Campbell knew this very young-looking commander.

'Your Grace, may I present Captain Holbrooke?'

The duke rose and returned Holbrooke's bow, with a degree of politeness calculated to a nicety. Yes, there were officers of Holbrooke's age and rank on his staff, but they were all known to the duke. He was aware of what patronage and money had brought them that far, whereas he knew nothing whatever of Holbrooke.

'Here's a man nearer our age, Duff,' the commodore said to his second-in-command with a laugh. 'Mister Holbrooke was made commander even younger than you!'

Faced with the duke's age and nobility, and his military rank – he was a lieutenant-general and master of the ordnance – Howe had evidently decided to make a virtue of youth and energy. The duke looked unimpressed.

'I'm sure you have a written report for me,' Howe continued.

'I do sir,' said Holbrooke removing the sealed envelope from his pocket.

'Well, you can give that to my secretary. For now, a brief summary of what you found, if you please.'

Holbrooke paused, putting his thoughts in order, this was no time to start with the usual formula, 'I proceeded in pursuance of your orders…'

'Take a seat man, if it will make you more comfortable,' Howe said not unkindly and swept a pile of papers off the only spare chair. 'You were to start with Cézembre Island, if I remember correctly,' he prompted.

That was the nudge that Holbrooke needed.

'Yes sir. The island is fortified, as you expected. There's a battery looking west over the approach channel. There are at least two thirty-six pounders, high up on the northwestern cliffs.'

Howe shuffled the papers on the table.

'There's a chart here somewhere…'

'I have one here,' said Holbrooke, taking Fairview's copy from his pocket.

Howe turned the chart so that the duke could see it.

'The guns are here, sir,' said Holbrooke, 'and you can see the extent of their arcs to the east. They're sited to cover the channel.'

'How do you know their arcs?' asked Howe.

'That was when they stopped firing at us, sir,' Holbrooke replied simply. 'I saw gun emplacements stretching to the west, so I'm sure there are more than two guns in the battery. I'm certain those that fired on us were the only ones that would bear.'

He looked at Howe who almost winked. He had no need to ask that question, but he wanted the duke to know that his officers weren't shy of taking fire.

'You see, Your Grace, we know that the fort on Conchée Island is armed and manned so there's no approaching Saint-Malo from the north. If Cézembre wasn't armed, then it may have been possible to force the channel, but even then, there are two more forts on the way through, and then the three forts in front of the town. It really is impossible.'

'Well, I'm disappointed,' replied the duke. 'An attack right into the town, or a landing under the walls would have saved a great deal of time. However, I see there are *naval* reasons for not making a direct assault. Proceed, if you please.'

Holbrooke cleared his throat, not entirely happy to be caught in the crossfire between a duke and a commodore.

'I sailed around Cancale Point into the bay,' Holbrooke continued, 'arriving at midday…'

'That would be yesterday wouldn't it?' asked Duff.

'Yes, sir, this all happened yesterday.'

Holbrooke was starting to understand; Howe and Duff were gently educating the duke in the utility of naval power. They were ensuring that he understood that this whole stretch of coast had been covered in a single day, not the three or four that it would have taken on the land.

'The beach south of Cancale is ideal for a landing, so long as we understand the tides. There's a garrison here in Cancale and they have a battery of guns that face south across the bay. They command the beach up to this small village of La Houle.'

'How big is La Houle,' asked Howe.

'Perhaps twenty houses, sir. The beach in front of the village is crowded with fishing boats. Then the shoreline continues south, curving towards the east as you see here,' he pointed at the chart.

'There's a small battery being constructed just here, south of La Houle,' he continued.

'How do you know about that,' asked Duff. 'It must have been hard to spot if it didn't fire at you.'

'The guns aren't mounted yet, sir. I went ashore at night and found the battery. It looked like the emplacements were being made for twenty-four pounders. I estimate that they could be mounted as soon as today.'

'One moment, Commander,' the duke interrupted. It was significant that he was pedantically using Holbrooke's rank rather than the more usual courtesy title of *captain*. 'You went ashore at night, alone?'

'Not alone, Your Grace. I had my bosun and a man who speaks French like a Frenchman, just in case it was needed.'

The duke nodded thoughtfully.

'Then you will know what this land is like above the beach.'

'That was partly why I asked Captain Holbrooke to go

ashore, Your Grace,' said Howe.

'The sand is firm and flat and depending on the tide there could be anything up to three hundred yards of it between the high and low water marks. Above the sand there are dunes around twenty feet high covered in tussock grass. The battery is being built on top of one of those. The land behind the dunes is flat and it appeared to be good going.'

Howe looked pleased.

'And what does this battery command?'

'The bay south of La Houle, sir,' replied Holbrooke. 'It's well-sited and from what I saw, it was commanded by a regular artillery officer, not the local coastguard militia.'

The last thing that Holbrooke wanted to do was to be drawn into explaining how he knew the Austrian major in command of the French guns at the army's landing site.

Howe looked at the duke.

'Your Grace, in light of this information I must formally state my position. For you to attempt anything against Saint-Malo, this is where you must land, here at La Houle,' he said jabbing a finger at the tiny hamlet with the stubby church tower. 'We can deal with this battery and then your army can be put ashore in good order. It's only seven miles marching to Saint-Malo, and most importantly the anchorage is sheltered from the west. I can guarantee to take you off from Cancale, if need be.'

'Then so it must be, Commodore. I would have preferred to be landed at the town itself, but you tell me that it's impossible. You command until I am ashore, and this is your decision.'

The duke looked as though he was lining up his defence already.

'This map, may I have it?' asked the duke.

'Do you have another, Mister Holbrooke?' asked Howe.

'I brought three, sir. My sailing master asked that I give one to his colleague in your flagship; it's marked with additional soundings and clearing lines.'

'You'll see Campbell's sailing master sooner than you think, Captain Holbrooke,' he replied with a subtle emphasis on the *captain*, for the duke's benefit. 'I have another duty for you. We must anchor over the tide, but I need a clear marker for the flagship's berth, so that there's no disorder as we approach the anchorage. *Kestrel* doesn't have a station in the squadron, so you'll be our marker. I'm sending you ahead to Baleine Bay with a pilot and you're to anchor half a cable beyond where the flagship should be. 'The pilot's a Guernsey man… remind me of his name, would you?' he asked the secretary.

'Renouf sir, Ishmael Renouf.'

'Of course, thank you.' Howe looked stern for a moment. 'Renouf is a good man, but the responsibility to place my flagship so that the squadron can anchor safely as they come up astern of me is yours, Mister Holbrooke. That must be understood.'

'Aye-aye sir,' replied Holbrooke.

'And after Baleine Bay we will need to anchor again before we make Cancale Bay, unless this damned wind picks up. Perhaps south of the Minquiers, but that depends upon the wind. Speak to the master before you leave, he'll tell you how much space the squadron needs, and you can give him that chart of Cancale.'

Holbrooke turned to leave.

'Captain Holbrooke,' said Howe before he'd reached the cabin door, 'I'm sure His Grace will agree that we owe you our thanks. This has saved us making an abortive attempt at the Saint-Malo channel. Now we can steer directly for the proper landing site.'

***

CHAPTER TEN

Wind and Tide

Saturday, Third of June 1758.
Kestrel, at Sea. Baleine Bay, Sark.

It was one thing to decide on a destination, but in the English Channel with fickle and uncertain summer winds and a relentless tidal stream, it was quite another to get there. *Kestrel* had powered ahead of the squadron as soon as Holbrooke had set foot on his quarterdeck, and yet as the sun rose the forest of sails started showing on the northern horizon, closer than Holbrooke would have wished. For all Fairview's effort, *Kestrel* would only be an hour or so ahead of *Essex*, barely time for the sloop to lay back on its anchor and show Howe's sailing master where he should steer.

Renouf chewed his knuckles, infecting the whole quarterdeck with his nervousness.

'How far to run now, Mister Renouf?'

Holbrooke was doing his best to appear calm, but it was a ponderous responsibility that Howe had laid on his shoulders. The squadron needed the best part of a mile for its anchorage, and even a mile was only safe so long as they weighed before the tide turned. If they stayed over a tide, the transports and storeships would inevitably collide as they swung. This Baleine Bay offered a bare mile from north to south.

'Two cables, sir, or thereabouts,' the pilot answered, 'when Baleine Rock is on the beam.'

'There's a bare cable between the rock to starboard and shoal water to larboard,' said Fairview confidentially. 'Just enough space to swing if we need to.' The master had no good opinion of the pilot's skill, but that wasn't personal, he had no good opinion of any pilot's ability.

'Fifteen fathoms you said, Mister Renouf?'

'Aye sir, fifteen fathoms or thereabouts at the bottom of the tide. You'll need to veer sixty fathoms to allow for the flood.'

Fairview nodded in agreement. If they placed themselves directly between Baleine Rock and the shoal to the east with sixty fathoms of cable, then they could swing safely and have some margin for error.

'Deck ho! Sail, sir. Sail five points on the larboard bow.'

'Very well,' Holbrooke replied.

'Mister Turner, run up to the masthead and let me know what you see.'

'Half a cable to run,' said the pilot.

Fairview was ready to order the topsails backed, Lynton was on the fo'c'sle at the cathead, ready to slip the anchor, but they were all staring at him. Didn't they understand? Whatever that sail was, it couldn't possibly be more important than the safe anchoring of the squadron. He opened his mouth to snap at them, to remind them of their duty, but at the last moment thought better of it. With a tricky anchorage coming up, it was no time to unsettle his people.

'Proceed with the anchorage, Mister Fairview,' he said in a calm voice.

As the cable snaked through the hawse, Turner hailed from the main topmast head.

'It's a man-o'-war, sir,' he shouted, a little too excitedly for Holbrooke's taste, 'and there's a sail beyond her that could be another man-o'-war.'

'Very well,' Holbrooke replied through the speaking trumpet. If one was a man-o'-war, then probably the second would also be.

'Mister Lynton, can you leave the anchoring to the bosun? Very well, I'd welcome your opinion on those two sails, if you please. Let me know when you can tell whether they're French.'

Lynton ran up the shrouds, perhaps not as fast as a topman, but certainly without discredit to his rank

It was a racing certainty that this frigate was French and that the second sail was also a frigate or corvette. As soon as Turner identified her as a man-o'-war it had narrowed the field down to British or French; no other nation had cause to cruise in this Gulf of Saint-Malo. As for her being British, well it was a possibility. Anson may have found the need to send a frigate or two to find Howe, but it was unlikely, and in any case, they'd be coming from the west, not the southeast. Holbrooke was confident that the next hail from Lynton would identify them as French, but it was worth waiting a few minutes for confirmation before committing himself.

'Mister Edney, bend on the signal for an enemy in sight to the southeast, and the supplementary flags for two frigates.'

It was only Howe's new list of signals that allowed Holbrooke to be so specific in his report to the flagship. Never had such a comprehensive list been issued to a squadron. It remained to be seen how robust the system would prove under the stress of action.

'Mister Matross, prepare to fire a gun to windward.'

With so many matters to occupy the flagship as it led a hundred-and-fifty ships to an anchorage, it would be easy for them to miss a flag hoist if their attention wasn't drawn to it.

'Deck there, they're two frigates, sir, or perhaps one's a sloop. Ship rigged in any case,' shouted Lynton. 'French for sure, they're tops'ls are fresh as daisies.'

'Make the signal, Mister Edney,' said Holbrooke.

Kestrel was laying back on her anchor, the fitful westerly wind having its own way while the tide was briefly slack at low water.

'Flagship's signalling, sir.' Edney leafed through the sewn pages of the squadron's fighting instructions.

'*Kestrel* prepare to weigh anchor,' he reported.

'Next signal will be to investigate the enemy,' said Lynton as he jumped from the gunwale back to the deck, 'A guinea on it,' and he looked expectantly at his gambling partner Fairview who grimaced and shook his head.

Holbrooke would have liked to take that bet. He knew Howe better than Lynton did, and he was certain that the flagship would anchor within hailing range, then the commodore could give detailed instructions to his sloop commander. It wasn't right to say that Howe didn't trust his subordinates, it would be more accurate to say that he left nothing to chance if he could avoid it.

***

'Anchor's at short stay,' Lynton reported, 'we can be underway in less than five minutes from when you give the order, sir.'

Holbrooke glanced across at Fairview who'd been in deep conversation with the pilot. The master saw the look and nodded.

'Yes, sir,' he replied to the unspoken question. 'We'll be safe enough at short stay, the tide's just making now and won't be more than a knot by the time the flagship reaches us. If we should drag, it'll be nor'-nor'east, but it's unlikely.'

'Nevertheless, Master, I'd be grateful if you'd watch the bearings.'

Holbrooke looked carefully at the rock that was only half a cable to the west and found a distinctive tree on the shoreline to take a transit. It was more accurate than the compass and he could watch it himself, getting the first hint of any drag.

'Mister Lynton, an experienced man's foot on the cable, if you please, and he's to sing out if he feels any movement.'

It took an hour for *Essex* to come to the anchorage, an hour in which the two Frenchmen beat ever closer. They were only five miles downwind now, sailing beautifully under those carefully cut sails that hadn't suffered the sun, the wind and the salt spray for the months on blockade duty that their British counterparts had. The largest was a small frigate showing ten gun-ports each side. She wasn't much bigger than *Kestrel* although her guns were probably eight-pounders rather than *Kestrel's* six-pounders. The smaller ship would have been called a sloop if she'd been British. She was what the French called a *frégate légèr* or sometimes a *corvette*. Whatever the owners called her, she had seven gun-ports each side, picked out in white against a black hull. Perhaps he'd been a little hasty in identifying them both as frigates, but Holbrooke thought he'd be excused.

'Mister Holbrooke,' shouted Howe from the bowsprit of *Essex*. The flagship hadn't even let go her anchor before the commodore was hailing *Kestrel*.

'Sir!' responded Holbrooke.

'Weigh anchor immediately and run down to those two. Stay to windward and don't engage them unless you can get that smaller one alone. I don't want to send any of the squadron's escorts, but if they come within two miles, I will do so to prevent them from seeing the flatboats. Just persuade them that they shouldn't be interfering.'

Holbrooke could see Howe's point. These Frenchmen could do no real harm and it wasn't worth breaking the cohesion of his force to see them off. *Kestrel* was ideal for this task for the same reason that she'd been the right choice for scouting the anchorage; she wasn't part of Howe's plan, and sending her away wouldn't alter his formation. Holbrooke could already hear the pawls of the windlass clicking more slowly as the sloop was hauled up to her anchor, and he could see the topmen running up to loose the sails.

'They can try to get among the transports all they like,' Howe shouted, pointing to the squadron behind him.

They were anchoring in the same formation that they'd used for cruising, with the exception that the escorts from the starboard wing had moved around to larboard, so that they protected the seaward side of the anchored formation. To reach the vulnerable transports and storeships, the Frenchmen would have to run the gauntlet of the two fourth rates and seven frigates that would soon be covering a flank only a mile long. It was an impossibility.

It was a tricky manoeuvre to get the sloop out of her anchorage without being set onto the shoal only a hundred yards to leeward or drifting down on the tide to collide with the flagship and the first division of transports immediately astern. To Fairview, however, it was another opportunity to show his skill. There was no doubt that a dozen pairs of eyes watched them from *Essex* even though the flagship was still engaged in anchoring. Under jib, fore stays'l and fore tops'l, *Kestrel* cast her head to the nor'east. The instant that it looked like he could take advantage of a sustained gust in the westerly wind, Fairview ordered the anchor to be broken free from the sandy bottom. *Kestrel* gathered way, still pointing directly at the flagship.

Holbrooke held his breath.

It was a race between two natural elements: the sloop had to gather speed from the wind to achieve steerage way before the sluggish tidal stream bore her down on *Essex*. For a few seconds it appeared that she wouldn't make it and Jackson's team on the fo'c'sle readied their fenders and bearing-off poles. Then, with only yards to go, the quartermaster nodded at Fairview. The rudder was biting!

'Bring her easy to starboard,' the master ordered.

A sharp movement of the rudder now, when the sloop was still only just moving through the water, could bring disaster by interrupting the flow past the stern.

Holbrooke watched as *Kestrel's* bows paid off the wind. Now that the flagship was on the larboard side – the windward side – the danger was over, and she slipped confidently past the huge third-rate.

'Neatly done, Mister …'

Holbrooke stopped in mid-sentence as something small and solid hit the crown of his hat. He looked to windward, just in time to see Howe waving a ship's biscuit at him amid the grins of everyone who could spare a moment from anchoring. Holbrooke looked momentarily perplexed.

'It's just the commodore's way, apparently,' said Chalmers. 'I fancy he's proving to the world that *Kestrel* passed a mere *biscuit-toss* away! I believe it may even be a compliment'

'Oh… Well…'

'You should raise your hat, sir,' whispered Fairview, 'to acknowledge the jest. Otherwise the commodore may think you don't approve.'

Holbrooke felt foolish, but he lifted his hat to the commodore and ostentatiously patted out the non-existent dent. He waved in what he hoped would be taken for a cheerful manner. It was all very well for a commodore and the second son of a peer to find amusement this way, but as a mere commander with no connections to speak of, Holbrooke felt far too vulnerable to take a risk with humour.

He replaced his hat, the wooden smile still fixed incongruously to his face.

'Are we clear of the shoal? Yes? Then bear away Mister Fairview and let's be after those gentlemen.'

'First Lieutenant, clear for action and beat to quarters.'

There was immediate bustle on the deck, as lashings were cast loose, and guns were run out. From below could be heard the carpenter's mates knocking away the wedges from removable bulkheads. Everyone appeared to be in motion – everyone except the poor pilot Renouf, who had expected to be back aboard the flagship by now. He'd been forgotten in the haste to be after the enemy. Now he seemed condemned to another day and night aboard *Kestrel*, and he didn't look pleased.

***

Holbrooke closed his telescope with a snap.

'They're trying to lure us away from the squadron in the hope that they can beat us before Howe dispatches a frigate or two.'

Kestrel had been chasing the two Frenchmen to leeward for an hour now. The sloop was in no immediate danger, having the weather gage, and they could easily beat back to the anchorage if the Frenchmen turned on them.

Lynton and Fairview nodded in agreement. They'd heard the commodore's orders as well as Holbrooke had.

'Mister Fairview. What's the distance to the flagship now?'

'Four miles, sir.'

'Then I suggest that's our limit. Bring her to, and we'll see what our friends do next.'

It was unnaturally quiet on the placid sea with the sloop lying-to under a backed main topsail and jib. The people were still at quarters and the guns were run out. The smoke from the slow match drifted idly to leeward, towards the enemy. The French frigate and the corvette were also lying-to, perhaps deciding on their next move.

'Excuse me sir, but I believe I recognise those two. They're from Saint-Malo, unless I'm sadly mistaken.'

'Saint-Malo, Mister Renouf?' replied Holbrooke. 'I thought that was just a privateer port.'

'Well, it is really, sir, there's upwards of fifty of the roving gentlemen that hail from there. But these two men-o'-war are also based at Saint-Malo, they anchor out in the Rance, but they have mud berths in the lagoon as well. They don't often go to sea,' he said with a gesture of contempt. 'Of course, the infamous Thurot's ship is berthed there when he's not cruising, but he's a King's officer now, although that hasn't changed his habits.'

'That makes sense, sir,' said Lynton. 'With the Channel Fleet at sea these two could hardly have come around from Brest and if they were from Cherbourg, they'd not want to be cut off from home by the squadron.'

'Well, we can be sure that they're here to find out where the squadron's bound. Probably a smuggler brought the news of the sailing. Then they saw us off Saint-Malo and decided that was too much of a coincidence.

'Yes, but whatever their orders, they'd be blocks of wood if they hadn't caught the privateering spirit in the port,' Renouf replied. 'There's neither a shopkeeper and nor a labourer that doesn't owe his employment to the privateers. They'll be on the lookout for an easy capture, for certain.'

Holbrooke looked gain at the pilot. He'd been quiet until now, but the idea of an enterprise on the edge of legality seemed to have enlivened him. Of course, the Guernsey men and Jersey men were famous smugglers, a trade that they didn't see fit to give up in wartime. He'd have better knowledge of the doings of Saint-Malo folk than any mainland Englishman.

'Then what'll they do next, Mister Renouf? If you were in their shoes, what would you do?'

Renouf stared wistfully to leeward, perhaps he was closer to these Frenchman than he would admit.

'I'd obey my orders and as soon as I was confident of the squadron's destination, I'd sail back to Saint-Malo as fast as I could. The captain of the frigate – she's the *Joli* incidentally – is a regular officer and has high notions of honour.'

'And they're unlikely to be sure yet. Even if they guess that it's Saint-Malo, they can't be certain. It could still be any of the ports between Cape La Hague and Ushant. Granville, for example,' said Holbrooke. 'No, I believe they'll want to see the squadron a little closer, but to do that they have to get past us. They won't want to tackle us with the squadron just to windward, there's too much chance of us crippling one or both, even if they should take us. If I was that captain, I'd be looking for a way of getting closer to the squadron.'

'Wouldn't it be grand if they split up?' said Lynton, almost licking his lips. 'We'd only need half a glass to take that little fellow. Two broadsides and he'd strike before we could board him. The commodore would surely send help when he heard the guns, and then there'd be no rescue from the frigate.'

'Wishes won't achieve anything, gentlemen. We'll hold this position until the commodore recalls us.'

'Mister Edney, can you see the flagship's signals?' asked Lynton, taking the hint.

***

Kestrel waited in vain. The French frigate and the sloop loitered through the day and in the first dog-watch *Kestrel* was recalled. The squadron weighed anchor and now there were seven British frigates underway; the odds had changed. If just two of them were dispatched to chase the French, it would be odd if they failed to take at least one of them. The Frenchmen were also of that opinion and they reached away across the bay towards Saint-Malo.

***

CHAPTER ELEVEN

Reconnaissance

Monday, Fifth of June 1758.
Kestrel, at Sea. Off Cancale.

Holbrooke stood stiff and straight, his hat hovering some inches above his head as the pipes screeched their greeting to the duke and the commodore, stopping just in time to avoid rendering those sacred to honours to the colonel and naval lieutenant that accompanied them. The people were at their quarters and the sloop was cleared for action – they were within long cannon-shot of the battery at Cancale – and yet still the ceremonial had to be observed. Holbrooke was aware that nobody else thought it a little strange that they should bother with these naval courtesies when round shot could be crashing around them at any moment. Certainly, Lynton and the master saw nothing incongruous, and by the bearing of the bosun's mate and the sideboys, neither did they.

The introductions were swift. Only Lynton and Fairview warranted the notice of the two great men, and Fairview only because they would be sharing a very small quarterdeck with him for the next hour. Swift, even perfunctory, and yet the introductions were hugely important to Lynton; this was how the men who could influence his career became aware of him as an individual.

'Well, let's go, Holbrooke. The duke and I want to see these beaches of yours.'

Holbrooke had already noticed that the lieutenant who trailed in Howe's wake was not carrying the customary bunting bundle. There would be no shift of the commodore's broad pennant, not for a mere unrated sloop.

'Wind's nor'westerly and the tide has just turned, sir,' said Holbrooke, 'we won't get much closer than a mile to the dunes.'

'Then so be it,' replied Howe, 'get me as close as possible but don't run aground under the enemy guns, not even on this flat sand on a windward shore and a rising tide.'

'Carry on, Mister Fairview, keep to the five-fathom line,' Holbrooke ordered.

'And a half, five,' intoned the leadsman from the starboard fore-chains, as if responding to a cue.

The colonel broke off from the duke, who was standing as far aft as he could go, beyond the number fifteen six-pounder.

'His Grace wishes to know the significance of the wind and tide as it relates to the possibility of running aground,' he asked.

Howe laughed. 'You tell him Holbrooke.'

'Well, sir, running aground is a bad business at any time but under enemy guns it could be disastrous. In this case the wind and tide are important because if we do run aground, the rising tide will soon float us again and the wind off the shore will help push us out to deeper water. It's all sand here, so with the sea almost flat, there's no danger to the ship's structure if we run gently aground. It would be a different case if there were rocks. Under these circumstances I can afford to take more of a risk.'

Holbrooke noticed the colonel's momentary alarm.

'Of course, I've no intention of putting the sloop aground with the two commanders of this expedition on board. You see we have two leads going so that we can respond quickly to any changes in the depth, one on each side.'

'Deep six,' called the larboard leadsman.

'Bring her up a point,' said Fairview to the quartermaster, responding to the report of deeper water. Howe nodded his approval

Holbrooke tried not to watch as the colonel relayed this intelligence to the duke. In a way, Holbrooke pitied the commander of the land forces. Both his rank of nobility and his rank as a soldier prevented him from getting involved in this kind of detail, but he could see that the duke was keenly interested. He sent the colonel off to study the operation of the lead-line.

'There's the battery at Cancale,' said Holbrooke pointing over the starboard beam.

Howe studied it through his telescope. It was a solid masonry emplacement for a battery of eight guns. Their black muzzles could be seen protruding through the embrasures.

'We're within range if they're twenty-four pounders. I wonder that they don't fire,' he said. 'Do they believe we can't see them? Are they hoping to lure a more succulent target?'

Holbrooke could see the sense now in not flying the commodore's pennant. And yet, he wondered. If Hans Albach was over there, he'd surely recognise *Kestrel*. Would he hold his fire for an old friend? Quite possibly. He'd committed worse military sins off Emden, coming close to colluding with Holbrooke in the downfall of the French garrison.

Howe looked over his shoulder at his flagship moving into the anchorage with the whole squadron of men-o'-war, transports and storeships following. The battery would be disappointed; Cancale Bay offered good holding ground outside the range of the guns. Also, the new flatboats with their vastly improved carrying capacity allowed him to conduct the operation at greater range than he could have done if he'd had to rely on ship's boats.

'They have no overhead cover,' remarked the duke, grudgingly joining the discussion, 'they're not bomb-proof.'

'Oh, I believe we can silence that battery without resorting to the bombs. I have only two and barely enough ammunition for a single landing. I'll reserve them until we really need them.'

'We could try a ranging shot now,' said Lynton, more in hope than any real expectation that the commodore would agree.

'No, I think we'll observe our side of this peculiar truce, Mister Lynton,' said Howe. 'I fancy we have more to lose than they do.'

Kestrel was making less than three knots under her topsails and headsails. The land slipped by slowly to starboard and soon any danger from the Cancale battery was behind them.

'There's a great deal of open beach for my men to advance over,' said the duke, looking at the expanse of flat sand between the lapping waves and the sand dunes.

'Yes, Your Grace. It looks quite daunting now, but it will be a long time before your men are ready to land and the tide will have risen by then. We'll be able to put them ashore under the very shadow of those dunes if we can make the landing at five o'clock. Every hour after that will increase the distance again.'

'What would be the last time for the landing today, commodore?'

'At eight o'clock there'll be about three hundred yards of sand, that should be the latest to put the grenadiers ashore. Of course, once they've taken the villages and the dunes, the remainder can be put ashore at leisure.'

'Deep four,' called the starboard leadsman. He had a soft accent that was bred somewhere in the Downs – sheep country – and it was quite distinct from the harsh Portsmouth accent of the larboard leadsman.

Holbrooke was prevented from interfering by Fairview's calm order to the quartermaster. *Kestrel's* head moved two points to larboard and the next call, from the Portsmouth man, showed that they'd moved back to five fathoms. Not for the first time Holbrooke blessed his good fortune in having Fairview as his sailing master. Most unrated sloops had one who was newly promoted from the ranks of master's mates.

'If you look just to the left of that tallest dune, sir,' said Holbrooke addressing the commodore, 'you'll see the gabions in front of the new battery.'

'Could they really have set it up in that time?' asked Howe. 'It's only three days since you were here, and you said that the guns weren't in place then.'

'Yes, sir. If the guns were available. I doubt whether they've registered them though, so their firing may be a little wild.'

The contours of Cancale Bay were steeper here and *Kestrel* could move closer to the shore, well within twenty-four pounder range.

'Mark five.'

That was the Downsman. He'd told Holbrooke once that his family came from the tiny hamlet of Idsworth, nestled in a valley of the Downs just a couple of miles to the east of the London road. It was close to one of England's main commercial arteries, but it marched to its own beat, a community turned in upon itself and not welcoming the attention of the outside world.

'Shot!' said Lynton. They could see the white smoke to the left of the high dune and a moment later they heard the dull boom of a cannon. A plume of water soared upwards half a cable ahead of the sloop, its moment of life ending in a frosting of spray blowing away on the wind.

'Stand on, Mister Holbrooke,' said the commodore. 'I want to see right down the throat of that battery. You may fire if you think you have the range.'

'Mister Lynton, fire by divisions and make sure every gun is well-pointed,' called Holbrooke to the first lieutenant who was already far forward among his guns.

The quarter gunners were fussing over the pointing and elevation of each of the forward two guns on the starboard side, levering hand-spikes and tapping quoins. Lynton took a last look and stood back. The ship was hardly rolling at all, providing the best of platforms for this kind of long-range gunnery. Nonetheless, it was a very long distance to expect six-pounders to hit a target.

'Numbers one and three, fire!' shouted Lynton, and the two guns bellowed and leapt back on their breechings. A spray of sand showed where they had struck the base of the dunes, a full thirty feet below the battery.

'Knock those quoins out a touch,' shouted Lynton, already deafened by the first discharges.

'Numbers five and seven, fire!'

Better this time; the shots had landed only just below the level of the embrasures but well to the right.

There was a whirring overhead. Holbrooke looked up to see a hole appear in the mizzen tops'l.

'Have you seen enough, Your Grace? I fear that those fellows will have our range in a few minutes and a sloop isn't a two-decker; it can't stand many hits from twenty-four-pound shot.'

'I've seen enough, Commodore. Let's return and start preparing for the landing.'

Fairview bore away and stood out into the bay with the wind directly abaft, taking the most direct path to increase the range from the battery. They only had to endure two more salvos, and they fell short as the French gunners struggled to adjust for the rapidly opening range.

'Deck there!' shouted the lookout from the main topmast head. 'On the dunes, sir, soldiers.'

Half a dozen telescopes trained aft over the taffrail.

'Dragoons!' exclaimed the colonel, 'and there's infantry there too.'

'Out of range,' muttered Lynton to Holbrooke so that he couldn't be overheard.

Holbrooke could see now without his telescope, which the colonel had unceremoniously taken up from its stowage on the binnacle. There was a group of around a hundred horsemen in blue tunics on the dunes half a mile north of the battery. They could have been dragoons, but he couldn't tell with the naked eye. What he could see was a long line of infantry behind them, an endless snake of white uniforms, black tricorns and moving patches of blue where their wide cuffs swung to the rhythm of their marching. There was a glint of polished metal above them as their bayonets reflected the noonday sun. They were marching along the dunes towards the battery and would be there in perhaps fifteen minutes.

'Deep eight,' reported the larboard leadsman

'Regulars or Militia?' asked the duke.

'I can't tell at this range,' replied the colonel.

'Can we get closer, Commodore?'

Howe glanced at Holbrooke who nodded in reply.

'Yes, Your Grace, Mister Holbrooke will move in as close as he can.'

'Bring her on to the wind, Mister Fairview,' said Holbrooke. 'Steer for the head of that column and stand in to four fathoms.'

'Aye-aye sir,' Fairview replied.

The men ran from their guns to haul on the tacks and sheets. By pinching the wind, *Kestrel* could lie two or three points off the desired course; it would need a tack in five minutes to bring her head onto the marching column.

'That's two companies of regular line infantry,' said the colonel after a long searching stare through Holbrooke's telescope. 'The dragoons could be either, they both have blue uniforms. They look like regulars though, unless the French militia is better drilled than ours.'

'Mark seven,' called the starboard leadsman. It was shoaling rapidly. They'd have to be careful that they didn't run aground between casts of the lead.

'Can you get a shot at them?' asked Howe.

'I'll go about in two minutes, sir,' said Holbrooke, catching Fairview's eye, 'unless it shoals any faster. We should get a shot at them then, but it's too long for grape or canister.'

Fairview brought *Kestrel* sweetly onto the larboard tack. The starboard side gunners had been released to work the ship, so the larboard guns were all manned and ready. Lynton was leaping from gun to gun, checking the elevation.

Another waterspout rose ahead of the sloop, the battery had started firing again now that they were back in range.

'Broadsides, Mister Lynton, we may get only one chance.'

'Broadsides, aye-aye sir!'

Kestrel steadied on her new course running parallel to the line of dunes. There was a breathless pause.

'Fire!' shouted Lynton.

Kestrel's Dutch builders hadn't anticipated her firing many whole broadsides in her life; her scantlings weren't made for it and her shallow draught meant that the recoil had a particularly noticeable effect. The sloop moved bodily sideways as all eight six-pounders spoke in flame and thunder. It was a good broadside, possibly the best of Lynton's career so far. At least four of the balls ploughed through the ranks of the dragoons. Holbrooke could see horses down and kicking, and blue-coated figures immobile among the tussock grass. He knew how difficult it was to manoeuvre on the top of those dunes. There was only a single winding path and as soon as the men and horses left it, all unit cohesion would be lost. It happened now. The officers were quick-witted enough to know that a second broadside would do an equal amount of damage, and they hastily pulled their companies and squadrons back below the crest. It must have been an ignominious retreat, made worse by their utter inability to fight back. By the time *Kestrel's* battery was reloaded, only dead men and wounded horses could be seen on the dunes.

'A salutary lesson to the French, I believe, Mister Holbrooke.'

Those were the first words that the duke had uttered to Holbrooke since he'd embarked.

'Yes, Your Grace.'

***

Kestrel quickly moved out of range of the battery again. It never failed to amaze Holbrooke how slowly artillerymen learned the lessons of firing at moving ships, even when they manned batteries overlooking the sea. No doubt they would do well if *Kestrel* had anchored within range or – God forbid – had run aground, but as long as she kept moving, the salvoes continued to drop ahead or astern. Apart from that one hole in the fore tops'l, *Kestrel* had suffered nothing from nearly an hour under the French guns.

***

'Will you take my longboat, sir?'

'If you please, Mister Holbrooke. His Grace and I must be back in *Essex* without delay. I want to do something about those batteries before they hold up the landing.'

The bay was starting to fill with ships, anchoring closer to each other than would ever have been countenanced at Spithead or the Nore. The ten transports that carried two flatboats each started immediately on the slow process of heaving them off their makeshift cradles and swinging them over the gunwales and into the water. Already the boats were pulling over from *Essex*, *Rochester*, *Deptford*, *Portland*, *Richmond*, *Pallas*, *Brilliant* and *Tartar*, carrying the post-captains who had been nominated to command divisions of boats. It still seemed a curious use of such an exalted rank, but the duty was vital to the mission and in any case, those men-o'-war had little else to do now that the squadron had been brought safely to its destination.

Kestrel's station now was at the southern end of the landing area, within sight of the small battery but out of range. Holbrooke had nothing to do but wait. The dragoons and infantry must have moved away because there was no sign of them. They'd taken their dead and wounded and departed.

The tide was flooding fast now, and the strip of sand was getting narrower by the minute. It was said that at the head of the Gulf of Mont Saint-Michel, near the castle on the mount, the flooding tide could out-run a horse. Holbrooke found that unlikely, but certainly a man would want to step out to keep ahead of it.

'Commodore's pennant's shifting, sir!'

That was Edney; he was becoming a good signal midshipman. There'd been little call for flags when they operated alone off Emden, but now, as part of a large squadron, his role had become more important.

'Hauled down in *Essex*, sir, broken out in *Success*.'

So, Howe had moved into a frigate, thought Holbrooke. What's afoot?

He trained his telescope on the new flagship. *Success* was underway and so were *Rose* and *Flamborough*, heading south towards *Kestrel*.

The three frigates had little space to manoeuvre and never did make it into the sort of neat line beloved by squadron commanders. Nevertheless, their objective was clear; the battery at La Houle! Howe was taking personal command to silence the three guns. Holbrooke hoped fervently that Albach wasn't there. A combined broadside of sixty nine-pounder guns was on its way to obliterate the battery.

'Signal from the commodore, sir. *Kestrel* to join the line.'

'Weigh anchor!' shouted Holbrooke. 'Bosun, get those men moving, I want to be underway in ten minutes!'

***

CHAPTER TWELVE

The Line of Battle

Monday, Fifth of June 1758.
Kestrel, at Sea. Cancale Bay.

The line of battle! Every sea officer dreams of the day that he'll walk his quarterdeck as his ship moves into its allotted place in the line, with the enemy in sight. In this case the enemy wasn't a noble column of ships-of-the-line, but a tiny battery perched precariously on the dunes of Cancale Bay. Neither was *Kestrel* a mighty third rate with seventy-four guns loaded and ready, but a humble sixteen-gun sloop. Nevertheless, it was a proud moment. He could see it on the faces of his crew. They'd caught the mood of the occasion: there was an eagerness, a delight in the prospect of the coming battle, one-sided though it was.

'Half a cable, sir,' said Fairview looking judiciously at the spacing of the three frigates. 'They're not leaving much room for error.'

'Then let that be our spacing also, Master, half a cable astern of *Flamborough*.'

Kestrel was sailing hard on the wind to join the line. It was a pretty sight, three frigates of twenty guns in tight formation under tops'ls – fighting canvas – making no more than three knots in the light west-nor'westerly breeze that swept over the dunes. *Success*, flying Howe's broad pennant, was an older ship. Like *Fury*, Holbrooke's frigate in the Mediterranean at the start of the war, she carried a small demi-battery on her lower deck and a pair of three-pounders on her quarterdeck. *Success* in fact carried twenty-four guns even though she was rated a twenty. *Rose* and *Flamborough* were new twenty-gun nine-pounder frigates, launched for this war and as alike as two peas in a pod. They were both spilling the wind from their main tops'ls to keep in their stations on the leading ship, the slower *Success*.

Holbrooke knew the histories of their captains. Eighteen months ago, they'd all been commanders, like Holbrooke, and they'd each been posted in the great rush to build and man the additional ships that were needed to fight the war. Holbrooke's fear was that if he didn't make post-captain soon, he'd miss his chance. Another six months – a year at most – and their lordships would move him out of *Kestrel* to make way for another newly-promoted commander to prove himself. There was no compromise. Either he was posted, or he'd be on half pay for the rest of his life, and the half-pay of a commander wasn't an appealing thought. He shook away that unprofitable line of thinking to concentrate on bringing his sloop into action. After all, that was the surest way of being noticed – and promoted.

'Bring her three points to larboard, quartermaster,' said Fairview. 'You may steer for *Flamborough's* ensign staff.'

Kestrel slid neatly into the line just as the flagship's broadside opened with a roar.

'Starboard battery ready,' reported the first lieutenant. 'I'd like to fire by divisions unto we get the right elevation, sir.'

'Very well, Mister Lynton. Remember we're a lot closer than we were last time.'

It was a shock to see how fast the day was slipping away. Already it was four o'clock and in two hours it would be high water. Albach's battery was only a quarter of a mile away. Once the frigates had found their elevation, it would be uncomfortable work serving those twenty-four pounders. Of course, it would be uncomfortable work in the ships too. Frigates and sloops weren't built to withstand shot of that size, and just a few hits could disable any of the three. Any single hit could disable *Kestrel*.

'Good shooting,' Lynton commented as he saw the sand erupt in small fountains, to subside quickly leaving dark patches where the sun-worn top layer was disturbed. *Success* was peppering the battery with her nine-pounders and now *Rose* was joining in.

'Good shooting, aye,' replied Holbrooke, 'but we'll need to put our balls right through the embrasures to have any effect. Look how that sand is just absorbing the balls. It's all held together by the roots of those damned great clumps of grass.'

Holbrooke watched as *Rose's* first full broadside threw up a storm of sand and grass without any visible effect on the guns.

'No gun captain is to fire until he's certain of his mark. We can fling as many of our balls into the sand as we like, and those gunners will just laugh at us.'

Now the French battery was replying. The sound of their guns was noticeably deeper and louder than the frigates' nine-pounders. They'd made poor practice in the morning, but with their targets so close they could hardly fail to score hits. There was another gun speaking too, not the great solemn boom of the twenty-four pounders, nor the sharp crack of the frigates' nine-pounders. It was something between the two.

'They've two twenty-fours and a twelve, I fancy,' said Fairview. 'Look, the flagship's taking hits!'

It was indeed. *Rose* and *Flamborough* had momentarily sagged away to leeward giving *Kestrel* a view of *Success* that they hadn't had before. There were holes in her mizzen, and it looked like a portion of the taffrail had been shot away.

'Her guns are still firing,' said Fairview.

'Mister Lynton, you may fire when your guns bear.'

Lynton raised his hat in reply and bent down behind his beloved number one gun. A brawny sailor had a handspike under the right-hand side of the carriage, and he was edging the gun sideways as the sand dunes slipped by them. Lynton held up his hand, the sailor whipped away the handspike and Lynton stepped clear.

'Fire!' he shouted and stepped forward to see the fall of shot.

Holbrooke too was watching, but it was hopeless. There were already sixty-two guns firing at the battery. It was impossible to distinguish the all-too-brief eruptions of sand caused by *Kestrel's* six-pounders from the others. The impact of a six-pound ball in dry sand looked much the same as a nine-pound ball.

'Broadsides, Mister Lynton,' shouted Holbrooke above the rising din.

Numbers one and three guns were still reloading, so the first broadside was a mere six guns, and yet it shook the sloop like a terrier shaking a rat. The gunners all had their elevations now, and it was a case of using the handspikes to keep the guns pointing at the target and to load and fire as fast as possible.

Holbrooke looked ahead. The smoke from the frigates was rolling away to the east, and the smoke coming down from the battery on the dunes wasn't thick enough to obscure *Success*, only four hundred yards ahead. She was hauling her wind!

'The flagship will be aground in a moment,' shouted Fairview. 'Look, she's handing her tops'ls and fore stays'l. She's using her jib to haul her bows off the wind. Too late, far too late.'

Success came to a graceful halt, her bows nudging into the sand and her broadside facing the French battery. Fairview had assumed it was an accident, her rudder shot away or some other calamity that caused her bows to fly into the wind. But Holbrooke knew better. The commodore was in *Success*, and Holbrooke knew him well enough to guess that he was sacrificing an old frigate to silence the French battery. There could be no landing until the battery had been silenced, and if that took another two hours, they would have lost the opportunity to land the army today. Tomorrow anything could happen. A French army could appear over the dunes – those dragoons and infantry they fired at this morning could have been but the precursor – or a gale could sweep in from the west. It must have been evident to Howe that after this first pass, it would take half an hour for his line to reach back to the north and make another attack.

That was too long, and in any case, it may still not silence the battery. Today was the day, and Howe would do whatever it took, make any sacrifices, to put the duke's army onto the beach. Holbrooke was as sure as he could be that *Success* had been deliberately run aground under the French battery to slug it out toe-to-toe.

Rose, the next astern, kept stolidly on her course, reinforcing Holbrooke's opinion. Howe would have shouted his intentions across to his next-in-line and now *Rose* was leading the frigates away from the battery.

'High tide's in half an hour, sir,' said Fairview.

Kestrel's guns were silent now as their view of the battery was masked by the grounded frigate, still flying the commodore's pennant.

'Boat putting off from the flagship, sir,' Edney reported.

Holbrooke trained his telescope on the yawl. There was Commodore Howe, sitting in the stern sheets, looking grim, his shoulders set in defiance. He was right to leave the grounded frigate, of course, but it can't have been easy to leave after giving that order; some would impute all sorts of dishonourable motives. The yawl set its lugsail and stretched away for the anchored *Essex*. Now that Holbrooke had a moment's leisure, he could see that preparations for the landing were far advanced. The flatboats were congregating around the flagship, each with its load of grenadiers, the shock-troops of the assault on France. The post-captains would be boarding now and as soon as the battery was silenced, they'd be underway for the shore.

'The commodore's signalling, sir,' said Edney, and then in a lower voice, 'well, waving his arms, not exactly signalling.'

Howe was pointing at *Kestrel* and then emphatically gesturing back to *Success*. His meaning was clear, *Kestrel* was to haul out of the line and support the grounded frigate. It was an obvious decision; *Kestrel* drew four feet less than the frigates and Howe had seen that she was well-handled in shallow water. So that was the end of *Kestrel's* career in the line-of-battle, a single pass in front of the battery and it was all over.

'Mister Fairview, we'll run a line to seaward of *Success*. Can we lie close enough on the northward leg?'

Fairview looked at the wind and squinted across the compass.

'Just about, sir, so long as the wind doesn't shift into the nor'west. We should be able to veer at the end of each run and keep close to the frigate.'

Holbrooke looked over at the commodore's yawl. He'd been forgotten already; Howe was moving on to the next phase of the operation, putting the army ashore.

***

Holbrooke knew why he'd been sent back to support *Success*, it wasn't only because of her shallow draught, nor because of any merit on the part of *Kestrel* or her commander. It was mainly because the sloop was surplus to requirements. Howe had set up a structure to his squadron that held good in both cruising and at anchor. It was strong in defence, mutually supportive and, most importantly, all the captains of the men-of-war had been briefed on the plans and the signals to carry them out; Holbrooke hadn't. He wasn't even wanted to fill the gap left by *Success*. Well, if he was to be merely a hewer of wood and drawer of water, then he would be the best of that oppressed breed.

'Mister Lynton, you'll need to control your guns positively, I'll be reaching across behind *Success*. You'll get the opportunity for one or two broadsides each time we move ahead or astern of her, but you mustn't let the men fire into the frigate by mistake.'

Kestrel's six-pounders hardly counted in this battle, but by appearing and disappearing from behind the frigate, he hoped to put the French gunners off their rhythm.

'You may veer now, Mister Fairview, and make the first reach. Take her as close you can without touching the ground.'

Kestrel had already moved to the south of the battery, but with the wind steady at west-nor'west it was a simple matter to turn to larboard and put the stern through the wind.

'Ready the larboard broadside, Mister Lynton!'

It was curiously quiet on the sloop's deck. The battle between the grounded frigate and the battery was raging less than half a mile away, but Holbrooke felt detached from it all. He could see the twenty-four and twelve-pound balls striking *Success*, raising showers of splinters where they impacted on the upper deck, or making the hull shake where they hit lower down. The frigate's masts all still stood, and she looked as though she could put to sea in a moment. However, a closer look showed the slightest slope on the frigate's deck as the tide receded. In an hour she'd be leaning over so far to larboard that her guns would be unable to bear on the battery, and then she'd be hulled again and again, and sure to flood when the tide turned.

Holbrooke looked along the deck. His sloop had taken no damage at all, the guns were in good order and the crews were crouched beside them, with their sponges, rammers and handspikes poised for their turn in the madness to come. Lynton was standing atop the windlass where he could see over the gunwale and control the broadsides. His was the responsibility of preventing his guns from firing into *Success*. The training and elevation would be the responsibility of the quarter gunners and the gun captains.

A few degrees of helm and *Kestrel* heeled a trifle to starboard, then steadied. The gun crews were behaving like veterans, tapping at the quoins to reduce the elevation so that the balls would carry true to the target and levering the handspikes to keep them pointing.

Holbrooke eyed the range. He'd been right, they'd only get one broadside in at each end of each reach. It was better to wait for the last moment before they were masked by *Success* so that they had the best chance of hitting the battery.

Lynton glanced over his shoulder at his captain.

Crash! A heavy ball from the battery slammed into the hull below the upper deck.

'Twelve pounder!' shouted Lynton, waving his hat. The plan was working and some of the battery's fire was being diverted from the frigate. They'd find it a frustrating task trying to hit the sloop as it appeared and disappeared from the shadow of the frigate. If only one gun fired at the sloop, that was a third of the battery's strength being wasted.

Holbrooke waved his hat at Lynton.

'Fire!' shouted Lynton. The feeling of detachment from the battle evaporated in a moment. The guns belched their iron and flame and the smoke rolled back across the deck. The eight larboard six-pounders hurled themselves back against the breechings and the worms were immediately thrust down the muzzles to hook out any remaining wadding.

The side of the frigate was blocking their view now, she was very close. Fairview was obeying his instruction to use every inch of water to close the range to the battery. The leadsmen were far up in the beakhead where they were clear of the guns, but that meant the possibility of Fairview not hearing their calls, so a midshipman was stationed with them to run back along the length of the deck to relay the soundings.

'And a half, three,' said the breathless youngster after he'd sprinted down the starboard side, hurdling the breechings and dodging the gun crews.

Fairview was cutting it fine. The sloop had only half a fathom under the keel. It would only take a modest irregularity in the surface of the sand to put her aground. Then Holbrooke remembered that Fairview had seen the ground at low water, and he would undoubtedly have noticed anything of that sort.

'*Kestrel*!' Captain Ourry, was shouting to Holbrooke.

'Good work, Holbrooke. If you can draw any of their fire, I'd be grateful. I'm going to shore the larboard side so that my guns still bear as the tide ebbs.'

'I'll run back and for and give them a broadside when I emerge from behind you,' replied Holbrooke. 'Do you need any men?'

'Not yet, but the time may come…'

Holbrooke knew what he meant. If his casualties became so great that he couldn't man all his guns, he'd call for reinforcements from *Kestrel*.

***

For two hours Holbrooke reached backwards and forwards to leeward of *Success*. The shoring took little time and the French gunners couldn't interfere as it all happened on the disengaged side. *Kestrel* was miraculously little damaged. The twelve-pounder that appeared to be devoted to their destruction achieved little, just three hits and no guns silenced, no men killed or wounded.

The tide ebbed and soon the frigate was lying in just a few feet of water, held upright by the spars lashed to her side and wedged onto baulks of timber on the sand.

'The battery's fire's slacking, sir,' said Lynton.

Holbrooke had noticed it. The twelve-pounder hadn't fired at all the last time it had an opportunity and by the interval between shots from the twenty-four pounders, it appeared that only one of those was still in action. If Albach was commanding, he'd take a pragmatic view of events, Holbrooke guessed. The final destruction of the battery was only minutes away, whether it was by Ourry's guns or by a storming party that the ebbing tide would soon make feasible. A prudent battery commander would spike his remaining gun and withdraw his gunners to fight another day.

There was a louder report than usual from the battery, and a cloud of black smoke, different in quality to the grey of a cannon discharge, rose rapidly from the dunes. The last gun had been disabled by over-charging it. That was the end of the gallant La Houle battery. Three days it had been in existence and it had held up the British landing by about as many hours. By any scale of military logic, it had done its duty.

***

Kestrel anchored to seaward of the squadron. The sloop's damage was minimal; the three shots in her hull had already been temporarily repaired by the carpenter's crew. Jackson had some knotting and splicing to do, but thankfully Harris' surgical skills hadn't been required. Even *Success* had fared surprisingly well for lying under a battery of heavy guns for three hours. All but one of her nine-pounders were still in action and she'd float off at the next tide.

Holbrooke was exhausted. He'd been on deck since before dawn and now it was nearly the end of the last dog watch. He'd seen the flatboats take the first wave of grenadiers onto the beach and seen the red coats move up the dunes to establish a defensive perimeter. Now the same flatboats were ferrying field guns, infantry, horses, ammunition, rations and all the myriad needs of an army in the field. They were proving their worth on their first day of use.

'Boat from the flagship, sir,' reported Edney, removing his hat as he entered the cabin. 'Orders from the commodore,' he added, handing over a sealed envelope.

He should be used to it by now, this nervousness whenever he opened orders. Yet Holbrooke was still a young man, three months shy of his twentieth birthday – an imposter in command of a sloop-of-war – and the thrill of the unknown gripped him. The contents of this letter could change the course of his life. Howe had already demonstrated that he would use his officers in any way he saw fit. It could be another expedition ashore, or a bombardment of another French position, temporary command of a larger ship, even. Anything, so long as he stayed at the centre of the action, gaining recognition and credit.

He forced himself to break the seal with his knife rather than ripping the paper in his haste, yet his trembling hand betrayed him. Serviteur looked discreetly away.

Disappointment flooded over Holbrooke; he could almost have wept after the stresses and anxieties of the past week. *Kestrel* was to leave Cancale Bay and proceed north to the Jersey Channel, to watch the squadron's northern flank. A hewer of wood and drawer of water indeed.

***

CHAPTER THIRTEEN

The Trap

Tuesday, Sixth of June 1758.
Kestrel, at Sea. Gorey Point, West 7 Nautical Miles.

The wind had backed a few points into the southwest and the June sun shone hot upon *Kestrel's* decks. Holbrooke had ordered the hands to quarters before morning twilight – the absurd hour of four bells in the middle watch – and when no enemy had appeared, he'd dismissed the watch below and taken a nap himself. Now he felt refreshed. The sloop's decks were clean, all traces of yesterday's battle had been removed and the men were in high spirits. The only check to his good humour was the gloomy presence of Ishmael Renouf on his quarterdeck. He was well named: an unwanted man, cast out from his fellows along with the equally superfluous *Kestrel*. The Guernsey pilot had been a late addition to his orders and now the wretched man was haunting the deck, watching with a critical eye every move that Fairview made.

Chalmers fell into step with Holbrooke, enjoying the company, silent though it was. After a few turns, he paused and stared east at the green shores of the Cotentin Peninsula.

'You truly believe that Hans Albach was commanding that battery yesterday? Yet I can't understand how you would know. By your own admission it was unlikely to be a major's command.'

'It's more of a feeling than anything else,' Holbrooke replied. 'Albach was certainly at the battery on Friday night, unlikely though that may sound, and I imagine that he would have stayed to supervise hauling the guns into position. When the battery was properly established, he probably left a junior coastguard militia officer in command – I conceded that there are a lot of assumptions here – and returned to the main battery at Cancale. When he saw the squadron anchor in the bay, he'd have guessed that the dunes to the south were the most likely landing site – that would be why he'd placed a battery at La Houle – and he'd have hurried down to take personal command.'

'As you say, a lot of assumptions,' Chalmers replied nodding thoughtfully.

'There are, but there's another thing. That battery was fought with more than usual resolve. It must have been obvious that it was a losing battle, and yet those militia artillerymen stuck to their guns until they had only one left. They bought valuable time for the French regulars to start a march for the defence – or relief if the duke moves fast enough – of Saint-Malo. That suggests a degree of determination that I wouldn't expect in a militia subaltern. That and the judicious withdrawal when there was nothing more to be gained; neither too early nor too late. I sense the hand of a professional at work, and after Friday night's encounter, there's a good chance that it was Albach. Furthermore, I believe that he survived Howe's onslaught. It was certainly his style to destroy his guns at the end rather than let the enemy have them.'

'He was particular about his guns,' Chalmers mused aloud, 'he'd have recognised *Kestrel*, I imagine?'

'Oh yes, we're very distinctive, even to a soldier. The only other sloop that looks remotely like us is probably wrecked on some Bahamas sandbar.'

'That was a strange encounter, wasn't it?' Chalmers asked, remembering that day when they captured this very ship.

'Yes,' replied Holbrooke. 'It's not every day that one of His Majesty's frigates fights two identical Dutch privateers-turned-pirates, captures one,' he patted the binnacle in affection, 'and sends the other scurrying away downwind to its near-certain demise.'

They walked on in silence for a moment. It was that day, ten months ago, that had led directly to Holbrooke's preposterously early promotion to commander and to the quarterdeck of the very sloop that he'd captured, the sloop whose deck they were now pacing.

'What are your intentions, if I may inquire,' asked Chalmers. 'I gather we've been sent here on a somewhat spurious errand.'

'I believe so.' Holbrooke paused, his mood changing like the snuffing of a candle. 'Commodore Howe is a most particular planner. His dispositions for the cruise to Cancale and for the landing are masterpieces; every man-of-war and every transport and storeship down to the smallest hoy has a role to play and a station to fill. He even has a plan for filling any gaps, so Captain Ourry's station has already been taken by another frigate until *Success* is patched up. *Kestrel* was a late addition to his squadron. He has no job for us, and we were becoming a hindrance to the smooth workings of his command. There's no need for a screen here to the north, not with Anson and the Channel Fleet blocking anything coming from Ushant, and this westerly wind preventing anything rounding Cape La Hague. We've been sent here to keep out of his way.'

He continued in a low voice, 'the pilot Renouf is with us for much the same reason.'

'Then we should make the most of it. This is tantamount to a cruise after all. Isn't that what you've been craving?'

'A cruise with no chance of a prize,' Holbrooke replied. 'That... that great squadron,' he said biting off an obscenity – he never swore in front of the chaplain – 'will have frightened off every innocent French merchantman and fisherman from the Chops of the Channel to Calais, aye and every not-so-innocent Englishman smuggler too.'

Holbrooke stopped abruptly and turned to the chaplain.

'But it's not the lack of prizes that troubles me, we've had more than our share of fortune already.'

Chalmers knew what was coming, he'd heard it or something similar from Holbrooke on many occasions.

'I have to get myself noticed. Time's running out for me

to prove myself fit to be posted. I know you believe that I've already done that, but as far as their lordships are concerned, my name will hardly have been mentioned. Commodore Holmes probably ignored me, certainly the published accounts don't give me any credit for the fall of Emden, and now Howe, with a plethora of captains to look after, will certainly overlook me. In four or five months the Admiralty will yield to pressure from the many deserving lieutenants and promote one into *Kestrel*. I'll be on the beach waiting for a vacancy in the post-captain's list that hasn't already been promised. I tell you truly, David, my wait will be in vain! I must distinguish myself, and that very soon.'

Chalmers knew that it was no good trying to shake his friend out of this frame of mind once it gripped him. He'd long ago decided that Holbrooke was a complex character; a great leader and a fine fighting seaman who saw neither of these aspects of his own character but was in the grip of the anxiety and self-criticism of a young man making his way in a veteran's world.

'Well, you know my view. Their lordships would be mad indeed to overlook your talents.'

'Ha, there you have it! Surely you see, they are mad — mad as hatters, the whole gang of them — and we are nothing more than their playthings.'

The ancient quartermaster had seen young captains come and young captains go and being no more than a few feet away at any point of their walk, had naturally heard every word. He nodded his grey beard in solemn agreement to this fundamental naval truth.

'Amen, halleluiah,' he said in a deep bass growl, not caring what the chaplain thought about this mildest of blasphemies.

It was hard to enjoy the sunshine now, and Holbrooke's humour had spread across the deck with the speed of a quick-match. The two men paced on, lost in their own thoughts and carrying their personal cloud with them.

***

'Sail ho! Sail a point on the starboard bow,' shouted the lookout from the main topmast. 'Looks like a ship's tops'ls.'

'Up with you, Mister Edney, and tell me what you see.'

Holbrooke swept a glance across the deck. The guns were already cleared for action and the yards had been chained, so there was little else to do except to turn the hands up, if it became necessary.

'What do you think, Mister Lynton,' he asked as his first lieutenant arrived on deck, as much to prevent him unnerving everyone by fussing over the guns as for any real desire to hear his opinion.

Lynton stopped in his tracks and looked to the northwest as though he'd never seen the sea before.

'Coming down this side of Jersey? If she's ship-rigged then she's either a man-o'-war or a privateer. Unless she's a merchantman that's slipped past the Channel Fleet and hasn't heard about Howe's squadron. In that case, she could be heading for Granville or somewhere else along the coast.'

'A victualler from Portsmouth for the squadron?' asked Holbrooke.

'Not with this wind,' Fairview interrupted, joining the conversation, 'she'd never have weathered the cape.'

That was true. With the wind in the southwest, anything coming from the east of Cape La Hague would have to tack and tack again to get this far.

'Mister Renouf, your expert opinion, if you please.'

Renouf had been hanging back, listening to the discussion but not joining in. He really was a timid man for a pilot, thought Holbrooke.

'East of the Écrevièr Bank, I take it?' Renouf lapsed into a very convincing Breton accent when using French words.

'Just so, it appears,' replied Holbrooke.

'A French merchantman, I don't doubt,' he replied with a curious sideways look, 'making for Saint-Malo perhaps.'

'No French merchantman would take that passage unless forced to, there are shoals everywhere and few of them marked,' said Fairview.

'I believe I know my own back-yard,' snapped Renouf in reply, and he turned away to study the wake.

'When's high water, Mister Fairview?' asked Holbrooke

'Midday, sir, or thereabouts.'

'Then the tides rising, what do you say now Mister Renouf? Would a homeward bound West Indiaman risk it?'

Renouf shook his head without turning.

'Not when the deep passage to the west of the Écrevièrs is open to him, but there are many other places that a merchantman could have sailed from.'

'Very well,' said Holbrooke, 'whatever that vessel is, you may beat to quarters, Mister Lynton. God send us a merchantman or anything less than a big frigate,' he continued, 'begging your pardon Mister Chalmers.'

To the sound of the drum, the Kestrels poured out from below decks. In just five minutes Lynton was able to report the ship at quarters, cleared for action. By that time the masthead of the chase – for that is what they now thought it – was just visible from the deck.

Jackson, his yards already chained, was busying himself with boarding nets. Not for the world would he forego his nets, not after the fight with the Dutch pirates last year.

'Sir!' shouted Edney from the main topmast. 'It's a man-o'-war. It looks very like that sloop that we met off Guernsey. The same tops'ls.'

Holbrooke looked unsurprised.

'Any sign of the other one?' he replied through the speaking trumpet.

'Nothing, sir, there's not another sail all around the horizon, not even a fishing boat.'

Holbrooke turned and smiled at Chalmers who bowed wryly in acknowledgement that Holbrooke's invocation had worked. Something less than a big frigate, it was; but not Renouf's merchantman.

***

The sou'westerly wind was on *Kestrel's* quarter and even under fighting sail she was making six knots. The French sloop – *Trois Poignards*, Renouf had thought was her name – was hard on the wind, beating up to *Kestrel* with every appearance of offering battle.

'What's her weight of metal, Mister Renouf,' asked Holbrooke.

Renouf looked embarrassed, more reticent than even his usual demeanour.

'If she's the *Trois Poignards*, and I say *if*, then she carries fourteen four-pounders, an easy win for you, sir,' he replied.

Holbrooke was almost certain that the pilot knew more than he was saying, that in fact he was very familiar with this ship. Probably it was nothing more than a little smuggling that brought him into contact with the enemy, but he would bear watching anyway.

'D'you hear that, Mister Lynton? Fourteen four-pounders in all probability.'

Lynton replied with a cheer, taken up by all the gun crews.

'Do you see anything else?' Holbrooke shouted up to the masthead.

'Nothing, sir,' replied Edney, 'clear all around.'

'Stay at the masthead, Mister Edney, and keep a careful lookout. There's a frigate around somewhere.'

Now, was there something about the look on Renouf's face? Probably not, just his shyness coming through and his irritation at being contradicted by Fairview.

'She's coming on boldly enough,' said the master. 'Look at her!'

The sloop – for that was what she was in British terms, whatever the French called her – hadn't shortened to fighting sail and hadn't deviated from her course. It occurred to Holbrooke that the French captain may be unaware of *Kestrel's* presence, but then he discarded that idea. No King's ship – British or French – could possibly keep that bad a lookout in the Channel.

'Mister Lynton, Mister Fairview. I plan to place her on our starboard bow, then at the last moment cut across her hawse and give her a broadside with the larboard battery from right on her bows. He'll have to turn one way or the other, and in either case I'll manoeuvre to rake her. Double-shot both batteries, Mister Lynton, the range will be pistol-shot, I aim to finish this as quickly as possible.'

'Aye-aye sir,' replied Lynton. Fairview just nodded, his mind already working on the helm orders and sail trimming.

'But remember, gentlemen.' Holbrooke continued, 'there's never yet been a fight at sea that went according to design. The enemy has a plan too and one thing's for certain, it won't fit in with ours. So be ready for changes. In any event, Mister Lynton, keep those guns firing!'

***

Now the two sloops were only a mile apart. The Frenchman still had not manoeuvred, not even when *Kestrel* made a distinct alteration of course to larboard. It was as though the French captain disdained tactics and manoeuvre in favour of a single broadside and a swift boarding. Closer and closer, in just a minute they would be broadside-to-broadside but passing each other at a combined nine or ten knots.

'Helm a-weather, Mister Fairview,' Holbrooke shouted from his position at the leeward mizzen chains. He was leaning far out to catch the first hint of movement from his adversary.

Kestrel came off the wind and the Frenchman moved from the starboard bow right across to the larboard beam. Still he held his course. The larboard guns were being levered around as the Frenchman's bows drew rapidly left. A moving target it may have been, but it was a moving target at a mere thirty yards and that first double-shotted broadside hammered into her bows. Holbrooke could see the splinters flying from her beakhead, the parted lines and the holes in her foresail. As they hurtled past, he caught a glimpse of the gammoning for her bowsprit, a shot had grazed it and half a dozen turns had parted. That would be a limiting factor for her manoeuvering; her captain would have to reduce the pressure on the headsails to avoid losing all her forward spars, the foremast included.

'He's following us around, sir,' said Fairview.

Sure enough, the Frenchman was turning his ship to larboard, chasing *Kestrel's* stern away to the east. It was an unusual tactic, rather like a playground game of tag where the pursued kept close behind the pursuer, just out of arm's reach. It was almost like a stalling tactic, as though…

'Sail ho! Sail on the starboard beam, close to the coast. It's another man-o'-war, sir.'

So that was it, a trap and an elegant one at that. The sloop's role was to lock onto *Kestrel* and pin the British sloop in position until the frigate could join the battle. Holbrooke glanced again at Renouf. His face was blank, and he gripped the gunwale capping with ferocious intensity. It was as though he was carefully showing no emotion. Could he have set this up? In a general sort of way, it was possible, although he'd had no contact with the shore since he'd joined the squadron at Portsmouth. And yet, he'd suggested this as the most profitable place to hunt, and here they were with a sloop to windward and a sixth rate reaching up to cut off the escape to the south. Only the channel between the Écrevièr bank and the Cotentin Peninsula offered a means of escape, and that meant leaving his station. If this sou'westerly persisted it would be days before he rejoined the squadron. An elegant trap indeed.

'She must have been hiding against the coast over by Portbail,' said Fairview, glancing sideways at Renouf, who looked the other way.

'Veer ship, Mister Fairview, and lay me alongside him.'

Holbrooke eased his sword in its scabbard.

'Mister Lynton,' he shouted, 'stand by the starboard battery.'

The fore-stays'l came down in a flash and, relieved of the windage forward, *Kestrel* spun around to starboard, bringing her stern through the wind.

'Fire!' shouted Lynton.

This time the load of sixteen six-pound balls was too much for the Frenchman's bowsprit, and it broke clear and fell into the sea under the sloop's forefoot, dragging a crazy mass of stays and halyards with it. Her foremast and topmast survived, but they would never stand for a hard beat to windward.

'She's veering,' shouted Fairview.

Holbrooke could see the bows turning towards *Kestrel*. It was an act of desperation but one that may yet work. He guessed that the Frenchman was attempting to fix himself alongside *Kestrel* and he could see the boarders mustering on the sloop's bows. They were making no attempt to either clear the wreckage of the bowsprit, or to rig a new forestay. A few intrepid souls had scrambled out on the foreyard holding grapnels, ready to catch in *Kestrel's* spars and rigging.

It was a race between *Kestrel's* increasing speed after she'd veered and the Frenchman's remaining forward momentum now that he was hard on the wind with no headsails.

Bang! The swivel gun beside Holbrooke fired and he saw a gap torn in the French boarders. He'd been unaware of the marines pushing forward between the guns, but now their muskets were popping away as well.

'Fire!' shouted Lynton again and the starboard guns erupted. He'd had the foresight to load with grape. The splinters flew from the enemy gunwales, and more men went down.

The French larboard guns could at last bear and now it was *Kestrel's* turn to receive a punishing broadside. The four-pound balls did little damage to *Kestrel's* sides, but where they found the gunports they were lethal. Men were falling all over the deck now as the French swivels joined in.

'Repel boarders sir?' shouted Lynton, almost in his ear.

'Be damned if I will. Stand by to board her! Away Boarders!' Holbrooke shouted. 'We'll take her, lads, and carry her into Portsmouth!'

Lynton waved his sword, urgently gathering the men at the starboard gunwale. There were only a few yards between the two sloops now. Neither had rigged boarding nets, each planning to board the other and neither wanting any impediment.

'Where's the frigate?' Holbrooke asked looking around. He was shocked by what he saw. There was the second Frenchman, *Joli* was her name, if Renouf was to be believed, only three or four miles away and reaching up fast under all sail. Even her windward stuns'ls were set in her haste to join the battle.

'Helm to windward, Mister Fairview, we must leave the boarding for another day.'

'Ready the guns, Mister Lynton. Load with ball. We'll have to fight the frigate before we can finish the sloop.'

Kestrel paid off slowly, fast enough to stay out of reach of the sloop, but not out of reach of the taunts that were flung after them. It was a bitter blow to muster the boarding parties and then send them back to the guns, but that frigate would be upon them in ten minutes.

***

CHAPTER FOURTEEN

Treachery

Tuesday, Sixth of June 1758.
Kestrel, at Sea. Gorey Point, West 10 Nautical Miles.

With the wind on her starboard quarter, *Kestrel* tore down towards the enemy frigate. Over his shoulder, Holbrooke could see the sloop frantically attempting to follow, but with no headsails it was difficult to keep her bows off the wind. They were trying manfully, the mizzen mast was already bare, and the main tops'l was flying, but her speed was down to about two knots and her steering was erratic. The frigate, however, looked majestic. She was hard on the wind, rushing to get between *Kestrel* and her obvious escape route to the south.

'How well do you know these waters, Mister Fairview?' asked Holbrooke.

'Pretty well, sir, I can keep you off the rocks and shoals in any case.'

'Then please do so, Mister Fairview, please do so.'

Chalmers appeared on deck. At quarters he assisted Harris the surgeon in the gunroom on the deck below, but with the two casualties now calm, he'd come up to see the general situation. The pilot, evidently no longer trusted if not under outright suspicion, was lurking gloomily near the taffrail. Holbrooke stood in front of the binnacle, his legs apart and balanced against the pitch and roll of the sloop as it sped downwind towards the frigate. He'd noticed before how Holbrooke's whole personality changed when they went into action, or in any other kind of crisis. Gone was the youthful uncertainty, the self-deprecation and timidity. It had been replaced by towering confidence and an assumption of command that would have sat as naturally on far older shoulders. Holbrooke gave his orders with not the slightest fear that they wouldn't be obeyed.

'Mister Chalmers, we'll be in action again soon, this is no place to linger. Perhaps you could take Mister Renouf below into safety.'

Chalmers bowed and gestured towards Renouf who, with a shrug, followed him to the gunroom where the surgeon was preparing for the next influx of wounded. He'd only had to deal with two so far, both with serious splinter wounds but neither requiring amputation. Two more were dead before they arrived in the gunroom, and they'd been moved into the space that was usually the first lieutenant's cabin.

'Batteries ready,' reported Lynton. 'I've lost two men taken below but I've still plenty to serve the guns.'

'How's her bearing doing, Mister Fairview?' asked Holbrooke.

'Near as damn-it steady, sir. If he doesn't go about, we'll shave his stern close as a Piccadilly barber.'

Holbrooke nodded and stared hard at the frigate, now less than two miles on the larboard bow, but crossing fast from larboard to starboard in an effort to get to the south.

'Starboard battery, sir?' asked Lynton.

'I think not,' replied Holbrooke, 'I can't believe this gentleman is going to tamely let us rake his stern. Ah, there he goes!'

The frigate turned her bows to starboard and tacked neatly across the wind.

'Mister Fairview, I'll leave the detail to you, but I want that frigate to believe that we're determined to rake his bows. Steer as though you intend to cross his jib boom at half pistol-shot. Then watch for my command because when he's convinced, I'll want you to come to starboard and cross his stern, very, very close.'

'I'll need to veer now, in that case, sir.'

'Very well, master.'

Kestrel put her stern through the wind and steadied with the French frigate five points on her starboard bow, emphatically declaring her intention to cross the

Frenchman's bow.

'Mister Lynton,' he shouted. 'Engage with the starboard battery as soon as your shot will carry, but I'll need a full broadside from the larboard battery when we cross his stern. You may double shot the larboard guns.'

Closer and closer. The frigate looked vast compared with the diminutive *Kestrel*. The officers on her quarterdeck towered above Holbrooke, having no real quarterdeck of his own – in the sense of a separate deck higher than the main deck – and with a low freeboard in any case. Five cables to go…

Bang! The number one gun fired, followed by the whole starboard battery in ragged order as the gun captains fancied their shot would carry.

The side of the frigate erupted in flame and smoke. She'd fired a broadside – all her larboard guns simultaneously – and *Kestrel* reeled as chain shot screeched overhead to tear through the sails and rigging. Holbrooke turned to find Jackson, but the bosun was already directing the repairs with the few men that could be spared from the guns.

Now here was something Holbrooke hadn't reckoned with. A solid bank of smoke lay between the two ships and the sou'westerly wind was pushing it back over the frigate. For a few vital seconds the French captain was blind.

'Now Master! Down with your helm.'

Kestrel turned five points to starboard; they were on a course to clip the frigate's stern. The smoke must be making *Kestrel* very difficult to see from the Frenchman's quarterdeck, and a five-point turn without either tacking of veering would be hard to detect.

'Larboard battery ready!' shouted Lynton. 'Double-shotted.'

'Fire by divisions as we cross her stern, Mister Lynton. Make every shot count!'

Bang, bang! Holbrooke was concentrating on the manoeuvre, so once again he was taken by surprise when numbers two and four guns fired. The frigate's high stern reached far above *Kestrel's* deck and even the upper deck was above the level of the sloop's guns. Nevertheless, the double loads of ball smashed through the stern, wrecking the transom while the swivels at full elevation made short work of the cabin windows and the gingerbread on the taffrail. It was a blow, but hardly a knockout. This was the hard lesson of taking on an adversary of a class above oneself – the frigate was bigger, stronger-built and a had a greater number of heavier guns. She had a harder punch and could endure more punishment. It would take luck or skill of a very advanced sort for *Kestrel* to win. Yet Holbrooke was in no mood to concede.

'Veer ship and put me alongside her Mister Fairview.'

'Aye-aye sir,' replied the master.

The gun crews were hauling in the larboard guns and feverishly reloading. Holbrooke could see the frigate's starboard eight-pounders; ten of the great ugly brutes, their muzzles thrust through the gun-ports. They looked big and powerful compared with *Kestrel's* six-pounders. He could hear Fairview giving the orders that would turn *Kestrel* to the nor'west, abreast of the frigate. Then it would be a bare-knuckle slogging match; the frigate having the longer reach, the strongest punch and the broadest chest. The fighting madness left Holbrooke in a flash, suddenly he was rational again and he knew this battle against two opponents could only end one way. It was the disappointment over being sent away from the landings and the probable – no certain – treachery of the pilot that had led him to this crisis.

'Where's the sloop?' he shouted to the quarterdeck.

'To windward and heading south,' replied Edney, keeping his head as always.

Then this was a well-planned trap. The frigate and the sloop had ensured that one of them would always block the escape back to Cancale Bay and the safety of the squadron, leaving the other free to deal with *Kestrel*.

'Belay the veering,' Holbrooke said, clapping the master on the shoulder to prevent the irrevocable helm order.

'Hold your course. Your piloting skills are about to become vital, Mister Fairview.'

The master looked in astonishment at his captain, then he saw the massive frigate over his shoulder and the sloop far astern, cutting off their retreat, and he nodded in understanding.

There was one thing to be said for this retreat; it put the frigate captain off his stride. His starboard broadside had been holding its fire until the little sloop ranged up alongside, but now its prey was running fast for the coast of the Cotentin Peninsula and every second was increasing the range. Holbrooke counted to himself. If the Frenchman didn't fire in thirty seconds, he'd have missed the best opportunity to disable *Kestrel*. Thirty seconds passed, and then another ten.

The frigate fired a ragged broadside. Her gun captains had expected to fire at maximum depression, but now had to knock out quoins for the greater range and shift the heavy guns around to bear on the quarter. It all took time and the precious seconds had flown away as fast as *Kestrel* sped east with the wind on her quarter. Nevertheless, the sloop took three hits. One of them harmlessly smashed into the larboard quarter; work for the carpenter or the yard but nothing to stop *Kestrel's* flight. The second was unlucky for the sloop. It hit on the transom as the stern rose to the swell, creating a foot-wide hole below the waterline. The third ball caused the most harm: it shattered the new wheel, bringing down the old quartermaster and one of the steersmen.

That should have been the end for *Kestrel*. Any other ship would have been unmanageable for vital minutes until the rudder tackles were manned. Even if the frigate hadn't come up to them in those few minutes, the sloop would have been slow to respond to helm orders and would have been a certain catch within the hour.

However, *Kestrel* was different. Her tiller was still on the upper deck, covered by nothing more than a grating that the carpenter – no lover of modern innovations – had covertly made removable by the simple substitution of battens and wedges for the yard's joints and nails. He was on the job in a flash, knocking out the wedges, throwing the battens over the side and lifting the grating to reveal the tiller. Two of the number fifteen gun's crew recognised the situation and grabbed the stout bar. It was awkward because instead of being three feet off the deck as it was before the wheel was fitted, the tiller now swung at ankle height. It was difficult to hold the tiller and still get a good grip on the deck.

'She steers, sir,' said Fairview as he saw the tiller moving from larboard to starboard and felt the sloop respond.

'Then shape a course to round La Hague, Mister Fairview, and set all sail. We need to keep out of range of that frigate until we're around the cape. I don't believe he'll follow us out into the Channel.'

Now it was sheer seamanship and navigation that would save them. Cape La Hague was thirty nautical miles away, perhaps four hours in this wind.

'Mister Lynton. Reload the guns, quick as you can, then you may give the bosun all the hands he needs.'

Within minutes the courses were drawing and the stuns'ls started to appear, along with the full suite of stays'ls and the infrequently seen spritsail. *Kestrel* was wounded, but not critically, and she could still show a bold spread of canvas. Forward of the mainmast, the pumps were already manned, the familiar sound drifting aft to the quarterdeck. The carpenter was hanging over the taffrail, looking at the hole below the waterline as the stern rhythmically rose and fell.

'I'll leave one of my mates to tidy up this mess, sir,' he said levering himself back inboard. 'That hole's my first concern now.'

The French captain was slow to react; a retreat was the last thing that he expected after *Kestrel's* bold approach. By the time the frigate fetched *Kestrel's* wake, it was a three-mile stern chase and not a gun could be brought to bear.

***

'Man Overboard!' shouted Edney, who happened to be the only one looking astern, 'It was Mister Renouf, sir, I saw him jump.'

'Mister Treganoc, a shot at that man, if you please,' said Holbrooke, 'quickly now.'

Treganoc took a musket from the marine standing beside the aftermost gun, checked the priming and strode aft to the taffrail. He'd seen the way that the trust between Holbrooke, Fairview and the pilot had deteriorated, and he'd come to the same conclusion as his captain. There had been treachery on the pilot's mind from the first time he came aboard. Renouf had taken this opportunity to jump overboard, carrying the lifebuoy with him, at the point where the French frigate was at its closest.

Bang! Treganoc's musket fired.

'Damn it! Missed,' he said.

The sergeant had brought a file of marines aft and they now lined the taffrail and fired a volley. Still the figure of Renouf could be seen clutching the lifebuoy and receding further and further behind.

'I beg your pardon, sir,' said Treganoc in a disgusted tone, 'the traitor still lives.'

'It was a difficult shot,' Holbrooke replied. He was watching Renouf through his telescope. The frigate was up with him in less than ten minutes. Now it would surely heave to and send a boat or throw a rope, but it neither slowed nor altered course. He saw a movement from the man in the water, Renouf's despairing wave as his would-be rescuers ignored his plight.

'Unfortunately, sir, he has a reasonable chance of survival. The tide will wash him up on the coast of France, or Jersey, in a day or so,' Fairview commented dispassionately, 'as long as he holds onto that lifebuoy.'

'Let's hope it's Jersey and I can send a letter before he can escape again.'

Fairview grimaced. There was so much illicit trade between the Channel Isles and France that Renouf need spend no more than a day waiting for a boat and a sympathetic skipper.

If he made it ashore…

They chased north through the midday sun and into the afternoon watch. To start with, the frigate gained on *Kestrel* and at one point was little more than a mile astern. However, as Jackson got the loose halyards and sheets in hand and replaced the damaged mizzen tops'l, the sloop's speed gradually increased. Soon she was running mile-for-mile with the frigate. The French sloop was nowhere to be seen, lost in the haze to the south. At six bells in the afternoon watch, with Cape La Hague abaft the beam to the sou'west, the frigate hauled her wind and with a parting gun in salute, started her long beat back to the south. The French captain had problems of his own. With his home port unlikely to be available for some time, the British Channel Fleet to windward and both of his ships requiring repair, he'd have to find a commercial harbour to refit.

***

'You know that I don't usually hold with councils of war,' said Holbrooke as he addressed his officers in his cabin. 'Nevertheless, I need your professional opinions and I must, I regret, record them,' he said motioning towards his clerk who sat at the desk holding his pen expectantly.

Holbrooke shifted uncomfortably in his chair. *Kestrel* was lying-to ten miles nor'east of Cape La Hague, gently pitching and rolling in the sou'westerly breeze. The forlorn sound of the chain-pump drifted back into the cabin, a reminder of one of the critical factors that he must consider.

'Commodore Howe is expecting *Kestrel* to return within four days of our departure, that would be Friday. We can still achieve that even with this wind, isn't that so, Master?'

'It is, sir,' Fairview replied. 'We'll have to make a bold beat nor'west into the channel and we won't round the cape again until tomorrow, but we can certainly be in Cancale Bay by Friday; sooner if the wind backs.'

The cabin was silent except for the scratch-scratch of

Pritchard's pen.

'Very well, Mister Fairview, so in navigational terms, it's still within my power to fulfil my orders.'

He turned to the bosun.

'Mister Jackson, what's the state of our sails and rigging?'

'I'd be happier with a new mizzen tops'l sir, instead of that old one I've had to bend on. It won't stand a blow. Otherwise we're all patched and spliced, sir…'

Jackson's expression was transparent, he desperately wanted to know what his captain wished him to say. He'd swear blind that he had not a stitch of canvas to hang on a yard if it helped, but Holbrooke was giving nothing away.

Pritchard wrote rapidly, catching the testimony of these ship's standing officers.

'Doctor?' asked Holbrooke.

'Two dead, as you know sir, and we'll have to bury them this evening or tomorrow at the latest, what with this heat. I've five men in the sickbay. One arm amputated above the elbow and four with deep lacerations. I have hopes for all of them and they'll do as well under my care as they will in Haslar,' he replied a little too emphatically.

Chalmers considered Harris. He knew that there was a degree of bravado in his answer. Haslar was probably the finest hospital in Britain. It was undoubtedly the largest, and surely his injured patients would have a better chance of survival inside that specialised institution? He glanced at Holbrooke and saw intuitively that he had the same opinion.

'Chips, what's the damage,' Holbrooke asked.

The carpenter pulled at his beard and thought for long seconds. He must have known that he would be asked this question, but apparently was only now considering how to answer it.

'The starboard gunwale's all knocked about, but my crew's working on that now, sir; it's nothing to worry about. The shot in the transom is awkward to come to, but it's well above the waterline.'

He paused, stroking his beard again.

'The wheel's a problem. I can't fashion a new one and I can't raise the tiller off the deck, not without a new rudder-head and that's a job for a yard. That ankle-breaker of a tiller is all very well in these winds, but it'll be unmanageable in a blow. I'm not happy to be at sea with it in that state.'

Scratch, scratch, scratch. Pritchard's pen and the clanking of the pump provided a doom-laden accompaniment.

'And the shot below the waterline?' asked Holbrooke, prodding the carpenter to continue.

'Ah, now that's the worst of it, sir. It's come in at a difficult place, where the lowest fashion piece meets the stern post. As you know, perhaps, they're held together by treenails from outboard. All I can do is push in a plug, and that's not really holding as the ship works. We'll be pumping every watch until we reach a yard. And the transom knees have been strained too.'

Silence again as Pritchard caught up. Holbrooke was determined that this council should be properly recorded.

'Mister Lynton, do you have anything to add?'

'Well, having heard the carpenter, it seems to me that we tempt fate by staying at sea, sir.'

'Thank you, Mister Lynton. I asked your opinion regarding the state of the sloop. Once I know that I'll decide on our next course of action alone.'

'I beg your pardon, sir. I spoke out of turn...' Lynton mumbled in reply, embarrassed to be checked – however mildly – by his captain. 'I'm lacking ten of our complement, sir, we sailed three short and we've lost seven, as you've heard...' He stumbled to a close.

Holbrooke ignored his first lieutenant's embarrassment.

'You've recorded everything, Pritchard?'

'Yes, sir,' the clerk replied. 'I'll just ask for these gentlemen's signatures before they leave.'

'Very well, then you may all return to your duties. Mister Chalmers, will you stay a moment?'

***

'If it's spiritual guidance you require, then I'm your man, George. But I can add nothing to the testimony of your officers, except possibly to note that the surgeon may be somewhat optimistic about the chances of recovery for those wounded men. I suggest that they'd do better at Haslar.'

'I agree, and certainly that's a consideration,' Holbrooke answered. 'And yet I still need your guidance, David.'

Serviteur brought sherry and departed to the scullery as silently as he'd come. He would hear what the captain and the chaplain said, but there were few secrets now that Serviteur had been on board for the past eight months.

'Rationally, I should cut and run for Portsmouth and let the yard have a look at the sloop. If I return to Cancale, I'll be more a hindrance than a help to the commodore.'

Chalmers said nothing, he just watched his friend.

'And yet, my motives could be misconstrued. I ran from a French frigate. I had such a fright that I didn't care to stay at sea any longer, it could be said.'

'Men will say whatever they wish to say. You've all the documentary evidence you need, and you didn't fall into the trap of taking advice, just gathered the facts from those best placed to offer them. The facts say go back to Portsmouth.'

'Even so…'

'George, this is one of those moments when only your opinion counts. I can't help. This is where you earn your princely pay. The last point I would make – and I say this from a desire to ease my fellow man's suffering – is that of the five wounded, in my opinion, two will be dead by the end of the week if they're not put ashore to a hospital…'

***

CHAPTER FIFTEEN

Penny for Your Thoughts

Wednesday, Seventh of June 1758.
Kestrel, alongside. Portsmouth.

The westerly wind carried *Kestrel* past the Round Tower and past Portsmouth Point, stemming the two knots of ebbing tide at the harbour entrance. Now the sloop was creeping towards the pontoon to the south of the wet basin. The sound of her pumps carried clearly to the men on the shore.

'Back the main tops'l,' shouted Fairview, 'brail the mizzen.'

The sloop's forward momentum was checked and converted into an irresistible sideways pressure from the wind on her beam.

'Move that fender for'rard,' called Jackson to the party of men detailed to preserve *Kestrel's* paint and woodwork. 'Drop it half a fathom, I want it just skimming the water.'

Yard by careful yard *Kestrel* moved towards the pontoon. The same master attendant was waiting for them and the same riggers, no longer standing back and watching but ready to take the sloop's warps.

'There's a gust coming, Mister Fairview,' Holbrooke warned as he saw a lugger over on the Gosport side heeling to the unexpected draught of wind.

'Aye sir, and it's coming a little more northerly,' he replied.

'Let fly the jib sheet,' Fairview called to the fo'c'sle party. 'That should be sufficient, I believe,' he said to Holbrooke.

The sloop was in competent hands, the easing of the sail area right forward would stop the bows being pushed hard onto the pontoon by the wayward gust.

Jackson flung the heaving line and the riggers were soon hauling the bow warp across. The aft warp could wait, a combination of the wind and the ebbing tide would naturally swing her stern into place.

The eye of the warp was safely dropped over the bollard and the rigger stood back, giving a thumbs-up to Jackson.

'Give it some slack… more, more. Avast, hold it there.' Jackson watched the bows carefully. If the forward warp was hauled in too far it would prevent the stern swinging into place.

The familiar crunching sound of the rattan fender being compressed between the sloop and the pontoon announced that they had arrived safely alongside. All that remained was to double up on the head and stern warps and rig springs.

'Well, here we are again,' said the master attendant. 'The first thing I heard this morning was that you'd sent in a boat requesting to come straight into the harbour; no dallying at Spithead for the good men of *Kestrel!* I came directly here, now what can we do for you, sir?'

Holbrooke left the carpenter to relate his tale of woe. There was no rush. They wouldn't be able to get into the basin until late in the afternoon, when the tide had risen, and meanwhile the preservation of the sloop was still in Holbrooke's hands. The hands would be pumping through the day, although the flow would slacken now that they were alongside, and the timbers weren't working with the sea. It had been an anxious night as the quartering wind increased. In the middle watch it was a strong tops'l breeze and Holbrooke wondered whether they could pump as fast as the water was coming in through the hole in her stern.

***

'What do you think, sir, two months again?'

Lynton was evidently looking forward to some more shore leave; the frustrations of their time with Howe's squadron had affected even him.

Holbrooke looked across at the master attendant as he disappeared below with Chips.

'They're short of work, with the Channel Fleet at sea and Howe's squadron away. Whether that means they'll throw all their shipwrights at the problem and get us back to sea quickly, or whether they'll take their time to spin out the employment, only the master attendant knows.'

Holbrooke broke off to wish the injured men well as they left to be taken across the harbour in Haslar's own lighter. Two of the lacerations could walk with assistance, but the other two and the amputee were being tenderly carried by their messmates on the stretchers that belonged to the lighter.

'I'll be back before you sail, sir,' croaked one them, with his chest swathed in an elaborate bandage. 'I'll heal quicker than that wheel in any case,' he said jerking his finger towards the strangely bare quarterdeck.

That seemed to exhaust the man's energy and his head fell back onto the canvas.

'Just rest easy now, Matthew Ogden,' his messmate said, gently shifting a bundled shirt to stop his head rolling. 'Just rest easy...'

Holbrooke shook his head as he watched them being carefully lowered onto the pontoon. What were their chances? The odds for the amputee were perhaps three-in-four for survival while the others had a somewhat better prognosis. An even chance that at least one of them would die, then. Better than the near certainty of losing two of them if they'd stayed at sea.

'Ah, here they come now,' Lynton said as Chips dragged himself aft muttering under his breath. The master attendant looked cheerful by comparison.

'Oh, it's a big job, no doubt about it, sir. We'll have to replace the knees and three of the larboard fashion-pieces; a big job for sure. Luckily, I have a dry-dock just waiting for you and plenty of men. I'll just get my tickets from the commissioner's office this morning. Sir Richard is away in London, so it'll go through quickly and we'll have you in the dock at the top of the tide. We'll be cutting wood tomorrow forenoon.'

Captain Sir Richard Hughes was the resident

commissioner, the senior Navy Board official in Portsmouth. His son of the same name had been the first to alert the Admiralty to the possibility of an Austrian garrison at Emden, when he commanded the frigate *Hind*. That information had profoundly influenced Holbrooke's actions at Emden earlier in the year. Evidently Sir Richard was free with delegating authority in his absence.

'And the wheel, master attendant, and the binnacle?'

'Oh, I've a few wheels in my store and we can make the plinth in no time; same for the binnacle. You'll have to write a letter for the compasses of course and I can't speak for how long that'll take; it depends on our affectionate friends.'

Yes, Holbrooke thought, it was the little things that caused the problems. The Navy Board, who bizarrely signed all their letters as *Your Affectionate Friends*, would have to authorise the issue of two new compasses, and that assumed there were compasses to be had. He tapped his pocket in reflex. He'd already decided that he wouldn't wait for the navy board to issue the compasses if there was a danger that he'd be delayed. Not when there was an instrument vendor behind the Hard, and Holbrooke's credit was good. He'd walk over there as soon as this business was concluded. After all, what was the point of prize money if he couldn't use it to further his career?

'You'll be wanting to know how long you'll be without a ship, Captain Holbrooke.'

'An estimate would be helpful, if you please.'

'Well, we've to dock her down, shift the stores from the after end, cut out the old fashion-pieces…' he counted off the tasks on his fingers; Holbrooke was prepared for the worst '… and then give her a splash of paint and flood the dock. Let's say seven weeks, if we can get a good run at it before Mister Anson and Mister Howe come back with a list of jobs reaching from here to Plymouth Dock.'

He was a jolly soul, this master attendant, but it was quite clear that his primary concern was to maintain a steady flow of work for the yard. The navy's ships were just a means to an end for him.

'I imagine you'll be looking for the port admiral, sir. Mister Holburne is using Sir Richard's office, so if you'll walk with me, we can kill two birds with one stone, ha, ha!'

***

Admiral Holburne carried the responsibility of a commander-in-chief and the powers that went with it. It was he who ensured that ships sailed on time and in sufficient numbers upon the occasions that their lordships demanded. He'd seen enough young captains who preferred to loiter in port, and he chose not to take the story of *Kestrel's* damage at face value. Holbrooke spent a worrying ten minutes in the outer office while the master attendant was called to describe the work that was required and its probable duration. By the time that Holburne had finished with him, the schedule was pared down to five weeks, and *damn your eyes, sir, if it's a day longer!*

Holbrooke's interview was equally difficult. He was quizzed on the circumstances of his departure from the squadron – *be so kind as to produce Commodore Howe's written orders, Mister Holbrooke* – and on the detail of the fight with the frigate and sloop. In the end, Holburne grudgingly conceded that perhaps Holbrooke had acted appropriately, while stopping short of an actual endorsement of his decision to return to Portsmouth.

'You're to report to this office every Monday, Wednesday and Friday forenoon with a statement of the whereabouts of your people and the progress of the repairs to your sloop. There's to be no straggling, and no trips to London for you or your officers, do I make myself clear?'

'Aye-aye sir,'

'I'll expect your first report the day after tomorrow, Mister Holbrooke. Now, I have much to do, so good day to you.'

Holbrooke felt as though he should have stood on his dignity and protested the admiral's use of the word *straggling* in the same sentence as he limited his own movements.

There was an implication that Holbrooke was planning a dereliction of duty that one may expect of a late returning libertyman. He felt sure that most captains would certainly object... or would they? Holburne was a fearsome man. He'd used an armed press gang to break up a meeting in his native Inverkeithing and – if the reports were correct – had drawn his sword as an argument for securing the office of Provost. No, probably most captains would have behaved much as he did, he decided. Some battles were better not fought.

***

Despite the daily running of the gauntlet when he delivered his report to Admiral Holburne's office, they were probably the most pleasant five weeks of Holbrooke's life so far. He had the Saturdays and Sundays free at a time when the concept of a *weekend* was unknown, and the remainder of the week to spend on his beloved *Kestrel*. The distinguished firm of Hawkins and Hammond of Bond Street, who acted as prize agents for both Carlisle and Holbrooke, had made the first distribution of prize money from the capture of the French frigate *Vulcain* in the Mediterranean two years ago. Now, at last, he had money to spend that hadn't been borrowed from the agents, nor did he have to negotiate a line of credit each time he made a purchase. It was a welcome reminder that there were prizes taken in the Caribbean and the North Sea that would provide a steady flow of cash for years to come. If he was careful, he could survive as a gentleman, in a modest way, even if he were to be cast onto the beach tomorrow and never given another ship.

He and Chalmers took their rooms again at the Dolphin and on Fridays they shared a carriage to Wickham. They spent the night at the Holbrooke cottage and on Saturdays Chalmers and the senior Holbrooke persecuted the brown trout of the Meon. The junior Holbrooke, however, pursued other endeavours and promptly at eleven o'clock every Saturday he lifted the brass lion-head door knocker of

Bere Forest House. He was expected. His courtship of Ann had become a settled state of affairs, and everyone appeared content with the arrangement. True, Ann's father quizzed him frequently, yet discreetly, on his prospects of becoming a post-captain; a genuine captain as far as the conservative understanding of a provincial corn merchant extended. They walked together through the Saturday market, they strolled along the banks of the Meon and they visited Ann's friends. On Sundays they each crossed the river and climbed the little grass mound to the church of Saint Nicholas where the Holbrookes and Chalmers met the Featherstones at worship. Those were idyllic days, a dreamlike time of growing understanding between Holbrooke and Ann.

**

It was Sunday evening and their carriage was jangling along the Fareham road, heading back to Portsmouth. Chalmers cradled a canvas bag with its dozen half-pound trout wrapped in the fresh green grass and wild garlic that he'd cut from the riverbank. They were destined for the tender ministrations of the Dolphin's cook and packed as they were, they should last until Wednesday or Thursday. Fried trout for breakfast for at least the next three days, the thought made him salivate.

Holbrooke was unusually thoughtful. He usually was bouncing with good humour after a couple of days in Wickham, but now he appeared... not depressed, nor disturbed, but quietly contemplative.

'A penny for your thoughts,' said Chalmers, a phrase from his childhood springing unbidden to his lips.

'Oh, nothing,' replied Holbrooke, 'I'm just a little weary.'

Chalmers made no response. He'd told his friend many times what a poor liar he was. In many ways he was as transparent as a pane of glass, and it was quite certain what occupied his mind at this moment. The coach rattled on along the flint-covered road with its occupants engrossed in their own thoughts. Ten minutes passed and the carriage swung left over the Wallington Brook and past the tidal mills at the head of Fareham Creek. The road was smoother now, a main thoroughfare that was kept clear of the worst of the potholes and boulders.

'Actually,' said Holbrooke, startling his friend who really was weary and had almost fallen asleep the moment the motion of the carriage eased, 'I was thinking of Ann.'

Chalmers thought for a second or two, trying to remember what had caused Holbrooke to speak so, then he remembered his question of fifteen minutes ago, *a penny for your thoughts.*

'Then if you were thinking of Ann, my friend, it's probably best for both of us if you keep your thoughts to yourself. I'll keep my penny if you don't mind.'

Holbrooke smiled; his face relaxed from the rigidity of hard thought.

'You can't escape from your offer so easily, my dear friend,' he replied laughing. 'I was thinking about Ann, but more specifically about whether I should ask your advice.'

'And your conclusion?' asked Chalmers.

'My conclusion is that I should. Ask your advice, that is.'

'Then it appears that I have no hope of escape. I'm trapped in this carriage with a madman for another hour at least, for only a madman would ask another's advice in affairs of the heart. It appears I must submit.'

'You must, it appears.'

Holbrooke paused, marshalling his thoughts.

'*Kestrel* will be ready to sail again in a week and a half, so next Saturday will be our last at Wickham for some time. Perhaps only for a week or two, but possibly longer.'

'That's a well-known difficulty of naval life, I understand,' replied Chalmers.

Holbrooke half-bowed in sarcastic acknowledgement.

'I'm sure you've noticed that Ann and I are becoming quite... *attached* to each other.'

'It would have been hard to miss it, my friend.'

'Well, I'm considering whether I should ask Martin Featherstone for his daughter's hand.'

Silence.

'Does that surprise you, David?'

'Not in the least. So far you have told me nothing that any reasonable person couldn't have guessed. I'm sure it's not for a statement of the obvious that you woke me from a fast-approaching nap. If you wish to propose marriage to Ann – and by the way, I believe that you'll make a fine couple – then you hardly need my advice. I wish you the very best in your future together. Now I believe I'll take that caulk.'

'If only it were so simple,' said Holbrooke, ignoring his friend's desire for sleep. He stared out of the window as the horses cantered past Portchester Castle. 'It's not Ann that's the problem, I believe she will agree to marry me. If not, then she's a very good actress. Nor is her stepmother any kind of hindrance, she appears to have a real regard for me.'

Chalmers nodded; he knew where this was going.

'It's her father who I feel may be a problem. He's always been probing about my prospects for being posted and I understand that he's been speaking to a long-superannuated sea officer from up Soberton way.'

'A famous haunt for washed-up sea officers, I understand,' said Chalmers.

'Naturally we haven't been specific in our conversation. Neither of us has candidly admitted what's on our mind, but I'm becoming certain that Featherstone is unhappy with his daughter marrying anyone below the rank of post-captain. He often hints that he has great ambitions for his only child, that she's his only heir and that his fortune is not inconsiderable.'

'I understand that huge great house belongs to him, it's not rented, and it's not entailed or mortgaged,' added Chalmers.

'Oh, I hadn't heard anything of the sort,' said Holbrooke.

No, you wouldn't, Chalmers thought. Even the inhabitants of Wickham have a rustic sort of sensibility in such affairs.

'Well, I take it from the general thrust of his conversation that he wouldn't welcome an offer from me until I'm posted. You know my view on the likelihood of that happening. I'd give myself no more than an even chance of being gazetted before this war ends, and then, God help me, all I can do is hope for another.'

Now is the time to cease the facetiousness that I'm becoming prone to, Chalmers resolved silently.

'I see your problem, George, but I also believe you know the answer. A proposal of marriage – unless you're a habitual proposer, which I know you're not – is something that you should only attempt if you're sure that it will be welcomed, by both the lady and her family. You'll probably only get one cast at this, so you would be best advised to wait until you're certain of your trout rising. You're both still young after all, there's plenty of time.'

Did I really compare Ann Featherstone to a rising trout? Good God, David, get a grip of yourself, Chalmers said to himself. But Holbrooke appeared not to have noticed.

'On the other hand, a bold move may win all,' Holbrooke mused. 'I may be misjudging Martin Featherstone. Perhaps he's just making idle conversation, trying to show me that he's taking an interest in the navy.'

Chalmers looked hard at his friend.

'I think you know that's not so. Mister Featherstone's not stupid, for all his air of detachment from domestic affairs.'

'You're right of course,' said Holbrooke in a tone of finality. 'I must wait until I'm posted. I can be patient, to a point, but it's the inaction that'll kill me. I'll while away the time thinking of that damned interfering superannuated sea officer in Soberton. If ever I get my hands on him, I'll wring his mischievous neck!'

***

It was fortunate for Holbrooke's peace of mind that the road from Fareham to Portsmouth followed the coast at the foot of the chalk escarpment known as Portsdown Hill. If the carriage had come over the top, he couldn't have failed to notice that the anchorage at Spithead was unusually crowded. While he'd been dallying in Wickham, Howe's squadron and the fleet of transports and storeships had returned!

***

CHAPTER SIXTEEN

Called to Account

Monday, Third of July 1758.
Essex, at Anchor. Spithead.

Holbrooke paced the flagship's deck uncomfortably. He'd been there for two hours, since four bells in the morning watch. The flagship's decks had hardly been holystoned before he's started his march of doom. His own boat's crew had rowed him out from the Sally Port. They'd been hastily rounded up by Jackson from their homes and lodgings around Portsmouth, and now they lay off the flagship, waiting. Holbrooke was stemming the tide, waiting to be called in to see the commodore. Nobody had spoken to him, and he had the feeling that Howe was deliberately keeping him waiting, to soften him up for the interview. At least that was how Holbrooke's guilty imagination anticipated the meeting. He'd damaged his ship, he'd failed to meet his rendezvous and now, when the squadron returned to Portsmouth, he'd been unable to be found. It didn't sound good.

His train of thought was interrupted by the doors to the commodore's cabin being thrown open. A string of clerks and staff officers thundered out, followed by the commodore himself, startling the marine sentry whose salute was a second too late; he saluted nothing more than the great man's receding back. Howe cast a rapid glance around the quarterdeck before descending to the entry port. He saw Holbrooke and inclined his head, his face grim and unfriendly. Then, to the howl of the pipes, he was gone, his boat's crew setting the lugsail to take him tearing down towards the harbour entrance.

Holbrooke gulped and tried to look unconcerned, but he knew he was making a poor attempt. He jumped when he heard Captain Campbell's voice behind him.

'Follow me if you please, Captain Holbrooke,'

It all sounded very formal; unlike the last time he'd met the flag captain.

***

'We missed you at Cancale Bay,' Campbell stated without any preamble. 'You were expected back by the ninth of June, if I correctly remember your orders.'

Campbell left the statement hanging. He hadn't invited Holbrooke to respond, he'd merely laid out the indictment.

'You've heard nothing of what occurred then, sir.' Holbrooke replied. 'I sent a report on the seventh.'

It was a poor attempt at regaining the moral ascendency, but it was the best that Holbrooke could manage. He didn't dare take too high an attitude.

'We've heard no news, except a rumour from a bumboat that *Kestrel's* in dock. You should be aware that the commodore's annoyed. He's delaying any action until he's heard your story. Now's your chance, Mister Holbrooke.'

Holbrooke opened the canvas satchel and extracted a copy of the report that he'd sent to Howe as soon as *Kestrel* had arrived at Portsmouth, and copies of the thrice-weekly reports to Admiral Holburne. This was his ammunition.

'The day after we left Cancale Bay we fell in with that French frigate and sloop, just inside the Écrevièr Bank. We damaged them both, but the frigate shot away our wheel and put a hole in our stern below the waterline, where we couldn't come at it. I have the carpenter's report here.'

'How much water were you taking?'

'Three feet an hour after the best plug that the carpenter could manage. We pumped continuously until we arrived at Portsmouth the next day.'

Campbell had served with Anson when he sailed around the world. He knew all about leaking ships, and probably three feet an hour didn't seem too disastrous to him.

'And where were the French ships when you broke off the engagement?'

'To the south of us, blocking our passage back to the

squadron.'

Campbell sat in silence for a moment.

'There's something else you should know, sir,' Holbrooke continued. 'It was a trap. That Guernsey pilot, Renouf, led us into that place and the two Frenchmen sprung the trap.'

Campbell's eyebrows went up.

'Renouf jumped overboard when he knew that the French were unlikely to catch us. He'd hoped to be picked up by the frigate, but it sailed straight past him.'

'Serves him right,' Campbell replied, smiling for the first time. 'Now where were you when we anchored yesterday afternoon?'

That was the most dangerous question. Holburne had forbidden him to go to London, the usual magnet for young sea officers, but he'd said nothing about Wickham, only ten miles away and just two hours at most by carriage.

'I was visiting my father in Wickham, sir. Admiral Holburne gave me leave to travel that far.'

Holbrooke gambled that Holburne wouldn't be questioned on the matter, and if he was there was enough elasticity in his verbal orders to justify Holbrooke's trip.

'And this is all in these documents?'

'It is sir. I expect *Kestrel* to be ready for sea on the tenth of July and I hope to rejoin that squadron on that date.'

'It's regrettable that your report didn't reach us in Cancale Bay,' Campbell mused. 'It sounds like you acted correctly, but I have to tell you that the commodore is very annoyed. He'd planned to give you command of a division of flatboats for the re-embarkation. You'd have been the only commander, you know, the rest of us are all post-captains. An opportunity missed, I'm afraid.'

Holbrooke felt sick. That was just the kind of chance he'd been hoping for. He'd have been compared directly with senior post-captains and it would have looked very well on the commodore's report.

'Still, I expect there's to be another landing soon and

perhaps – I cannot guarantee it – but perhaps you'll have another chance. The army will be camped on the Isle of Wight for the time being, but the commodore's on his way to London to meet Mister Pitt. You heard about Saint-Malo?'

'No sir, I've heard nothing at all.'

'You saw the duke and his army land, and that was a very creditable affair.'

'The flatboats performed well?' asked Holbrooke.

'Yes, very well indeed. The soldiers are bursting with enthusiasm for them. They landed the army in a time that couldn't have been contemplated before, and the same for the re-embarkation. Unfortunately, the rest of the affair was not quite so successful. The army marched unopposed to Saint-Servan across the lagoon from Saint-Malo. However, they decided that the town was too strong to take by assault, that it required a regular siege, and that they couldn't achieve it before a French army appeared. They satisfied themselves with burning all the ships that lay under the walls: three of the line that were being repaired, twenty-four privateers and sixty merchantmen of all shapes and sizes.'

Holbrooke nodded. It was a significant achievement, but it hardly justified the employment of such a large squadron and army.

'They marched back to Cancale Bay and we took them back on board without any trouble. It appears that the duke doesn't care to be involved anymore and he left for London yesterday. His staff say that he'll press for a command in Germany, where there may be some real soldiering to do. Lord alone knows who'll command the land forces if we have another go.'

***

'Then what appears to have started badly ended well, in fact,' said Chalmers, as they walked out through the gate in the city walls beneath the Dock Bastion.

'Yes, although I daren't visit Wickham. It appears that Howe will be ready to sail before the end of the month and however' much he is assured that I acted correctly, he'll be justifiably angry if I leave Portsmouth again. The only good to come out of this is that it's stopped me agonising over whether to propose to Ann. I cannot now, unless I do so by letter, and that would hardly be correct.'

'Certainly not,' replied Chalmers, privately relieved that his friend couldn't commit himself so rashly. It wasn't that Chalmers disapproved of the match, in fact he very much approved of it, but he thought there was a strong probability of Martin Featherstone withholding his agreement until Holbrooke was posted. In fact, he could sympathise with Featherstone, who wanted only the best future for his only child.

They crossed the swing-bridge over the Mill Pond, skirted the Gunwharf and struck out towards the Hard and the main dockyard gate.

'I shall write to Ann, of course' Holbrooke continued. 'We made no arrangements, but she'll be expecting me to call again on Saturday, and that I certainly cannot do. Then *Kestrel* will be ready next week, and we'll be sent away again.'

Chalmers cast a sideways glance at his friend. His voice wasn't as firm as it usually was, and he had a fixed, glassy expression.

'I believe you're wise not to travel again until you're back in the commodore's favour.' Chalmers was studiously looking ahead as he spoke. 'If you truly wish to marry Ann, then the shortest path to that goal lies through your posting in the Gazette, and that appears to be in Mister Howe's gift. With the sloop back in the water and ready to sail, you can make yourself useful. Until then he sees you as irrelevant to his plans.'

'You're right, certainly. I'll send a letter this afternoon.'

'And I shall write to your father. I have an appointment with his trout, but my place is here for the next few weeks at least.'

***

'Was the letter not to your liking, Ann,' asked her

stepmother as she peered around the half-open door of her room.

Sophie Featherstone had seen Ann take the letter that was addressed to her and retreat to the privacy of her room. It was quite clear who'd written the letter, and the joy on her stepdaughter's face as she recognised the handwriting on the envelope confirmed it. But Ann had been alone in her room for half an hour. Each previous time she'd received a letter from her Captain Holbrooke, she'd reappeared in five minutes, bouncing down the stairs to announce her happiness, her delight in the world and all its works.

Ann was sitting on her bed with the letter held in a lifeless hand.

'Oh Sophie! He's not visiting next Saturday, and perhaps not for some time. The commodore's returned and now he must stay in Portsmouth to get his ship ready to sail again.'

Sophie sat beside her stepdaughter and held her hand. They were very close, more like sisters than mother and daughter and with only twelve years separating them, they had an empathy that rarely existed across generations. And yet they were very unalike, both physically and in their manners. Where Sophie was tall and dark with an athletic bearing, Ann was of average height with golden hair that she wore loose. Sophie rode well, mixed easily in any company and could hold her own in an argument, while Ann, at nineteen, hadn't yet shaken off her adolescent diffidence.

'I…I know nothing of men. Tell me honestly Sophie, is he trying to put me off? It seems very strange that he's unable to travel just ten miles when he wants. After all, he's the captain of his ship. Who's to say he can't?'

Sophie smiled tenderly.

'Even the captain of a King's ship answers to a higher authority, Ann. I've heard of this commodore, Richard Howe's his name, and he's said to be very particular about how he wishes things done, and most insistent that his orders should be obeyed.'

'Then you think Captain Holbrooke may still care for

me?'

'He'd be a fool not to, and I do believe Ann, that between you and I, we may refer to him as George. I know you call him George, even if I still have to observe the formalities.'

'I don't want to appear stupid, but it's so difficult being courted by a sailor. He has no fixed home, unless you can count his father's cottage, and I don't know where he'll be from one day to the next. This letter gives no indication of when I may see him again. He could be off to the East Indies for all I know.'

Sophie thought for a moment.

'You know that your father is against you becoming too attached to George before he's been made a post-captain?'

'I do, and I understand his reasoning and of course I respect his decisions. But it's so hard to wait. I just feel as though I've no control over anything. It would be very improper, I suppose, to go to Portsmouth to see him.'

Sophie laughed.

'I'm afraid it would, although you'd give our friends in the town something to talk about for years to come! It would be very improper of you to seek him out in Portsmouth. But there is another possibility. Do you remember that we stood on the Round Tower last year to watch the fleet sail?'

'Yes, you could almost touch the ships as they came out. You're not thinking...'

'I am, but we'll need some information to make this work. I've already called once on William Holbrooke at his cottage and I can do so again. He's probably the best source of naval information in the town. I can ask him when he expects George to sail and I can at least attempt to understand this business of the naval ranks and their significance. I believe he's secretly afraid of me, so it shouldn't be difficult.'

'You won't embarrass me Sophie, will you?'

'No, have no fear. I know the man and I know how to

handle him. Just leave it to me and then at the least we'll know more. At best we'll fulfil your desire to see him again, although in the guise of interested watchers, no more. Not a word to your father now. I'll tell him when it's too late for him to object.'

***

They floated *Kestrel* out of the dry dock on the Monday, two days ahead of the date demanded by Admiral Holburne. Her new wheel looked dark and incongruous against the weathered oak and elm all around it that had been bleached white by the sun, the salt spray and the endless scrubbing. She lay in the wet basin for two days taking on stores and setting up the tops'ls and the running rigging, then on the Wednesday, exactly five weeks after they'd limped back into port, they warped out into the harbour. There they lay, waiting for orders. The commissioning pennant flying from her main truck announced to the world, and to Commodore Howe, that *Kestrel* was ready to re-join the squadron.

***

'Weigh anchor, Mister Fairview.'

'Boat coming alongside, sir,' said Edney. 'It looks like dispatches and mail.'

'Easy on the capstan until we get the mail on board,' Holbrooke said to the first lieutenant. 'You may weigh with a will as soon as the boat's clear.'

The strong nor'easterly whipped over the dockyard, laying *Kestrel* over under the minimal canvas that she was showing to cast her head to the east. The ebbing tide ran fast under the sloop's forefoot. The hands were already out on the yards ready to drop the tops'ls.

'Anchor's aweigh, sir,' shouted Lynton from the fo'c'sle.

The wind caught the jib and fore-stays'l and the bows fell away to starboard. Tops'ls and mizzen appeared as if by magic and *Kestrel* gathered way. They had two knots of tide under the keel, and the docks and Gunwharf slipped rapidly down the larboard side.

'There's a note you should see, sir,' said Pritchard, daring to step into Holbrooke's view during the tricky departure from Portsmouth. 'It wasn't covered or sealed, and I saw that it required your immediate attention…' he trailed off, unsure whether he'd done the right thing.

'Oh, give it to me then,' said Holbrooke in exasperation.

A single look at the note just deepened the mystery. He turned it over, there was nothing on the back, and no sender's name.

'*In haste. Look at the Round Tower as you pass.*'

'That's all?' asked Holbrooke.

'Yes, sir,' replied Pritchard looking wretched, 'there was nothing to identify it.'

It could just be his father's handwriting. And yet he was not the sort of sentimentalist to stand on the Round Tower and wave to his son's ship; that was for lovesick girls and heart-broken mothers, he would have said. In its three-and-a-half centuries the tower had seen plenty of both, but not many hard-bitten old sailing masters.

'Very well, you were right to show it to me.'

Holbrooke raised his telescope and trained it over the larboard bow towards the Round Tower. At first only the massive grey structure could be seen, with a few indistinct figures atop. In peacetime, when King's ships didn't so frequently leave the harbour, the Round Tower would be packed with people getting the closest view possible of a man-of-war under sail. But the people of Portsmouth had become jaded by the spectacle, and today only this small group was visible.

The sloop passed Portsmouth Point, and now the details were becoming clearer. It was a group of three. Holbrooke lowered the telescope and carefully wiped the eyepiece and objective lens with his handkerchief. When he looked again his suspicion was confirmed. There was Ann, flanked on one side by Mrs Featherstone and on the other by his father.

'Give a cheer, lads,' shouted Jackson who'd recognised the group as quickly as Holbrooke, even without a telescope.

Kestrel sped through the gap, wind and tide urging her on, to the loud huzzahs of her people. Holbrooke waved and waved and watched the group until the turn in the channel past Spithead became a matter of urgency.

***

Saint Catherine's was behind them and the sloop was running sou'-sou'west into a glorious evening – sky-blue-pink his mother used to call those colours – as the sun made its stately way towards the horizon on the starboard bow.

'There's nothing important in the official mail, sir,' said Pritchard, laying a small bundle of documents on the table. 'I've warned Mister Matross that there's a letter from the gun wharf about the honeycombing on number eight gun and that he'll see it after you've read it.'

Holbrooke glanced at the letter; it didn't require his attention and he passed it back to the clerk without a word.

'There's a personal letter, sir,' he added, handing over a neat paper package.

'Thank you, Mister Pritchard, just give that letter to the gunner and I'll read the rest later.'

The personal letter was from Lady Chiara. He could easily recognise her hand, so much more cursive than the style taught to ladies in England. It was neatly if incorrectly addressed:

Captain Holbrooke of the Navy Royal, His Britannic Majesty's Ship Kestrel, at Portsmouth, England.

He cut through the seal and the ribbons beneath and unfolded the five sheets of clean, white paper. Trust Lady Chiara to use only the best materials. She'd written on one side only, and her writing was far from small. Thus delivered, five sheets conveyed less information than perhaps two sheets from the Admiralty or the navy board. However, her prose was so concise that he knew there would be enough information to hold his attention for some time.

'Serviteur, a sherry would go down well now,' he called into the scullery.

My dear George, the letter started.

It was the first letter that he'd received from either Chiara or her husband since Carlisle's ship had called at Hampton – a short ride from Williamsburg – on the way to Louisbourg. He was aware that there'd been some uneasiness about introducing Chiara to her husband's family, but the frankness of Chiara's description of the events left him gasping in astonishment. The sheer hostility of Carlisle's elder brother and father, the way that the antagonism had lasted through the visit, the reconciliation between Chiara and her father-in-law – but not his brother – after Carlisle had left. They were all stories that were best kept close within a family. He was surprised that Chiara was so freely confessing the sordid details to him, her husband's sometime first lieutenant.

He was pleased to read that Carlisle's cousin and her husband had made up for his brother's unpleasantness by opening their home for Chiara. As she pointed out, her baby was due in only three months – two now after the letter had taken a month to reach him – and she needed a comfortable and secure home.

She'd heard nothing from Carlisle since he'd left but that wasn't surprising given the state of the land communications in the American colonies. Holbrooke had heard that the expedition against Louisbourg was well underway and the fortress may already have fallen. He hoped that Carlisle had found a way to return to Williamsburg before the birth, but he knew that it was unlikely.

Chiara ended with her best wishes and her hope that she'd soon see Holbrooke's name in The Gazette. She made a point of asking at the governor's palace to see the latest copies whenever she took a walk in the town.

It was a good letter that nicely complemented his unexpected send-off from the Round Tower. He wondered how Chiara and Ann would agree; very well he thought.

***

CHAPTER SEVENTEEN

Cherbourg

Thursday, Thirteenth of July 1758.
Kestrel, at Sea. Off Cherbourg.

The night had been warm, and *Kestrel* ran fast across the channel, stuns'ls set, driven by the same nor'easterly that had sped them out of Portsmouth Harbour just the previous afternoon. The sloop had been cleared for action all night, but the people were in their regular watches with the lucky watch below already snoring in time with their swinging hammocks.

'I make it sunrise at twenty-one minutes past four,' Fairview declared, checking his watch as the vast orange orb heaved its nether regions clear of the cloudless horizon. He stooped low over the binnacle. Protecting his eye with a piece of smoked glass, he squinted through the nearer slit on the wooden stile attached to the compass. Then, with infinite care, he turned the inner box until the cat-gut thread that was stretched vertically through the slit in the furthest stile bisected the sun.

'Now, Mister Turner.'

'Nor'east half east… no, three-quarters east,' announced the midshipman, looking squarely down at the compass card from above.

Fairview straightened and held his hat formally across his chest. 'The binnacle compass is correct, sir, allowing for variation,' he said with a look of satisfaction.

'Thank you, Mister Fairview,' said Holbrooke whose gaze and attention was directed south, towards Cherbourg.

'You may unship the stile and return the compass to its drawer, Mister Turner,' Fairview continued, not in the least perturbed that his captain had hardly registered a word he'd said.

Whenever the horizon was clear Fairview made a point

of checking the accuracy of the compass against the known bearing of the rising and setting sun. Of course, it was possible to verify the accuracy during the day, but it involved complex calculations. And then there was the practical difficulty of taking an accurate bearing of the elevated sun using the shadow of the horizontal cat-gut line stretched between the two stiles. A bearing at sunrise or sunset was altogether more desirable and more reliable. Nevertheless, most masters of anything less than a flagship would seldom bother to be on deck so early or so late without good reason. It was one more facet of Fairview that made him such a boon as a sailing master.

'That'll be Pelée Island, Mister Fairview?'

'Aye, that's it,' Fairview replied. 'There's a fort on the west side and a battery on the north.'

'I can't quite see the causeways.'

'The one to the south is hidden behind the island. It almost makes a complete pathway to the mainland, but there's a small channel for boats right up against the Tourlaville shore. If you look to the right of the island, you'll see the other causeway; it's more of a breakwater really. That leaves a nine-cable channel into the anchorage.'

Holbrooke could just make out the breakwater now with its stone pillar at the western end. It was a strange arrangement that left the anchorage exposed to winds from the north and west. An uncomfortable anchorage, Holbrooke decided.

'What's the depth, Master?'

'Oh, there's plenty of water until we're five cables off the island, sir, but I'll have the lead heaved anyway.'

'Then let's stay two miles clear and set a course to the west. We should be able to see all we need to see in this clear air. Get the stuns'ls in, if you please.'

It was rather like Saint-Malo all over again, he thought. The fortified island lying to seaward guarding the approaches to a French port. The difference here was that Cherbourg wasn't anything like as important to the French as Saint-Malo. It had been strongly fortified in the previous century, but the castle had been demolished seventy years ago. There were only a few privateers based at Cherbourg, and no King's ships refitted there.

There had been great plans to improve the defences, both landward and seaward, but they hadn't yet been put into practice. Now only Pelée Island defended the seaward approach and a small fort guarded the land approach from the west. The little Divette river and its marshy banks covered the east flank of the town and hosted its rudimentary port facilities.

Nevertheless, Cherbourg's anchorage was large, and it was well sheltered from the south and east. Holbrooke's mission was to probe and to determine whether the batteries on Pelée Island had been occupied since Howe's postponed attempt at the end of June – while *Kestrel* had been in dock – and whether any naval force had moved into the vicinity.

The quartermaster put the helm down and came four points to starboard. Now they were coasting west-nor'west along the shallow indentation at the northern end of the Cotentin Peninsula, with Cape La Hague ahead of them.

Holbrooke leaned his telescope on the hammock crane and focussed carefully on the island. It was tiny, no more than a cable across, and it was barren. There were no trees, just a bleak expanse of rock and the low walls of a small fort and an even smaller battery. Every inch of the island was open to his inspection. He could see the black muzzles of the guns at the battery – it looked like about ten of them, all pointing north – and the profile of the nearest gun in the fort was just visible with twelve embrasures reaching away to the west. That was all he needed to know. There was no need to draw their fire, particularly as he could see soldiers moving about in some agitation at the prospect of engaging this English intruder.

'Keep well out of range, Mister Fairview. I have no desire to put the sloop into dock again.'

The defenders of Cherbourg had been busy since their last alarm. Defensive works were being hastily thrown up all along the shore to the west of the town, extending some five or six miles to the headland beyond Querqueville. It must have been evident to the military commander that a landing to attack Cherbourg had only been postponed by the bad weather two weeks before.

'Do you know anything of these shores, Mister Fairview?' Holbrooke asked.

'Foul ground, the whole coast from Barfleur to Cape La Hague, sir,' he replied. 'Every beach is encumbered with rocks. Oh, they look safe enough on the chart, but when you get close you can see that there's precious little chance of putting twenty or thirty flatboats in together.'

Holbrooke nodded mutely and continued his study of the shore as it slipped by to larboard. The Bay of Cherbourg looked attractive enough, but with close observation he could see the patches of white where the waves broke on the rocks. There was a fort being hastily repaired on the point at Equeurdreville and a line of entrenchments overlooking the shore. At Querqueville there was another fort – more of a battery really – but if it mounted twenty-four pounders then the area between Equeurdreville and Querqueville was covered. The bay beyond Querqueville started to open beyond the point.

'Mister Fairview. I'd like to see that bay a little better. It appears that the guns haven't yet been mounted at Querqueville, so you may move in as close as you see fit.'

At the master's word, *Kestrel's* bows paid off from the nor'easterly wind.

'No bottom on this line,' called the leadsman.

That was a twenty-fathom line, Holbrooke thought, and they were two miles offshore. He'd expect the water to shoal quite fast.

'I think we'll stand in under tops'ls, Mister Fairview.'

Jackson had been ready for this sail reduction and in only a few minutes the courses were furled. Now the sloop had only the three tops'ls, the mizzen and the jib.

'Stream the log, Mister Turner,' Fairview ordered.

The battery at Querqueville was a hair off the larboard bow and the Bay of Saint-Marais was right ahead.

'Will you be going ashore tonight?' Fairview asked winking at Turner and the quartermaster.

'I think not, Mister Fairview. This coast is looking far too alert. I doubt whether a stroll along the shore would be conducive to my health.'

He paused for a moment while Fairview contemplated how some jokes fall on stony ground.

'I thought you might enjoy a stroll instead of me,' Holbrooke continued in a flat voice, still looking through the telescope. 'You can take Smithson with you,' he added, 'and Mister Turner.'

He turned in time to see Fairview and the quartermaster's horrified faces quickly replaced by guilty grins.

'Four knots and a quarter,' said Turner who had just returned from the taffrail, wondering whether he was in trouble and, if so, how it had happened without him opening his mouth.

'By the deep, eighteen.'

'I'd like to haul our wind at twelve fathoms,' said Fairview sheepishly. It had been his first attempted humour at his captain's expense and it had rebounded on him. He resolved never to try again.

'If you please, Mister Fairview.'

'Mark fifteen.'

It was shoaling rapidly now.

'Helm a'weather, quartermaster,' ordered Fairview.

Kestrel's bows moved to starboard.

'Start those sheets there,' called Jackson.

Now Holbrooke had a clear view of the bay. It was a mile wide and the sandy beach between the rocky outcrops that enclosed the bay rose gently towards fields and patches of woodland. At the eastern end there was a small village.

All along the shoreline he could see the bare earth where entrenchments were being dug.

'What do you make of it, Mister Lynton?' Holbrooke asked.

Lynton had been gazing equally earnestly at the shore. Rock-bound though it was it appeared more promising than Cherbourg Bay.

'There's a space of perhaps half a mile between the rocks,' he said, 'but I believe I can see a patch of white almost in the centre, sir.'

Holbrooke turned his telescope to where Lynton was pointing. Yes, there was a hint of white where the waves were breaking, presumably on a patch of rock.

'Mister Fairview, mark off the extent of that beach, if you please, and lay down the position of those rocks.'

That would give the master something to do other than make poor jokes. It could also be useful if Howe decided to land the army at Saint-Marais Bay.

Fairview busied himself with the compass and a notebook.

'Deep twelve,' called the leadsman.

'Haul your wind a point, Quartermaster,' said Fairview.

Holbrooke looked up. They had almost reached across the little bay and that twelve-fathom sounding would be the underwater extension of the point at the western end of the bay. There was a battery being established there also, but like its fellows, its guns hadn't yet been mounted. He looked across the deck, the gun crews were all at their quarters, lounging in the warmth of the early morning sun. Their breakfast would be late today. So far, they looked happy enough, but Holbrooke knew how quickly they would come to resent being sent to quarters for no apparent reason.

'Mister Lynton, what's the range to that battery, do you think?'

He could see the unfinished wall of gabions and the empty spaces between them temporarily filled with fascines. At the eastern end, there was a party of soldiers digging furiously. It looked like they were filling more gabions to provide a solid wall of packed earth at that end.

'Half a mile, barely,' the first lieutenant replied.

There was a stirring of interest all along the eight guns of the larboard battery. Quarter gunners and gun captains started rousing their crews and blowing on the slow match.

'Nearer three-quarters,' said Fairview with a snort.

'Then you may stir them up a little, Mister Lynton. Fire by divisions until you have your elevation, then broadsides as long as we're in range.'

Lynton rubbed his hands.

'Aye-aye sir!' he replied with a broad smile.

'Steer small quartermaster,' Holbrooke ordered, to give the guns the best chance.

Bang, bang! The first two guns fired together.

'Short!' exclaimed Lynton as twin white plumes appeared off the point.

'Nearer three-quarters, as I said,' Fairview commented, not entirely under his breath.

The wind blew the gunsmoke away most conveniently over the larboard bow. Numbers six and eight guns were already easing the quoins back to give their guns more elevation.

Holbrooke watched the working party through his telescope. They were close enough to distinguish the officers in their white coats from the soldiers who had stripped to their shirt sleeves for the hard manual work. They seemed to find *Kestrel's* first attempt amusing.

Bang... bang! The second two guns fired with a greater interval between them. This time it was more difficult to see the fall of shot, there was no plume of white water but two puffs of dust where the balls hit the rocks below the battery.

Bang, bang! Numbers ten and twelve guns made Holbrooke start, they were so close, and he was so intent on watching the reactions of the soldiers at the battery. One of the officers was waving madly. He'd seen that the ranging salvoes were creeping ever closer and he was trying to get his men behind the gabions.

As Holbrooke watched, he saw the two balls fall right among the working party. Two men fell and lay still, the others retreated to the safety of the gabions. Those huge wicker baskets filled with hard-packed earth would keep out *Kestrel's* six-pound balls. The gun crews cheered and the numbers fourteen and sixteen guns fired, their balls kicking up the turned earth in front of the gabions.

'Broadsides while you can, Mister Lynton.'

Kestrel managed four broadsides before they were out of range. The men cheered as the earth erupted in modest fountains where the balls landed. They'd done precious little material damage, but the effect on morale must have been considerable. Perhaps only half a day's worth of work had been destroyed, but those soldiers had been routed without any hope of retaliation. They'd felt the destruction that a tiny sloop could inflict upon them; they could only tremble when Howe's ships-of-the-line appeared before their puny defences. That was one advantage of this bay, the third and fourth rates could approach close enough to cover a landing.

***

CHAPTER EIGHTEEN

A Measure of Redemption

Saturday, Fifteenth of July 1758.
Kestrel, at Anchor. Spithead.

The nor'east wind gave Fairview an interesting exercise in working the tides to cross the English Channel. It was only seventy nautical miles, but it took *Kestrel* two days to make the passage. In the end, they had to wait for the ebb to drop down from the east of Selsey Bill into the Solent. They anchored at Spithead late in the dog watches, but not so late that they couldn't see their identifying flag and the *captain* pennant hanging out in the flagship.

Holbrooke entered the great cabin with some trepidation. He hadn't met Howe since the squadron's return from Saint-Malo, in fact his only sight of the commodore had been the frosty glance that he gave before that awkward interview with the flag captain. Time seemed to have healed some of the antagonism, yet his welcome was not as warm as it might have been.

'Take a seat, Mister Holbrooke, and give me an account of your reconnaissance. I'll read your report later,' Howe said, indicating that the envelope should be handed to his secretary. 'This wind can't have made it easy to get back. I heard you were seen off Selsey this morning; had to wait for the tide, eh?'

Holbrooke expected no quarter from the commodore, and this mild allusion to a landfall that was less than exactly accurate was the least of his fears. He knew, and the commodore knew, that there was no shame in being set a few miles up the channel on the flood. The tides could be predicted, more-or-less, but the wind was much less certain and the sudden shift into the west had taken both he and Fairview by surprise. Holbrooke was comforted by knowing that Howe's fleet had taken three days to get to its anchorage at Spithead; three days and the loss of a transport on the Horse Tail Sand.

'Yes sir, the wind veered this morning and caught us the wrong side of the flood. We anchored on a long cable off Selsey until the ebb.'

Howe nodded grudgingly.

'Then what did you find at Cherbourg, Mister Holbrooke? Are the Pelée Island batteries manned?'

Holbrooke recognised the mild rudeness in the insistent use of *mister* rather than *captain*. It represented the finest of distinctions. When applied to a post-captain or a commodore the use of *mister* was perfectly normal. When applied to a master and commander, it stressed the fact that he was not a post-captain. He was in fact a *captain* only by courtesy, and perhaps only temporarily, and Commodore Howe evidently didn't care to offer that courtesy.

Still, there was nothing that Holbrooke could do. He saw that Campbell looked embarrassed and turned away to gaze out of the window, fidgeting with the notebook that he habitually carried. Howe clearly had developed a poor opinion of this youngest of his commanding officers, Holbrooke thought. He still had suspicions of his conduct in the affair with the French frigate and sloop and *Kestrel's* return to Portsmouth. Perhaps Howe had heard about his weekly visits to Wickham and their purpose. Well, there was no point in hoping that Howe would change his mind without some stimulus. Holbrooke knew that the burden was on himself to prove his value.

'The fort and the battery are both manned, sir. Ten guns in the battery facing north. The guns weren't run out in the fort, but I saw one and a total of twelve embrasures facing west. There was a lot of activity, much more than would have been required for that one gun, so I assume each of the twelve embrasures had its own gun out of sight. The guns that I could see all looked like twenty-fours, sir...'

'Did you see any men-o'-war?' the commodore

interrupted, 'anything in the road or up the river?'

'Five ships and two snows, all merchantmen, in the anchorage, sir, and two vessels up the river. I couldn't get close enough to see them but I'm sure they weren't men-o'-war. They could have been privateers.'

'Very well,' Howe replied, 'then I'll read your report later,' he turned back to his desk loaded with papers. The meeting was at an end as far as the commodore was concerned.

'Sir…'

Howe looked up again in irritation.

'With the tide not turning for another four hours, rather than fight against it, I cruised the coast to the west of Cherbourg, to determine the state of the defences.'

Howe's expression changed, he looked interested.

'They're fortifying the whole of that coast for eight miles beyond Cherbourg…'

Holbrooke described what he'd seen: the earthworks, the batteries with their gabions and fascines, the absence of guns.

'I fired four broadsides into the gabions at the battery at the western end of Saint-Marais Bay, perhaps setting the work back half a day, sir.'

Howe nodded. It was always good to annoy the enemy.

'You've noted all this in your report?'

'I have, sir, and this chart summarises what we saw.'

Howe gave Holbrooke a curious look.

'Then unroll it, man, a picture's worth any number of words.'

Holbrooke spread the chart out on the table.

'Here's the battery that we attacked, sir, and here's the bay to the east of it.'

Howe studied the chart systematically, running his finger along the coast from east to west.

'This is by the same hand that drafted the chart of Cancale Bay, isn't it?'

'Yes, sir,' Holbrooke replied. 'Josiah Fairview, my sailing

master. He's a meticulous surveyor and draftsman.'

'He was my mate in *Centurion* in the last war,' added Campbell.

'Then you're certain of Saint-Marais? The extent of the rocks at either end and of the bay and this foul ground in the centre?'

'The rocks showed white in the swell, sir. It was almost low water and they were the only obstructions that we could see.'

'A battery at either end,' Howe continued, 'probably twenty-fours like the island.'

'The guns hadn't been mounted two days ago, sir, but the placements looked the right size.'

'Earthworks all along the shore as well?'

'Yes, sir,' Holbrooke replied, 'they were still throwing them up, but the work was well advanced.'

Howe exchanged glances with Campbell.

'Defended then, and yet still possible, I believe, Campbell,' he said to his flag captain.

'It still looks the best place, sir. Even if we silence the Pelée Island guns, there's no good landing in Cherbourg Bay.'

Howe stared at the chart for a moment.

'This is most valuable, Captain,' he said. 'You've done well.'

So, it was *captain* now? Holbrooke recognised the significant step towards the commodore's good opinion. Significant but still not enough. He needed Howe to be at least his advocate if not his patron if he was to be gazetted after these expeditions.

'Oh, and Captain Holbrooke,' said Campbell, 'you won't have seen the general order that the commodore issued on the thirteenth. As you predicted, the lack of gang-boards was found to be a serious matter for the army, although why they didn't forecast that is beyond me. The carpenters of the fleet are building them now, a pair for each flatboat. That hoy, *Forester*, that caught up with us in Cancale Bay, it was loaded with deals and carpentry stores, enough for the gang-boards for a whole fleet of flatboats. Your specification has been immortalised, Captain,'

Holbrooke bowed in acknowledgement. For some reason Campbell had appointed himself his mentor. Although he was wary of contradicting his commodore, he was adept at helpful interjections. Holbrooke could see that Howe had registered Campbell's compliment yet chose not to comment.

'Holbrooke's Plank!' added Campbell. 'It has a ring about it, don't you think?'

Howe ignored the jest.

'Would you send Mister Fairview over to talk to my sailing master?' Howe asked, already moving on to other matters.

***

'A measure of redemption, then,' Chalmers declared after Holbrooke had told his story of the interview with Commodore Howe.

'Yes, I believe so, but there's still a long way to go. He didn't entirely believe the urgency of *Kestrel* returning to be docked last month, you know, despite the master attendant's word on the subject and the port admiral's endorsement. I suspect that he knows about my visits to Wickham, although God knows they were innocent enough. How he heard I cannot tell.'

'It's a family, this navy of yours George, and this part of Hampshire is nothing more than a small village, full of gossip and speculation. He could have found out from any number of sources, and the telling didn't need to be malicious, just the normal to-and-fro of information in a family, in a village.'

Holbrooke thought about it for a moment.

'You're right, of course, David. There are few secrets in the navy.'

'And I can see how his train of thought would lead him to suspect your conduct. As you stated, from his perspective, you took the first opportunity of some more-or-less exaggerated damage to run back to Portsmouth. The fact that there's a lady involved just made his suspicions more certain. It's all circumstantial, but we're not dealing with a court of law here.'

'No. If Commodore Howe wishes to blight my career, he can do so without concerning himself with any kind of official action. He can achieve it by mere inaction. If he doesn't mention my name in his report to the Admiralty, then they'll assume that I made no significant contribution.'

Holbrooke strode across to the windows and checked himself. He'd become aware that this habit of staring into space had become known to his officers. He'd seen no signs of amusement from them, but he wanted to avoid any appearance of strangeness. He turned quickly back to Chalmers, who hadn't missed his captain's abrupt change of direction.

'It's infuriating, David. The ironic thing is that I value Mister Howe's opinion of me more than any other senior officer that I've met. If I could choose a mentor, a patron, it would be him. Not merely because he has influence, but because I'd like to model myself on him. He's energetic, decisive, intelligent and he can command men. He's the sort of sea officer that the service is crying out for, and yet I'm failing to impress him.'

This time Holbrooke did stare out of the cabin window. *Kestrel* was at the western end of the Spithead anchorage and the tide was flooding. The rest of the squadron was invisible, forward of the beam, but the whole of the Solent was open for his inspection. He watched the coastal traffic hurrying on its occasions and saw the sea break on the shingle of Gilkicker Point. The bright flag that flew over the field gun battery on the point made a pleasing splash of colour on this sparkling day.

Chalmers made no comment, but he watched his friend's back as he stood in mute introspection. One can discern much of a person's mood from the set of his shoulders, Chalmers thought. He was aware that Holbrooke loved Shakespeare's plays and acknowledge that there was much wisdom in them, although somewhat less than the bible. In this case his friend appeared to be giving too much weight to Cassius: *The fault, dear Brutus, is not in our stars, but in ourselves, that we are underlings.*

'I can't see Ann, of course,' said Holbrooke, turning briskly back to the cabin. 'We're all forbidden to stray outside Portsmouth and the Yard without the commodore's written permission, and I don't feel that my case would be improved by applying to spend tonight in Wickham!'

'Indeed not. Will Miss Featherstone have heard that *Kestrel's* at Spithead?'

'Oh, certainly. As you pointed out, this area's no more than a dispersed village. The comings and goings of the squadron will be common knowledge as far north as Alton and Guildford.'

'Then you must write without delay. Imagine how the poor young lady will feel when she hears that *Kestrel* has returned! A letter now, sent by the morning carrier, will reach her by noon tomorrow. Perhaps not ahead of word-of-mouth, but maybe not far behind.'

***

Holbrooke chewed the end of his quill. It was a nasty habit, a hangover from his childhood, and a sign of his agitated mind, and he started guiltily when he realised what he was doing. How to write to Ann? He'd written to her before, but now it was a more delicate matter.

On the one hand, they had no formal relationship. He and Ann had no understanding about a joint future and her father hadn't given his agreement to anything more than his calling on Ann in her own home. On the other hand, he felt a strong attraction to Ann, and he was sure that she felt the same for him. After all, she'd travelled down to Portsmouth Point when *Kestrel* had sailed away only three days ago. A letter that sounded over-familiar could well be resented by her father, but probably not by her step-mother.

He realised that he didn't know enough about the family to know whether she could open her own correspondence. It was quite common for the parents of unmarried daughters to intercept letters before they were delivered. And yet a cold, impersonal letter may do more harm than good, particularly after the way that he'd left her less than two weeks ago.

The bell struck twice, seven o'clock in the evening.

'Will you take supper, sir?' asked Serviteur, breaking in on his thoughts.

'In thirty minutes, if you please.'

He'd fallen into the habit of addressing Serviteur as though he were a gentleman; it was an inevitable consequence of the man's own bearing and manner.

'Would you also tell Mister Pritchard that I shall have a letter to be dispatched, and let Dawson know that he's to take the yawl and row Mister Pritchard to the Sally Port?'

It was close to an abuse of his position, Holbrooke knew, and Pritchard, probably Dawson as well, would immediately guess the message that was being sent to Miss Featherstone of Bere Forest House, Wickham. Damn them all he thought. No other captain in the fleet would hesitate for a moment.

'And Serviteur,' he called as his servant opened the cabin door, 'tell the bosun to pass the word. If any officer or man has a letter to be sent, he's to deliver it to my clerk in the next thirty minutes.'

A small sop to his conscience, perhaps.

Alone in the cabin now, Holbrooke could stare out onto the beautiful summer evening undisturbed. He was almost sure that Sophie Featherstone, Ann's stepmother, was a friend to his cause. They'd been together on the Round Tower, waving as he set out to sea. How much influence did she have over Martin Featherstone? Considerable if he was any judge of character. She'd certainly bullied his father into joining in the enterprise. She'd needed an escort to negotiate Portsmouth Point, even if only as far as the Round Tower, and the elder Holbrooke would have had no chance against her will.

Dear Miss Featherstone.

No, that would never do. It sounded like a letter from a bank manager. He crumpled up the paper and drew out a clean sheet. Strangely, that false start had hardened his resolve.

My dear Ann, he wrote purposefully. Now that he was resolved to be bold, he found the words came quickly.

What a pleasant surprise to see you at the Round Tower with your mother and my father. I waved until you were out of sight, and I do hope you saw me.

That was not entirely true, of course. He'd waved until the sloop's navigation had claimed his attention, but by then he'd have been too far away for Ann to see. A white lie.

You cannot imagine how it lifted my spirits to know that you had made the journey to Portsmouth to see me sail away…

Holbrooke wrote on, making quite sure that Ann knew how much he appreciated the pains that she'd taken to see him navigate out of Portsmouth Harbour.

You may know by now that Kestrel is at anchor at Spithead again. I really don't know how long we will be here, probably days rather than weeks…

This was the hard part, telling her that he wouldn't be able to see her until these expeditions were completed. He didn't know how close she was to his father; it had come as a real surprise to see him on the Round Tower. If they were on calling terms, then the senior Holbrooke would no doubt explain the constraints that his son was under.

Holbrooke finished the letter as the ship's bell struck three times. He could hear the noises of the yawl being hauled alongside and the crew scrambling down the side. His clerk knocked and came in.

'Ah, Mister Pritchard. Would you take this letter to the Dolphin and ask the landlord to deliver it to the Alton carrier before seven in the morning? He should add the cost to my account.'

'May I, sir,' he said.

Holbrooke nodded. Pritchard held the sealing wax over the candle and dripped a pool of red, molten wax onto the flap of the envelope. He sealed it with a gold guinea that he kept in his pocket.

'You should consider having your own seal struck, sir,' he commented.

Holbrooke knew very well that most captains had their own seal, perhaps a heraldic coat of arms for their family, or a copy of the seal from the county or town they called home. He also guessed that Pritchard saw it as a slight upon his own dignity, his captain not having a personal seal. Holbrooke, however, felt his hold on his rank was too tenuous to tempt fate in that way. A common guinea would do until he was posted, regardless of Pritchard's dignity.

***

It was four bells in the first watch, and still quite light this close to the summer solstice, when he heard the yawl returning. Probably Pritchard had given the crew an hour to wet their whistles at one of the sailors' inns that were only a few hundred yards up Broad Street. Most likely he'd also gone to meet some of the other young gentlemen, perhaps at the Blue Posts only a short walk from the Sally Port. It was a humane indulgence; they weren't under sailing orders and with the sloop at Spithead, that was the only way for any of the people to get a run ashore.

There was a knock at the cabin door and Pritchard came in. It was apparent that he'd taken a drink. Not enough for Holbrooke to object, but enough to put a broad smile on the clerk's face.

'Dispatches from the flagship, sir. We were hailed alongside as we were returning, it saved them sending a boat.'

'Thank you, Mister Pritchard.'

The clerk showed no sign of leaving. He wanted to know what was in the orders before anyone else.

'Thank you, Mister Pritchard,' Holbrooke repeated

emphatically, looking hard at his clerk.

When he was alone, he broke the seal. He found that he was strangely nervous. The meeting with the commodore today, he felt, had gone some way to repairing his relationship with his superior. Perhaps this was the fruit of that reconciliation.

You are hereby requested and required to take His Majesty's Sloop Kestrel to the vicinity of Cherbourg, there to watch the port and await the arrival of the squadron under my command in the first week of August…

***

CHAPTER NINETEEN

An Opportunity

Sunday, Sixth of August 1758.
Kestrel, at Sea. Off Cherbourg.

The cutter *Grace* had brought news of Howe's squadron the evening before, so the arrival of over a hundred vessels was no surprise to Holbrooke. Nevertheless, the sight of such an armada of ships silhouetted by the dawn stirred the blood. One by one, the rays of the hidden sun illuminated the t'gallants and royals, picking them out in gold against the still-dusky sky. It was hard to imagine how such an armament could fail in its purpose.

The squadron was welcome. For three weeks *Kestrel* had patrolled between Cape La Hague and Cape Levi, never sighting an enemy man-o'-war or privateer and rarely a merchantman. For the first few days the fishing boats of the coast had sulked in their ports and sheltered beaches, but gradually the urgent need to make a living had tempted the bolder souls to take the risk. Soon, when the word got around that *Kestrel* wasn't interested in them, the bay was again dotted with fishermen in their distinctive lug-rigged flambards and bisquines, the local craft of Normandy. But never anything large enough to tempt the English cruiser. Holbrooke had noted the development of the batteries and earthworks along the coast and Fairview had run lines of soundings and laid down the positions of any rock that showed itself above the waves.

The squadron made its leisurely way into the bay, the flagship *Essex* in the lead with frigates and fourth-rates on the flanks.

'Flagship signals for captain of *Kestrel*, sir,' announced Midshipman Edney removing his hat for this formal report.

He was growing into the job. He'd learned to keep a

constant watch on the flagship and to anticipate the most likely signals that would be directed at *Kestrel*. An hour before, Holbrooke had spotted him refreshing his memory of the signal for *captain report aboard the flagship*, and it would have been surprising if he didn't already know his own ship's pennant.

Edney wasn't the only one who could anticipate the squadron commander's needs. Jackson had already warned off the captain's coxswain, and the longboat was on a short painter with Dawson and the crew waiting in the waist, dressed in matching blue jackets from the slop store. Holbrooke saw that Dawson sported a tall, black, glazed hat with the ship's name picked out in yellow, a new addition to his wardrobe that the sailmaker had run up, deeming that the sloop's dignity was being compromised by a captain's coxswain without appropriate headgear.

Here was Treganoc, his regimentals adding a patch of colour to the blues and whites on the quarterdeck. Holbrooke had warned him to be ready, so that he could add his professional military analysis to the plans and drawings of the French defences.

Holbrooke cast a sweeping glance around this little patch of sea that he'd come to think of as his own. There were no fishermen this morning. It was Sunday and in this part of France that still meant mass in the morning and the afternoon spent with wine and boules and calvados. Those few free-thinkers or those whom poverty drove to sea on a Sunday evidently didn't like the look of these newcomers.

'Keep two miles clear of the island, Mister Lynton, and look out for the flagship's signals. I expect you'll be given a station soon; you're to take it up with all possible speed.'

***

It was always a shock to see the tall sides of a third-rate after *Kestrel's* low freeboard. From the sloop's waist, Holbrooke could step down into the longboat with ease, but to even reach the entry port of *Essex* he needed to climb the sea-slippery cleats keeping a grip on the side ropes. It was a difficult feat at sea and Campbell had thoughtfully positioned strong and agile seamen either side of the cleats to prevent a fall. The seamen themselves were clinging onto the coaming of the gun-ports with practised ease and grinning at the careful progress of the officer. Holbrooke's precious rolls of charts had been given into Dawson's custody, and it was in his competent arms that they were carried into the flagship.

Campbell met Holbrooke at the entry-port. It was a handsome yet surprising gesture; it would be more usual for the first lieutenant of a flagship to meet a commander.

'Good morning, Holbrooke. It's a pleasure to see you again. I trust your watch hasn't been too dreary,' Campbell said smiling pleasantly.

He was clearly in good spirits even though the prospect of commanding a division of flatboats must have been weighing on his soul. Campbell's welcome had all the appearance of sincerity and it seemed to warrant a response from Holbrooke, who was still unsure of how he was perceived by Howe, and by extension his flag captain.

'Very quiet, sir,' he replied as they walked towards the cabin. 'I've seen nothing other than fishermen for the whole three weeks. The coast seems to be holding its breath.'

'As well it might,' Campbell laughed. 'The commodore is looking forward to meeting you again. He's in an easier frame of mind now.'

That short conversation carried them to the door of the great cabin. Holbrooke would have liked to have had the time to probe Campbell about this *easier frame of mind*, and how it related to his own standing with the commodore, but it was a difficult subject to raise, and he wasn't at all sure how much Campbell would be prepared to reveal.

'Would you wait outside for a moment, Mister Treganoc?' asked Campbell.

Inside the cabin, a very senior looking soldier was deep in conversation with Howe at one end of the dining table, while at the other end their principal aides were talking quietly.

'Good morning, Captain Holbrooke,' Howe said looking up.

Captain Holbrooke. That was a good start.

'General, I don't believe you've met Captain Holbrooke. He's been keeping a watch on Cherbourg for me. Captain Holbrooke, this is General Bligh.'

This was a surprise. When Holbrooke left Spithead three weeks before, the Duke of Marlborough still had command of the field army, although he was openly manoeuvering for an appointment in Germany. Bligh was an old man, he looked to be in his seventies, but he smiled and extended his hand. He appeared an easier man to work with than his predecessor.

'You have charts, I see,' said Howe, gesturing at the thick paper rolls under Holbrooke's arm. 'That sailing master of yours must be a prolific surveyor.'

'He is, sir,' replied Holbrooke. 'He's laid down every rock and foul ground along the coast and he's run lines of soundings for all the approaches. If you intend to land between Cape La Hague and Cape Levi, these will be useful.'

'And the French defences?' asked Howe.

'They're separately laid down here,' he replied indicating the second bundle. 'My marine lieutenant is waiting outside to add his knowledge, if you please, sir,'

'Yes, please call him in.'

Introductions were made and Treganoc was soon in a deep and detailed conversation with Bligh's staff officers. Holbrooke could add little to the discussion and Howe had soon seen as much as he needed.

When everyone else was too deeply engrossed in the maps and charts to notice, Howe moved closer to Holbrooke so as not to be heard. 'Mister Holbrooke, join me on the gallery for a moment, if you please,' he said quietly, 'and Campbell, you too.'

***

The squadron still had a few miles to run to its anchorage in the bay, and from the flagship's stern gallery the three men had a glorious view of the squadron with the sun now a few hand-breadths above the horizon. They all paused a moment to take in the grandeur and the beauty of the scene.

The gallery was a narrow platform running the width of Essex's stern outboard of the cabin windows. It had a guardrail at chest height that prevented two people passing without an undignified shuffle. Having politely ushered Holbrooke out first, Howe found himself placed irrevocably between his flag captain and his youngest commander, with no easy way of exchanging places. Probably he would have like to face both Campbell and Holbrooke, but that was no longer possible.

Howe gave Campbell a meaningful glance. The flag captain replied with a nod.

'I wanted to get away from the soldiers, Holbrooke, but particularly from the general who doesn't need to hear this.'

An unpromising beginning, Holbrooke thought. What was coming next? Was he going to be replaced in command of Kestrel? Had Howe promised the sloop to one of his own staff? His legs felt suddenly weak and he touched the guardrail to steady himself.

Howe appeared not to notice, but Campbell did, and he winked encouragingly at Holbrooke over the commodore's shoulder. Howe plunged on obliviously.

'You're aware that each division of flatboats is commanded by one of my post-captains?'

'Yes, sir,' replied Holbrooke, weakly.

'Well, I've decided to give you Captain Campbell's division. Temporarily, on approval as it were.'

A wave of relief flooded over Holbrooke. This was good news.

'Captain Campbell and I have discussed this at length. It will come as no surprise that I really would prefer my flag captain by my side during these landings. I need the freedom to shift my flag yet leave the elements of the squadron command intact in the flagship.'

Campbell nodded approvingly.

'However, there's another reason. I was a commander once, Holbrooke, and so was Campbell, and we both know how important it is for you young fellows to have a chance to distinguish yourselves. Through no fault of your own, your service in command has been overlooked so far. I know the role you played at Emden, yet your name has less prominence than your marine lieutenant,' he gestured towards Treganoc through the cabin windows. 'I'm giving you that chance.'

Campbell winked again from behind Howe. It occurred to Holbrooke that it would suit Campbell to be relieved of this duty. There was little honour and less recognition to be gained by a post-captain in command of four boats, even on such a vital service. For a master-and-commander, however…

'Thank you, sir, for this great honour,' Holbrooke said, trying to master his emotions.

'Of course, you know all about the flatboats after the landing trials up Fareham Creek. I suggest you take Mister Treganoc with you as your coxswain, you may find him useful. He can steer a boat, I presume. There's no opportunity to practise.'

'Oh yes, sir. In fact, he's already steered a flatboat, the day after the trials.'

'It will be a little cramped in the stern sheets,' said Campbell, 'but you're both slim fellows and the soldiers will just have to move up the bench.'

'We found that the divisional commanders can't effectively steer their boat, attend to the direction of their division and look out for the flagship's signals all at the same time. They need a coxswain to second them. I'm reluctant to tell the army that they must embark one less soldier, so as Campbell says, it will be a tight squeeze.'

'Is your sloop in good hands for an hour or so,

Holbrooke?' Campbell asked, 'I'll need to go through the signals with you.'

'Yes sir, my first lieutenant is quite competent.'

'And you have that sailing master of course,' Howe laughed. 'You'd better put him under lock and key or I'll be looking for him on my own quarterdeck! Now, move along there Campbell and let me get back to the cabin. God only knows what those soldiers are planning in my absence. They've probably already decided that the whole thing's too difficult and they'd be better employed at Horse Guards or disporting themselves on Rotten Row!'

***

The peace of the flag captain's day cabin was welcome after the business of the commodore's quarters. Campbell's secretary was there, and he'd made a bundle of all the letters and instructions that Holbrooke would need. There were signals for advancing and withdrawing, signals for the bomb vessels to engage the targets ashore and flags to direct the sloops – *Kestrel* would be one of them, without Holbrooke in command – to fire over the advancing boats into the shore defences.

Campbell guided Holbrooke through the mass of paperwork. He was a meticulous man and unlike many of his contemporaries, he recognised the need for exactness in an enterprise of this sort.

'Now, you'll have a division of four boats from *Ruby*, *Amity's Assistance*, *True Briton* and *Eagle*.'

He named the transports that had brought the boats from Spithead, resting on booms in their waists.

'The boats' crews will come from *Essex*. You'll have Fitzalan and Johnstone, the two master's mates that were with you in Fareham Creek and another, Tomlyn, who you probably don't know. They're all good officers as I hope Fitzalan and Johnstone showed themselves on that previous occasion. They've been steering these flatboats for three or four months now and know their business. Mister Treganoc of course will steer your boat.'

That's good, Holbrooke thought. He was happy with those coxswains and it was reassuring to know that Treganoc would be close at hand.

'You'll be taking the grenadiers of Effingham's in the first landing and Lambton's regiment – the Sixty-Eighth – in the second. They're well drilled, they've been in and out of those boats a dozen times now. Of course, you know Captain Overton, he'll be in your boat commanding the two companies.'

There was little more to be said of a formal nature, and they drank their coffee while Campbell gave Holbrooke the benefit of his experience at Saint-Malo and the first abandoned attempt at Cherbourg.

'You know, Holbrooke,' said Campbell, watching the younger man's face, 'I wouldn't blame you if suspected me of palming this duty off on you because it didn't suit me.'

Holbrooke was unsure how to respond to that statement. He'd begun to believe that Campbell had a liking for him and had worked quietly in the background to secure this opportunity, this chance for Holbrooke to prove himself. Campbell saved him by plunging on.

'The truth is that there *is* an element of self-interest. Oh, I'm not shy,' he added, 'it's not the danger to my person that concerns me, but the danger to my ship.'

He looked around to confirm that his secretary and steward had left.

'The fact is that my first lieutenant's sick on shore and my second's not the best of officers, he's hesitant and he doesn't have any command of the men. My sailing master's a drunkard. The commodore was only partly jesting when he said that he coveted your Josiah Fairview!'

Holbrooke nodded. He was being included in sensitive matters by a post-captain of considerable seniority, ten years at least, Holbrooke had heard. Campbell made the comments on his sailing master from first-hand experience of the rank, being one of the few officers to be commissioned after holding a master's warrant himself.

He'd been with Anson on his famous voyage around the world and the shocking loss of life had propelled him from midshipman to master's mate to sailing master in a short space of time. He'd navigated Centurion home from the Far East, loaded with the spoils from the capture of the Spanish treasure ship. Best to make no comment, Holbrooke thought.

'There's another reason, and the commodore mentioned it. You've no more than a year – probably less – to prove yourself, and time is passing. You need to make it easy for Commodore Howe to mention you in his report, you need your name in the Gazette. In this expedition, the command of a division of flatboats is certainly the best way to achieve that. I've done my best to get you that opportunity. It's up to you now!'

***

CHAPTER TWENTY

Assault Commander

Monday, Seventh of August 1758.
Number Five Flatboat, at Sea. The Bay of Saint-Marais.

Little wind and fair weather, the master's mate had written in *Kestrel's* log yesterday. *Ditto weather* today. That about summed it up. There was just enough wind to give a sloop steerage way, but the frigates and ships-of-the-line weren't stirring from their anchor berths without a favourable tide and a pair of longboats to tow them.

The signal for the flatboats to be manned had been hung out in the flagship as the first hint of morning twilight started to show. Holbrooke and Treganoc had been rowed over to *Ruby* where they were met by twenty of the oarsmen that *Essex* had provided. Campbell had to strip his ship of eighty of his best seamen to man the four flatboats. With a weak set of officers under him, it was no wonder that he was reluctant to leave the ship himself.

The flatboat had already been hoisted out and it was a matter of seconds for the oarsmen to take their places. *Essex* must be a good ship, Holbrooke thought, because every man carried a canvas cushion stuffed with oakum. The sailmaker and his mates had been busy. The cushions looked like they'd had hard use already, perhaps they were always issued to the boat crews when they expected to be rowing for long periods. But of course, he'd met Campbell, and that was just the sort of spirit of co-operation that he would foster among his people. He was beginning to regret that he hadn't thought of such a convenience for himself, the oak thwart was no more yielding than any other he'd sat on. Never mind, he thought, once they were clear of the flagship he could sit on his coat.

'Here you go, sir,' said a middle-aged seaman, the stroke oar, knuckling his forehead. 'Compliments of Mister Upton, our sailmaker. There's one for you and one for the marine gentleman.'

He offered Holbrooke two cushions just like those that the oarsmen had, but they were new, and the word *Kestrel* had been done in stitches of red wool diagonally across each cushion. It was a handsome, thoughtful gift; Holbrooke imagined that Campbell would have been involved. In any event, they were most welcome and would become more so; it would be a long day.

They rowed over to the anchored flagship where they met the other three boats and lay alongside in turn as the swivel guns and ammunition were lowered into the bows. They were big, these flatboats, but with fifty soldiers embarked, rations and water for the oarsmen, ammunition for the swivel gun and the gang-boards stowed over the keel there would be no spare space at all. God help them if they came within range of French cannister shot! Holbrooke cast that appalling image from his mind. There was nothing to be gained by dwelling on the possibilities of bloody disaster.

The next task was for Holbrooke's division to embark its load of grenadiers. Each flatboat had a number painted on its transom, and the landing units were allocated to boats by the numbers. Holbrooke's boats were marked five, six, seven and eight.

These grenadiers were the shock troops of the infantry, picked from the biggest and strongest of the ranks. They came into the flatboats to the beat of a drum, each man swinging himself over the gunwale and into the boat in perfect unison, so that in a matter of a few minutes they were all seated, those in the centre facing inboard and those at the bows and stern facing forward or aft. Each man carried his small knapsack with a day's rations and fifty rounds of ball and powder, and each man's musket was gripped vertically between his knees.

Fifty-one, Holbrooke thought as he saw the small drummer-boy stow his sticks in his shirt and drop into the boat, one more than he'd expected. The youngster sat on his drum over the keel between the knees of the grenadiers.

It seemed odd – from a sea officer's perspective – that the soldiers had to do everything to the beat of a drum. It was so unlike the freedom of action that seamen had. Yet Holbrooke knew that it was necessary. The big, cumbersome smooth-bore land pattern muskets were most effective when fired *en masse* by a disciplined body of men. It was the shock effect of fifty lead balls weighing a little over an ounce each and travelling at six hundred yards in a second, arriving simultaneously at the target, that won battles. To achieve that shock effect a company must form up quickly, each man in his allotted place and load and fire in unison. There was no room for independent action and no room for hanging back; the beat of the drum was essential.

Now it was a matter of waiting for the signal to start towards the shore.

Since before sunrise they'd heard the dull, flat booms of the bomb vessels pounding the town. It was a diversion of course, to hold the enemy's main force in Cherbourg. But now the guns of the third and fourth rates and the frigates started pounding the forts and batteries guarding the bay. As Holbrooke had guessed, the Bay of Saint-Marais had been selected for the landing. He felt a surge of pride that the beach and its enclosing headlands had been surveyed by his own ship. It was Fairview's diligent work that would ensure that none of these flatboats struck a rock before they had disgorged their load of soldiers.

'They won't be deceived for long,' said Overton, cocking an ear to the east, 'not when they see this bombardment. It must be apparent that Saint-Marais Bay is our objective, even to the French.'

He sounded a little nervous, the trepidation of soldiers the world over before they go into the attack. It would pass, Holbrooke knew, as soon as the bows of the flatboat hit the sand.

'I'm not sure, sir,' replied Treganoc. 'From Cherbourg,

it can't be obvious where we are concentrating. The transports are so spread out, and it's hard to ignore the bombs that are dropping around your ears. We may create enough doubt for the French commander to hold his force at the town until he's certain that we're not just demonstrating off Saint-Marais. Enough time for you to establish yourself ashore. Remember, we can shift our point of attack from the sea much faster than an army can march from one landing site to another across the land.'

'I hope you're right, Mister Treganoc, because even with twenty flatboats we can still land no more than a thousand grenadiers and guardsmen in this first wave. I'd be surprised if the French can't muster at least three-thousand men on this coast. If they concentrate at the right place, we won't get ashore at all.'

It was just nerves, thought Holbrooke, yet he was surprised to hear it from Overton. He must be well regarded to have been given the command of the battalion's grenadiers, and yet he sounded unsure of himself.

'Let's concentrate on our task, gentlemen,' he said to break Overton's cycle of pessimism. He was pleased to see that Overton collected himself and moved on to studying the shoreline with his sergeant-major.

Holbrooke's division was on the left flank of the assault. They were to secure the eastern end of the beach and then, with reinforcements, march on the fort that perched on the point. The fort would be a continuing problem until it was silenced. Fortunately, the French engineers had been forced to compromise on its position so that it looked both east towards Cherbourg and west over the approach to the Bay of Saint-Marais. Although its guns would be a threat during the run-in, they couldn't cover the beaches themselves. Holbrooke had only to bring his division safely through that first danger, then they would be shielded by the point itself. Overton would have to deal with the entrenchments on the beach, but not the big guns.

Overton's patch of beach was perhaps a hundred and

fifty yards wide, but to reach it the flatboats would have to thread their way between Querqueville point and a large patch of rocks in the bay, a gap of just sixty yards at this state of the tide. Holbrooke knew his mark, a gable-ended barn, probably the French equivalent of a tithe barn, that sat back a quarter of a mile from the shore. With the barn bearing south-by-west on his approach, the Querqueville guns would have him in range for just a mile. At full stretch even the slow flatboats could cover that mile in fifteen minutes. That meant he'd have to brave three or four shots from each gun, perhaps sixteen shots in all. Holbrooke knew how difficult it was to hit a small moving target at sea when under fire from the men-of-war offshore. It would be sheer chance or excellent shooting indeed if his flatboats were hit. At least they were out of range for grapeshot, that was a comfort.

***

Holbrooke felt as though he was at the centre of a gathering drama. The flatboats were clustered now around the frigate *Pallas* where Howe had shifted his flag for the assault. The third and fourth rates were anchored two miles offshore along with all the transports. From that position the French would be uncertain whether the landing would be at Cherbourg or anywhere five miles either side. The bombs were anchored a mile-and-a-half offshore for their bombardment and the frigates and sloops were gathering to the west ready to start their approach to cover the landings.

'There's the prep,' said Holbrooke, watching the flag soar up to the masthead of *Pallas*.

Five minutes to go. Treganoc gave a few orders to the oarsmen, two strokes starboard, a stroke larboard, backwater starboard, to keep the bows pointing south.

'Any moment now…' said Overton, fighting to hide his nervousness. One or two of the soldiers shifted uneasily in their seats, and some knees jigged with a life of their own, but otherwise they sat with the infinite patience of their calling. The oarsmen spat on their hands and rolled their shoulders, ready for the outpouring of energy that they knew would be required.

'Signal's executed, Mister Treganoc, take us in.'

'Give way!' Treganoc called to the stroke oar, the man who'd given him the cushion. Treganoc wasn't sitting on it now and neither was Holbrooke sitting on his, they needed to stand to see over the heads of the soldiers. It was horribly exposed, and the commander and the marine lieutenant had just made themselves the most vulnerable people in the boat. Holbrooke noticed that Overton had wisely decided to stay seated. The number six boat was extended on his starboard side and the numbers seven and eight followed the leaders two boat lengths astern. Holbrooke had deliberately put himself nearest the danger.

'Easy!' called Treganoc.

The stroke oar eased back on the power and the other oarsmen followed him. Holbrooke waved to the number six flatboat to slow down, then repeated the signal to the other two. He wanted to conserve the rowers' energy until the guns on Querqueville fired. That would be the time to stretch out. There was a theory going around the squadron that it may be better to approach the beach as though the boats were tacking, making a turn of four or five points every few minutes to throw off the French gunners' aim. The counter theory said that all that would be achieved would be to spend longer in the killing zone. Both hypotheses had merit, but they failed to address the morale factor. These soldiers needed no fancy manoeuvres; they were out of their element on the water and wanted nothing more than to feel firm ground under their boots. Rapid and direct was the only option.

Holbrooke heard a sound like the rotten stitches of an old sail being pulled apart. A plume of water rose astern, conjured into life only to instantly subside, leaving a patch of disturbed water and a plume of spray blowing away on the wind. There was another ahead and yet another on the larboard side. Three guns had fired. He could imagine the difficulty of traversing the guns fast enough to keep up with the crossing rate of the target. Holbrooke was about to make the problem a whole magnitude greater. He nodded at Treganoc.

'Now men! Stretch out for all you're worth,' Treganoc shouted. 'Show them how it's done, stroke oar!'

The flatboat leapt forward over the rippling waves. Treganoc's full attention was upon the steering now. The boats performed most shockingly as their flat bows lifted clear of the water, it took the utmost concentration to keep them on course.

The second salvo came in. There were four splashes this time, all astern of the flatboats. The battery commander hadn't imagined that their speed would increase so rapidly and it was almost impossible to correct their aim once they were loaded and ready. Far better, Holbrooke knew from experience, to let the battery fire and try to aim better with the next salvo.

The point was coming closer now. Holbrooke was straining to make out his head mark. He'd seen it often enough before, but even a slight change in the aspect could make it hard to identify. It should be just to the left of that clump of trees...

'I have our head mark, Mister Treganoc. Steer half a point to larboard.'

He had to remember that he wasn't steering a single flatboat but a rectangular formation thirty-five yards in width and forty-five yards in length. The gap between the rocks was only sixty yards so he needed to keep close to the larboard side – and that meant close to the guns.

It was just a little difficult waiting for the third salvo. The gunners knew the speed of the flatboats now and they knew exactly where they were heading. Again, the sound of rotten stitching being pulled apart. Three of the splashes were right in among Holbrooke's division. He looked behind, the boat following him, number seven, was in trouble. Had it been hit? No, but a ball had fallen among the larboard oar blades.

It looked like two of the oars were damaged. The boat kept moving as the seamen jettisoned the broken oars and pulled the two spares from underneath the gang-boards. No lasting damage then, but that boat was far out of station now. Better to keep going and let it catch up, Holbrooke thought.

Were they too far into the bay for the fort's guns to reach them? Holbrooke thought so, but the laggard boat was still in danger, and now it would have four guns firing at it.

Holbrooke turned around in time to see the boat disappear amongst the splashes as the battery vented its fury upon this last remaining target. He held his breath, and then he saw the flatboat emerging from the spray apparently undamaged.

Focus now on the gap.

'You can see the headmark, Mister Treganoc?'

'Yes, sir. I'm keeping it a hair on my starboard bow to keep to larboard of the gap.'

Holbrooke could see the rocks now, and so could Treganoc. Better to let the marine lieutenant con the boat through the gap; he was in the best place to ensure that he left enough space to starboard for the number six boat.

They sped through the space between the partly submerged rocks and as they emerged Holbrooke spread his arms side to side, an emphatic order for the numbers seven and eight boats to move up onto the wings.

'Let them catch up,' he said to Treganoc.

The stroke oar eased a little and the bows of the flatboat dropped. Steering suddenly became easier although it still made a longboat appear the model of good behaviour.

There was a battery of field guns to the west, but they'd probably been under orders to leave the east end of the beach to the fort. They were banging away at the boats to Holbrooke's right; for the time being no artillery was bothering his division.

Now he could see puffs of smoke from the earthworks at the top of the beach. Some undisciplined militia were firing before the boats were decently in range.

Holbrooke looked to his right; the four boats were in line abreast. With a vigorous forward motion of his arm, Holbrooke gave the order to make for the beach at maximum speed.

The oarsmen gave a cheer that was echoed by the musketeers and the flatboats sped towards the shore.

Half a cable to go. Splash! The grapnels were released from the transoms.

They weren't exactly in line abreast, nor was their spacing even, but nevertheless they made a brave spectacle as their flat prows mounted the wet sand and their momentum carried them clear of the waves. The bang of the swivel gun startled Holbrooke even though it had been in his orders. There was only one opportunity for the swivels to contribute, and that was before the grenadiers had landed, so he'd ordered that they should fire at the best target they could see, or at nothing at all if there was no target. There was value in firing the first shot; it gave the grenadiers a taste of powder-smoke.

All four swivels fired their load of canister towards the defences that were only a hundred yards away now.

'Gang-boards!' shouted Holbrooke, and the four oarsmen at the bows ran the deal planks out over the bows and dropped them onto the cleats that had been made to hold them in place. *Holbrooke's planks*, he remembered as he saw the other boats of his division deploy their own.

The drummer started his steady beat. Overton and the sergeant-major had scrambled to the bows and were first ashore. The sergeant-major's halberd directed the grenadiers; those from the larboard side wheeled around and formed a long rank on the sand. The men who'd been sitting on the starboard side formed the second rank behind them. As if by magic, the grenadiers from number six boat extended the line further to the right. It was far less than two minutes before the company was in position, and further to the right, the second company had also formed up. Captain Overton strode purposely into the gap between the companies, followed by the sergeant-major. There was no sign of nerves now; it must have been the anticipation rather than the reality that unsettled him.

'The First and Second companies of the Thirty-Fourth will advance ten paces. Quick March!'

The drum sounded ten beats as the whole body of soldiers moved forward. A man in the front rank fell, the first casualty of this day, he was utterly ignored by his fellows.

'Halt!' the sergeant-major shouted. All hundred men stopped together.

At the top of the beach, the French militia could be seen abandoning their defensive positions in the face of this overwhelming force.

The sergeant-major went through the litany of orders for the front rank to present their weapons. There was a breathless moment as the sergeants adjusted the aim of those who were overcome by the occasion.

Another man fell, well over to the right of the line.

'Fire!'

The two companies disappeared briefly in the cloud of powder smoke. It had barely cleared before the second rank fired over the kneeling front rank.

'Fix bayonets!'

'The First and Second Companies will charge to the front!'

The sergeant-major stepped back and Overton moved four steps forward. He drew his sword.

'Charge!'

A great cheer from a hundred pairs of lungs powered the two companies on their way. Yet it was to little avail. All that could be seen of the militia was blue-clad figures withdrawing rapidly inland. The eastern end of the beach at Saint-Marais Bay had been captured for the loss of two grenadiers.

***

Holbrooke had seen all that he needed to see. The urgent need now was to reinforce the grenadiers and guards who had secured the beach. Once more he had to run the gauntlet of the guns of the Querqueville battery, but that second wave, the grenadiers of Lambton's regiment, provided the force that was needed to take the fort. Again, the French saw no purpose in standing to be massacred and they withdrew in good order towards Cherbourg as the Thirty-Fourth and the Sixty-Eighth formed up for the attack.

Six times that day Holbrooke led his division back to the beach, loaded with the musketeers of the Thirty-Fourth regiment, then the Sixty-Eighth, then the stores that they needed to sustain themselves, then the ammunition and all the other logistic requirements for an army going into action. When the battalions and their stores had all been put ashore, he ferried ammunition for the artillery. It was indeed a long day, but as a breeze came in from the southwest, they were able to sail back from the beach each time, although they still had to row in. A long day, but at the end of it, Bligh's army held a foothold on French soil and in the morning, they would march on Cherbourg.

***

CHAPTER TWENTY-ONE

September Gales

Saturday, Ninth of September 1758.
Kestrel, at Sea. Off Saint-Malo.

The first gale of September had come booming in from the west, a foretaste of the changing weather as summer gave way to autumn. Howe's squadron was again on the coast of France, caught unawares in this Gulf of Saint-Malo and battling now for survival on the lee shore. *Kestrel* was well offshore having been sent to the north as a screen against French commerce raiders hoping to snap up a disabled transport or a storeship heading home. The sloop was lying to under fore-and-aft sails and the watch on deck was huddled under the gunwales. Only the lookouts kept their lonely vigil, relieved at every glass by fresh eyes.

'I'm trying to tally up the profit and loss of these expeditions,' said Chalmers. 'Would you tell me again how many vessels were destroyed at Cherbourg?'

The chaplain was wedged into a chair in the cabin, and the chair itself was lashed between two ringbolts. Every lee lurch stretched the lashings and the knots, making a sixteenth of an inch more play each time. It would soon be advisable to call Serviteur to tighten the lashings, but that would mean that Chalmers would have to move, and he was perfectly comfortable where he was. Another fifteen minutes, he thought.

'Well we sunk, burned or made prizes of about thirty vessels,' Holbrooke replied. 'Three of them were substantial ships but the rest were snows and brigs and some smaller craft.'

He'd been sent ashore by the commodore to supervise burning the vessels at the wharves and the timber-built warehouses. It had been a simple task to prepare them and set them alight. He'd seen ships burn before, but it had always been under fire. Somehow this cold-blooded destruction of merchantmen alongside the wharves seemed more like arson than warfare. He couldn't stop thinking about the livelihoods that were being laid waste by his actions.

'I saw with my own eyes the levelling of the port facilities, so that must count in the balance,' Chalmers added.

The army engineers had dealt with the masonry structures. The pier, the docks, all the loading wharves, the magazines, five different forts and a dozen batteries, all were torn apart and where they were too massive, they were blown asunder by well-laid charges of gunpowder.

'And the guns that were carried away, a hundred and fifty pieces in all, I understand. Then if we combine that with the damage at Saint-Malo in June, three ships-of-the-line, twenty-odd privateers and sixty merchantmen, we come up with a substantial tally.'

'Don't forget that a foreign army was roaming the French countryside for some days each time. I don't imagine that was without cost to the inhabitants,' Holbrooke replied.

'Indeed, and the tales of wanton destruction make for unpleasant hearing,' Chalmers said reflectively.

'On the debit side, a good portion of the Channel Fleet has been taken away from its normal employment and the navy board has chartered what? A hundred and thirty storeships and transports? A very great number in any case. Then there's the army. I believe the least we've had this summer is twelve line battalions and nine squadrons of dragoons, not to mention the artillery and engineers.'

'What's your conclusion then, David? Are we the winners or losers?'

Chalmers thought for a moment, tapping his finger gently on the table as his chair continued to work at its lashings.

'If, and I say *if*, the army can take Saint-Malo this time and hold it long enough to deal with it in the same way that

Cherbourg was served, then I believe we may say that Britain is only marginally the loser.'

Chalmers saw that Holbrooke was about to object and he held up his hand to prevent him interrupting.

'Also, if we have forced the French to withdraw regiments from Germany, then we may say that we are slightly in credit, although that will be a difficult thing to prove.'

Holbrooke saw Serviteur in the scullery and hailed him over. He could see that Chalmers would end up in a heap against the leeward side of the cabin if his chair wasn't soon secured.

'That's all very well, David, and I can't fault your credit and debit account, but you sound like a clerk rather than a chaplain. Sure, in the hard game of profit and loss, it's difficult to justify these descents. Yet there's more to the art of war than numbers. Don't forget the morale effect of having a foreign army marching unimpeded on your soil. France, particularly, is not used to suffering invasion, and here they are, impotent in the face of a mere eight thousand British soldiers. Imagine what our parliament would have to say about it if Britain suffered such an attack! The government would be toppled in a day'

Chalmers looked cunning, as he did when he was about to announce a checkmate.

'That's true, my dear Mister Holbrooke, and parliament would certainly be a factor if these descents — these raids — were on the south coast of England. But they're not, they're in France, and France has no regular body such as parliament to hold the government to account.'

Chalmers was becoming agitated in his eloquence; his face was flushed, and he was stabbing the table with his forefinger.

'King Louis doesn't have to keep looking over his shoulder and gauging the reactions of a few hundred commoners each time there is a twist in the story of this war. He can force through his own strategy to the bitter end, or until he runs out of his money and his subjects' money.'

'Then you believe this is all futile?'

'Yes, probably. Oh, Commodore Howe is putting his heart and soul into it, and the foot soldiers march where they're told, but I don't detect much enthusiasm from the general or his staff. Do they have somewhere they'd rather be, do you think?'

Holbrooke laughed. 'Oh, that's for certain. There's a British army being sent into Germany through Emden. That's where the real soldiering's to be done, that's where the glory is. You know that the duke called in every ounce of influence that he had to be relieved of these raids and given a command in Germany? The new man, General Bligh, has no desire for this duty and neither does his staff, and I think you may be right, that lack of enthusiasm infects the rank and file.'

'Breaking windows with guineas, indeed,' said Chalmers with finality.

***

Sometimes, it was depressing spending time with Chalmers, Holbrooke thought, and yet he spoke the truth without fear or favour and would do so at the highest level if he were invited. For himself, Holbrooke was satisfied with the way the last month had gone. He knew that he'd performed well in the landings at Saint-Marais and he'd heard from Captain Campbell that it hadn't gone unnoticed by the commodore. If he needed proof that his stock was rising, he had it in the orders that again gave him command of a division of flatboats to withdraw the army from Cherbourg and then again for the landings at Saint-Lunaire a few miles west of Saint-Malo. This second attempt at Saint-Malo had started well and the soldiers had been landed with little opposition. They were now marching east towards the town and perhaps this time they would be successful. It was certainly possible, but Holbrooke worried about how they would cross the Rance, its broad estuary lying between them and Saint-Malo. The squadron could hardly help, the guns on Cézembre Island were still in place and the ring of forts around the town had been reinforced rather than diminished. Holbrooke just hoped that General Bligh knew what he was about.

Nevertheless, it was comforting to know that he'd redeemed his reputation with Commodore Howe. It would only take a modicum of goodwill for his name to appear alongside the post-captains who had commanded divisions of flatboats at two landings, and he hoped not without good cause that Campbell would see that Howe remembered.

He was also pleased to know that Lynton had behaved well in his absence. He'd risen to the challenge of command. He hadn't run the sloop ashore and nor had there been a mutiny. Holbrooke's greatest fear had been that Fairview would have tried to take advantage of the situation, to usurp a portion of the command responsibility, but it seemed that all had gone well. In fact, his two principal subordinates showed every sign of being on better terms of mutual respect than they had ever been.

The only cloud on this glittering horizon was his inability to cement his relationship with Ann. After Cherbourg the squadron had returned to England, but to an anchorage off Portland, not to Spithead. It was deemed an easier place from which to return to France if the wind was in the west. True enough, but it meant that he and Ann had communicated only by letter and hadn't seen each other for two months. Two months! And that while *Kestrel* was operating in home waters.

There was another angle that had just occurred to Holbrooke. Was it such a good idea to be known in the navy as a sea officer who understood the management of boats? For the post-captains it would do no harm, they were secure in their ships-of-the-line and frigates. But for a master and commander…

***

Even through the planks of the deck above his head, Holbrooke heard the cry of *Sail ho!* He'd barely risen from his chair when there was a knock on the door, followed by a very wet midshipman.

'Mister Lynton's compliments, sir, sail in sight to the south,' he said, holding his round hat in his hand. 'The lookout believes it's a cutter beating up to us from the squadron, sir.'

'Very well. My compliments to Mister Lynton and I'll be up directly.'

He turned to Chalmers who was having difficulty extricating himself from the chair that was now so tightly attached to the deck and the table that there was no space for a body to squeeze past its arms.

'If you'll excuse me David. No, do stay in the cabin, if you wish. I believe Serviteur has some coffee brewing.'

By the time Holbrooke reached the quarterdeck, the cutter's gaff tops'l could be seen from the deck. She was hard on the wind with only her mains'l, tops'l and heads'ls showing, and she was making her way north as fast as the opposing wind would allow. In fifteen minutes, she was under *Kestrel's* lee and the lieutenant in command was leaning far out through the weather shrouds, using a speaking trumpet to pass his message.

'Orders from the commodore, sir. You're to rejoin and prepare to command a division of boats to take the army off the shore.'

This was terrible news. If they'd taken Saint-Malo, they certainly wouldn't be withdrawing so soon. A French field army must be marching to the Brittany coast to cause this rapid retreat.

'To Saint-Lunaire?' replied Holbrooke. His words carried easily downwind to the cutter.

'No, sir. It's too exposed. Saint-Cast, further west. You're to make all haste, sir, begging your pardon, and you're to report to the commodore for orders.'

Saint-Cast! It was undoubtedly better sheltered than Saint-Lunaire where Bligh and his army had been put ashore, but it was a long march from Saint-Malo, probably twenty miles allowing detours for the rivers. Holbrooke could imagine the naval imperatives that were causing this change of plan. This westerly gale didn't look as though it would subside soon, and even when it did, the exposed beach at Saint-Lunaire would be difficult, and the anchorage positively dangerous. He could only speculate what had happened on land.

'Get her underway, Mister Fairview,' he said to the master who had appeared unbidden on the quarterdeck. 'Set a course for Saint-Cast, sou'west by south should be about right, I believe.'

***

Holbrooke met the flagship long before he saw Saint-Cast. The westerly wind was trying its best to prevent the squadron of men-of-war and the vast fleet of transports from moving the five miles across the bay, it was dead to windward. Howe was forced to stand far out into the channel before beating back into the new anchorage. So far out that he needed to put his escort force into its proper formation to protect the main body of the convoy, and that was causing mayhem. The masters of the transports and storeships didn't know why they were putting out to sea again – there had been no time to pass the word around them all – and they obstinately refused to stay in formation. Howes frigates and sloops were ranging far and wide bringing in the lost sheep, and like any flock, when one decided to stray, the idea infected all the others. It was less like a convoy than a haphazard collection of ships, each master intent on steering the course that he saw fit.

'Under the flagship's lee, Mister Fairview,' said Holbrooke, studying the figures on *Essex's* deck through his telescope. He could see the commodore and Campbell, but neither was looking at him, they were looking earnestly to windward, presumably willing the gale to abate. Holbrooke had seen Saint-Cast once, and he'd studied the chart; it was an obvious choice if they had to land an army in a westerly gale; or to recover an army. It had a smooth sandy beach between protective rocky outcrops, and it offered the only real shelter from a westerly within a march this side of Saint-Malo. Nevertheless, it was an act of desperation. Immense and overwhelming though Bligh's army appeared, it couldn't stand against a French force of the size that King Louis was likely to send against it. Its only refuge lay in the ships that had put it ashore, and now they were moving far from Saint-Malo. It was uncomfortable at sea in this first of the autumn gales, but on land, with no shelter except the peasant huts that the lucky few could commandeer, it would be miserable. By now, not a man of the army would be dry. There would be sore feet and raging fevers in the ranks, damp powder and a long march to an uncertain deliverance.

'Captain Holbrooke,' shouted Campbell when they were in the flagship's lee, 'we're to bring the army off at Saint-Cast. You're to have a division again.'

'Tomorrow, sir?' replied Holbrooke having to use the speaking trumpet against the howling wind.

'Perhaps,' Campbell replied. 'It depends on how fast the army marches. Some at least will be there tomorrow. You're to come aboard *Essex* as soon as the weather moderates, or tomorrow morning at the latest.'

Both knew the absurdity of that order. This westerly had at least two more days of life before it blew itself out and a transfer by boat in this weather was all but suicide. If they could reach the shelter of Saint-Cast bay by tomorrow morning it would be possible, but otherwise Holbrooke would be bound to his ship.

Fairview was demonstrating his mastery of his trade by keeping the sloop close alongside the much larger third rate. It was an interesting problem with *Essex's* broad sails blanking the wind while her high sides protected *Kestrel* from the worst of the sea.

'There's a French army on the march, Holbrooke.'

He was no soldier, but nonetheless that news chilled him.

'Stay in signalling range,' Campbell shouted and then waved for *Kestrel* to move into her night station.

***

'No night for campaigning, sir,' Treganoc said, his body just a dim shape to leeward of the binnacle.

'No, I expect not,' Holbrooke replied then realised that it sounded as though he were cutting off the conversation. 'What will be the state of the army tonight, do you think?'

The lean figure of Treganoc moved into the dim illumination of the compass light. He was a seasoned seafarer but still he had difficulty keeping his footing in this short, steep sea. He steadied himself with one hand on the binnacle.

'If I understand it correctly, they were probably stopped at the Rance with no way of getting across. They'd have moved upstream, but the French will have destroyed the bridges. Eventually they'd have had word of the forward elements of a French army and decided quite correctly that they are in no fit state to fight a general field engagement. That's when they'd have sent a message to Mister Howe to be ready to take them off.'

Holbrooke grimaced in the dark. He could picture it all too well.

'That would have been the last thing that the commodore wanted to hear,' said Holbrooke. 'He'd have been relying on the gale blowing through so that he could use Saint-Lunaire to embark the army. He'd have had to make a fast decision to divert them west to Saint-Cast, the nearest beach with shelter from a westerly.'

'It's strange, isn't it, how each of the services finds it so difficult to imagine the constraints that the other is subject to. I don't imagine General Bligh or any of his staff imagined that the weather could prevent them using the same beach that they landed on to re-embark.'

'And there won't be many people on Howe's staff who can imagine the difficulties of withdrawing across a hostile territory in this weather with the French army snapping at your heels. You marines have the advantage of seeing both sides.'

Treganoc smiled in the darkness, his teeth showing momentarily white in the gloom.

'You'll be my coxswain again, Mister Treganoc?'

'I will if you'll have me, sir.'

'I don't believe this will be as easy as the last time we cut this caper. We may yet look back at the guns of Querqueville with nostalgia!'

***

Through that long, dark night *Kestrel* kept her station to windward of the squadron. They tacked in the middle watch and as the day dawned and the marks on the land started to be identified, those responsible for the navigation of the squadron began to have faith that they could fetch Saint-Cast on this tack. In fact, with the tide set to turn at three bells in the morning watch, possibly they'd be able to bear away a little.

They reached the blessed shelter of Cape Frehel before the forenoon watch was called. The sea abated dramatically but the wind continued its howling. The swell still swung around the cape, but it was no longer breaking, and it was striking their quarters rather than their bows, an altogether more comfortable motion.

The squadron, the transports and the storeships anchored in Saint-Cast Bay in the forenoon watch. It was still a wild scene with the wind shrieking through the standing rigging and the halyards while the ships tossed and bucked under the swell that found its way around the point and into the anchorage. Still, it was perfectly safe to take the longboat to the flagship and Holbrooke and Treganoc stepped through the entry port only slightly dampened by the elements.

***

CHAPTER TWENTY-TWO

Grenadiers

Sunday, Tenth of September 1758.
Saint-Cast Bay.

Captain Overton led his horse through the close defile that ran from the low plateau, down the slope of the escarpment onto the beach at Saint-Cast. Behind him marched the hundred grenadiers that the Thirty-Fourth had contributed to the army's advance guard. And behind them marched the grenadier company of the Sixty-Eighth. Since they'd been landed at Saint-Lunaire a week ago, he and his two companies had ranged across this odd little part of Brittany largely unhindered by the French Army. In the unusual late summer weather – they were not to know how quickly it would turn – they'd marched the couple of miles to the estuary of the Rance, and there they'd paused, waiting for General Bligh and his staff to decide what to do next. The river was half a mile wide at the point where it flowed past Saint-Malo and the army had no apparent means of crossing it.

General Drury had been given command of the guards and the combined grenadier companies from the line regiments. He'd marched them twelve miles up the left bank of the river almost as far as Dinan, looking for a ford or a bridge, but at Dinan they'd met stiff resistance and withdrew without finding a means of crossing the river. Probably the bridge in the town was still intact, but it couldn't be taken by Drury's small force and it was clear that General Bligh was nervous about taking his army too far from the landing beach.

Drury's force had returned to the army to find them preparing to withdraw. Bligh had received word of a French force on the march from Brest, commanded by the Duke d'Aiguillon. Brest was no more than a hundred miles to the west and the duke could be expected on the Rance in days. To make matters worse, the first Autumn gale had swept in from the Atlantic bringing torrential rain to torment the British soldiers. Overton's horse had suffered from the constant rain and now he was leading it by the bridle to conserve its energy for when it may be needed.

Captain Overton looked behind him as he carefully picked his way down the defile. His men were in good order, but their spirits were low. There wasn't a dry stitch of clothing among them. Their oiled ponchos had kept them dry for the first few hours, but the incessant rain and the gale-force winds had soon found the chinks in their armour. The men were wet, their equipment was wet, but worst of all their powder was damp. His company sergeant-major was fond of telling the men that their long land pattern muskets were merely spears that may occasionally – if they were lucky – be used to fire ball. Well, his cynicism was about to be tested, because Overton expected at least half the muskets to misfire at the first attempt.

It was a relief to see the beach as he broke through the scrubby trees, and a sheer delight to see the squadron anchored off the bay, the hundred-odd ships blocking the view out to sea. But best of all was the long line of flatboats anchored by their sterns just beyond the point where the waves broke as they rushed up the slope of the sand. All was in order.

There were two tarpaulined figures in the centre of the beach, and seeing the column marching down, they walked towards Overton.

'Good afternoon Captain Overton,' said Holbrooke as he and Treganoc strode up the beach. 'You'll be the advance guard of the army, I presume.'

'Good morning, sir,' Overton replied. 'Good morning Mister Treganoc, you'll forgive me if I don't remove my hat,' he added with a strained smile. 'We are indeed the advance guard, in fact we are the very point of the bayonet, being the advance of the advance. However, when the main body of the army arrives, we must transform ourselves into the rearguard.'

He paused to allow his two friends to admire his witty reply, but to no avail. Disappointed, he continued.

'I'm to hold this southern end of the embarkation,' he said sweeping his arm from the defile to the point of land to their south, at the furthest extent of the beach.

'Who commands the advance guard, is it still General Drury?' asked Holbrooke.

'Yes. He has all the grenadiers and a half battalion of guards. Perhaps fifteen hundred men in all. And that reminds me, excuse me a moment.'

He turned to dispatch a lieutenant to tell the general that he'd made contact with the beach.

'One moment, Captain,' Treganoc interrupted. 'Before the messenger goes, have you seen these defensive works?'

Now it was pointed out, Overton could see the earthworks in front of him. He'd seen Holbrooke and Treganoc scramble down from what looked like a sand dune when he approached, but now he looked more closely he could see that it was a trench-line dug at the point where the sand gave way to soil. He followed it with his eyes and saw that it extended the whole length of the beach. Surely the navy hadn't had time to dig this in anticipation of the army arriving. Of course not, he must have been blind, the works had been in place for months if not years. They were weathered and crumbled in places, and they were constructed to face the sea. They were surely French defences, presumably dug by the local militia during some earlier alarm in case Saint-Cast was used as a landing site.

'They face the wrong way, of course, but something could be made of them if the French appear before you're all embarked,' Treganoc continued.

'Thank you, Mister Treganoc, much obliged.' It was an essential piece of information and Overton would have looked particularly dull if he'd failed to mention it in his report.

Overton scribbled a brief message and gave it to the lieutenant who turned and made his way back up the escarpment with a file of grenadiers.

***

'Have you seen anything of the enemy?' Overton asked.

'Nothing at all,' Treganoc replied. 'We kept off the beach until we saw you at the top there; this is the first time we've touched the sand…'

A skirmisher on the left of the column, with lungs of brass shouted, 'cavalry, sir, on the beach.'

There was an instant stirring among the soldiers. Overton took a quick look then swung himself into his saddle, the better to be seen by his grenadiers.

'The Thirty-Fourth will form a line!' he shouted, restraining his capering horse, indignant at being mounted after such a pleasant walk. He gestured with his drawn sword for the line to be formed facing the horsemen.

The sergeant-major turned to face the column that was still entering the beach from the defile and issued his orders in a voice calculated to carry in the heat of battle. As the last men of the two companies slid down, they moved automatically into their places at the left of the line. Each man cast off his tarpaulin coat and left it on the ground behind him. The red and yellow of the Thirty-Fourth Regiment of Foot gleamed in the sodden air.

Now there was a double row of bayonets facing the French horsemen, stretching from the base of the escarpment to the line of the earthworks. The grenadiers couldn't be outflanked either on the left or the right, not without the horsemen risking being trapped between the trenches and the sea.

'Hussars,' announced Treganoc who'd borrowed Holbrooke's telescope. 'About a half squadron, probably the first scouts for the Duke d'Aiguillon's army.'

The French hussars commanded the beach above the earthworks, but only as long as they stayed out of musket range of Overton's line. They wheeled and gestured, unsure what to do next.

'The Thirty-Fourth will advance,' Overton announced. The drummer struck up a preliminary roll that turned into a marching beat. At the sergeant-major's command, the whole line stepped purposefully towards the hussars.

Holbrooke stayed close behind the line, partly for security and partly out of curiosity. He'd never been in a land battle before. He could see the hussars' indecision. A hundred and fifty yards separated them from the line of bayonets now and they were withdrawing as the British advanced. It was a stalemate, but the hussars were at the greatest peril of unforeseen circumstances. Were they leaving it too late?

Overton stood in his stirrups. 'The Thirty-Fourth will charge!'

The drummer's rhythm increased. The officers on foot drew their swords and the sergeant-major gave the order. With a mighty cheer, the whole line broke into a run, their muskets and swords levelled at the enemy. Overton wasn't trusting his damp powder; he'd settle this stalemate by the bayonet!

Holbrooke ran awkwardly behind, clutching his sword to avoid it becoming entangled in his legs. Treganoc's uniform was better suited to this kind of activity and he ran smoothly behind the line.

The grenadiers were shouting now, and the hussars saw their imminent peril. At a command they wheeled away to withdraw at a canter along the beach. All but two, who tragically chose to turn towards each other. They collided and down they went, horses and riders entangled in stirrups and reins. The two men made frantic efforts to get to their feet, one even drew his sword while still trapped under his horse, but too late. The line of red and yellow surged over them. There was a bulge as the grenadiers nearest to the fallen Frenchmen paused. The muskets rose and fell. Holbrooke didn't see the bayonets do their bloody work, but when the line had passed on, both men were already mortally wounded. No less than three bayonets had pierced each of them and their lifeblood was pouring out on the sand. The horses were untouched, and they scrambled to their feet, looking puzzled as to how to rejoin the herd. It was a pitiless action, but there was little room for chivalry in a bayonet charge.

The hussars were chased halfway along the beach, turning in their saddles to voice their fury at the British infantry. When he was satisfied, Overton halted the line. He knew that there was no chance of catching them, but he'd at least given them a bloody nose.

The grenadiers were breathing hard, but there were smiles and slapping of backs as they re-formed the line. This was their business; they had no feeling whatsoever for the wreckage of good men that lay on the sandy soil behind them. They were the enemy, not fathers and husbands and sons, not men who they could share a drink with. They were the enemy, and not a man in the ranks gave them a moment's thought.

***

'Well, that answers the question about the whereabouts of the French army,' Treganoc commented. 'They won't be less than twenty miles behind the hussars, and now they know where we are. They'll certainly be here tomorrow.'

'In that case, we're ready to take you off the shore now,' said Holbrooke, 'we should have you all back in the transports before dark,' he continued looking at his watch.

'Unfortunately, that won't be the case,' said Overton, looking away. 'The main body is planning to make camp for the night at Matignon; that's nearly three miles from here.'

Treganoc glanced at Holbrooke. Sheer madness, he thought. Today General Bligh could enjoy an orderly withdrawal from the beach. Tomorrow he would have to fight even to get onto the beach.

'Will the general change his plans when he hears that the French scouts have found us?' Treganoc wasn't prepared to let this go.

Overton paused, embarrassed to be discussing his general's thoughts in front of a sailor and a marine.

'I think not, he's fixed in his purpose once he's decided his course of action. He wants his army to march onto the beach after having refreshed overnight.'

They were saved from further speculation by the sound of a drum. The escarpment above the beach was pierced by four defiles, and down the one nearest the centre of the beach he could see a much larger body marching. There were more horses in this group – General Drury's staff presumably – although it was still predominantly infantry.

***

The commander of the French hussars held his squadron out of musket range; he was evidently counting the companies coming off the escarpment. When he was satisfied, he turned away and dictated notes to a junior officer who wrote on a piece of paper. Then, anxious not to be encircled and having seen all he came to see, he wheeled his horse's head around and cantered away to the north.

The advance guard was an impressive sight. Tired and wet they may be, but they were the pick of the army, and they carried themselves accordingly. Column after column marched down onto the beach, just over a thousand men after the half battalion of guards had been left at the small town of Saint-Cast to hold the top of the escarpment. The companies of grenadiers wheeled to the left and the right in turn and formed up in lines along the top of the beach.

'Here comes Captain Rowley,' said Holbrooke seeing a longboat hastening towards the shore. 'He commands the embarkation, and this time he'll do it from the shore. Five of us division commanders will stay on the beach until the army is embarked. Three of the others are post-captains and one's a commander like me. We're to see to the orderly loading of the flatboats.'

That made Overton stare. Three post-captains and two commanders to organise the embarkation and be the last to leave the beach! That was a perilous duty indeed. It was all very well if the enemy wasn't pressing from behind, but that was hardly likely to be the case now that the hussars had found the embarkation beach.

'Sergeant-Major,' said Overton, 'let the men rest for a moment. When I return, we'll have to do something about these earthworks so that they at least make a pretence of facing inland. I'm going to report to the general.'

'And I must report to Captain Rowley,' said Holbrooke.

***

CHAPTER TWENTY-THREE

Delay and Frustration

Sunday, Tenth of September 1758.
Saint-Cast Bay.

Holbrooke had met General Drury during the landing. He commanded the guards brigade but had been extracted to lead the combined grenadier companies taken from each of the line regiments and a half battalion of his guards. It had always been an important service, but now it was vital. This rearguard would have to hold the beach against a French army and perhaps extricate itself and re-embark under fire; a complicated and dangerous manoeuvre that had rarely been accomplished before.

'As you see, general,' said Rowley, 'we are ready to embark the army immediately.'

Rowley had been briefed by Holbrooke on the army's overnight plans but chose to pretend that he imagined the army would be following close behind the advance guard.

'That won't be necessary, Captain,' Drury replied. 'The main body of the army will embark tomorrow. I would be grateful if you would kindly arrange for your boats to be on the beach at first light.'

Rowley paused, regarding Drury with a thoughtful eye. A major-general was only one rank higher than a post-captain and the stakes were high.

'General, as I understand it, tomorrow we will have a French field army about our ears. It will be a bloody business to embark the army even with Mister Howe's squadron providing covering fire. If the army marches now, we'll be clear of the beach before the French arrive. Surely that's worth attempting?'

Drury was not an inflexible man. He was a good soldier and understood better than Rowley the dangers of staying on the French shore another night. Even a quite modest enemy force could disrupt the embarkation. His guards and grenadiers would be in the greatest danger, having to hold the beach while the main body embarked, then withdraw to the boats under fire from the top of the escarpments. He knew well the efficiency of the French field artillery and could easily visualise the speed of the horse-drawn guns taking position on the escarpment when the British rearguard vacated it. He and his men would be subjected to canister and ball from commanding positions as they hurried to the boats. He considered Rowley before replying.

'You make an eloquent point, Captain Rowley. I'll send a message to General Bligh, but don't hold out very much hope. I'll have a reply in perhaps two hours, can you hold your boats off the beach that long?'

'I'll hold them all day and all night if I have to, sir. They'll follow the tide in as it rises. The sea isn't too bad at present, but if the wind veers much more northerly this beach will be untenable. I implore you, general, to do whatever you can to hasten the army.'

***

The reply came in just an hour. The main body would be on the beach at nine o'clock on the morrow. No explanation, but then nobody had expected one. It was just one of those fateful military decisions that would be inexplicable to future historians.

The boats lay off the beach until there was no possibility of their being employed that night. The sun set in the last dogwatch but there was still an occasional illumination from the quarter moon that appeared between the scudding clouds, until that also set in the first watch. Then there was no point in remaining and Rowley made the signal for the flatboats to return to their mother ships.

During the middle watch the wind did indeed veer, a full four points into the northwest and the anchorage felt the force of the swell as it was funnelled and shortened in its passage around Saint-Cast Point.

***

As the ships' bells rang eight for the end of the middle watch, the boats and their crews were underway again, nosing up to the shore, hoping for an early start. There was no sign of the main body of the army.

Rowley's boat came within hailing distance of Holbrooke's.

'It's time for us all to go ashore, Captain Holbrooke,' he called, 'the other three are on their way.'

There were to be five sea officers on the beach: Joshua Rowley of *Montague*, a sixty-gun fourth-rate; Jervis Maplesden of *Portland,* a smaller fifty-gun fourth-rate; William Paston of *Jason*, a forty-gun fifth-rate; John Elphinstone of the eight-gun sloop *Salamander*, a commander like Holbrooke, and Holbrooke himself. They each had an older midshipman or master's mate as a runner. Holbrooke had selected Edney as his second. It was a prodigious outpouring of the squadron's leadership and a tangible demonstration of the navy's determination to extract the army from this perilous shore.

The boats were silent as they rowed to the beach. Only Holbrooke's was rowed by men who were not from his own ship, but even they had become attached to Holbrooke over the past weeks and they well understood the gravity of the situation. Treganoc looked tense, the first sign of nerves that Holbrooke could remember in his marine lieutenant.

'Can't I come with you, sir,' Treganoc asked in a whisper. 'I'm not one for signs and omens, as you know, but I've a bad feeling about today. I'd be a lot easier if I was with you, guarding your back, as it were. Mister Edney can manage this boat.'

'You know that's not possible, Treganoc. You're needed here.'

'That's right, sir,' said the stroke oar, eavesdropping shamelessly and imposing on the freedom of the pre-dawn.

'Ain't nobody can steer this old hulk like you can.'

'Look!' said Treganoc, and he pointed to the northern part of the bay. The first grey light of the morning played on the high ground above the beach and showed a column of marching men, their forms indistinct in the dim light.

'Friend or foe, I wonder,' asked Holbrooke, but in his heart, he knew the answer.

'The French for certain, sir,' Treganoc replied. 'They've come from the west, along the shore of the Fresnaye Bay, not from the south. That's the advance guard of the Duke d'Aiguillon's army come from Brest and they must have marched through the night. They're moving towards Saint-Cast. They'll be held for a while by General Drury's guards, but only until their line regiments arrive, then our rearguard will have to withdraw and give up the town. It'll squeeze General Bligh and our own main body.'

Holbrooke could see the problem for himself. If the French took Saint-Cast before the British main body had passed the town and was on the beach, they could threaten the long column and perhaps even cut off a part of it, leaving it with no way down to the waiting boats. The question now was which of the two armies would reach its objective first.

They rowed on in silence, the flatboat bucking and rolling to the waves that were slanting around the point, it's head repeatedly pushed from its right course by the gale-force winds.

Holbrooke felt rather than saw Treganoc slip the kedge. In these conditions it would be essential in getting the heavy boats through the surf on their return journey.

The flatboat's bows slammed onto the beach. This was a real test of the boatbuilders' skill as the whole weight of the boat was dropped from three feet onto the hard, wet sand. There was no sound of splintering wood or clench nails being ripped out of timber, just a solid thump.

At least there was no need to run the boat far up the beach because only Holbrooke would be disembarking. He felt Treganoc shake his hand before he left, the first time he'd presumed on such intimacy in their eight months together. It was strangely touching and left Holbrooke with a sense of foreboding.

Edney looked nervous as well. Holbrooke was starting to regret bringing him, not because he doubted his capability or his steadiness, but because Treganoc's fears were well-founded. This most certainly *was* a dangerous mission.

***

This time the beach was secure, even if the heights to the north were in enemy hands. There'd be no French hussars to cause an alarm. Only a regular force of infantry could overwhelm General Drury's rearguard positions. The earthworks were just visible now, the freshly turned soil showing dark against the sand and bleached grasses. The grenadiers and guards hadn't wasted the night. The inland face of the earthworks was now a steep, high obstacle, and the seaward side had been improved with firing steps and enough depth to shield the defenders. It wouldn't stand a regular attack but perhaps it would hold back the French until the main body of Bligh's army had been embarked in the transports. However, it wouldn't help the rearguard when their turn came to run for the boats. Holbrooke did a mental calculation, the same one that he'd worked on a dozen times before. There were sixteen hundred men under General Drury's command and each of the boats could take fifty. The whole rearguard would need about forty boats to take them off the beach in one go. The squadron didn't have that many, even if the flatboats were augmented with ships' longboats and yawls. They would have to extract the rearguard in two waves. The last eight hundred or so men would have to hold a portion of the beach for thirty minutes while the boats ran back to the transports, unloaded their cargo and returned to the beach. It could be a long thirty minutes.

***

'You know your orders, gentlemen,' said Captain Rowley as the five captains stood in the centre of the beach. 'We'll need to use the whole beach, even though the northern end will undoubtedly be under French artillery fire within the hour.'

He didn't flinch at all even though that was the part of the beach that he'd allocated to himself.

'At all costs the embarkation must be carried out in an orderly manner, and that's our job. I've agreed with General Drury that we may override any orders from his officers in the interests of getting the army off the beach as swiftly as possible. Mister Elphinstone and Mister Holbrooke, the army doesn't understand the subtlety of our ranks, so you will conduct yourselves as though you are both post-captains. I don't intend to enlighten the soldiers.'

Holbrooke glanced at John Elphinstone. He was a master and commander like himself but considerably older, perhaps in his thirties. He'd languished through the peace as a half-pay lieutenant and it was only the coming of the present war that had brought him his promotion. He'd been in command for over a year and would certainly be more anxious about his future than even Holbrooke was. He looked keen and eager but couldn't hide his tension.

'My final thought, gentlemen, is this,' he paused, but there was no need, he already had their attention. 'It's our duty, as I see it, to be the last men off this beach. No soldier should be able to say that he was left behind while one of us five rowed away to safety.'

The gale howled over their heads, the waves pounded on the beach and blown sand stung their faces. Without a word they each shook hands and moved away to their posts. Holbrooke had the southern end of the beach, furthest away from the advancing French as befit his status as the most junior of the company. He and Edney turned their backs to the wind and walked the half-mile south to their sector.

***

It was growing lighter by the minute and now the grenadiers of the Thirty-Fourth could be easily recognised by their red uniforms with yellow facings and tall distinguishing hats. They were spaced along the hundred-and-fifty yards that made up their portion of the defensive earthworks. There was a grenadier for every three yards and a reserve fifty yards in the rear, still hurriedly constructing a semi-circular embankment of their own: a shelter against direct artillery fire until they were called to the part of the line where they were most needed. The grenadiers of the Sixty-Eighth occupied the other half of Holbrooke's sector on the right of the Thirty-Fourth. It was comforting that Captain Overton commanded both companies in Holbrooke's sector, it would make the control of the beach so much easier.

***

'There's no sign of the army yet,' said Overton. 'They'd better be marching otherwise they'll be cut off. You can hear the French skirmishers now; they must be on the outskirts of Saint-Cast already.'

Holbrooke looked at his watch. The time was flying by and it was already eight o'clock. His only contribution so far was to insist that Overton levelled his earthworks in two places to make a road for the main body of the army. He could just imagine the disastrous delay and confusion if the marching column with its ammunition carts and baggage should be faced with a five-foot wall of compacted earth and sand while the French artillery played upon them.

Now everything was ready. Behind him the four flatboats and a mixed bag of ships' boats were straining at their bow anchors fifty yards off the beach. He could see Treganoc, at the far southern end, saying something to the quarter gunner in the bows and testing the training and elevation of the swivel. The oarsmen looked relaxed even in this strong wind, lounging on their thwarts, their oars inside the boats.

'Do you hear something, sir?' asked Edney, cocking his

ear to the south.

At first Holbrooke could detect nothing but the howling of the gale. Then he heard it faintly, the sound of drums beating the time for a march. Not a single drum, he realised, but a great number, all beating the same rhythm each at a slightly different time to the others, so that it was a constant hum of sound. That's why he hadn't heard it before, it sounded like another part of the harsh melody of the gale.

They stared hard at the top of the escarpment. The dragoons came first, riding with their swords drawn and looking warily in all directions. They would have heard that the rearguard held the town and the beach, and that the enemy was approaching from the west, but this was no time to let their guard slip. Two companies of horsemen split off and moved north along the escarpment, and two more moved south. The remainder held their positions, leaving a lane for the marching column.

Holbrooke and Edney hurried forward to meet the column before it reached the earthworks. Holbrooke glanced at his watch. Nine o'clock.

Very faintly now came the sound of fifes as well as drums. Between the groups of dragoons, a splash of reds and blues and whites and yellows burst into view; the colours of the leading line regiments of the First Brigade. Down they came, in a long line, losing some of their formation as they scrambled down the escarpment, but the barking of the sergeants soon brought them back to order as they marched onto the flat surface at the bottom of the hill.

General Bligh's army had arrived, but so had the Duke d'Aiguillon's and the scene was set for a bloody day's work.

***

CHAPTER TWENTY-FOUR

A Fighting Withdrawal

Monday, Eleventh of September 1758.
Saint-Cast Bay.

A horseman at the head of the leading regiment cantered up to Holbrooke and stopped in a spray of sand. He was a staff officer by the look of his gear and by the way he appeared to have no function in directing the regiments behind him.

'Major Vaughan, at your service,' he said, 'I second General Mostyn of the First Brigade...'

This was the moment for Holbrooke to assert himself. He cut off the major before he'd finished explaining himself.

'Captain Holbrooke of the navy,' he said just in case there was any chance of the major confusing the land service rank of captain with that of the sea service. 'Take your brigade to the north end of the beach,' he said, waving his arm to the right. 'Captain Rowley will give you your orders for embarkation.'

Without waiting for a response, Holbrooke turned to Edney.

'Run to Captain Rowley, Mister Edney, and tell him the First Brigade is on its way. Be sure to name Major Vaughan. Hurry, you must be there before the column.'

It was half a mile to where Rowley was waiting, and Edney set off at a steady jogging run, muttering to himself in time to the beat of his feet on the sand; 'First Brigade, Major Vaughan. First Brigade, Major Vaughan. First Brigade...'

For a moment it looked as though Vaughan may demur, may have his own orders, or his own ideas of where his brigade should embark. Perhaps he was less than entirely happy to be marching his men towards the sound of the

238

field artillery. However, with his commanding general far to the rear of the brigade, and with the urgency of the situation plain in the imperious way that this naval captain directed him, he doffed his hat and marched on with the colours of his leading battalion, from the Fifth Regiment of Foot, following close behind.

Holbrooke breathed a sigh of relief. Although he was furthest from danger at this southern end of the beach, he was the first contact that the main body of the army would have with the navy. It would be all too easy to allow disagreement and confusion as to who commanded. It may be different when the first of the army's generals came down the slope, but he would face that problem when it arrived. He looked over his shoulder for the reassurance of General Drury, but he was far up the beach, confronting the French artillery.

***

Battalion after battalion came down the slope of the escarpment. The soldiers marched quickly, never looking back, and the baggage trains rattled along behind them. Seeing the carts, Holbrooke realised that they posed a danger to the embarkation. If just two of them lost their wheels as they followed the infantry through the gap in the earthworks, they would hold up the whole operation.

'Captain Overton!' Holbrooke called. 'If you have an officer you can spare, send him forward to divert all the carts to the left-hand path. They can catch up with their battalions on the beach.'

'Yes sir,' Overton replied. He appeared glad to be having positive orders. So far, his men had not been engaged and they and he were growing nervous again. They could see all their fellow soldiers heading towards the boats and safety while they had to hold their positions for an uncertain length of time.

Now the frigates and sloops and the bomb vessels started their bombardment to cover the withdrawal. The bombs were concentrated at the north, anchored close in for the greatest accuracy, while the frigates and sloops sailed slowly to their own anchorages spread across the beach. Holbrooke spared a glance for *Kestrel*. He was pleased to see his sloop move into position opposite his own sector of the beach. No fuss, and as soon as the anchor touched the sandy bottom, the spring was passed aft, and the sloop was hauled around so that her broadside was pointed at the centre of the beach. It was a matter of minutes before the first guns – fired by divisions – threw their shot at the French infantry column that was advancing south along the top of the escarpment. It was perfectly executed. No doubt Fairview was conning the ship while Lynton commanded the guns, a perfect sharing of responsibility for the best performance.

In only twenty minutes the battalions had filled up the north and centre of the beach and it was the turn of the boats in Holbrooke's sector. By now the soldiers had been into and out of the flatboats many times, and their embarkation drill was slick. With the twin gang-boards extended, and the soldiers moving forward to the beat of a drum, they marched up and into the boats, going straight along the centre in two columns and filling up the seats from the stern. Holbrooke used the other ship's boats for the supplies and the horses. There were wounded too, more and more as the embarkation continued. The peasantry was rising against the invaders, the militia was snapping at their heels and the French field army was threatening their flanks. It was hard luck on any soldier who fell out of the column before it reached the beach.

***

'How many more do you think, Mister Overton?' asked Holbrooke.

'That must be two-thirds of the main body now, sir.'

Holbrooke looked at his watch; eleven o'clock.

'You see the French are skirmishing past the town now. The guards will have to withdraw soon if they're not to be cut off.'

'Is General Drury with them?'

'As far as I know, yes. He'll try to hold on until the last of our men are past the town and fall in behind them. That could be any time now.'

Those were *Kestrel's* balls falling among the French skirmishers, but they had little effect, and still the white-clad figures crept ever forward.

***

Crack! Holbrooke heard the unmistakable sound of field artillery, probably a six-pounder. He glanced to his right but couldn't see where the ball landed.

Crack! The second shot, then two more.

'Up there, sir,' said Edney, urgently pointing to the arm of land that jutted out on their left side, 'field guns!'

A battery of horse artillery had galloped up from the left. Now the tail end of the British army was hemmed in from the left and the right and from behind. It was impossible to see the size of the force behind the field artillery, if there was a force at all. It could be an isolated battery of the militia, but whoever they were, they were placing their guns in the worst possible position. Point de la Garde that spit of land was called, and a battery of guns on that peninsula could command the whole of the southern end of the beach.

'Look over there,' said Overton. He'd seen the battery too. 'They can't be part of the Duke d'Aiguillon's army because they would have had to cross our line of march, it must be a militia unit.'

'Orders sir,' said a subaltern, removing his hat and offering the slip of paper to Overton.

He read it once, then again. He looked up at Point de la Garde and nodded his head sagely.

'I'm to dislodge those guns, sir,' he said to Holbrooke. 'You won't have the pleasure of my company for a while.'

***

Without another word Overton turned to his sergeant-major and issued brief orders. A company of grenadiers, half his force, formed in a skirmish line and started moving up the rocky incline towards the guns. Holbrooke watched them with his heart in his mouth. They were in dead ground, below the crest of the escarpment, and the guns couldn't see them, but when they showed above the rim, they'd be at point-blank range for grape and canister. It was frustrating. Holbrooke could see what was needed but had no way of achieving it. If *Kestrel* were to shift her target onto this battery, the artillerymen could be distracted long enough for the grenadiers to reach the top and charge in amongst them.

Holbrooke looked at the sloop. There was no sign that Lynton had seen the new situation and it was too far for him to signal. No amount of arm-waving would be correctly interpreted at that distance.

Then he saw a flatboat veer off its course. For one moment he thought it had been hit, but then he realised that it was a deliberate move to get close to *Kestrel*. It was Treganoc's boat. It spent no more than a few seconds under the sloop's stern, but he could see Treganoc motioning towards the point and the French field artillery. The flatboat pulled fast away for the shore and as it did, *Kestrel* started to turn. The bars of the windlass could be seen pulling through a vertical arc as the spring was hauled in and the larboard battery turned to face Point de la Garde. A pause, then the whole larboard battery fired together. At least one shot reached the French artillery and the shaft of a limber pointed disconsolately towards the sky. It was good but not good enough. That artillery commander wasn't going to be distracted, not when he knew his position was about to come under attack from grenadiers. Holbrooke could see the guns pointing at the rim, waiting.

As the red-and-yellow figures reached the crest the first of the French guns fired. Down they came like toy soldiers. More came pouring over the top and the horse artillery blasted a gap in their ranks too. It was pitiful to watch. Three times Overton's grenadiers tried to come to grips with the artillery, and three times they were repulsed. Surely Overton would withdraw, if he still lived.

The toy soldiers gathered for one more try. Holbrooke watched in horror. The depleted band was going to burst over the rim into the face of four six-pounders loaded with canister. *Kestrel's* balls were still landing on the point, but an artillery battery was a difficult target and they had little effect after their first broadside.

A trumpet call sounded. Holbrooke realised that he'd been guilty of not keeping abreast of the embarkation. Those were guardsmen now scrambling down the defile – they could only be the rearguard – and that meant the main body of the army was all on the beach. The French infantry was pressing hard on the retreating column. And there was Overton, at the head of his company, running and sliding back down to the beach from the point. What had looked like a failed attack on the battery had in fact been a successful diversion to allow the army to retire in good order. A dozen grenadiers sacrificed for the greater good.

Now the only thing for Holbrooke to do was to get the men into the boats as fast as possible. The rearguard still held the earthworks along the whole length of the beach, and the frigates, sloops and bomb vessels still pounded the top of the escarpment. Nevertheless, the French were on the heights in force now, and their artillery commanded the beach. It was a stalemate, if a bloody one, where the French weren't yet ready to make an assault on the beach, and the British still had about three thousand men waiting to be evacuated.

The bay was a mass of shipping and boats. It appeared that everything that could float was on the water, down to the captain's gig of the cutter *Grace*. Every boat was loading soldiers and stores to the limit of its freeboard. With a sweeping glance Holbrooke could see that the boats weren't all escaping damage. Up to the north where the artillery fire was hottest, a flatboat and a ship's yawl were sinking. So far in his sector they were all safe, but for how long?

And the gale still howled, and the waves crashed, and the blown sand whipped across the beach, blinding the grenadiers when they turned to look to seaward.

***

'Here they come,' said Overton, pointing to a white-uniformed column mustering on the escarpment right opposite the Thirty-Fourth's position.

Not just here, but all along the heights above the bay there were columns of infantry gathering for a final push down onto the beach. They were being punished mercilessly by the guns of the squadron. The bomb vessels had found the range of the top of the rise and every minute or so the puff of an explosion in the air indicated where a few more Frenchmen lost their lives. It couldn't be long now before the French commander gave the order to attack. It would soon be more dangerous for his army to hold its position than it would be to charge down onto the thin line of the British rearguard.

Holbrooke looked around. The boats were still hurrying to and fro, the oarsmen hauling on their oars for all they were worth. There appeared to be about a thousand men left on the beach now. The entire rearguard and a few odd units that hadn't yet made it to the boats.

General Drury still had his horse, the only one left on the beach, and he was galloping towards Holbrooke.

'Captain!' He shouted over the sound of the wind, the guns and the drums. 'I'm going to send half the rearguard back now. I can't hold the French for long with the numbers I'll have left. You see they press me on every side.'

'You'll need to hold for twenty minutes, General,' Holbrooke replied, that was the time they had pared it down to for the fleet of boats to make a round trip.

He looked at the boats arriving, many of them just holding now on the beach waiting for their cargoes. One of his own flatboats – he'd come to regard the boats in his sector with proprietorial affection – was struggling, it looked like a part of the bows was missing. As he watched, the stern lifted and the boat capsized, scattering soldiers and sailors into the waves. There was nothing he could do; he tore his eyes away from the pitiful scene.

'Send your men back as soon as you like, sir,' he said, and the general galloped away again.

He noticed Edney beside him, a bloodied bandage around his hand. The lad was wild-eyed and filthy; he'd seen horrors today that would stay with him for the rest of his life.

'Mister Edney. You're to go back in Mister Treganoc's next boat.'

He saw the start of a protest.

'That's a definite order, Mister Edney, and I don't have time to discuss it,' he said harshly.

Then he softened his voice.

'You've done well, Mister Edney, very well, and I'll be sure to mention you to the commodore. There's nothing more for you to do here, you can be of more use with Mister Treganoc. Now go!'

He didn't know how prophetic his words were. Edney turned to run back to the shore then paused. He swung around, removed his hat and said solemnly, 'aye-aye sir. God go with you, sir.'

***

Here they came. Every second man was leaving the earthworks and running back to the boats. The bugles sounded, harsh and imperative, and the enemy infantry columns came scrambling down the defiles towards the beach. It was lucky that they were constrained to four narrow approaches, because they had enough men to roll right over the thinly defended line on the beach. On they came, the drummers in front of the columns dropping back as they came closer, leaving the wickedly gleaming bayonets at the front.

Holbrooke eased his sword in its scabbard and checked the priming of his pistol then replaced it on his right side. There was that sound again, the sound of ripping stitches in old canvas. The sand a few feet away from him erupted in a fountain. That was the work of the battery on the point that Overton's men had expended so much blood upon. He ran down to the water's edge. Everything now depended upon the rapid embarkation of the rearguard.

The right column of the French army smashed into Overton's grenadiers on a narrow front, only four soldiers wide. No thin line could stand against that shock and the grenadiers gave way, falling back towards the beach.

Holbrooke could see Overton. He turned to the trumpeter at his side who blew a few distinct notes. That was the signal for the company reserve, a platoon-and-a-half of fresh grenadiers just fifty yards from the head of the French column. The lieutenant in command waved his sword from side to side and they formed a line. It was line against column now. Each tactic had its advocates for the attack. The French generally preferred the column, it gave more of a shock effect on a small front. The British, on the other hand, preferred the line as it offered the possibility of enveloping the enemy, and that is what happened. The small group of grenadiers ran headlong at the French column just as its momentum was fading. They stopped the French in their tracks, and their wide right wing swung inwards taking the head of the column in its left flanks. Thirty Frenchmen died by the bayonet, not knowing whether to face right or left when they had anticipated charging straight ahead. The right column of the French army was thrown back in gory ruin and the grenadiers summarily bayonetted the few who remained behind the earthworks.

But it was only on the British left that the columns were stopped. All over the beach to the north the earthworks were penetrated, and the French columns were spreading out and encircling the defenders. Bitter little battles were breaking out all over the space between the escarpment and the sea.

Holbrooke saw General Drury, sitting tall in his saddle and slashing down at French soldier. He saw the horse rear up, then fall back and the general disappeared from sight. A mass of white uniforms converged on the spot where he fell, and even from here Holbrooke could see the musket butts rising and falling as the commander of the British rearguard was slain.

Holbrooke was out of the battle for the moment, although he knew it couldn't last. The last wave of boats was just leaving the ships where they had disgorged their cargoes and they were heading back for the beach. In Holbrooke's sector it was still possible to embark the last of the grenadiers, but he could see that it would be suicide to try over the rest of the beach. He could see his fellow captains wildly waving the boats away. That was their own salvation they were dismissing, theirs and the hundreds of grenadiers and guards still fighting on the beach.

Holbrooke's boats were in the surf now, just a few yards from him.

'Now!' he shouted to Overton. 'Now or never!'

Overton's bugler sounded the retreat. The grenadiers of the Thirty-Fourth and the Sixty-Eighth came surging down the beach. There was no drum-beat for their embarkation in the boats, they just threw themselves over the gunwales and into their seats. Most of the flatboats left their gang-boards behind in their haste to get away.

The last of the grenadiers were barely in the boats before the French, realising that they were missing their chance, came rushing down the beach, bayonets levelled.

'Get in the boat, Overton,' shouted Holbrooke.

He leaned hard onto the bows of the boat and pushed it off the sand. That was it, all he could do now was try to join his fellows further up the beach.

Then he saw a boat turning back. It was Treganoc's flatboat with Edney sat beside him with a musket at the ready. The fool was coming back for him, Holbrooke realised. It could be done; the French were still a hundred yards away and coming on cautiously now in the face of half a dozen swivel guns from the boats that were backing off from the shore.

Holbrooke waded out until the water was at his waist. The boat was so close, and then a fountain of water thrown up by a French ball hid it. When it cleared, he saw the boat had slewed to starboard and was pointing away from the beach. Then he saw why. Treganoc was slumped over the tiller, holding it hard over to the larboard side of the boat. Edney was frantically trying to move him, but there was no room in the boat to get any leverage. Holbrooke looked back at the beach. It was all too late. The nearest Frenchmen were just twenty yards away. He waved emphatically to Edney. 'Go back!' he shouted.

Holbrooke didn't even know whether the midshipman had heard him because the next thing that happened was a blow to his side. A musket ball he thought, and then he fell into the waves. The gale roared and the waves tumbled, and Holbrooke swallowed saltwater as his face hit the sand three feet down.

He surfaced and drew a great mouthful of air and water, then the surf took him under again. He felt the bubbles around his face and neck, the sand in his eyes and an overwhelming numbness in his right side. His lungs were on fire. Then he saw the light again and took another breath, agony this time. The grey sky offered no promise and his last image before the waves rolled over him again was of white-clad figures thrusting their glinting bayonets towards him. He was wounded and helpless in the grip of the sea with a relentless enemy closing in on him.

***

CHAPTER TWENTY-FIVE

Disaster at Saint-Cast

Monday, Eleventh of September 1758.
Saint-Cast Bay.

Holbrooke was vaguely aware of a blue uniform and a moustachioed face that hung over him; a French voice.

'*Il se réveille. J'ai d'autres devoirs alors. Je vais le laisser avec vous, monsieur.*'

The blue uniform was leaving, he had other duties to attend to, that much he could understand.

Holbrooke's vision was restricted to a narrow tunnel with an opaque ring around it, the colour and texture of the inside of an oyster shell. The blue uniform drifted through the opaque ring and disappeared. Another figure moved into sight, wearing darker clothing; a uniform perhaps, and there was something undefinably familiar about it... But he was so tired, and he couldn't keep his eyes open. Was this death? If so, it was a peaceful end to existence, and Holbrooke found he didn't mind it at all, if only he could rest, if only he could remember. He drifted off with a nagging feeling that he'd missed something important, an unfinished thought before the opaque ring closed and light faded.

***

When Holbrooke next awoke his eyes opened involuntarily and he had enough recollection of his situation to close them again quickly. He lay still, taking in his surroundings before committing himself to consciousness in this unknown company. For perhaps five minutes he lay still, listening to the sounds around him and not daring to move. He ached all over and he desperately wanted to cough as each shallow breath brought the air into contact with his salt-ravaged lungs. But the pain was nothing to the numbness on the right side of his chest. Pain, as his father often said, was just God's way of reminding you that you're still alive, but this lack of feeling, this coldness, was truly terrifying.

The voices were French, a great number of them. He could hear the cries and moans of wounded men, but they weren't close, and they were muffled. Either the gale had ended, or he was in a shelter because there was no wind over his face. He was alone, he thought, probably in a tent. That would account for the lack of wind and the muted cries. If he was alone, then he could risk opening an eye. He allowed his left eyelid to just flicker slightly, enough to confirm that he was under canvas and that the day was far advanced from when he'd been struggling in the surf. Then he closed it again. Several hours must have passed since he'd been left on the beach, he thought.

He jumped involuntarily when a voice spoke, close at hand now, just inches away perhaps, and it spoke in a guttural, accented French.

'My dear Captain Holbrooke. You've been playing dead for the last five minutes, but even I can see the increased rate of breathing and the movement of your eyes under your lids. Don't concern yourself, you have a laceration and bruising of the ribs, nothing broken and nothing internal. You'll live to see old age!'

Holbrooke kept his eyes closed for a few more seconds, composing himself.

'Major Albach. It's good to see you, sir.' He croaked in the French that was their only common language.

Albach thrust Holbrooke's rolled-up waistcoat further under his head to raise it from the horizontal.

'The good doctor has washed his hands of you. It seems he has more pressing duties among the truly injured. May I ask how you do?'

'Well, now that I know this lack of feeling is just bruising,' he felt cautiously with his hand. 'Or possibly it's these bandages, they are a little tight perhaps? In any case, now that I know that I'm not injured, I feel almost well.'

'I saved your life, you know, and I hope you appreciate it. You'd have been skewered by half a dozen bayonets if I hadn't been there. I had to give your sword away, I regret to say, to compensate your attackers. I hope it had no sentimental value. I saved your watch but it's rather wet.'

Holbrooke shook his head. The sword was a workmanlike article that he'd kept when they'd taken *Kestrel* from the Dutch pirates. His best sword was still in the sloop.

'But I'm amazed that you showed no surprise when you saw me, Captain. Surely you can't have been expecting me. After all, when we last met on the Ems, I was returning to the Austrian army.'

'Would it be possible to have some water, then I'll be able to talk,' said Holbrooke, his voice sounding like an old rook in the autumn, cawing at the falling leaves.

Albach reached behind him for a canteen and a metal cup.

After Holbrooke had drained the cup, he leaned to his side and vomited into the sand. He took another cup and felt far more refreshed.

'My apologies, Major,' he said as without flinching Albach scooped up the sand and the meagre contents of Holbrooke's stomach and threw the wet stinking mass out of the tent door.

'I saw you at Cancale Bay,' said Holbrooke simply, when Albach returned 'In the first few days of June, you were setting up a battery outside that little village, La Houle.'

Albach didn't immediately catch the significance of *the first few days* and *setting up a battery*.

'You must have eyes like a hawk to have distinguished me from so far away. I knew *Kestrel* as soon as I saw her of course, but that's a very different thing to recognising a man at nearly a mile, even with a telescope.'

Holbrooke wondered how much he should say. It was entirely possible that the French army would consider his exploits ashore in Cancale Bay as an act of espionage and treat him accordingly. He looked either side to assure himself that he and Albach were alone. It was curious how he trusted the Austrian.

'For your ears only, Major Albach,' and he gave the Austrian a most particular look. 'I was but fifteen yards away from you on the night of the...' Holbrooke thought quickly, '...the second of June.'

Albach's face took on a comical aspect as he counted backwards from the day that he was sure of, the fifth of June, the date of the British landing at Cancale Bay.

'Yes,' he said cautiously. 'I stayed the night there to advance the work before the guns arrived the next morning.' He looked at Holbrooke in wonderment.

'Well, you'll be distressed to know, my dear Albach, that if I had crawled away a bare minute later than I did, you would have relieved yourself on this very head,' he declared, laughing.

Albach looked confused, then the realisation dawned. Yes, he'd walked over to the edge of the camp just before turning in. Yet he looked dissatisfied, still unsure about what he was hearing.

'You were alone on enemy soil, engaged in a reconnaissance?'

Holbrooke noticed the careful use of words. Albach called it *reconnaissance*, not *spying*. There was a deadly distinction between the two. It meant the difference between being taken up as a prisoner-of-war and being marched to the gallows.

'Not alone. You perhaps remember Jackson, the bosun and I'm certain you'll remember Serviteur. They were with me.'

Now Albach could laugh out loud.

'I was congratulating myself on knowing just where you were without you having any idea that I had left the Netherlands, and all the time you were stalking me in the night!'

'I was. But why are you in France, and how did you come

to save me today? It was today wasn't it? I haven't slept through twenty-four hours?'

'Yes, just about one o'clock, or two bells in the afternoon, if you prefer. You see, I did learn something in my time in your ship.' He looked pleased with himself.

'My superiors found me to be an embarrassment. My own regiment is in Silesia and Colonel Reutter's detachment was necessarily being dispersed. You remember the colonel from Emden? But of course you do; you were kind enough to carry him and his gun to Ostend,' he said looking with affection at Holbrooke.

'It so happened that a letter came from the militia of Brittany asking for volunteers who were experienced artillery officers. My superiors wished to oblige the French and so I was sent to Dol de Bretagne to command the militia artillery.'

He fussed with Holbrooke's pillow for a moment.

'The militia officers are willing enough, but they have no experience at all. You can't possibly conceive of their fanciful perceptions of a battle. It's been my policy to go wherever it looks likely that they'll be in action, and that's why I was with the militia battery that deployed to Point de la Garde this morning; you saw us I'm sure. I was watching you. You're quite distinctive you know, among all that red and yellow. When I saw how it was going and that you were determined to see all the soldiers off the beach, I ran down to give myself the honour of being the officer to whom you would have to surrender. It was quite heroic; I do assure you. Those French peasants have no idea what an officer in the Imperial Artillery looks like, and I ran the risk of being taken for an enemy. In fact, I arrived just in time. I saw you go down, and I saw those French savages charging at you. I stopped them by sheer force and the flat of my sword. A guinea for each of the five of them was the price of your life, and in exchange for your sword they gave you into my custody and helped carry you to this dressing station.'

Holbrooke digested this information. He was fortunate,

he knew. If Albach had arrived a few seconds later, he'd have been dead.

'Your ships ceased their bombardment at that moment, and in recognition the duke declared a general quarter to the thousand or so of your soldiers left on the beach. It was fortunate, it prevented a bloodbath.'

'Did you see Mister Treganoc?'

Albach looked solemn.

'His boat managed to escape, and I saw it return to the fleet. Your midshipman did very well, but I believe Mister Treganoc was badly wounded, or he may even have died. He wasn't moving when I saw them pulling away. I very much hope he survived. I remember so well his generous remarks about my field guns when we first met. Certainly, he didn't move while he was still in my sight.'

He looked solemn and stared at the sand.

'If I may say, it wasn't my guns that wounded him; it was a musket ball from one of those who would have bayoneted you. Luckily that was one of the last two loaded muskets in the group, the other one was used to shoot you. By the time they had reloaded the boat was beyond their range.'

'I'm relieved to hear it. There were enough lives lost in this misbegotten adventure,' said Holbrooke and his head fell back on his pillow.

'And I do believe that the midshipman – I regret that his name eludes me – recognised me. He certainly looked shocked when he saw me.'

'You were a popular visitor to *Kestrel*, Mister Edney would know you well enough.'

Albach nodded.

'You must rest now. You're in my keeping, you know, and we can talk later. I'll bring you a glass of wine, but then you must sleep.'

***

The light had faded when Holbrooke woke again. He felt much stronger now and sat up, looking around him. The only illumination was from a campfire some yards away, and it gave a strange orange glow to the tent. He realised that the canvas was no longer being buffeted by the wind. The gale had expended its fury and moved on up the channel and across to the Netherlands and Germany. It would be a hard night for soldiers of both sides in Hanover.

He was alone. No, there was a sentry outside the door of the tent. His musket was slung over his shoulder, so he evidently wasn't expecting any trouble from his captive. What now? He was a prisoner of the French, although Albach had somehow managed to take him into his own custody. That couldn't last, he knew. At some point he would be given up to the French navy. That was the convention, each service looked after the captives of its adversary service. Probably he'd be sent to Brest, or perhaps to Saint-Malo, although there would be little enough naval presence there after their ships had been burned back in June. Thinking of the French navy brought him to wondering what had become of the other British captains who had been on the beach. He'd last seen Rowley and the others waving away the boats, deliberately stranding themselves with the trapped remnants of the rearguard, faithful to Howe's order to be the last men off the beach. He hoped that they had held out until the French blood-lust had been slaked.

Holbrooke realised that he was hungry and thirsty. He felt filthy after vomiting and he dearly wanted some water to wash his face. He looked down at his chest and stomach. The bandage that had been wrapped around and around was showing a seepage of blood on the right side, not a great amount, but enough to make Holbrooke wonder about the extent of his injury. The rest of his clothes, his waistcoat and his coat and hat, had been folded beside him. His pistol had been placed under his hat; he could see its muzzle poking out under the gold trimming. That was a strange omission of Albach's; even as a friend it would be a fundamental precaution to keep a firearm away from a prisoner. He lifted the hat in curiosity, then saw that it was no omission. The flintlock mechanism had been destroyed and there was a bright splash where the soft lead of a musket ball had scored the barrel and shattered the wooden handle. The ball had expended its energy in demolishing this weapon and it seemed likely that his wound was caused by the pistol being smashed against his ribs by the force of the shot. The good sea-service pistol had evidently sacrificed itself to protect its owner.

Holbrooke sat up. For a fleeting moment it occurred to him that he could try to escape. With the gale still raging, the squadron could hardly have left the bay yet. It may be possible to find a boat…

Then common sense came to his rescue. He was wearing a bloodied naval uniform and was surrounded by ten thousand enemies who had just won a hard-fought battle. His chances were slim at best, and in the likely event that he was taken, he could expect summary execution. There would be little sympathy for a man who caused trouble now, and he doubted whether Albach's influence could help him a second time. It appeared to be one of those occasions in life when he must await his fate, but in the meantime, he could try to clean himself. Although his shirt was nowhere to be seen, his waistcoat would cover the bandage and his coat would complete the transformation from an anonymous wounded man to a wounded King's officer. The canteen of water was still there where Albach had left it. He paused for a moment; his thirst balanced against his desire to wash. He reached a compromise and poured a handful of water that he rubbed vigorously into his face. The rest he drank, the cool water soothing his salt-sore throat.

His refreshment complete, Holbrooke found a barrel to sit upon. He decided that it would be best to stay in the tent until Albach returned. He didn't want to risk his life roaming the camp unescorted, however pure his motives. In any case, from the sounds around him, he was still in the temporary dressing station on the beach, and he'd no desire to see the damage that his squadron and the rearguard had done to the French infantry.

Well, he was a prisoner-of-war and he'd survived the most dangerous phase – the initial moments of capture and the hour after – when the passions of the victors were at their height. He didn't appear to be too severely wounded although now that the feeling was coming back, the pain of his bruised ribs and broken skin was starting to make itself felt.

Presumably he would be exchanged within a few months. It rarely took longer as the British navy had a credit balance in captured sea officers. The important thing now was to be transferred to the custody of the French navy as soon as possible, where he could expect much more sympathetic treatment.

He thought back over what Albach had told him. It was likely that Treganoc had been badly injured, or perhaps he was dead. Most likely dead from Albach's tone. Holbrooke felt regret at the thought, but it wasn't yet grief, maybe it never would be. He'd seen death and mutilation aplenty during two years of intense warfare at sea and perhaps he was becoming hardened to it. He remembered that Treganoc had aged parents living across the Tamar in Cornwall, but to his shame he knew almost nothing more about the marine lieutenant's life outside the service. He must of course write to the parents if Treganoc had indeed died, but he couldn't do that until he knew the facts, and that probably wouldn't be until he was exchanged.

Edney had survived, evidently. That led him to a more encouraging thought – and Holbrooke recognised its selfishness – that Edney had witnessed his rescue from the waves. But what had he seen? He didn't remember being conscious when he was dragged ashore, so all that Edney would have seen was Albach preventing him from being bayoneted out of hand. What report would he give to Lynton?

There was another thought. What of his command of *Kestrel*? This wasn't the Jamaica Station. There were dozens of hopefuls waiting for a sloop and it was unlikely that Lynton would be given temporary command in his absence. Unless he was exchanged very, very quickly, it was probable that *Kestrel* would be given to another newly-promoted commander.

His heart raced at the thought. Would he be posted? He'd done well on the beach at Saint-Cast, at least he thought he had. Would it merit Howe's recommendation, and would that be enough for their lordships to take notice of him? It made sense, but sense rarely had anything to do with it. He knew that he was still woefully short of influence. At the Admiralty, only Admiral Forbes knew him, because he'd been the motivating force behind the Emden blockade.

He was forgetting the Admiralty Secretary, Clevland. He may also have a good opinion after their two meetings. Holbrooke had acquiesced in concealing a scandal when his then first lieutenant had attempted to murder him. Yes, Forbes and Clevland probably had a fair opinion of him.

His mind strayed to his father, and then to Ann. They were the only two people outside the service who would feel much regret at the news of his possible death – at least he *hoped* that Ann would feel regret. How long before the story of his survival reached them? The Duke d'Aiguillon was presumably an honourable man; his staff would be making a list of the officers and men that they had captive, and the names of the dead where they were known. It was entirely possible that the list would be sent to Howe before the squadron left the bay. Then the fact of his survival would be known at the same time as news of his capture was received. It was possible, but hardly likely, he acknowledged to himself. The victorious army would have plenty to do before they dealt with the niceties of communicating with the vanquished. It was more likely that a letter would be sent by a cartel, and that would take at least a week. He had to accept that there would be a period, days or weeks, when his father and Ann may think the worst.

***

CHAPTER TWENTY-SIX

The Prisoner

Tuesday, Twelfth of September 1758.
Saint-Cast Bay.

Holbrooke woke early. His bruised ribs were sore, and he was hungry. He had to force himself into civility when Major Albach drew aside the flap of the tent.

'I apologise for apparently deserting you, Mister Holbrooke,' said Albach brushing the dust off his uniform, 'and I regret that you've been confined to this tent since yesterday, but as you can imagine, it's necessary for your own safety.'

'Yes, I understand, and thanks for your consideration,' Holbrooke replied, forcing a smile. 'The guards have been good enough to bring me food and drink, but they haven't been very communicative.'

Albach moved closer and leaned in towards Holbrooke, cupping his hand around his mouth so that they weren't overheard.

'They're my men, the local militia of the coast,' Albach continued in a low voice, barely more than a whisper. 'Most of them speak French more-or-less although they're Bretons. I've forbidden them to speak to you unless it's necessary for your comfort. You know, your soldiers didn't always behave in the best manner ashore and there's genuine anger among the people of this area. My main concern has been your safety. I've stationed a whole platoon within a shout of this tent and the lieutenant has his orders to protect you. I've let it be known that you're a valuable captive.'

'I'm not sure my skin has ever been described as valuable before,' Holbrooke chuckled, quite recovered from his early-rising grump, 'but I'll be careful what I say. I heard the guards changing and guessed they were speaking Breton.'

He paused for a moment, hardly daring to ask the next question, dreading to hear the answer.

'Have you heard anything of the other sea officers who were on the beach? There were four of them and I believe none of them got off in the boats.'

'They're well,' said Albach, now speaking in normal tones and striding stoop-shouldered around the tent. 'They're at the other end of the beach under the custody of the Boulonnais regiment. The colonel of the Boulonnais has no idea what he should do with them. He finds them an embarrassment, and I've offered to take them off his hands.'

He turned to face his friend.

'Now listen, Holbrooke,' he continued changing to a more intimate form of address, 'I've arranged to have all five of you moved away from here before the duke decides what he's going to do with the British soldiers. You don't want to be mixed up with them; they're far too many to receive any sort of gentlemanly consideration.'

He looked knowingly at Holbrooke. Soldiers captured *en masse* could expect to be treated *en masse*, and they had no general officer to speak for them, Drury having died on the beach and all the rest having made their escape.

'The soldiers will be taken to Dinant, but that's too close for comfort to the scene of their depredations; the locals won't treat them well. You and the other sea officers will be going to Saint-Malo, eventually. However, the navy owns no buildings in the town and your men burned all their ships, so until they can arrange suitable accommodation, they've agreed that I may take the five of you to Dol. The bishop there is a friend of mine. I sent my best horseman to him yesterday and I had his reply a few minutes ago. He's agreed to make accommodation available in the cathedral. It's a long ride, at least thirty miles, and we must make it in one day, tomorrow, on horseback. Do you think you can manage that?'

Holbrooke nodded cautiously. He hadn't yet tested his

wound by even gentle walking let alone a day in the saddle on rough country roads. He was too well-bred to ask how on this earth Major Albach had become good friends with the Bishop of Dol.

'There's one thing that I'll need your assistance with.'

Albach looked embarrassed, so much so that Holbrooke feared that he was going to be asked for something that his rank and commission couldn't allow. Some information, perhaps, in exchange for his comfort and safety.

'All five of you will need to give your unconditional parole for a month, otherwise the duke will insist on keeping you under his eye. It will need to be signed in the presence of the adjutant-general, and I'm sure you know the likely penalty of breaking parole.'

He held up his hand to forestall Holbrooke's interjection.

'I only state this because it was so particularly pressed upon me by the adjutant-general himself, not because I imagine for one moment that you would break your sworn bond.'

It was fortunate that they knew each other so well, because Albach's spelling out of the obligations of parole could be resented by any gentleman. Holbrooke thought for a moment. In any event, it was highly unlikely that he would be exchanged in less than a month, in which case there was nothing to be lost and much to be gained.

'I agree of course. And Albach, thank you again for your consideration.'

Albach made a self-deprecating gesture.

'There's a second part that I must ask you to agree. The other gentlemen; they must also sign the parole. I've committed myself to be their custodian and the parole must be signed by all. All or none. Do you think you can convince them?'

Holbrooke thought it would take minimal persuasion once the alternative was explained to them. He knew none of the four well, but his impression was that they were all reasonable men. It wouldn't do to be confident and he'd have to put it to Captain Rowley with delicacy, he was a post-captain after all, but they were very likely to agree, he decided.

'I believe I can put the case to them, Albach, and frankly they'll be fools if they don't agree. Could you give me, let's say an hour, to speak to them? It may take that long to explain how I know you so well before I even touch on parole.'

'You'll be circumspect of course, regarding my role at Emden?'

'Certainly. The details of the fall of Emden are known only to you, Chalmers and me.'

Albach's actions at Emden, his confidential discussions with Holbrooke that at the very least *nudged* the French garrison into withdrawal, would be dangerous in the wrong hands.

'Then I'll bring them here within the half-hour, within a turn of the glass' he added with a grin. 'You'll be uncomfortable here tonight, but tomorrow I'll have horses and an escort for you, and you'll spend the night under a roof with a good bed.'

***

The meeting with the four captains went much as Holbrooke had expected. He was the only one injured in the withdrawal, and he had the advantage of a measure of sympathy because of it. It did take some time to explain how he knew Albach, the story was so incredible, the coincidences so unlikely. However, when he put the question of parole to them, knowing the alternative arrangements, they quickly agreed. Rowley and Maplesden knew sea officers who had fallen into French hands in the last war, and they'd all stressed the vital importance of coming under French navy jurisdiction as soon as possible. There was a much greater fellow-feeling between the sea services.

By the start of the dog watches it was all concluded. The

adjutant-general sent his compliments and regrets; he was too busy to attend in person. His place was taken by a brisk, active French major, festooned with the aiguillettes and badges and lanyards of a general officer's staff. He arrived in the afternoon, trailed by a harassed looking clerk with a folding desk and a portfolio of papers, inks and pens. The major witnessed their signatures on the parole documents and the clerk affixed a wax seal. Hats were removed, bows made, and the transfer was complete. They were now the legal property of Major Hans Albach of the Austrian Imperial Artillery, presently commanding a battery of field guns in the Bretagne Milices Gardes-Côtes.

***

Albach's escort turned out to be the entire field battery of the Dol-de-Bretagne regiment of coastal militia. They mustered before first light at the top of the escarpment, just outside the town of Saint-Cast. That was where the attacking column came pouring down the defile, Holbrooke thought, looking at the narrow path to the beach. And over there was Point de Garde where Overton's grenadiers had shed so much blood. The place where he'd nearly died was covered by the tide and the bay was empty now. Not even the wreckage of a flatboat was left; the only one to be salvaged by the French had already been removed for inspection.

Four French militia officers, forty Breton-speaking artillerymen, thirty-four horses, four six-pounder guns and limbers, one of them squeaking along on a jury-rigged axle and wheels, four baggage carts, five British naval captains and an Austrian major. They made an exotic spectacle as the rattled along the road through the small villages and past the isolated farmhouses.

The evidence of war, of violent conflict, was all around them. The crops that hadn't been harvested in time were trampled, barns were burned, and the stench of death hung in the still air where horses, men and farmyard animals lay yet unburied. After two hours riding, they passed the wreckage of the bridge over the little Argeunon river. Whether it had had been destroyed by the French in anticipation of invasion or by the retreating British wasn't clear, but the river was impassable at this place. They turned southwest and pressed on by an unmade road along the left bank until they came to a ford where they stopped to rest the horses and share a late breakfast.

There were likewise no bridges over the Rance, and the ferries and boats had all been destroyed, as Albach's messenger had reported. They'd continued to Dinan, the lowest point on the river that hadn't been touched by the armies and the first place upriver that had not destroyed its bridge. The farmers and peasants of this part of Brittany had fled to the regional centre of Dinan for refuge in the face of the invading army. They hated the British for what they had done to their land. The five sea officers were fortunate to suffer nothing more than insults and taunts as they rode through the town, surrounded by Albach's militia. That was the most worrying part of the journey. The militiamen were all drawn from the country around Dinan. They knew the inhabitants and were known by them, and there was no hiding the identity of their captives. Albach left the talking to the largest of his lieutenant's; his own foreign accent would only make things worse. The lieutenant evidently didn't relish the job, but he performed it manfully, alternately ordering and threatening the crowd, at one point even drawing his sword. There were harsh words from the people who knew him, people he'd grown up with as neighbours. It was hard to explain why it was his duty to defend these Englishmen who had put the ravaging army ashore.

They were lucky that their uniforms so obviously identified them as navy. It's doubtful whether an Austrian major could have held the discipline of his men if their prisoners had been British soldiers. The sight of the hated red coats would have inflamed the crowd beyond the ability of the militia to control them.

Over the bridge and they were out in the country again and free from the town's mob. Now they could pick up the pace again. Holbrooke set his teeth against the pain, refusing to be the cause of a delay in their arrival at Dol. Albach had warned them that the city gates were closed an hour after sunset, and it would take more than his authority to have them opened. A night under the stars among a hostile population appealed to none of the sea officers, and the militia were all eager to reach their billets.

The sun had already set, and the short twilight was ending as they reached the ancient city of Dol. The moon, just past its first quarter and high in the sky on their right hand, shone down on the six horsemen who clattered through the city gates and into the cathedral close, to be welcomed by the vesper bells of Saint Samson.

This was the city where Albach had been stationed since April. He'd been a regular worshipper at the cathedral, and his genial good humour and his appalling Austrian accent had endeared him to Bishop Jean-François-Louis. It was that friendship that had led him to agree to accommodate the Austrian's British guests, away from the hurly-burly of the French army and in the bosom of a city that had not experienced the horrors of the invader.

Paston and Elphinstone helped Holbrooke down from his horse; he would have fallen otherwise. During the ride his wound had opened, and the good shirt that Albach had lent him was covered in blood. His only possessions were the clothes that he stood up in, his drowned watch, a small, discreet purse of guineas and the ruined pistol that had saved his life. He'd held onto that pistol as a memento of the event to show to his father. He fancied that the scar in his side would match the lock mechanism, it was too good to leave behind. The others were no better off, except that their clothes were intact, if somewhat less clean than their servants back in their ships would have wished. Their swords, like Holbrooke's, had been claimed by the victors.

The militia led their horses away to the stables at the

other end of town. The four field guns rattled away over the cobblestones bound for the barracks. There were no friendly farewells, the lieutenants and the soldier had expended a great store of local goodwill in their defence of these British invaders. They knew it would be months before they were again cheered in the streets as they used to be.

***

The ride through the devastated countryside had been a harrowing experience and riskier than any of them could have imagined. They were used to the martial values of the navy and to a lesser extent of the regular army. They had reckoned without the blind hatred of the peasants and townspeople. The five of them stood in the close at the door to the cloisters, blinking in astonishment at this peaceful place that they'd been brought to.

'Good evening, gentlemen.'

They hadn't seen the dark figure emerging from the gathering shadows of the cloister gate. He was all in black except for a tiny flash of a white clerical collar around the neck. His black cassock reached to the ground and his close black biretta covered his head. Even his buttons and the tassel on the biretta were black.

'I am the dean of the cathedral of Saint Samson, and in the name of His Grace, Bishop Jean-François-Louis Dondel, I bid you welcome to the cathedral close. His Grace is occupied at vespers, of course.'

Holbrooke and the others were still looking cautiously around them, yet not quite believing that they had reached safety.

'There's no need to be alarmed, gentlemen, nobody would dare to even consider insult against you in the close. In fact, your person becomes more and more inviolate the further we penetrate. In the close you are free from insult, in the cloister you are free from even a raised eyebrow, and in the sanctuary of the cathedral you are as close to heaven as you will be until the day of your deliverance.'

The dean kept up his smooth patter as he led them through the next door into the cloisters and on to a suite of two rooms that looked out onto the close.

'There are four rooms here, gentlemen. They are usually reserved for passing pilgrims, but His Grace has agreed to set aside two of them for your use, for a month if necessary. I expect you are hungry. Supper will be served after vespers; my servant will bring it to you. Until then, I expect you want to wash,' he said looking dubiously at their travel-stained clothes. 'The doctor will come to look at the gentleman's wound,' he said motioning towards Holbrooke who was being supported by Paston and Elphinstone.

'I will call again in the morning after prime.'

The dean could see the blank looks all around him.

'That will be at the hour of sunrise, more-or-less. About six o'clock. I'm sure you naval gentlemen are used to rising early.'

And with that he was gone, moving soundlessly across the flagstones of the cloisters.

***

There was no settling in to be done. The rooms were bare except for two beds in one and three in the other. There were no conveniences of any kind except a chamber pot and none of the men had any belongings to be organised. They sat in silence, gazing out of the windows at the darkening world beyond. Albach caught the mood and left for his own lodgings, promising to return early the next morning.

After half an hour, there was a knock at the door and the promised servant brought supper. It was bread and cheese, hardly a meal for men who hadn't eaten since a hasty breakfast on the banks of the Argeunon. Nevertheless, what it lacked in imagination it made up for in quantity. As they were finishing the same servant returned carrying two bottles of wine and five glasses. The man spoke only Breton but managed to convey – by tracing an imaginary tall hat above his head – that it was a gift from the bishop.

The doctor arrived soon after. He had a competent air, spoke excellent French and carried the essentials of his trade in a black leather bag.

'Sit, if you please, sir,' he said in a firm voice. He unwound the bandages – Holbrooke noticed that he was surprisingly gentle – and called over his shoulder for the servant to bring warm water. When the water came, he washed the wound. It didn't look so bad once the filthy bandages had gone and the dried blood had been washed away.

'This may hurt a little, sir,' he warned.

Holbrooke would swear later that he jumped involuntarily two inches from the seat. The doctor was pushing hard on the bruised bones one by one, starting at the lower rib. The pain increased as he moved up the chest.

'Very well,' he announced. 'As my colleague in the army appears to have decided, there is no fracture, just a general bruising over five of your ribs and an area where the skin has been removed almost to the bone. May I ask what caused this bruising?'

Rowley produced Holbrooke's pistol. The doctor smiled wryly and offered the smashed weapon up to the broken and bruised skin.

'You see, it's a perfect match.'

He produced fresh bandages and started winding them expertly around Holbrooke's chest, watched by the fascinated sea officers.

'Now sir, are you a student of the illustrious William Shakespeare?' he asked as he finished the last turn of the bandage. 'Good, then you'll remember King Harry's words before the skirmish, for that is all it was, whatever Shakespeare may have imagined,' he wagged his finger in admonishment, 'before the skirmish at *Azincourt*.'

He suddenly stood erect and to the amazement of his audience, in a solemn, ferociously accented English he declaimed:

He that shall live this day, and see old age,
Will yearly on the vigil feast his neighbours,
And say 'To-morrow is Saint Crispian:'
Then will he strip his sleeve and show his scars.
And say, 'These wounds I had on Crispin's day.'
Old men forget: yet all shall be forgot,
But he'll remember with advantages
What feats he did that day.

'We're not so far from Saint Crispin's day,' he continued in French. It appeared that his English was limited to the works of the bard, 'although quite far from Azincourt. You must keep that pistol, sir. It is visible, irrefutable evidence of your courage.'

He closed his bag and washed his hands in the remains of the warm water.

'Now, I must leave you. I'll call again on Wednesday when I expect a scab to have formed and to find you feeling more comfortable.'

'Well, I've not heard better at Drury Lane,' exclaimed Paston. 'Do you realise that nobody else spoke the whole time the doctor was here? The man should be on the stage. We're certainly getting our money's worth in entertainment.'

***

CHAPTER TWENTY-SEVEN

The Exchange

Monday, Eighteenth of September 1758.
The Cathedral of Saint Samson, Dol-de-Bretagne.

The days passed. The doctor visited again, but they were disappointed of another theatrical performance. He seemed a much more workaday person in the light of day and merely removed the bandage and recommended Holbrooke to let the wound have the air.

After six days in Dol they were visited by a French naval captain who had come up from Saint-Malo. He asked them questions about Howe's squadron, about the flatboats and about the plans for future raids. The Frenchman evidently had no experience of interrogation and he utterly failed in the most basic of techniques. The captives weren't separated, and they were offered no inducements and no threats. It was easy to talk without giving away any information. Rowley told him what he already knew about the squadron, he offered shameless lies about future expeditions and described a flatboat that he knew the French had already captured, omitting details of the larger kind that they had not.

The French captain could give no estimate of when they would be moved to Saint-Malo. There were no King's ships there yet and the navy owned no houses in the town. The yard at Saint-Servan had been destroyed and with it the foremen's homes and the workers cottages. There was nowhere for them at Saint-Malo. He would send for them when the navy was ready to receive such senior prisoners.

He brought new parole papers that superseded the army's agreements. They restricted the parolees to the limits of the city of Dol unless escorted by an officer of the French navy. They were under the jurisdiction of the French navy now and not even Albach would be permitted to take them outside the city walls.

'Our exchange, sir?' asked Rowley. 'Is there any word of a cartel?'

'Your Admiralty has been informed of your presence here and has been invited to offer French equivalents in exchange; we are awaiting an answer. You know of course that these things take time.'

Then his father and Ann would already know his whereabouts and would hope for his speedy return, Holbrooke realised with a start. He'd written letters, of course, but their safe delivery was nowhere near as assured as a cartel letter addressed to the Admiralty. He was surprised at how much he wanted Ann to know that he was safe. Yes, he was concerned that his father should know, but that concern was fading into the background of his preoccupation with Ann.

Their days were pleasant enough. It took a little while for the people of Dol to warm to them, but they'd each had a purse of guineas – a standard precaution when there was a danger of being captured – that they'd managed to hide from their captors. They were able to drink coffee and wine at the inns and offer small coins to the beggars who hung around the cathedral close. Nevertheless, they were captives and the war continued without them. They thirsted for news like shipwrecked mariners craved water.

***

The first letters started to arrive after two weeks. Rowley had a short note from the naval secretary, *by command of their lordships*, to inform him that the formalities of exchange had been started, that equivalent French prisoners had been identified in Portsmouth, that no objections had been raised by Paris and that he anticipated a fast conclusion. Holbrooke had a letter from his father, but nothing from Ann. He was surprised at how nervously he awaited the next delivery.

Only three days later Albach rode up to the cathedral with another packet of letters.

My dear Captain Holbrooke, Ann's letter started. There was something infinitely comforting about that familiar use of *my dear…* That single short additional word made all the difference to the intimacy of the letter. Holbrooke savoured the thought for a moment.

Ann went on to congratulate him on his deliverance from the jaws of death and his hoped-for recovery from his wound, and to look forward to the day when he could return to England. It was a cautious letter, naturally, but within the bounds of convention it expressed warmth and hope for the future of their relationship that Holbrooke was beginning long for. He'd heard the romantic poets speak of love at first sight. It had been nothing of the sort for him, and he didn't believe Ann had felt anything of that nature when they met at Christmas. It was a slow-burning mutual regard, a relationship that they both wanted, without the flowery sentiments and the embarrassing changes in mood. And it was the sort of romance that Holbrooke needed, the kind that he felt he could manage. Unbeknown to him, Ann also thought it was the sort of romance that *he* could manage, and she suited her own actions accordingly. There was more to Ann Featherstone than met the eye, but Holbrooke hadn't even started to suspect that truth.

There was also a letter from his prize agents, the illustrious and respectable company of Hawkins & Hammond, resident at Bond Street, London. Not only had the prize money for *Vulcain* been distributed, which he knew about already, but so had the money for some of the prizes that *Medina* had taken in the Caribbean. Besides, the partners anticipated an imminent distribution from the capture of the frigate *L'Arques* off Montserrat. He was a wealthy man and there was more to come, for *Medina* had taken prizes aplenty in the Leeward Islands and off Jamaica and *Kestrel* had done well in the North Sea.

If he wished, Holbrooke could afford to give up the sea and take to the study of law at Oxford. That had always been his ambition and it had only been thwarted by a family lack of funds. The irony wasn't lost on him. Just two years ago, when there was no question of raising the money, he would have given anything to cast off his master's mate's uniform and take up the gown. Now that he could pay the fees and buy his board and lodging with ease, and support a family at the same time, if that should be necessary, he no longer had the desire for a career in law. Nor would his sense of duty allow him to leave the service in the middle of a bitter war.

He recognised that he had twin reasons for wanting an early exchange. There was Ann, and he longed to see her again. But above all there was a desire to get back to sea, to earn his promotion to post-captain and to command a frigate. He was becoming single-minded, he knew, but as he told himself a dozen times a day, this war wouldn't last forever, and when it was over, he could whistle for his promotion, for all the good it would do him.

It appeared that a letter took about ten days to reach Dol from Wickham. Of course, it had to travel through London and down to Dover for the regular cartel ship, thence to Paris and so to Brittany. Ten days seemed not unreasonable for such a journey. Nevertheless, it raised the question of whether it was worth replying. Exchanges had been made in less than a month, and in this case, with both parties separated only by the English Channel, it seemed possible that they would be home faster than a letter. The next step though, was to be transferred to Saint-Malo, although it would be hard to leave this pleasant spot.

***

Then there was a letter from Chalmers, it was perhaps the most disturbing of all. He regretted to inform Holbrooke that Treganoc had died on the deck of *Kestrel*. He confirmed that it wasn't the six-pound ball that had landed close to the boat's transom, but a musket ball from one of the soldiers that were advancing on Holbrooke. Edney had tried to turn the boat, but by the time he'd pushed Treganoc's body to the side, they were thirty yards from the shore, and he could see that there was nothing they could do for their captain. They'd feared the worst until a letter arrived from Albach, just hours ahead of the formal communication from the French navy suggesting an exchange.

Chalmers had gone straight to Wickham to tell William Holbrooke. The old man took it very calmly. He'd been a sailing master through the last war, and it was very much part of a sea officer's expectation that he may at some time be a prisoner-of-war. At least the French were a civilised nation and his son could expect reasonable treatment. William gave little weight to the tale of an Austrian artillery major looking after his son; he knew nothing of Austria except that they were a landlocked people ruled by a self-styled empress. He had no truck with landsmen nor with empresses.

They'd sent a boy with a note to Bere Forest House, and Chalmers had visited briefly to tell Martin Featherstone the news. He hadn't seen fit to call his daughter, or his wife, into the conversation, so Chalmers could offer no opinion on how the ladies of the house took the news.

At the time of writing, Lynton had command of *Kestrel*, but they expected some change by the day. Lynton of course hoped to be made commander, but he was realistic enough to temper his hopes. Portsmouth wasn't Port Royal, and it would be much more unusual for Lynton to be given *Kestrel* when Portsmouth was full of senior lieutenants than it was for Holbrooke to be given her in the faraway Caribbean.

Chalmers' letter was in many ways unsatisfactory, except in that he'd delivered the news to his father. Holbrooke still wasn't sure that Ann knew of his deliverance, nor whether *Kestrel* was under new ownership.

***

The French captain appeared again, unannounced, on a still, clear day in the first week of October. As before, he came in a carriage, but this time it was followed by another. Both vehicles drew to a halt outside the gate to the cathedral cloisters.

'Gentlemen, there's no time to lose or you will most certainly miss your tide. We must be underway in ten minutes, no more!' he exclaimed as he jumped down onto the cobbles.

'Are we being transferred to Saint-Malo, sir,' asked Rowley. They had all become most comfortable at Dol and the prospect of a French hulk or a damp waterside house had little appeal.

'Saint-Malo? No, certainly not, although we must go through there. Have you not received a letter? Oh dear, then that's why you aren't ready. Your exchange has been agreed and I must have you away from France today!'

They stared at each other as the reality dawned upon them. They shook each other's hands vigorously, then they shook the Frenchman's hand, everyone was smiling. Maplesden almost skipped with joy because in the last mail he'd been informed that a new command awaited him, a third rate, *Intrepid*. If only he could be home before the end of October when it would surely be given to another.

Holbrooke remembered *Intrepid* from the engagement off Minorca two years before. *Byng's Nemesis*, she was called in the taverns of Portsmouth Point. She'd been sixth in the line when she'd lost her foretopmast to French chain shot. Her bows had flown incontinently up into the wind, preventing those ships astern of her from coming into action. Byng's battle was lost at that moment, and he never recovered.

Nevertheless, a ship was a ship, and a third rate was a jump up from the fifty-gun *Portland* that Maplesden had left vacant. Holbrooke had a moment to reflect that he'd received no such letter. In fact, Maplesden's joy at his letter had cast a gloom over the other four. It was evident that their lordships were busy offering their ships to new captains in what could only be termed unseemly haste. They knew that now, and they rejoiced in Maplesden's good fortune, but they had no word of ships for themselves.

Holbrooke's moment of reflection was shattered as Albach chose that moment to ride through the gates of the close, whipping his horse into a lather. He reined in when he saw the busy, happy group beside the cloisters and immediately recognised the significance of the two coaches.

'I'm too late, it seems, to be the bringer of glad news,' he shouted as his horse turned and capered, caught up in the excitement. 'I rode hard to tell you that you're to be exchanged immediately, but I see I'm forestalled.'

He gave a package of mail to Rowley.

'Gentlemen, I implore you, don't stop to read your letters. Ten minutes, no more, and then we must be on the road,' said the French captain. 'The cartel is drying out over the tide at the town quay but when she floats, she must be away. The tide waits for no man, gentlemen, as I'm sure I don't need to remind you. Hurry, I beseech you! There are fifteen miles to cover and when we arrive, we'll still have the documents to be signed and witnessed. There's no time to lose!'

It wasn't ten minutes, but it was certainly less than fifteen. They gathered up their meagre possessions in the handkerchiefs that they'd bought in town. Rowley took up a subscription to give a purse to the bishop for the relief of the poor, and they were away.

It was a wild ride, with Albach cantering alongside the madly swaying coaches. Just past Chateauneuf one of the carriages lost a wheel on the tight bend as the highway joined the road that followed the river. After a few minutes' consternation, while the French captain scratched his head, four of them squeezed into the remaining carriage with the Frenchman while Holbrooke rode astern of Albach on his horse. The French captain fretted and fumed and pulled out his watch every five minutes. He was more nervous than the prisoners on their way to freedom.

They bypassed Saint-Servan and its shocking destruction at the hands of the Duke of Marlborough's army and headed straight for the causeway to the town. There were more delays as the French captain explained himself at the first gate, then again at the second gate. Documents were examined and the officer of the guard called to authorise this fresh invasion by the British. Then a mad dash for the town quay. There was a scribe with his desk already set up as the master of the cartel waited patiently for his brig to float. A passing colonel of the militia, his lady on his arm, was dragooned into witnessing the exchange documents.

And then suddenly it was all over. The brig made its first tentative stirrings of freedom as the incoming tide freed it from the thick mud of the harbour. Final farewells were flung at Albach and the captain.

The master of the brig backed his jib to haul his bows out into the stream. He was being watched by an interested group on the quay and by Holbrooke and the other four sea officers. Perhaps it was the unwanted attention, but he ordered the jib to be sheeted home too soon and the brig hung in stays, drifting on the incoming tide, deeper into the harbour. The skipper of a passing lugger saw the problem and under the brute force of eight brawny Breton oarsmen he pushed the brig's bows off the wind and into the stream. The southerly wind caught the topsail, and the brig started to move forward against the tide. The catastrophe was averted and in fifteen minutes, they were past Cézembre Island and nosing out into the bay, bound for Cape La Hague, the Channel and, by the next morning, the Solent and Portsmouth harbour. Holbrooke breathed the clean salt air of freedom, mixed with the cloying scent of fear – fear for the future, fear for his career and sorrow at the almost certain loss of his beloved *Kestrel*.

***

CHAPTER TWENTY-EIGHT

A Disappointing Return

Saturday, Seventh of October 1758.
Brig Sister Susan, at Sea. Off Saint Catherine's, Isle of Wight.

The near-grounding on leaving Saint-Malo was no isolated incident. The master of the brig was incompetent, and his ineptitude was compounded by a profound nervousness at his every move being watched by a parcel of critical naval captains.

The winds had been light and baffling ever since they had left France, but the master appeared to have no idea – none whatsoever – of the tides in the Gulf of Saint-Malo or the Channel proper. When the stream was against him, he sailed offshore where it was strongest, and when it was with him, he hugged the coast where it was weakest. They narrowly missed foundering on Jersey, the Écrevièr Bank, Alderney, Cape La Hague and, astonishingly, the Casquets. How they came to be near the Casquets was a complete mystery. It was like a drunken game of shove ha'penny with the brig *Sister Susan* being carelessly pushed around the narrow seas instead of a coin on a board in the local tavern. Then, on the Saturday morning, they found themselves becalmed off Saint Catherine's on an ebbing tide and slipping further and further west away from their destination.

It was only a providential sou'wester that saved Holbrooke from spending a third night in the brig and prevented the world from witnessing the unedifying spectacle of five senior King's officers being tried at court-martial for mutiny.

***

'Wish you joy of your new command, sir,' said Holbrooke as brightly as he could, as they passed *Intrepid* at anchor at the tail of Spithead. *Kestrel* was nowhere to be seen, and Holbrooke wondered whether she'd been sent back to sea.

Maplesden was acutely aware of his own good fortune in stark contrast to the uncertain future that his companions faced. The letters that Albach had brought included a note from the Admiralty secretary informing him that his commission would be waiting for him at the port admiral's office, and that he could take command any day in October after Tuesday the tenth. If the master of the brig managed to get alongside in Portsmouth Harbour without drowning his passengers on the Point, he'd be the captain of a French-built third-rate in only three days. He made a polite attempt to conceal his glee, but it fooled nobody.

'I'm sure their lordships will see you right, Holbrooke,' he replied while lustfully studying the handsome lines of his new ship, 'Mister Howe will certainly have a good word for us all.'

He might, thought Holbrooke, but many captains had distinguished themselves that summer, and after all Howe was only a commodore and likely to be a captain again with the campaign season coming to its end. Possibly Maplesden's commission was the extent of his leverage at the Admiralty. No, he was wrong, Rowley could look forward to a ship with some confidence. Paston was already a post-captain and a spell ashore would be no disaster for him. That was not the case for himself and Elphinstone, both commanders and both acutely aware of the fragility of their rank.

***

It can only have been divine intervention that brought *Sister Susan* safely alongside at the very spot where *Kestrel* had berthed after leaving the wet dock, certainly it owed nothing to the master's skill. And there was *Kestrel* herself, looking bright and jaunty at anchor further up the harbour. Holbrooke wondered what he should do. He hadn't been informed that he'd been superseded. As far as he was aware, he was still the captain of the sloop, unlikely though it seemed. Should he hail a boat and be rowed over to his ship? That risked an embarrassing scene on the deck. If he'd been replaced, he wouldn't be entitled to the honours of a commanding officer. His own bosun's mates would have to put away their pipes, and he would be greeted with merely a doffing of hats by whichever officers were available.

He was still deciding what he should do when the gangway was laid onto the quay. The first person to come aboard was a messenger from the port admiral requesting that the five captains should meet him in his office before proceeding further. It was ominous that he didn't say they shouldn't proceed to their ships. The implication was clear; they had no ships.

As befitted his seniority, Holbrooke was the last to be called. Rowley came out looking glum, *Montague* already had a new owner, so had Paston's *Jason*, and they were both bidden to the Admiralty *at their leisure*. They could look forward to a spell of idleness until they again reached the notice of their lordships. Elphinstone too should visit the Admiralty at his leisure. By the time Holbrooke was called, he was reconciled to the worst of news. He was already planning how he would fill his time and calculating the earliest date that he could decently call on their lordships.

Admiral Holburne gave a wintry smile as Holbrooke entered his office.

'You managed to be wounded and captured, then, Mister Holbrooke,' he said before Holbrooke was quite in the room. Holburne was one of those officers who were suspected of using their leisure time in practising the art of putting their juniors at a disadvantage.

'Yes, Sir Francis, but my wound has healed and I'm ready to rejoin *Kestrel* immediately,' he replied. It was as well to play a losing hand to the end, as his mentor Carlisle had taught him. 'I see she's anchored up the harbour.'

The cold smile turned to a withering glare.

'Don't play games with me, Mister Holbrooke, it won't wash. You'll know by now that their lordships have given the ships that each of the five of you *previously* commanded to other captains. They could hardly do otherwise, with the date of your return not known and a war raging. Ships need captains and the country needed those ships last month, not when the French choose to honour their exchange obligations.'

He stared at Holbrooke until the younger man dropped his eyes. His point made; he took a softer tone.

'I happen to know that Mister Howe gave a good report of your conduct to the First Lord. Now, what the board will do with that I don't know, but unlike your fellows you have a definite appointment in Whitehall.'

Holbrooke looked up with hope starting to show in his face.

'Don't get carried away, Holbrooke, there's many a slip twixt cup and lip.'

He looked pleased with his aphorism.

'Lord Anson's still flying his flag over the Channel Fleet, but you're to meet Admiral Forbes at two o'clock on Tuesday.' He looked Holbrooke up and down. 'I suggest you contrive in some way to look a little more presentable by that time,' he added.

'Thank you, Sir Francis,' Holbrooke replied lamely, ignoring the calculated insult. He could think of nothing more useful to say.

'Your property's already been removed from *Kestrel.* My secretary will direct you to the store where it's being kept. Now, I think that's all the business that we have for today.'

'Excuse me Sir Francis, my followers in *Kestrel*, what's become of them?'

'Eh? Oh, I heard something about them. Your chaplain and your servant have removed themselves to lodgings ashore. In compliment to you I've restrained the impress captain from taking up your servant. I believe you'll find them at the Dolphin. All the others; officers, warrants, midshipmen, seamen, marines remain on *Kestrel's* books. I understand that Commander Rickets wishes to make some changes, to bring in some followers of his own, so you may have more of 'em on your hands. Anyway, I'll leave that to you.'

Rickets, thought Holbrooke, he'd never heard of him. Of course, he'd have been an anonymous lieutenant a month ago, fretting on a promotion. Now he was master and commander of Holbrooke's precious *Kestrel*, the ship he'd fought the Dutch pirates for in the faraway Caicos Passage, *his* ship. He already had an irrational hatred of this unknown Rickets.

'Captain!' called Holburne, as Holbrooke turned to leave the office. 'My condolences on the death of your marine lieutenant.'

Holbrooke nodded his acknowledgement. The port admiral didn't even know the name of the dead lieutenant, he thought with disgust. Treganoc. Treganoc of Emden and Treganoc the hero of Saint-Cast. He'd have a memorial set up at his home church in Cornwall.

***

The secretary directed Holbrooke to a storeroom a hundred yards away near the rope-walk. The key was held by a grizzled, stunted old man whose sole responsibility appeared to be the custody of officers' effects. Holbrooke imagined that he did a decent business when the owner of a trunk didn't return to pick it up, which must be a frequent occurrence. His own things were neatly piled against a wall; his desk, his cot, a few chairs and a small table that he'd brought into the sloop. There were his chests of books and his navigational instruments and another for the cabin stores that he hadn't consumed. It was strange to see it all there, all his worldly possessions in one place, neatly labelled and piled alongside similar trunks and bags. All his worldly possessions if you didn't count his growing wealth under the protection of Hawkins and Hammond, but even that thought didn't lift his gloom.

He noticed the absence of his uniforms, and they were the reason for his coming to the storeroom.

'A black fellow was here, with a parson, sir,' said the old man. Clearly Serviteur had made enough of an impression that he was mentioned before Chalmers. 'He had a note from the commissioner's office. They took away your uniforms, sir, but I made the parson sign a ticket for them.'

He waved a printed form in Holbrooke's face and there was undoubtedly a signature along the bottom, and it could have been Chalmer's, but the man wouldn't part with it.

Holbrooke would have given a guinea to see this creature try to prevent Serviteur reclaiming his master's uniforms.

Nevertheless, it was a nuisance. Now he would have to walk to the Dolphin in the ragged coat that he'd worn for the last month in captivity. It had been shot through, doused in seawater and bled upon, and then it had been lived in day and night for a month. The word disreputable hardly did justice to its sheer squalor. The waistcoat had suffered similarly, the shirt was borrowed, and he had on the duck trousers that he'd worn in the flatboat rather than the breeches and stockings that the sartorial standards of Portsmouth demanded. His wig was lost in the surf of Saint-Cast, his hat would never be the same again, he had no sword and as for his shoes...

'Welcome home, Captain Holbrooke.'

A familiar voice. There at the door was Chalmers, and behind him Serviteur.

'I apologise for not meeting you at the port admiral's office, but we only had news of the cartel after it had already berthed. We hurried here as fast as we could.'

'Chalmers, how good to see you, and Serviteur, how do you do? I gather you are both homeless.'

It was like a ray of hope in the abyss of despair.

'I took the liberty of taking your uniforms away, sir, to see to them,' said Serviteur. 'They're in the cart now all spruced up,' he added indicating a hand-cart pulled by a man who could have been the twin of the storekeeper. He grinned fiendishly from between the shafts, uglier than any pot-house nag.

Holbrooke looked helpless for a moment. The transition from ragged poverty to a man with a loyal friend and his own servant and the imminent prospect of fresh uniforms was too much for him to take in.

'This man will leave us while you shift into your shore-going rig,' said Serviteur, towering over the startled storekeeper, daring him to demur.

They talked rapidly while Serviteur helped Holbrooke into his clean uniform. In fifteen minutes, he was a changed man. From the crown of his hat to the soles of his shoes he looked the part, a successful sea officer in the home of the King's navy.

***

'First stop is the Dolphin, I think. You look remarkably thin, Holbrooke. Didn't they feed you in that cathedral? I warned the landlord to expect you for a late dinner and he's promised not to let us down.'

'Then tell me all the news, Chalmers. And Serviteur, how did you come to leave *Kestrel?*'

'I didn't like the look of Mister Rickets and he certainly didn't like the look of me, sir. He had his own servant and Mister Jackson was kind enough to swear that I'd never make a seaman, *not so long as my arse points downwards*, were the words he used, and even the afterguard duties are apparently beyond my powers. My discharge was mutually agreeable.'

'Per order of Sir Francis himself,' added Chalmers, 'who incidentally, for all his gruff and sarcastic manner, has a liking for you, Holbrooke.'

'He has a strange way of showing it,' Holbrooke replied with a laugh.

'You should know that Mister Lynton and Mister Jackson are only waiting for the word to join you in your new ship. *If you'll have them*, they told me to say, not wishing to presume.'

'Let's hope, Chalmers, let's hope.' He never thought he'd hunger for a ship in this way.

'Meanwhile, Serviteur has been keeping me company at the Dolphin for the past two weeks,' added Chalmers, 'and I must say that it's worked very well. My French has improved enormously.'

***

They talked all the way back to the Dolphin. Treganoc had been the only casualty in the flatboat. Edney had incurred the wrath of Howe's staff by steering straight for *Kestrel* rather than disembarking the soldiers first. Treganoc was still breathing when they hoisted him into *Kestrel*, but he was unconscious and with a bullet through his chest it was only a matter of time. He died as eight bells struck for the end of the afternoon watch.'

'Buried at sea?' asked Holbrooke.

'No. Mister Lynton wouldn't hear of it. We brought him home and the chaplain at Fort Cumberland collected his body.'

'I'll never forget how he walked – almost strolled – back to the boats at that jetty on the Ems, with a howling mob of French infantry behind him,' said Holbrooke. 'The coolest thing I've ever seen. Was it only six months ago? It seems like a lifetime. England lost a hero when Treganoc fell.'

They walked on in silence for a moment.

'Edney saw Major Albach rescue you from the bayonets, but he also saw you fall and saw the blood on your waistcoat, so we didn't know how you were until Albach's letter arrived. Curiously, it was the first we heard of you. It came ahead of a note from the Admiralty to say they'd had the exchange notification, and ahead of your letter. And it came the same day as Mister Rickets appeared with a commission in his pocket.'

'I can't really blame the board for rushing to get a new captain in place. Sometimes an exchange takes years to accomplish, if there are any complications or the slightest ill-will,' Holbrooke said. 'Did I tell you I have an appointment at the Admiralty for next Tuesday? Perhaps it's a ship!'

I do hope so, Chalmers thought, for this young man will fret himself into a decline without one.

***

'I'll go to London on Monday,' Holbrooke announced as they finished their pudding. 'That will allow Tuesday morning for my business in Bond Street and I can visit the Admiralty fortified by a feeling of wealth, if the hints in the letters from Hawkins and Hammond bear any truth.'

'You'll need a visit to your bank also, I suspect,' said Chalmers, cleaning up the last of the raisins that had fallen out of his portion of duff.

Holbrooke looked perplexed.

'I have no bank,' he replied, 'Do you think I should?'

'My dear Holbrooke. I'm not a man of money, but I'd have to have my head firmly in the sand to be unaware that your share of our prizes over the last two years will come to a substantial sum. Now, I have nothing to say against your prize agents, except to observe that they're as fallible as any others. You should certainly leave a small sum in their keeping, but the great bulk of your wealth must be in a bank.'

Holbrooke looked thoughtful. It hadn't yet occurred to him that he should have a bank account. A year ago, it would have been pointless, and no respectable bank would have considered him a worthwhile customer, and he'd been so busy since returning from the Caribbean...

'I don't even know where to start,' Holbrooke complained. 'I know that Carlisle uses Campbell & Coutts on the Strand and I believe they do quite well for sea officers. Do you think I should take advice from Hawkins and Hammond?'

Chalmers considered for a moment.

'It would be better not to rely on the advice of your agents. I'm not suggesting that they'd do anything dishonest, but it would be better if you're not beholden to them for this side of your affairs. They may have any number of reasons for recommending a banking house, and not all of the reasons would be to your advantage.'

'Then Campbell & Coutts it is. I'll write a letter now to go by the first carrier. They'll have it on Monday, and they'll be expecting me on Tuesday.'

Chalmers nodded his agreement. His own share of prize money would be substantial, although not nearly as great as Holbrooke's. He'd also need a bank, but that could wait.

Holbrooke had lapsed into that vague look that Chalmers recognised

'Do you think I should visit Ann tomorrow?' he asked.

Chalmers was expecting this question. He paused, pretending to think it through.

'On the whole, I believe not. Apart from the question of Sunday travel which I must officially abhor, while occasionally practising when the trout are rising, I think it would be a little premature.'

'How so?' asked Holbrooke, ready to argue.

'You know that I visited Bere Forest House to tell Mister Featherstone of your deliverance?'

'Yes, but you didn't see Ann, I understand.'

'I saw Mister Featherstone, but he didn't offer to call for either his wife or his daughter. I found that significant. How can I put this? You'll know that he has great hopes for his daughter, that he sees her making a good marriage that befits his growing prosperity and his importance, in a small-town sort of way.'

'Yes, I know that he would be reluctant to part with Ann to any sea officer less than a post-captain. That's why I've been so cautious, and I'll continue to be until I'm posted.'

'Well,' Chalmers continued, 'it's gone beyond that. Your wounding and capture have persuaded him, I believe, that sea officers as a class of people carry a risk… Now, hear me out. He wasn't direct at all and I didn't push him, but he mentioned the rank of post-captain so often that I'd have to be a blockhead to have missed his meaning. I believe it would be better if you *heave-to* for a while.'

Holbrooke sat in silence. The sounds of the high street

filtered through the bay window and the landlord could be heard clattering dishes in the room below. The clock on Saint Thomas' church wall struck six. He walked over to the window and stared out at the still-busy town. It was that intermediate time between day and night, when objects became indistinct and distance indefinite. A blind beggar – a seaman by his manner – stood outside the church doffing his cap to passers-by. He saw an old lady drop a coin in the cap and briefly touch the beggar's arm.

'Serviteur. Take this guinea and give it to the man across the road when nobody's watching. You see who I mean? Make sure he knows it's a guinea and that he secures it well.'

He continued watching as Serviteur fulfilled his commission. He saw the beggar bowing repeatedly and then walk quickly off in the direction of the Point, tapping his stick against the walls for guidance. Even a whole guinea would soon be expended in the taverns and ale-houses, and that was on the assumption that it survived its first contact with the ladies of the Point.

'I find the honourable course is to break off our communication until such time as I'm posted,' he said, turning back to Chalmers. 'Their lordships may do with me as they will, but God send a speedy promotion, if that's not too impious.'

'You are, as always, in my prayers,' murmured Chalmers

***

CHAPTER TWENTY-NINE

London

Tuesday, Tenth of October 1758.
London.

A cold, hard nor'westerly was bringing pelting rain to the capital. The streets were muddy and obstructed by people running from one area of shelter to the next. Holbrooke and Chalmers, however, had taken a carriage from their lodgings and it was with dry shoes and clean stockings that they reached their destination.

The banking firm of Campbell & Coutts had an ordinary double-front of bow windows with a door between them, opening onto the busy Strand. A clerk let them in and took their names and their rain-sprinkled coats. There was an atmosphere of hushed concentration as pens scribbled, wigs bobbed and the immensely important business of looking after other people's money proceeded with due gravity.

'Mister Coutts is expecting you, sir,' said the clerk.

He led them down a hallway to a small reception area with two polished doors leading from it. *Mr. George Campbell*, the brass sign on the left hand door proclaimed and *Mr. James Coutts*, the right hand door.

Campbell & Coutts, Chalmers thought. How strange that they should use the ampersand in the bank's name while the prize agents, *Hawkins and Hammond*, used the full conjunction. Was there a convention that he wasn't aware of? His ruminations were ended as the door was opened for him and Holbrooke.

James Coutts was the junior partner in this banking business. He'd married into the Campbell family just three years before, but now his name was on a brass plaque and he shared the responsibilities with the older George Campbell.

The business of opening an account took surprisingly

little time. Coutts was gratified to have another sea officer on his books, particularly one who had been so successful at taking prizes in this war. Everyone thought there was a good few years to run, and there were more fortunes to be made by active, aggressive sea officers. As soon as he'd received Holbrooke's letter, he'd enquired among the prize agencies to discover who looked after Holbrooke's affairs. It took very little time; they all knew each other and which sea officers they acted for. They needed to do so, because much of a prize agent's work was involved in untangling the complementary and competing claims to payouts. Thus informed, he'd called on his friend Mister Hammond on Bond Street, and what he learned there convinced him that Commander Holbrooke represented a sound investment in the future prosperity of the bank. Of course, Holbrooke didn't know that his new bank was already in contact with his prize agent, nor would he ever know that the link had been made before he'd even visited Bond Street.

Holbrooke left Campbell & Coutts with little to show for his visit; just an open letter confirming his status as an account holder. He had a vague recollection of interest rates being discussed, terms of deposit and the potential for investing in funds in the future, but it was a new language to him, and try as he might, he could take in very little. He was comforted by the assurance that his terms were identical to those of his friend Carlisle, who had kept his money at Bankers of 59 Strand, now Campbell & Coutts, for some years.

Nevertheless, he was quietly proud of having an account in a London bank. Now all he needed was some money to deposit, and that was their next destination.

***

They stepped out of the bank to find that the squall had blown through and in the way of autumnal showers it left behind a keen breeze and rapidly drying pavements. London looked scrubbed clean, if a little moist around the edges.

'I think we may walk, don't you, Chalmers,' said

Holbrooke as a hopeful hackney carriage pulled up alongside them.

Chalmers looked doubtfully at the mud-covered roads and the still-puddled pavements.

'I think not, Holbrooke. You'll arrive looking like a half-pay officer and I'll look like an unbeneficed parson. Let's take a carriage.'

'But I am a half-pay officer, at least until this afternoon,' he replied crossing his fingers behind his back, 'and you, to my knowledge, have no living,' he laughed, 'but I take your point.'

The hackney carriage bowled along through the streets of the capital. Charing Cross, Pall Mall, hard right at Saint James's Palace, a mad dash across Piccadilly and thence to Bond Street, and the relative quiet of this prosperous London backwater.

Holbrooke had corresponded with his prize agents since he'd first brought *Kestrel* back to England, but he'd never had the leisure to visit the premises. In truth, he'd never been invited. It was only in the past six months that Mister Hammond had really started to see the value of Holbrooke as a client and could map out a revue stream that may, possibly, flow from his depredations of the enemy's men-o'-war and merchants.

They were made most welcome. Coffee, brandy perhaps? Mister Hammond was most pleased to make Holbrooke's acquaintance and that of his friend.

'Now then, sir, we have quite an account building up for you. There's the *Vulcain* of course, and you take a master's mate's share in that capture; still a significant amount, oh yes, a good sum. Then there's *L'Arques*,' he added thumbing through a ledger, 'a lieutenant's share, and the merchantmen in the Caribbean. Let's not forget the *Torenvalk* that you so aptly renamed *Kestrel*, another lieutenant's share. Now it becomes much more interesting, sir. The gun money for l'Outardé is very substantial. The court agreed that you should have the captain's share even though you were only *in locum*. There was a pair of very valuable French West Indiamen that you shared with *Two Brothers* and *Blandford*. Finally, the privateer that you took off Dunkirk was bought into the service – did you know that? – another delightful addition to your portfolio.'

Mister Hammond sat back in his chair with the air of a man who had dined well or was exhausted by fruitful labours.

'A most useful sum, sir, and the funds are coming in month-by-month. Now, do you have a bank that I should talk to?' Hammond asked this with a straight face born of years of practise, despite his lengthy conversation with James Coutts only the day before.

'Campbell & Coutts, if you please,' Holbrooke replied, not without a certain satisfaction, presenting his letter of introduction.

Hammond made a creditable impression of surprise, and handled the letter with awe, as though this was the first time that he'd been entrusted with such a precious document.

'Very good, sir, very good. Now, our clients, our more *successful* clients, generally keep a certain amount lodged with us for expenses and emergencies. In your case I suggest that fifty guineas would be an appropriate amount…'

Holbrooke nodded, agreeing with each new proposition that Hammond made as though these sorts of decisions weren't new to him. He felt as though he was sinking deeper and deeper out of his depth. Yet in the end it was concluded, and he was assured that the funds would be transferred to his bank by the end of the week. In the meantime, Hammond graciously gave Holbrooke a sum to keep himself in London, 'for this is an expensive city, sir, if you don't mind me advising you.'

***

'I'll leave you to your visit to the Admiralty,' said Chalmers, 'and we can meet again at the lodgings. How long do you think you'll be?'

'I can't tell. My appointment is for two o'clock, but it

would be unusual if I'm seen on time. I expect to be with the admiral no more than half an hour.'

He hailed a passing hackney carriage; it wouldn't do to arrive with mud splattered all over his white stockings.

Holbrooke felt alone and vulnerable again. Somehow his friend Chalmers gave him strength simply by his presence, and now he felt his confidence evaporating with each yard that the carriage made towards Whitehall. That familiar feeling of being an imposter was returning at full strength.

A porter showed him into the well-remembered waiting room. He couldn't tell whether it was the same man as the last time he was here; they had all grown to look alike by their shared calling. He had an unreasoning suspicion that he could read his fate in the porter's demeanour, that the old man knew already what would be said to him by the admiral. Each smile, each familiar or condescending gesture had significance, or so Holbrooke thought. But if that was true, then the signals were obscured and unreadable, like a flag hoist seen from dead to windward through wisps of powder smoke.

There were half a dozen other sea officers in the room. He knew only one of them, a classmate of his at the naval academy. His old friend had his passing certificate and was hoping for a lieutenant's commission. It was slightly embarrassing to be chatting with him while waiting to see whether he'd been made a post-captain. The gap between the two men who had started their naval career as equals had grown to a huge chasm, one that was unlikely to be bridged in this war.

He'd spent some time deciding how best to conduct himself, what was the best attitude to take. It all depended upon what Forbes was offering him. He could be posted today, and his name could appear in the gazette tomorrow. He could return in triumph to Wickham to claim Ann as his bride and then to Portsmouth to the unimaginable splendour of a frigate. On the other hand, he could be told that their lordships had no present employment for him, and he could be facing the prospect of half pay for months or years, perhaps until this war was over. Then there would be no hope in the doldrums of peace. It largely depended on what Commodore Howe had said in his report, and despite the hint from Holburne, and his furtive reading of the porters' expressions, he really had no clear idea of where he stood.

On the whole, it was better to wait until the admiral had given his news, then he could choose whether to exult or take offence. But what would be the good of taking offence? No, better to put a brave face on whatever fate had in store for him in the hope of better days to come.

The clock ticked. It chimed the quarters, and every ten minutes a hopeful left the waiting room for his own personal appointment with destiny. Two o'clock came and went, then half-past two. His nerves were well and truly rattled when eventually he was called.

'Ah, Captain Holbrooke, welcome. Take a seat.'

Forbes was as bluff and hearty as ever, and surely this *Captain* Holbrooke was a hopeful sign, or was it nothing more than ordinary politeness?

'You're recovered, I hope?'

'Yes, sir, completely well thank you,' Holbrooke lied. He still had trouble walking long distances and his nights were interrupted by pain when he rolled onto his bruised ribs. 'I'm ready for any duty now, sir.'

Holbrooke regretted that last sentence before it was complete. The phrase *any duty* opened a plethora of appointments that didn't require a post-captain in command of a frigate. But it was too late, the words were said.

'I'm pleased to hear that, because the board has in mind a most extraordinary commission for you.'

Forbes paused for effect. Holbrooke waited, he didn't much like the sound of that *extraordinary commission*.

'We need a man who understands boats, a commander with experience…'

***

No, his words couldn't be unsaid, and in any case, it would do no good. Their lordships only changed their minds on appointments under the most intense political pressure, or very occasionally in the case of a senior and valued admiral. A commander had no hope; it was quite literally a case of take it or leave it, and Holbrooke knew that declining this commission would end his career here and now.

Holbrooke's mind was in such a turmoil that he could hardly take in all that Forbes was saying. It was an expedition into the wilderness of North America. There was a fort to be captured that would cut the French off from their settlements on the Great Lakes, that would open the interior to the English colonists. It was of the utmost importance strategically and Mister Pitt had a personal interest in the outcome.

An army had to be taken from New York up the Hudson River to Albany and then westward, across the wilderness to Lake Ontario, far beyond the limits of English settlement. There were rivers to navigate, and that meant there were boats to be built. There was at least one French sloop on the lake. The army had asked for a sea officer to command the boats and deal with the French navy.

'Are you following me, Holbrooke?'

'Y…yes sir. It's just such a surprise…'

Forbes pushed away the paper that he'd been referring to.

'You know, Holbrooke, I was a commander once, and I know what's going through your mind. You feel you've sufficiently proved yourself to be posted. Am I correct?'

Holbrooke studied the table for a moment, he was starting to be wary of sentences that started *I was a commander once…* Then he squared his shoulders and looked up at the admiral. This was probably the only opportunity he'd have to state his case.

'Yes sir, you are. May I explain myself?'

Forbes nodded cautiously. He was reckoned an

impatient man, but that was by people who had not heard him sit through the sixth sea officer that day *explaining himself*.

Holbrooke took a deep breath. He guessed the danger of what he was doing.

'I had *Kestrel* for nearly a year, sir, and before that I had temporary command of *Medina* for two months. I commanded *Medina* at Cape François and I destroyed a frigate and took prizes. In *Kestrel* I took more prizes, I blockaded Emden, captured the enemy's guns and I took a large Dunkirk privateer. I commanded a division of flatboats alongside post-captains and I fulfilled my duty by seeing the last soldiers off the beach at the cost of my own skin and my own freedom. Now I've come home to find *Kestrel* given to another and yes, sir, I had hoped that my actions would speak for me. I had hoped to be posted…'

Holbrooke finished with a helpless wave of his hand. He didn't know whether he'd helped his case or destroyed it, but it was done.

Forbes fiddled with the paper before him. Unlikely though it was, he appeared embarrassed.

'There's no frigate for you,' he stated bluntly. 'Whether you deserve one or not, there are none available and you can't be posted without a ship.'

There was a pause while Holbrooke took that in.

'Now, don't think that we haven't considered your case. If we put you ashore on half pay, then you run the risk of being…' he thought for a moment, '…not exactly forgotten, but there'll be new officers with their own claims that are fresh in the minds of the members of the board. You run a grave risk as a commander on half pay during a war.'

Holbrooke heard all that and he'd known it before he'd walked through the door. He also knew, and he could see it in Forbes' eyes, that the admiral was being disingenuous. Ships *were* becoming available. New sixth rates were being built and there were older ships whose captains were being moved up to fourth or fifth rates, or to flagships. But there was a long list of commanders and junior post-captains with far, far more interest than Holbrooke, with many more influential friends.

As though reading his mind, Forbes continued.

'You suffer from a lack of patronage, Holbrooke. With the best of intentions, the board can't ignore the cries from important men demanding that their friends be noticed. That's how the war is carried on, by people in power supporting the navy, and they demand something in return. This appointment is in your best interests. It's an important position and when you come back, you'll have some more solid achievements to claim the board's attention.'

Forbes talked on. Holbrooke acknowledged to himself that, in a way, he was being treated with more consideration than he should have expected. It was a wonder that he wasn't thrown out of the office and damned for his presumption. Instead, Forbes was taking the time to outline the duty he was being sent on and further explaining the naval facts of life.

'You'll take passage in the *Lord Halifax* from Plymouth on the first of November. She's a packet and she'll carry dispatches for Savannah and Hampton before she reaches New York. Now, you'll need a lieutenant to second you, a bosun and a carpenter, and of course you can have two servants. You'll report to Brigadier-General Prideaux in New York, and I understand he'll want to move up to Albany at the first hint of spring.'

When Forbes ended, he passed a sealed letter to Holbrooke, his orders. With the receipt of that letter, Holbrooke became legally committed to the enterprise, the capture of Fort Niagara and the strangulation of the French lines of communication in North America.

***

CHAPTER THIRTY

The Packet

Friday Third of November 1758.
Packet Lord Halifax, at Sea. Ushant, East 66 Leagues.

Every telescope on the deck was trained on a speck of white far to leeward, right over towards Ushant. In an innocent packet ship, that usually meant a single glass, the one owned by the master. However, today *Lord Halifax* boasted three telescopes, two of them quite superior instruments that had been bought with the proceeds of prize-taking.

'If you'll lend me your glass, sir, I'll hop up to the masthead and get a better look.'

As a bosun holding a navy board warrant, Jackson could just about get away with leaping around in the rigging of a packet. Lieutenant Lynton, as a commission officer, most certainly could not. The dignity of his station could countenance no such activity.

'Please do, Mister Jackson,' Lynton replied handing over the telescope, 'much obliged.'

Jackson ran up the weather shrouds as though they were library steps. He ran straight past the astonished lookout at the main top and continued to the topmast head. Seating himself comfortably on the cross-trees he drew the telescope to his eye and looked intently to leeward. From this position and with the help of Lynton's telescope, he could see more than a flash of white; he could see two distinct t'gallants and a mizzen tops'l.

'It's a ship,' he shouted. 'On the starboard tack, all plain sail to her t'gallants.'

No merchantman then, unless she was an East Indiaman. Yet she was in the wrong place to be a *Compagnie Française* ship and she'd hardly be a John Company ship barely out of the Chops of the Channel without an escort.

In fact, this odd patch of the sea with no regular trade routes had no right to be hosting a ship at all, let alone two.

'Squeeze her,' said the master. The helmsman eased the bows closer to the westerly wind. 'Let her shiver then drop off half a point.'

'That'll be *Frere Joseph*,' the master said to Lynton, 'or my name's not Jonathan Harley. He chases us almost every time we poke our noses out of the channel. It appears he has the word on our sailings, which isn't surprising. You'd think he had better things to do with his time.'

'A fast sailer?' Lynton asked.

'Fast on a bowline,' the master replied, 'but not so fast sailing large. Much good it'll do him today, but he's very persistent. Last year we lost him at dark only to see him again two miles to leeward at dawn.'

Lynton looked shocked.

'How were you not taken?' he asked.

'Two frigates hove over the horizon just as he was beating into range. Another fifteen minutes and I'd have struck. I've never been so glad to see a King's ship!'

'This wind will veer, don't you think?' asked Holbrooke, wishing Fairview was here to give everyone the benefit of his weather-lore.

'That's what worries me. It'll force us more to the sou'west. Further even, to the west perhaps, when we want to be heading sou'-sou'west.'

Holbrooke looked non-committal. He had no right to tell the master of a packet what to do, and it would be impolite to even suggest a course of action. Nevertheless, he knew what *he* would do, when the night hid their movements.

The master looked thoughtfully at the sails.

'We must pinch to windward as hard as we can while the daylight holds, but after dark? well, we'll see,' he said.

Holbrooke nodded. That was undoubtedly the right thing to do for now. If the ship down there to leeward was a French privateer, and a big one by the look of her, then they needed to be cautious. With the whole day before them, it was essential to keep the weather gage and to steal every yard to windward that the packet could manage. The Frenchman would undoubtedly be a more weatherly ship, as the master said, but even so she could hardly come up with them before sunset. At this time of year in the southwest approaches a cloud-covered night sky was a safe bet – perfect weather to allow the packet to slip away.

Holbrooke retired to his cabin, satisfied that the master knew his business. He'd been on board three days, after four on the road and two in lodgings below the Citadel. With a party of five, the navy board clerks had grudgingly agreed to a hired post chaise for the run down to Plymouth. Even then, it had been a cold and dreary trip as the chaise rattled through the brown and windswept counties. They'd picked up a carpenter in Plymouth. He was a young man by the name of Abraham Sutton and although he'd been to sea as a boy, he'd served his time at the navy yard at Plymouth Dock up the Hamoaze. He came recommended as an expert in the building and repair of boats and best of all he was a willing volunteer, looking for excitement and a taste of the new world. Holbrooke privately wondered whether he'd ever return to his native Devon. It seemed as though his heart was already halfway to the colonies.

Lord Halifax had sailed on time, but a steady westerly wind and a natural desire to give Ushant a wide berth had meant a tack up to the northwest, past Land's End, past the Scillies and halfway to Cape Clear at the southern tip of Ireland. This second leg was taking them over sixty leagues clear of Ushant, but apparently even that wasn't far enough to avoid the attentions of the ever-hungry French commerce raiders.

***

The wind did indeed veer into the northwest in the afternoon and *Lord Halifax* obediently followed it around. As the daylight faded her course was sou'west by west, three points off her required course; no, four points now that she'd already moved so far to the west. Then, as soon as the night had fallen and the privateer just three miles under her lee could no longer see her, she veered and headed east with the wind on her larboard quarter. By daylight *Frère Joseph* should be out of sight to windward wondering where her prey had gone.

Holbrooke, Lynton, Chalmers and Jackson were on deck before dawn. The faintest loom of the still-invisible sun could be seen leaching over the rim of the earth in the southeast. Not enough to see a horizon, or a privateer, but enough to give notice of the coming day.

They stood in a companionable huddle watching the daily miracle of dawn and casting furtive glances for a privateer. A King's ship would be at quarters now, possibly even cleared for action, but a humble packet with a crew pared down to the minimum couldn't afford such profligate use of manpower.

'Good morning, sir,' said Sutton coming up the companion ladder, raising his hat to Holbrooke. 'No sign of our friend of yesterday, I take it?' he added to Jackson.

'He'll be far over the horizon chasing our shadow,' Jackson replied. 'We've seen the last of him.'

The pale light in the southeast spread wider and slowly but surely figures on the deck became clearer. The light spread gradually into the west, showing the low clouds and a grey sea.

'Sail ho!' came the shocking cry from the maintop. 'Sail to windward!'

There was no need for Jackson to run up the shrouds. Now that they knew where to look, the vague outline of a ship could be seen plainly from the deck of the packet. The master of *Frère Joseph* had guessed their overnight course. He'd probably reasoned that the packet wouldn't wish to stray too far off the direct route that took them down to Madeira and the trade winds, and he'd gambled and won. He was close, too close for comfort and he held the weather gage. He could come down and claim his prize any moment he chose. He wouldn't wait long, not with the channel fleet at sea.

'He's put his helm up,' said Lynton.

Sure enough, the privateer was coming off the wind and running down to the packet.

Holbrooke looked at the master.

'All hands,' shouted the master. 'All hands on deck.'

He turned to the steersman.

'Helm up,' he said calmly and deliberately. 'Bring her before the wind. I'll be damned if I'll tamely strike to him. Let's see how fast he is on a run.'

The packet swung off the wind and the sheets and braces were checked away.

'Stuns'ls,' shouted the master. 'Rig the fore and main stuns'ls.'

The privateer was three miles dead astern now and Biscay lay ahead. If *Lord Halifax* really was a fast ship sailing large, then they still had a chance; there was a British blockading squadron off Rochefort. Again, the important thing was to stay out of reach during daylight, about nine hours Holbrooke reckoned.

The master looked around him, at the stuns'ls being laboriously rigged, at the privateer astern of them.

'Would you gentlemen lend a hand to clear away the guns?'

'You'll fight?' asked Holbrooke in surprise.

'No, sir. I don't want to antagonise him, chances are we'll be in his power before noon. Oh, I'll hurl a few balls from our four-pounders, just for form's sake, but I won't hit him, that would be unwise.'

Holbrooke nodded; it was only good sense. After all, this was essentially a commercial transaction. The privateer had no desire to hurt anyone on the packet and if he were afforded the same courtesy, then there need be no unpleasantness when they were boarded. Still, there was a decent chance of escape. If they could stay clear through this day and the next, they'd be quite likely to meet the blockading squadron, or some patrolling frigate. There could even be a convoy crossing the bay. Any one of those would frustrate the privateer. His best chance now was to close as fast as he could, then hope to get his prize home without meeting any British men-o'-war.

The stuns'ls started to draw and the packet's speed increased noticeably. Holbrooke watched the privateer carefully.

'What do you think?' he asked.

Lynton pulled a face. 'We're evenly matched, I would say, sir.'

'Then the race favours the pursuer,' said Holbrooke. 'It will only take one mistake, one piece of gear carried away and he'll be on us. Look at those stuns'l yards.'

They all gazed upwards. The wind was increasing, and the yards were flexing dangerously.

'He'll have to strike them, or they'll carry away in the next squall,' said Jackson.

'I suggest we make our preparations,' said Holbrooke, trying not to let his despair show.

It appeared very likely that he'd be a prisoner of the French again before the day was out. Nevertheless, it was entirely possible that the captured packet would never make it to a French port, she could easily be retaken by a British man-o'-war. That, however, wouldn't help him and his colleagues. Theirs were valuable bodies and they'd certainly be taken into the privateer.

Holbrooke was in the cramped cabin with Serviteur. He was loading pistol balls into the envelope containing his orders and distributing his purse throughout his clothing in the faint hope that his captors would overlook it.

It was hard not to let his misery show. This was quite possibly the end of his career. There'd be no rapid exchange once he was in the hands of a privateer. He'd have to wait while the owners negotiated with the French navy over his head money, and only then would he be eligible for exchange. It would certainly take months and quite possibly years. He'd be forgotten, and the war could well be over before he was repatriated.

He was stowing the last of his gold guineas into a waistcoat pocket when he heard a hail faintly through the skylight.

'Sail ho! there's a brig or a snow four points off our larboard bow.'

Holbrooke rushed to the deck. If this was a British cruiser, then they could be saved. A brig would have a hard fight against a ship-rigged privateer, but it would be easy for the packet to escape while the two were locked in battle. The privateer may even decide it wasn't worth it; after all it was none of his business to be fighting men-o'-war. Even if he won, the monetary balance would be against him. A little armed brig wasn't worth much and both vessels would certainly be extensively damaged.

Holbrooke studied the newcomer intently. A snow, not a brig, he decided, but she didn't look very British. Those topsails had never been approved by a navy board official in a King's yard. She looked very much like the smaller kind of ocean-going privateer that the French fitted out at Dunkirk.

Jackson shook his head.

'French for sure,' he said. 'One of those four-pounder snows, eight guns probably.'

Holbrooke kept his face immobile. His hopes had been dashed, and now he must continue preparing for a lengthy period of captivity.

'I can see the white of his colours now,' said Jackson. 'French without a doubt.' The snow was bows-on to the packet and the ensign could be partially seen through the tangle of masts and sails.

Holbrooke looked astern at the privateer. The distance had appreciably shortened; she was certainly the faster ship off the wind, whatever the packet's master thought. But something was happening. The privateer had put the wind on his starboard quarter and he was steering to the south of the packet's course. Holbrooke swung back to look at the snow. He had to wave Sutton aside, the carpenter had just reappeared on deck and was looking with interest at the newcomer, blocking Holbrooke's view. It had altered course a point or so to starboard and now the ensign was showing clear of the mains'l.

'Look again, Mister Jackson,' Holbrooke said with some complacency.

'Well, I'll be damned! That's a white ensign! She's part of the Channel Fleet!'

'Oh, didn't you know?' said Sutton in a matter-of-fact way. 'That's *Hazard's Prize*, taken in fifty-six. We didn't see fit to change her rig at Dock. I expect she'll be sold soon, but here she is and just in time too!'

***

'I feel the tide turning against me, Chalmers,' said Holbrooke when they were alone in the cabin that they shared with Lynton. He'd been turning over in his mind the linked objectives of promotion and marriage.

Chalmers considered for a moment before speaking.

When clouds appear, wise men put on their cloaks;
When great leaves fall, the winter is at hand;
When the sun sets, who doth not look for night?'

He gave Holbrooke one of his significant looks, the sort that said, *there, you see!*

'I know the quotation,' said Holbrooke peevishly, 'Julius Caesar.' He turned back to his gloomy study of the passing ocean. *Hazard's Prize* was in sight to windward. Her captain had agreed to accompany the packet until it was south of Finisterre and had offered to take mail back to Plymouth for them.

Chalmers made no reply. It wouldn't help his case to point out that the lines were penned for a different play entirely: Richard III. A little education is a dangerous thing, he reflected. He sat in silence with the patience of a hunter who knows the habits of his quarry.

At length Holbrooke raised his eyes.

'Then what should I gather from your morsel of Shakespeare, Chalmers? Other than a vindication of my mood.'

'Signs and portents, my dear fellow,' Chalmers replied, and again lapsed into silence.

Holbrooke looked puzzled. He knew that to say anything more on the subject was to walk straight into the trap that the chaplain had set. Yet, he couldn't help himself, as Chalmers knew full well.

'Surely that quotation leads us to expect the worst from signs and portents.'

'Just so, and yet here we are, happily on our way to the colonies and not in the hold of a French privateer.'

More silence.

'At sunrise the signs suggested that we should prepare for being captured,' Chalmers continued, 'but an hour later the situation had changed. My point is, don't put your faith in signs and portents, they're treacherous things.'

'You think I'm too pessimistic?'

'I do. Yes, I do. And I believe you should write to Mister Featherstone this very day so that the snow may carry it back to England.'

Holbrooke sat up with a start. It was as though Chalmers had been reading his mind. They'd determined weeks ago that he shouldn't write to Ann under the present circumstances, and it would surely be wrong to write to her stepmother, a married woman. But Martin Featherstone? He was the fly in the ointment, the impediment to his attachment to Ann. It would be a bold move to write to him. And yet, a frank letter stating his case could do no harm and possibly a lot of good.

'And furthermore, the time has come to let Mister Featherstone know that you have a fortune of your own, that you could live as a married gentleman without the need of a day's further employment. I sat with you in Mister Hammond's office last month. I have a shrewd idea of your wealth, and it's more than enough to recommend your suit to a provincial corn merchant.'

Holbrooke was aware of the scale of his wealth, but he hadn't yet connected it with the approval of Ann's father. His pulse started to race as though he was going into action.

'What would I do without you, Chalmers?' he exclaimed. 'Serviteur, my writing case, if you please.'

***

HISTORICAL EPILOGUE

The Legacy of Pitt's Strategy of Descents

The effectiveness of Pitt's strategy of descents has been argued for a quarter of a millennium. Certainly, there was considerable destruction of shipping and port facilities, and the privateers of Saint-Malo slept less comfortably, but whether it resulted in a significant reduction in French forces in Germany is not at all clear.

What is not in question are the considerable advances in command arrangements for combined operations, the leap forward in naval signalling and the development of the first mass-produced, purpose-built landing craft. These flatboats were used again at Quebec in 1759, at Belle Isle in 1761 and at Havana and Saint Lucia in 1762. During the American Revolution they provided vital littoral mobility to the British commanders and the design lineage can be traced through to the twentieth century. The descendants of the flatboats landed allied marines and soldiers at Okinawa and Salerno and nearly two hundred years after Saint-Malo they came full circle by landing the greatest seaborne invasion force of all time on the Normandy beaches.

Yet there are unanswered questions: why did Pitt persevere with the campaign after the failure at Rochefort; why was Saint-Malo chosen for a second attempt; and why was General Bligh's army landed to the *west* of Saint-Malo with no means of crossing the Rance? We will probably never have clear answers. Perhaps Pitt was merely going through the motions; appeasing King Frederick and Prince Ferdinand while carefully avoiding continental commitments.

However, with the disaster at Saint-Cast in 1758, the campaign of descents on the French coast came to an end. A British army was sent to the continent, through Emden, and the French homeland was molested no more until 1761.

***

309

Where Fact Meets Fiction

The descents on Brittany and Normandy in 1758 happened much as I have described them. The ships and people are real except for *Kestrel* and her crew, Major Albach, Captain Overton and some of the minor characters we met along the way.

***

The third Duke of Marlborough should not be confused with his illustrious grandfather, the first duke, who was the victor of Blenheim and Ramillies in the War of Spanish Succession. After the first raid on Saint-Malo in 1758, he successfully lobbied to be given command of the expeditionary force being prepared for Germany. However, the duke didn't live to distinguish himself on the continent, as his grandfather had done. He died of dysentery in October 1758, just months into the campaign.

***

Richard Howe was a remarkable man who served his country well through the Seven Years War, the American War of Independence and into the French Revolutionary War. He is best remembered for his great victory at the Glorious First of June which is still celebrated in the Royal Navy. He went on to become the First Lord of the Admiralty.

In 1758 while still a junior post-captain, he was plucked out of obscurity to command the naval element of Pitt's strategy of descents. The effect this had on his superior, Edward Hawke, is well documented. He was principally responsible for the early development of coherent amphibious warfare principles that can be traced forward to the doctrines in use throughout the world in the twenty-first century

***

There were three post-captains and a commander on the beach at Saint-Cast in September 1758; Joshua Rowley, Jervis Maplesden, William Paston and John Elphinstone.

They were all captured and quickly exchanged only to find that their ships had been given to others in their absence. Each of them was given a new and larger command within six months. I added the fictional George Holbrooke to this brave quartet. I hope that their shades will forgive me. At least I've brought their heroism to a new audience.

**

It's an interesting social commentary of the time that there was a Mrs Winter who owned, in her own name, a boatyard at Deptford Wharf in 1758. As far as I can tell she was the widowed daughter-in-law of the founder of the yard, but in any case, she managed the yard as a going concern. She appears to have lost money on building the prototype flatboat and, in recognition, the Admiralty allowed her another shilling per foot for the production models. A shilling is equivalent to five pence in late-2019 British currency, or about six-and-a-half cents in American. That's inflation for you!

**

Chris Durbin

OTHER CARLISLE AND HOLBROOKE NAVAL ADVENTURES

Book 1: The Colonial Post-Captain

Captain Carlisle of His Britannic Majesty's frigate *Fury* hails from Virginia, a loyal colony of the British Crown. In 1756, as the clouds of war gather in Europe, *Fury* is ordered to Toulon to investigate a French naval and military build-up.

While battling the winter weather, Carlisle must also juggle with delicate diplomatic issues in this period of phoney war and contend with an increasingly belligerent French frigate.

And then there is the beautiful Chiara Angelini, pursued across the Mediterranean by a Tunisian corsair who appears determined to abduct her, yet strangely reluctant to shed blood.

Carlisle and his young master's mate, George Holbrooke, are witnesses to the inconclusive sea-battle that leads to the loss of Minorca. They engage in a thrilling and bloody encounter with the French frigate and a final confrontation with the enigmatic corsair.

***

Book 2: The Leeward Islands Squadron

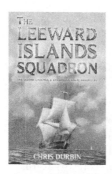

In late 1756, as the British government collapses in the aftermath of the loss of Minorca and the country and navy are thrown into political chaos, a small force of ships is sent to the West Indies to reinforce the Leeward Islands Squadron.

Captain Edward Carlisle, a native of Virginia, and his first lieutenant George Holbrooke are fresh from the Mediterranean and their capture of a powerful French man-of-war. Their new frigate *Medina* has orders to join a squadron commanded by a terminally ill commodore. Their mission: a near-suicidal assault on a strong Caribbean island fortress. Carlisle must confront the challenges of higher command as he leads the squadron back into battle to accomplish the Admiralty's orders.

Join Carlisle and Holbrooke as they attack shore fortifications, engage in ship-on-ship duels and deal with mutiny in the West Indies.

***

Chris Durbin

Book 3: The Jamaica Station

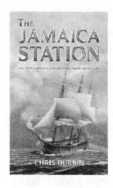

It is 1757, and the British navy is regrouping from a slow start to the seven years war.

A Spanish colonial governor and his family are pursued through the Caribbean by a pair of mysterious ships from the Dutch island of St. Eustatius. The British frigate *Medina* rescues the governor from his hurricane-wrecked ship, leading Captain Edward Carlisle and his first lieutenant George Holbrooke into a web of intrigue and half-truths. Are the Dutchmen operating under a letter of marque or are they pirates, and why are they hunting the Spaniard? Only the diplomatic skills of Carlisle's aristocratic wife, Lady Chiara, can solve the puzzle.

When Carlisle is injured, the young Holbrooke must grow up quickly. Under his leadership, *Medina* takes part in a one-sided battle with the French that will influence a young Horatio Nelson to choose the navy as a career.

***

Book 4: Holbrooke's Tide

It is 1758 and the Seven Years War is at its height. The Duke of Cumberland's Hanoverian army has been pushed back to the river Elbe while the French are using the medieval fortified city of Emden to resupply their army and to anchor its left flank.

George Holbrooke has recently returned from the Jamaica Station in command of a sloop-of-war. He is under orders to survey and blockade the approaches to Emden in advance of the arrival of a British squadron. The French garrison and their Austrian allies are nervous. With their supply line cut, they are in danger of being isolated when the French army is forced to retreat in the face of the new Prussian-led army that is gathering on the Elbe. Can the French be bluffed out of Emden? Is this Holbrooke's flood tide that will lead to his next promotion?

Holbrooke's Tide is the fourth of the Carlisle & Holbrooke naval adventures. The series follows the exploits of the two men through the Seven Years War and into the period of turbulent relations between Britain and her American colonies in the 1760s.

***

Chris Durbin

Book 5: The Cursed Fortress

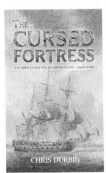

The French called it *La Forteresse Maudite*; the Cursed Fortress.

Louisbourg stood at the mouth of the Gulf of St. Lawrence, massive and impregnable, a permanent provocation to the British colonies. It was Canada's first line of defence, guarding the approaches to Quebec, from where all New France lay open to invasion. It had to fall before a British fleet could be sent up the St. Lawrence. Otherwise, there would be no resupply and no line of retreat; Canada would become the graveyard of George II's navy.

A failed attempt on Louisbourg in 1757 had only stiffened the government's resolve; the Cursed Fortress must fall in 1758.

Captain Carlisle's frigate joins the blockade of Louisbourg before winter's icy grip has eased. Battling fog, hail, rain, frost and snow, suffering scurvy and fevers, and with a constant worry about the wife he left behind in Virginia, Carlisle will face his greatest test of leadership and character yet.

The Cursed Fortress is the fifth of the Carlisle & Holbrooke naval adventures. The series follows the two men through the Seven Years War and into the period of turbulent relations between Britain and her American colonies in the 1760s.

***

BIBLIOGRAPHY

The following is a selection of the many books that I consulted in researching the Carlisle and Holbrooke Series:

Definitive Text

Sir Julian Corbett wrote the original, definitive text on the Seven Years War. Most later writers use his work as a stepping stone to launch their own.

> Corbett, LLM., Sir Julian Stafford. *England in the Seven Years War – Vol. I: A Study in Combined Strategy:* Normandy Press. Kindle Edition.

Strategy and Naval Operations

Three very accessible modern books cover the strategic context and naval operations of the Seven Years War. Daniel Baugh addresses the whole war on land and sea, while Martin Robson concentrates on maritime activities. Jonathan Dull has produced a very readable account from the French perspective.

> Baugh, Daniel. *The Global Seven Years War 1754-1763*. Pearson Education 2011. Print.

> Robson, Martin. *A History of the Royal Navy, The Seven Years War*. I.B. Taurus, 2016. Print.

> Dull, Jonathan, R. *The French Navy and the Seven Years' War*, University of Nebraska Press, 2005. Print.

Sea Officers

For an interesting perspective on the life of sea officers of the mid-eighteenth century, I'd read *Augustus Hervey's Journal,* with the cautionary note that while Hervey was by no means typical of the breed, he's very entertaining and devastatingly honest. For a more balanced view I'd read *British Naval Captains of the Seven Years War.*

Erskine, David (editor). *Augustus Hervey's Journal, The Adventures Afloat and Ashore of a Naval Casanova*: Chatham Publishing, 2002. Print.

McLeod, A.B. *British Naval Captains of the Seven Years War, The View from the Quarterdeck.* The Boydell Press, 2012. Print.

Life at Sea

I recommend *The Wooden World* for an overview of shipboard life and administration during the Seven Years War.

N.A.M Rodger. *The Wooden World, An Anatomy of the Georgian Navy.* Fontana Press, 1986. Print.

***

THE AUTHOR

Chris Durbin grew up in the seaside town of Porthcawl in South Wales. His first experience of sailing was as a sea cadet in the treacherous tideway of the Bristol Channel, and at the age of sixteen, he spent a week in a tops'l schooner in the Southwest Approaches. He was a crew member on the Porthcawl lifeboat before joining the navy.

Chris spent twenty-four years as a warfare officer in the Royal Navy, serving in all classes of ships from aircraft carriers through destroyers and frigates to the smallest minesweepers. He took part in operational campaigns in the Falkland Islands, the Middle East and the Adriatic and he spent two years teaching tactics at a US Navy training centre in San Diego.

On his retirement from the Royal Navy, Chris joined a large American company and spent eighteen years in the aerospace, defence and security industry, including two years on the design team for the Queen Elizabeth class aircraft carriers.

Chris is a graduate of the Britannia Royal Naval College at Dartmouth, the British Army Command and Staff College, the United States Navy War College (where he gained a postgraduate diploma in national security decision-making) and Cambridge University (where he was awarded an MPhil in International Relations).

With a lifelong interest in naval history and a long-standing ambition to write historical fiction, Chris has completed the first four novels in the Carlisle & Holbrooke series, in which a colonial Virginian commands a British navy frigate during the middle years of the eighteenth century.

The series will follow its principal characters through the Seven Years War and into the period of turbulent relations between Britain and her American Colonies in the 1760s. They'll negotiate some thought-provoking loyalty issues when British policy and colonial restlessness lead inexorably to the American Revolution.

Chris lives on the south coast of England, surrounded by hundreds of years of naval history. His three children are all busy growing their own families and careers while Chris and his wife (US Navy, retired) of thirty-seven years enjoy sailing their classic dayboat.

***

Fun Fact:

Chris shares his garden with a tortoise named *Aubrey*. If you've read Patrick O'Brian's *HMS Surprise*, or have seen the 2003 film *Master and Commander: The Far Side of the World*, you'll recognise the modest act of homage that Chris has paid to that great writer. Rest assured that Aubrey has not yet grown to the gigantic proportions of *Testudo Aubreii*.

***

FEEDBACK

If you've enjoyed *Perilous Shore*, please consider leaving a review on Amazon.

This is the latest of a series of books that will follow Carlisle and Holbrooke through the Seven Years War and into the 1760s when relations between Britain and her restless American Colonies are tested to breaking point.

Look out for the seventh in the Carlisle and Holbrooke series, coming soon.

You can follow my blog at:

www.chris-durbin.com

***

Made in the USA
Monee, IL
21 May 2024

58708437R10194